The
Bounty Hunter

P. R. Garcia

This is a work of fiction. Names, characters, places, and incidents are either the product of the author's imagination or are used fictitiously. Any resemblance to any person, living or dead, events, or locals is coincidental.

DEDICATION

To my granddaughter. May she always possess the heart of an adventurer, the soul of a warrior, and the dignity of a Huntsman.

Contents

Coming Summer, 2025, The Bounty Hunter II

Please leave an honest review.

You are fascinated.
Don't be.
My mind is feral, savage,
My life is feral, savage,
You would not understand,
You are not of my clan,
You are not of my life.
You think to know me
Is to know The Way.
You Cannot.
The Way —
Harsher than hottest deserts,
Colder than blackest space,
Deeper than ocean worlds.
You wish to be as I am.
Live as I do, Fight as I Live.
You cannot.
You are not of The Way
To live
Under the Helm,
Is to know a Code,
As one knows Life
For the Way and Life,
Are Intertwined,
They are Blood and Bone,
They are Life and Death.
That is The Way.

Ben Snow

ACKNOWLEDGMENTS

At an early age, my father introduced me to the big screen and ignited my passion for Science Fiction. With such classics as *The Day the Earth Stood Still, Mysterious Island, Journey to the Center of the Earth,* and The *War of the Worlds,* my realm was transformed to accept the unimaginable was feasible. In high school, Gene Roddenberry affirmed that space flight was credible. We could have a better world, and we were not alone. *Star Trek* became my inspiration. During my mid-twenties, Steven Spielberg with *Close Encounters of the Third Kind* and George Lucas with *Star Wars* expanded my imagination further. For the first time, I had life-size visual experiences of the airships and aliens that inhabited those alien systems. Today, Jon Favreau continues this greatness in *The Mandalorian* and deepens the work that those before him began. I thank the visionaries for their worlds and characters who have defined my life.

A special thank you for the following:

To Ben Snow for permitting me to include his poem "The Way". He captured the spirit of the men and women who remain protected behind the armor and vow allegiance to the ideology.

I

"Do you have a name? Something I can call you?"

"I am known as the Hunter."

"Not very original."

"It is sufficient."

1 SOMETHING'S WRONG

The ramp hissed as it lowered, releasing a breath of chilled air into the stagnant heat. BiiJun's gut clenched. He wasn't a man easily rattled, Kolorian-trained, an elite-class Huntsman Bounty Hunter. But something about this place, this forgotten planet, felt wrong. Deeply wrong.

His visor fogged with breath. Static danced across his inner helmet display as his boots struck the metal ramp with practiced ease. And yet, he paused. A violent shiver tore down his spine. Something unseen stirred at the edges of his instincts.

Something ancient, primal. Not fear.

Worse.

Premonition.

He toggled to infrared. The world flared red and gold, small animals scampering among the trees like whispers. No predators. No enemy heat signatures. But that didn't matter. Danger had a scent. And it was thick here.

He unlatched his long rifle with a quiet *snick*, stepping forward, muscles tense, breath shallow. At the ramp's edge, he froze. His foot hovered over the grass, his every nerve ending screaming.

Leave. Now.

The warning was so loud in his mind that he could almost hear it spoken aloud.

BiiJun withdrew a breath, tried to force calm, but the bile in his throat surged up instead. The only thing stopping him from returning to his ship was the crimson glow on his tracker.

Ting D'ton - Wanted for rape on three planets. 185 quibs.

That was why no other Hunter had bothered. The bounty was garbage. But BiiJun made an oath long ago: never leave a rapist breathing. Not for any price.

Having no choice, BiiJun stepped off the ramp and onto the grass. If his destiny awaited him on this forgotten world, he'd meet it head-on AND arrest his man.

He followed the locator's beeping to a slight mound of earth above a green basin. Dropping behind the dirt, BiiJun lifted his spyglass and scanned the valley below. Somewhere hidden amongst the timbers, bushes, and undergrowth existed his quarry.

Filaments of yellow flickered like ghost lights across the inside of his visor. BiiJun activated his heat vision. Within seconds, the thermal scan swept through the forest, slicing through foliage and shadow like a blade of fire. Images of deer, warm-bodied and unaware, grazing deep in the underbrush, burned brightly. Birds, tiny heat signatures, fluttered through the upper canopy. Squirrels darted along branches, their movement erratic, harmless.

He swept left.

There. A slow, steady glow - centered, still, and far too calm.

Target locked.

Three-point-six miles out, high in the limbs of a duskwood tree, the fugitive crouched with eerie stillness. BiiJun narrowed in, adjusting the zoom. His quarry wasn't running. He wasn't hiding.

He was *waiting*.

Through the visor, BiiJun saw his eyes locked on something below. He was watching prey.

Focused. Cold. Dangerous.

BiiJun's breath slowed. So did the forest.

BiiJun shifted his scope. A woman. Alone. Two canines were at her side.

His heart kicked into overdrive.

The woman. She was the reason he felt it. The danger wasn't for him. It was for her.

He calculated distances. The fugitive was closer to her. If BiiJun went for the arrest now, she might be dead before he arrived. But if he ran, really ran, he could reach her first.

Fifteen minutes. No mistakes. No detours.

He turned and bolted down the slope, rifle secured, boots eating up the dirt. Branches lashed at his armor. The wind shrieked in his ears. He had to make it. He had to reach her in time.

A roar exploded from the underbrush.

BiiJun skidded to a halt. A bear munching fresh berries stood ten feet off the trail. Upon seeing the Hunter, it spun around and roared. BiiJun went for his weapon, but the bear was too close, too fast.

The fanged bear charged, a blur of rage and claws.

The beast hit him like a meteor, smashing his breastplate with one earth-shattering swipe. His handgun flew in one direction and his rifle in another. His body lifted.

Then pain. Nothing but pain.

He slammed into the earth. Before he could crawl, the bear was on him again, teeth driving into his ribs, lifting him, shaking him like a limp rag doll. BiiJun pounded on the bear's head, hoping the animal would let him go. It did. He sailed through the air and slammed into a nearby tree, the sound of breaking bones filling his ears. The bear pounced and bit down on BiiJun's head. The enraged beast groaned in frustration as the *kolorite* metal of his helmet prevented the bear from penetrating Hunter's skull.

BiiJun screamed.

And then, pure survival instinct. His hand searched desperately across his belt for his weapon. Pulling it free, he jammed it upward and fired into the bear's throat. The monster howled and vanished into the trees.

BiiJun didn't move. Couldn't.

He lay in the grass, vision swimming, breath like fire in his lungs. His armor hissed, venting fluids. Blood pooled beneath him, his body torn, useless.

Far off, he heard the sound of barking. Laughter.

The woman. She was still alive. Still unaware.

He had to reach her.

He dug his fingers into the earth and pulled his body forward. One inch. Then another. Every tug was agony. Every breath cut like a razor.

But he moved. Because if he didn't, he would die. And she would, too.

His world narrowed to a single thread - the woman's voice. It drifted through the trees like music from another life. BiiJun followed it. Crawled toward it. One hand forward.

Pull.

Drag.

Repeat.

His body screamed. His vision blurred. Blood soaked through the shattered plates of his armor, warm and constant. He couldn't tell how much he'd lost. He only knew it was more than he could afford.

He didn't dare call out. The bear might still be nearby. Or the fugitive. Or worse.

Branches scratched his helmet. The forest swayed above him like a living thing. But the voice, her voice, pulled him onward like a gravity well.

She was close. He could almost see her.

Another step.

And the world went black.

2 THE STRANGER

Li-ara lived at the edge of nowhere. And that was how she liked it: a simple life in a cabin in the desolate countryside far from other beings, existing peacefully with her two guard canines. But today, she wished she had at least one other person with her.

A disturbance drifted through the air, a sound that didn't belong.

Not wind, not the usual hush of leaves or the whisper of wings above. This was heavier. Uneven. A dragging weight slicing through brambles, snapping twigs, crunching dry leaves with no care for silence. Whatever moved through the forest wasn't hunting. It wasn't stealthy or sharp. It was loud. Labored. Wrong. The cadence of its steps was off; one heavy, one light, a stagger between. Something wounded, large, and coming closer.

Li-ara halted mid-step, her basket heavy with tingleberries, vines still clinging to the rim. Her heart pounded so fiercely it rattled her ribs, each beat a frantic drumroll in her ears.

She crouched low, knees bending, and slid the basket gently to the mossy earth. Her fingers curled around the worn grip of her rifle, lifting the barrel slowly until it aligned with the tree line. She exhaled through her nose, steadying her breath like she'd trained herself to do. This wasn't her first encounter with the wild. But something about this sound, this approach, unsettled her. It wasn't just wounded. It was desperate.

Kii and Beta were already moving, ghostlike in their precision. Her *Gloxdirian* canines fanned out in near silence, communicating with glances and instinct. Kii took the left flank, low to the ground, tongue flicking the air for scent. Beta crept right, her steps so measured they barely disturbed the underbrush. Then, from Beta's throat, a low growl rumbled - deep, uncertain, not quite a threat. Something about it made Li-ara's spine stiffen. It wasn't the sound of aggression. It was confusion. A primal warning, yes, but laced with hesitation. Curiosity. Something was wrong.

Then the scent hit her.

Blood. Thick and metallic. Not fresh, not yet sour. Just strong. The copper tang rode the wind, carried across leaves and bark, and into her lungs. Someone, or something, was bleeding. A lot. The kind of blood loss that meant dying was close.

Her finger moved toward the trigger.

Then the forest exploded.

Leaves scattered. Branches snapped. The underbrush erupted in a violent tremor, and from it burst a figure, tall and imposing. Armor-clad. Covered in blood and half-collapsing, he staggered into the clearing like a shadow falling apart. Kii shot forward but stopped short, barking once. Li-ara froze, eyes wide, breath locked in her throat.

The figure took two more broken steps. Then dropped.

Hard.

He lay still.

Time stretched thin. The forest went silent again, as if holding its breath. Li-ara stared, rifle unmoving, mind racing. This wasn't an animal. It wasn't a beast or some wild scavenger. It was a man. Or at least what was left of one.

Her instincts fought with each other—fight, flee, protect. But in the end, something else took hold. Compassion. Something deep and involuntary. She dropped her rifle and ran.

Beta and Kii flanked the collapsed figure, not in aggression, but in anxious vigilance. They sniffed the blood-soaked armor, ears alert, but made no move to attack. That alone told Li-ara everything - this man wasn't a threat. Not now. Maybe not ever.

She fell to her knees beside him, her hands hovering, unsure where to touch without causing pain. His armor was covered in thick blood, cracked along the ribs, dented at the shoulder. The blood loss alone should've killed him. Yet somehow, he was still breathing.

A helmet hid his identity. Seamless. Sleek. It bore no markings, no insignia. But Li-ara recognized it for who the stranger was - a Kolorian Huntsman. An elite Bounty Hunter of the highest grade.

She pressed a trembling hand beneath the armor above his chest, waiting.

A flutter.

A heartbeat.

Alive.

Just barely.

And in that moment, Li-ara realized something terrifying and profound. This man had clawed his way through death itself. Not by accident. Not by chance. He had *chosen* to come here. Through the forest, through the pain, through whatever nightmare had torn his body open - he had come to her.

"Need help," came a weak, masculine voice. "Attacked."

"Yes, by a most ferocious beast," Li-ara said. "You are lucky to be alive. Few ever live to tell of a fanged bear attack. I am going to help you, but first I need to take your helmet off so I can tell how badly you are injured. And to help you breathe."

Without warning, the Hunter grabbed her wrist. "No, you cannot remove my helmet."

"But you're having trouble breathing. And I can't judge your injuries with the helmet and your armor on."

"You cannot remove my helmet. It is forbidden to reveal my face."

The Hunter's grip on her arm slackened, his body going limp as unconsciousness overtook him. Li-ara slipped her fingers beneath the edge of his helmet, ready to remove it, but stopped at Kii's sharp bark. The young canine's piercing gaze was locked on her, a silent warning - or was it rebuke? Either way, she hesitated. Removing the helmet would have to wait. Right now, she needed to get him home to attend to his wounds. But if she were going to save him, the helmet would have to come off, eventually.

"Beta, bring Fillo," she commanded, dropping her hand.

The older canine darted off to fetch the pack animal, which had wandered past the berry bushes, lazily pulling at the grass. Kii stayed behind, circling the fallen man. He sniffed the stranger's bloodied clothes, then gave a soft, uneasy whine, his ears pinned back. Lifting his gaze, he looked to her, seeking direction, unsure of what to do next.

"I know, boy. He's dying."

She pressed her fingers to the man's side. Blood oozed around her hand. The armor had fractured, buckled inward from some massive impact. Yet, its integrity held and prevented the bear from ripping him apart.

Fillo arrived in a thunder of clattering reins. Li-ara leapt up and yanked a blanket from the saddle and unlatched the stretcher poles in one swift motion. The wooden frame hit the ground with a dull thud as she flung it open. She spread the blanket across it, her fingers working fast, precise, every movement fueled by urgency.

She jerked open the saddlebag and pulled out her medical kit, along with the few precious bandages tucked inside. They wouldn't be enough. Without hesitation, she tossed them beside the stranger and reached for her own shirt. Gripping the hem, she ripped it into long, jagged strips, each tear echoing in the still air as she turned the fabric into makeshift bandages.

Dropping to her knees, she grabbed the coagulant powder from her kit and poured it straight into the open wounds. The powder hissed on contact, darkening as it met blood. She pressed hard, then wrapped him tightly, her hands swift, steady, and stained with red. His body twitched as she worked, but he didn't fight her. He didn't have the strength.

"I need to get you home," she said, her voice low but steady. "To do that, I have to move you onto this blanket. It's going to hurt, but I'm not going to let you die out here. Not today."

She stepped carefully over him, planting her feet on either side of his head, and leaned down. "Can you help me at all?"

Silence.

Her hands slid beneath his arms. "All right then," she breathed. "We do it my way." With a steadying breath, she began to pull.

She tightened her grip beneath his arms. With a sharp inhale, she heaved, every muscle straining, her back arched, legs locked. But his body barely shifted, dead weight soaked in blood and mud. Gritting her teeth, she tried again, grunting with the effort. He moved, but it wasn't enough. Her arms trembled. Fire lit through her shoulders and down her spine.

Sweat dripped from her brow, stinging her eyes, blurring her vision. This was impossible. He was too heavy. Too broken. But she didn't let go.

"I'm getting you out of here," she muttered through clenched teeth. "Even if it kills me."

Kii lunged forward, sensing her struggle. He clamped his jaws around the Hunter's shoulder pauldron, trying to help drag him. But the curved metal repelled his grip, slick with blood and dirt. Frustrated, he tried again, his claws scrabbling in the dirt, desperate to do something to help.

Li-ara dropped to her knees beside him, gasping for breath. "I can't move him alone," she said. She looked down at Kii, who stood anxiously at her side. "If you and Beta are going to help …" Her gaze shifted to the gleaming metal on the Hunter's shoulders. "Those damn shoulder shields have to come off."

She crawled to his side, fingers fumbling for the release clasps beneath the heavy plates. The metal was slick with blood and grime, the locking mechanisms jammed tight from the attack.

"Come on," she muttered, digging her nails under the first latch. It wouldn't budge. Li-ara grabbed the handle of her knife and jammed it under the seam, prying hard. The latch gave with a sharp *click*, the pauldron sliding an inch before catching on another strap.

"You better be worth this," she whispered to the unconscious man, then bent back to her work.

One strap loose. Then another. The first pauldron clattered to the ground with a thud.

She moved swiftly to the second pauldron. The first strap snapped with a sharp pop, the brittle leather giving way under her force. But the second strap refused to budge, wedged deep beneath the joint, mangled into the armor like it had fused with the metal itself.

"Damn it," she hissed, dropping to her elbows. She wedged her fingers underneath, wincing as the metal bit into her skin. Gently at first, then more aggressively, she rocked the strap back and forth, trying to find the angle that would free it.

Behind her, the Hunter let out a faint groan, a sound so weak it barely registered. It chilled her blood.

"Hold on," she said, voice tight with strain. "I'm trying."

The strap refused her again, binding itself like a vice. She shoved harder, twisting her fingers deeper. Finally – *snap*. It broke free. The second pauldron dropped.

She spun back around and pressed two fingers to the man's neck. His pulse was still there, but faint, slipping fast.

Too much time. She'd already taken too much time.

"Beta!" she called, her voice rough with urgency. The older canine trotted over, eyes wide and alert.

"Kii, Beta, shoulders," she ordered, pointing. The two dogs moved without hesitation, each gripping one shoulder with their jaws.

Li-ara crouched at his head, slipping her hands beneath his arms once again. "Okay, we do this together. Pull with me. One … two … three."

Together, the three of them dragged the Hunter inch by inch onto the blanket. His body jolted with every movement, metal scraping against the earth, a soft groan escaping his lips. But she didn't pause. She couldn't.

When his full weight finally rested on the blanket, she slumped back on her heels, chest heaving. "Good canines," she whispered, reaching out to touch both dogs. "Now, let's get him home."

Li-ara forced her battered limbs into motion. She bound his arms to his sides with strips of torn cloth, each knot pulling tighter than the last. She lashed down the corners of the blanket, then threaded thick rope through the stretcher loops, anchoring them firmly to Fillo's harness. Fillo snorted, but held steady as she worked.

She tossed the armor and her gear onto the blanket, then wrapped the edges up and over the injured man, tightening the last fold. The final knot she secured with her teeth, fingers too numb to finish the job.

She slumped back for a breath, then stood tall, wiping blood and sweat from her brow with the back of her hand. Her gaze swept the landscape ahead - an open stretch of rugged, uneven road leading away from the tree line. The sun had dipped lower, dragging long shadows across the brush.

Behind her, the forest watched - dense and silent.

Too silent.

She didn't need to look back to know eyes were watching from the undergrowth, their hunger crawling up her spine. But the danger was behind her now. Ahead lay her cabin - and hope.

"We're going home," she whispered, gripping Fillo's reins. Li-ara stepped onto the road, dragging death behind her, daring anything to try and stop her.

They moved fast. Too fast for the terrain. The pack animal stumbled over a rock, nearly veering off the path. Li-ara yanked hard, forcing her straight with a sharp murmur, not slowing.

Every few strides, she snapped a glance over her shoulder. Still no movement.

The stranger's body bounced with each bump in the dirt road, wrapped tight. His face, pale and still. Wrapped in the blood-soaked blanket, he looked less like someone clinging to life and more like someone already claimed by death.

The road ahead twisted like a cruel riddle, ruts, stones, dips that threatened to tear the stretcher free.

The journey home would take an hour, maybe more. She wasn't sure he had that long. With each step, her unease grew, but she kept moving.

Behind them, the forest stirred.

A branch cracked. Sharp. Deliberate.

Then came the howl. Low. Guttural. Too close. Another howl answered. Then another closer still.

Wild canines. They were tracking. Hunting.

Fillo balked, ears twitching, hooves stamping nervously. Li-ara yanked the reins and hissed, "Move! Or you're canine meat."

The stretcher bounced behind them. Her pulse thundered. Every instinct screamed to run, to flee. But there was no speed fast enough, no path smooth enough.

The forest behind them was waking.

Forty minutes into the journey, Beta let out a sharp bark. Li-ara drew her weapon, flicking off the safety with a practiced thumb. Her eyes scanned the open terrain, every sense sharpened. She listened. Nothing but the distant flap of wings as a night swallow darted overhead.

Still, something wasn't right.

"Stay," she said to Kii, handing him Fillo's reins. Then she sprinted to Beta. The moment she saw the Hunter, her gut twisted. A dark red stain bloomed across his chest, seeping through the blanket like a warning bell.

"No," she breathed, dropping to her knees.

She ripped the laces open and pulled the fabric back. The rough terrain had torn the wound seals wide open. Two of the chest wounds were bleeding freely now - fresh, wet, and angry.

Working fast, she peeled back the cloth bandage, blood coating her fingers. She poured the last of the coagulant powder over the open wounds. The gritty seal hissed as it met raw flesh. He groaned, a sound half-conscious and broken.

"I know," she whispered, pressing down to help it set. "I'm sorry."

She repacked the wounds, tightened the blanket, and retied the laces as fast as her fingers allowed.

Li-ara leaned close, her voice barely a breath. "Just hold on. We're almost home."

"Okay," came a whisper, surprising Li-ara.

"Let me take that metal contraption off your head so I can know if you are dead or alive. At least until we're home."

"No."

"This is ridiculous. I'm taking this stupid helmet off now." Li-ara slipped her fingers beneath the rim and began to lift. Something hard jabbed into her side. Looking down, she saw the barrel of a pistol pressed against her ribs.

"You've got to be kidding me. I'm out here dragging your half-dead body through the wilds, patching you up every time you start bleeding out, and *this* is how you thank me? You're going to shoot me for trying to save your damn life?"

"You cannot remove the helmet."

"Then die!" Li-ara snapped, storming forward and yanking Fillo's reins with a furious jerk.

3 HOW TO SAVE HIM

The sun was sinking fast, and the shadows had grown long, twisting across the road. Darkness blurred the dips and stones beneath her feet, turning each step into a gamble. A cold wind whispered through the trees, cutting through her thin clothes and raising goosebumps along her arms.

Her coat was wrapped around the Hunter. Which meant this journey, already desperate, was about to turn frigid. And the cold might finish what the blood loss had started. Their situation just passed critical.

She was running again. Fillo, Kii, and Beta trotted beside her. The fields of grain opened up just as the last rays of the sun disappeared. Her cabin stood like a lighthouse, beckoning her forward. But joy turned to ice as she saw the problem.

Steps.

The porch waited ahead, three steps too many. There was no way to get him inside. Not like this. He was barely conscious, his body limp and heavy with the weight of death pressing in. And she - she didn't have the strength to carry him. Not anymore. Not after everything.

Dropping Fillo's reins, she sprinted to the porch, heart hammering, eyes darting wildly. Another howl cut through the trees. Nearer, sharper, echoing off the fields like a blade.

They were nearly here.

Her breath came in short, uneven bursts. Panic clawed at her throat, but she couldn't give in. Not yet.

Think.

THINK.

She stumbled inside, boots slapping the wood, mind scrambling for a plan, anything that could help get him inside. Her fists clenched and unclenched in her hair. Her heart pounded in her ears. A scream of frustration started to rise.

Then, in a flash of madness or brilliance, she saw it. Fillo's stretcher.

It was insane. The thing was huge, awkward, barely maneuverable outdoors. But maybe, just maybe, it could work.

She ripped off her belt and flung it across the doorframe, using it as a rough measure. Then she bolted down the porch steps, slid to her knees beside the stretcher, and stretched the belt across its width.

Only an eighth of an inch stood between success and failure.

It would fit.

It had to fit.

Running on raw adrenaline, she rushed into the cabin. She shoved furniture aside, her boots slipping on the floor. Chairs toppled. A table scraped across the boards, screeching in protest as it skidded into the wall.

A path opened, but barely.

Li-ara's pulse was a hammer now, pounding behind her eyes.

The pack was coming. The Huntsman was dying.

"Hold on for a few more minutes," Li-ara shouted. "I'll get you inside before they get here."

Her eyes scanned the yard, sweeping across weeds, rocks, half-buried junk. She needed something, anything, to bypass the steps. But everything she saw was useless. Nothing was large enough, flat enough.

Then, her eyes locked on the front door.

Of course. The door. It was solid wood. Heavy, but available. It would work if she could get it off its hinges.

Li-ara flew into the kitchen, yanking open the drawer with a clatter. Her fingers closed around the hammer and chisel. She didn't pause. Didn't breathe. She spun on her heel and raced back to the porch, dropping to her knees in front of the door. Driving the chisel against the first hinge pin, she slammed the hammer head against its head. The metal shrieked in protest. but the bottom hinge pin slid out with three quick strikes. The middle one followed with a screech and a stubborn twist. But the top hinge jammed. Halfway out, it stuck fast, refusing to move.

"Come on," Li-ara hissed, bracing herself against the frame.

She grabbed the pin with bare fingers, twisting, wrenching. Nothing. Standing on her tiptoes, she dug her ring finger into the hinge gap for leverage.

Pain exploded through her hand.

She jerked back with a cry. Blood welled instantly, the torn skin along her finger already beading crimson. A jagged sliver of metal glinted back at her, mocking her effort.

A distant howl rose on the wind. It was close. Closer than the last. Her chest tightened as cold urgency gripped her.

No time for pain. No time for caution. They were coming.

Screaming in frustration and desperation, Li-ara wrapped her arms around the door and pulled with every ounce of strength she had. The wood groaned violently, the top hinge resisting her, crying in protest. She rocked it hard, over and over, her whole body shaking. With a final *crack* like a gunshot, the hinge tore free, and the door wrenched sideways off its frame.

Sweat stung her eyes as she dragged it across the porch. It scraped and bounced, nearly slipping from her grasp. She shoved it forward and maneuvered it over the landing until only the top edge teetered on the porch lip, ready to fall with the slightest push.

Beta barked, a sharp, frantic warning. Kii lowered his head and growled, the sound vibrating deep in his chest. The pack wasn't coming, they were here. And they had come to kill.

Li-ara grabbed Fillo's reins and moved her in front of the steps, lining up the stretcher with the door.

"Come on, Fillo, just one step at a time," Li-ara urged, tugging gently at the reins, coaxing her backward onto the wooden platform. Fillo's back hooves clattered against the board, her head lowering as she tested the first step with a cautious hoof. After a moment of adjustment, she ascended slowly, one careful step at a time.

Li-ara kept the reins tight, guiding Fillo with steady hands. But her alignment was off. The stretcher slammed into the doorframe with a jarring *crack*. She hissed under her breath, stepped forward, and coaxed the animal two more paces ahead. Then, crouching low, she shifted the stretcher's angle and gave the reins a sharp pull.

Fillo snorted loudly, ears pinning back as she stomped the ground with a sharp crack of her front hoof. Without warning, the animal jerked her head and lashed out with a powerful kick. Li-ara scrambled aside just in time. The hoof whooshed past her leg, missing by inches.

"Come on, you stubborn beast. Just a bit more to go. Move."

Her hooves planted firmly, Fillo refused to move another inch. Her nostrils flared, ears flicking nervously as the tension in the air thickened. Behind her, the stretcher creaked against the doorframe.

Beta didn't hesitate. The canine trotted to the front of the stubborn pack animal and let out a low, guttural growl. It wasn't loud, but it was commanding. Authority rippled through it. A flash of teeth followed, not savage, but enough to make a point.

Fillo snorted, stomped, and took a step backward. Then another. And another. The creaking resumed as the stretcher inched backward, Fillo pushing through the tight doorframe. Then she was inside.

Li-ara quickly unhooked the straps and tossed the reins to Beta. "Take her to the barn, girl." As Beta ran down the steps with the pack animals, movement caught Li-ara's eye. She turned to her right, blood draining from her face.

Five canines stood at the curve in the road, silhouettes like living shadows in the moonlight. Watching. Silent. Calculating. She counted again. Five. But were there more hidden behind them, veiled by trees and shadow?

She turned her attention to the door. It still lay flat on the porch, massive and heavy. All her hard work, all the sweat and sacrifice, meant nothing if she couldn't get that door back up. It was more than just wood and nails now. It was the only thing standing between them and the pack, between life and death.

Kii took his position on the porch, a loyal sentry standing watch. His back hairs rose. His stance was rigid. A low rumble vibrated from his chest. His lips peeled back, exposing white fangs. He leaned forward, poised to strike.

Li-ara didn't have time to be afraid.

She ran down the steps and dropped to her knees. Digging her hands into the cold dirt beneath the door, she lifted with everything she had. Her muscles burned. Her wounded hand throbbed. The door groaned.

But it **moved.**

She shoved it forward across the landing, inch by inch, until the edge slammed into the molding of the doorway.

Not stopping, not thinking, she bent low and heaved the bottom up, using her shoulder to brace the weight. With one final, desperate cry, she twisted the heavy slab and slammed it back into the frame.

She grabbed the hinge pins and drove them in with her palms, blood smearing the metal as they slid into place.

Two hinges.

The third was shattered.

Would it hold?

It had to.

"Kii, inside, now!" Li-ara looked toward the stable and saw Beta closing the barn door. "Beta, come, hurry inside. They're coming."

The moment Beta ran inside, Li-ara slammed the door shut. Her chest heaved as she thrust her body against the wood.

They were safe.

Her hand flew to the lock. Li-ara froze. In her haste to reattach the door, she'd mounted it upside down. And backward. The lock, meant to secure their safety, was now on the *outside*, completely useless. Worse still, the door swung outward directly toward the enemy.

A blood-chilling howl ripped through the stillness, rising from the trees behind the cabin. Then came another from the front yard. They weren't circling anymore. They had closed in. The cabin was surrounded.

Snarls echoed just beyond the walls. Claws scraped the porch. Wood creaked beneath the shifting weight. They were at the door.

Li-ara's gaze flew around the room, heart hammering. What could hold them back? What could secure the door?

Another snarl. Then a thud. A heavy body slammed into the door, rattling it on its hinges.

Li-ara lunged for the nearest kitchen chair, dragging it across the floor with a screech of wood on wood. She jammed it beneath the doorknob, angling it hard, wedging it tight.

Would it hold? She didn't know.

Another slam. A snap of teeth. The door jolted but held.

Li-ara took a step back. The silence was suffocating. Her ears strained for the sound of the first crack, the first sign they could break through. The seconds stretched, each one more excruciating than the last.

Kii and Beta stood rigid, their ears pinned back, their eyes unblinking. They were listening, too. Waiting. Watching. Every muscle in their bodies coiled like a spring.

Then, from behind her, a low, broken sound. A groan.

Li-ara's head snapped around.

The Hunter.

The terror outside would have to wait. She couldn't control what was out there. Not now. Not yet. But inside, someone needed her. Someone who she had risked everything for. She wasn't about to lose him now.

She turned and ran to him.

"I need to get you into bed so I can properly dress your wounds. But after our journey here, I don't have the strength to pull you. I need your help. If I help you, is there any way you can stand?" She detected no response. Again, she contemplated removing his helmet to discover if he was still alive. "I can't lift you by myself. Can you help me?"

A faint "I think so" reached her ears.

"Together, we can do this," she whispered.

Li-ara dragged a living room chair to the side of the stretcher. Slipping her arm around his waist and anchoring herself to his battered body, she lifted. Gripping the arm of the chair, the Hunter pushed. His legs quivered violently beneath him, but he rose, his muscles one command away from surrender.

"It's only about ten steps. We'll do this one step at a time," Li-ara said, her voice low and steady.

The Hunter moved his right foot, scraping it across the floor forward. He dragged the left foot behind, hesitant and weak. Each movement was a battle, each breath a ragged, desperate gasp. Li-ara took more of his weight, her knees nearly buckling under the effort. She could feel him fading.

Another step. Then another.

But seven steps in, he buckled.

"Wait!" she gasped, but his legs folded beneath him. Li-ara twisted her body, pivoting his weight toward the mattress. With a heavy thud, he dropped onto the bed, limbs sprawled, utterly still.

Li-ara staggered back, chest heaving. Her hands trembled. But he was on the bed. He was breathing.

Outside, the howls began to fade, receding into the woods and the night.

She dropped to the floor, chest heaving, blood on her arms, her shirt, her hair.

The cabin was silent.

Calming her breathing and her heart rate, Li-ara pushed herself up from the floor. She didn't have the luxury of resting. The Huntsman's wounds needed attending to, or he'd never survive the night.

Li-ara moved swiftly through the kitchen, her footsteps slapping against the wood floor. She grabbed what she could: clean towels, her sewing kit, bottles of medicine, a flame igniter, a cutting board, wooden spoons, the last of her bandages, and the strongest liquor she had. She did not take the time to think, only act.

"I need to stitch those bear bites first," Li-ara said as she pulled three needles and a thick spool of carpet thread from the sewing kit. Flicking the igniter, she passed the needles through the flame, disinfecting them. Cutting off long strands of thread, she threaded each needle and set them aside.

"I'm going to remove your helmet so I can give you something for the pain."

"The helmet stays on," came a weak voice.

"But you need something for pain."

"Do you have something I can bite down on?"

Li-ara thought. "I can give you a piece of kindling wood."

"Do it."

She dashed to the fireplace and selected a short, solid piece from the bucket - smooth, unburned, unyielding. Returning to his side, she hesitated only a second before lifting the front of his helmet just enough to see his mouth.

Blood.

Dry and cracked, streaked across his chin. Her stomach twisted. She wanted to see more, but she didn't lift the covering higher. She placed the stick gently between his teeth and lowered the helmet again.

"I can't stitch your wounds or attend to your injuries with your armor on. Can I at least remove that?

"Yes."

Li-ara exhaled sharply and reached for the knife at his waist, removing it and setting it aside. Li-ara unbuckled the empty holster. The belt dropped heavily to the floor. Then, she pried off the shredded breastplate, wincing at the wet sound of a seal breaking. She rolled him carefully to the side and slid the backplate away, fingers slick with blood. His undershirt, soaked and torn, ripped easily as she pulled it back. She gasped.

His chest was a roadmap of pain. Claw marks, fresh and angry, ran from rib to hip, but beneath them were countless scars. Old wounds. Deep ones. Layers of healing stacked across years of battle. Some were jagged. Some surgical. Some looked like they'd been burned shut.

What kind of life had this man lived?

Pouring water over the fresh bear bites, she began gently scrubbing away the dried blood and crusted powder. The Huntsman flinched, his jaw tightening on the stick, but he didn't make a sound.

"There are five deep punctures," Li-ara murmured, mostly to herself, eyes narrowing as she examined the torn flesh. "Looks like side-mouth bites - grabs, not a full clampdown. One's definitely from the main canine." She pressed a cloth to the worst of them, noting the dark, sluggish bleed.

"The bleeding's slowed, but these will still need stitching." She poured the liquor straight across the wounds.

His body convulsed. A low groan emerged, muffled by the wood in his mouth. Sweat burst across his skin, his chest heaving. She patted him dry, then positioned the first needle, breath held.

"This will hurt," she whispered.

His muscles coiled beneath his sweat-slicked skin. The veins in his neck stood rigid.

She drove the needle through torn flesh with surgical precision. The resistance - skin, then fat, then muscle - gave way with a sickening pop.

His body convulsed violently off the blood-soaked bed. The wooden stick splintered between his clenched teeth, fragments cutting into his gums. A metallic tang filled his mouth.

The next stitch tore through him like molten iron. A primal howl erupted from somewhere deep within. It was the sound of a man being broken. The raw agony in his cry reverberated through the cabin walls.

Her hands trembled uncontrollably, warm crimson coating her fingertips. Tears welled in her eyes, blurring her vision as she fought to maintain composure. Each ragged breath he took sent tremors through her own chest as if their pain had become one shared torment.

"Stay with me," she commanded, though her voice betrayed her terror. "Do you want me to stop?"

"No," he choked out.

Using her shirt, she wiped the tears from her eyes and the sweat from her face. She braced herself and pushed on. A second stitch. He screamed again. She clenched the needle as it slipped in the blood. Another stitch, another horrific scream. By the fourth pass, Li-ara was shaking so badly she could barely hold the needle.

"I'm done with that one. That was the worst," she whispered, even though she knew it wasn't true.

She moved to the next bite. His body arched, and a scream tore from his throat, a cry from the damned, echoing with pain so deep it felt inhuman.

The thread bit into his skin as she pulled, but instead of holding, the flesh tore wide open. The suture ripped clean through, shredding the fragile tissue like wet paper. Blood spilled fast, fresh and dark, pulsing from the reopened wound. His skin was too damaged, too thin.

"No more," he gasped.

"I need to close these wounds, or you could bleed to death," she said. "Please, let me give you the pain medicine."

"The helmet stays on."

Frustration flared in her, but so did mercy. He was soaked, half-conscious, and trembling. And she couldn't bear to hear him scream again. She nodded, even though he couldn't see it.

"All right. I'll disinfect the others and seal them with powder. Maybe it'll be enough."

The stranger didn't reply. He'd slipped into unconsciousness once more, drifting into the only place left that was free from pain.

Thankful he wasn't conscious, Li-ara removed the remainder of his armor with quiet movements, allowing her tears to flow freely. Beneath his leg armor, his pants were shredded, barely clinging to his hips. She cut away what little remained. His legs were scraped and gouged, but mostly intact, yet covered in scars, like his chest. One stretched from thigh to ankle, long and pale and cruel.

How was this man still alive?

Li-ara covered his naked body with a sheet and turned her attention to his arms. Her fingers fumbled over buckles and clasps slick with blood. She unfastened the rerebraces, lifting the battered upper arm plates free and tossing them aside with a metallic thud.

Next came the vambraces. The right forearm armor was wedged tightly from swelling beneath. She pried it loose, biting back a curse as it resisted, then finally gave with a jolt.

Last were the gloves, heavy, jointed things meant for battle and hunting. She tugged them off one finger at a time, revealing bruised, blood-caked hands beneath.

He looked fragile without the armor. Human. Vulnerable. But at least now, she could reach what mattered.

His right arm was badly swollen, the flesh bruised and angry beneath the skin. It hung at a crooked angle, bones misaligned as if the limb had been wrenched and forgotten. Li-ara sliced the sleeve open. She gently pressed her fingers along the length of the bone, feeling for a break. The skin was hot, the swelling tight. She found two fractures. Gently, she moved the arm to the side.

Li-ara sliced away the remains of the tattered garment, exposing the raw, dirt-smeared gashes along his arms and hands. None were deep enough for stitches. She dipped a washcloth into the disinfectant and dabbed it gently across every scrape and cut.

Her bandage supply once more depleted, Li-ara crossed the room to her closet and pulled out a clean shirt. She tore it into long, narrow strips as she returned to his side.

It was time to move the fractured radius and ulna back into alignment. She positioned her hands on either side of the break, fingers pressing into swollen tissue. She felt for the breaks and manipulated the bones back into alignment with a swift, decisive motion. The sickening crunch of calcified tissue finding its proper place again turned her stomach. Cries escaped the stranger's throat, a response to the pain she inflicted again.

Positioning the wooden spoons parallel to the realigned bones, Li-ara improvised a splint. With meticulous care, she wound bandages around the makeshift cast and secured it to a cutting board. A crude but effective immobilization device.

The left arm was in better shape. No fractures, just a deep, angry bruise stretching from elbow to wrist. Still, as a precautionary measure, she wrapped it tightly.

Exhausted, Li-ara stumbled to the kitchen, dumped the basin of red water, and refilled it with clean. She rewashed every inch of him she could reach, then replaced the blood-stained, sweat-soaked sheet.

She leaned close, whispering into his helmet, "Please live." Then she crawled to the chair and curled inside, pulled a blanket around her, and closed her eyes.

Li-ara had collapsed into the heavy silence of exhaustion, her body surrendered to sleep she hadn't meant to take. She didn't hear the soft, sinister padding outside - the return of the wild canines, noses pressed to the door, breath fogging the seams. She didn't notice Kii and Beta rise from their posts, muscles taut, tails rigid, pacing in anxious loops. Their claws tapped a restless warning across the wooden floor.

Then the screaming began.

It shattered the night like glass, high-pitched, primal, filled with pain.

Li-ara jolted upright, her heart slamming against her ribs, the nightmare still clinging to her But this scream wasn't in her head.

It was *real*.

"I'm here," she gasped, bolting upright.

The Huntsman's back arched violently off the bed, a cry tearing from his throat like fire. His body trembled with agony.

"What do you need?"

"Pain," he rasped. "Too much … pain."

She ran to the kitchen, mixed a tablespoon of pain powder and water, and rushed back. "Here, drink this. It should ease your pain. I'll leave so you can remove your helmet."

"I… I can't." His voice cracked. "No strength."

Li-ara froze. She stared at the mask covering his face. He needed the medicine. Now. Her mind spun.

"Can you hold the glass?" she asked, desperation edging her voice.

"No."

Panic clawed at her throat. She looked around, eyes darting over the room, searching, pleading for something, what she didn't know. Then she saw it.

"My scarf," she breathed, lunging for it.

She yanked the thick wool scarf off the coat and ran back to his side. Sitting beside him, she wrapped it around her head, tying it tight. Then, she closed her eyes.

"I'm blindfolded. I can't see. I promise. I'm going to help you drink."

"No," he whispered.

"You *have* to trust me," she said firmly. "The helmet's coming off, whether you like it or not. If I wanted to see your face, I had plenty of chances while you were unconscious. It's the only way to ease your pain."

Silence.

"Will you let me help you?"

"Yes."

She reached forward, fingers reaching out, searching for the helmet. Her fingers hit the covering, its metal cold against her fingertips. Slipping her fingers beneath the rim, she lifted. It was lighter than she expected.

Still blind, she located the glass, then his hand. Wrapping his fingers around it, she lifted his hand to his lips.

"Can you guide it?"

"I think so."

He drank half. Then, she felt the glass slip, his strength gone.

"I've got it," she whispered. "I'll tip it to your mouth. Tell me when it's gone."

Slowly, drop by drop, she poured the liquid into his mouth.

"Done," he whispered.

She groped for the helmet and placed it carefully back over his head, securing it in place. Then she slipped off the scarf and sighed in relief. "There. That wasn't so bad. The medicine should hit soon."

"Thank you," came the voice behind the mask.

She reached out and took his hand. His fingers squeezed hers weakly, but it was enough to make her chest ache.

"You're welcome," she whispered. "Now sleep. I'm right here if you need me."

She returned to her chair, curled up with the blanket again, and held his hand beneath the covers until morning.

4 EMBARRASSMENT

A chorus of morning birds called from the trees, crisp and sweet, drifting through the window boards like a soft knock on her senses.

Li-ara stirred. Her eyes fluttered open, blinking into the hazy gold light pouring across the floorboards. Judging by the lengthy sunbeams across the walls, the sun had been up for hours.

She shifted with a wince. Her back ached. Her legs were stiff. She hadn't meant to fall asleep in the chair, but exhaustion had anchored her there. The cushion, though beautiful, offered no kindness. She rubbed her neck, rolling her shoulders with a grimace.

A soft breath of air passed over her toes. She glanced under the bed. Kii's tail gave a lazy wag. Beta, still curled tight against the wall, let out a small huff, stirring only slightly.

Stretching, Li-ara felt the stiffness in her limbs as the memories of yesterday surged back like a flood: the bloodied Huntsman collapsing, the relentless wild pack circling, the trembling precision of needle and thread as she stitched flesh not her own. She turned toward him. He was so still. Cautiously, she leaned in, holding her breath as she hovered just above the edge of his helmet. Then, barely audible, like a whisper caught in sleep, came the faintest snore.

Noticing Li-ara was awake, Beta and Kiss slipped out from beneath the bed, their bodies low and tails already swaying. After a long, luxurious stretch, back arched and paws extended, they trotted toward the front door, tails whipping with urgency and purpose. Nature was calling, and waiting wasn't an option.

"Let me check and see if it's okay to go outside," Li-ara said, padding across the floor toward the door.

Halfway across the room, walking around the forgotten stretcher, Li-ara stopped. Her gaze locked onto the door. Her stomach sank. The door was upside-down and backward. Again, the night surged back in jagged flashes: the frantic heaving to lift the door upright, hammering the hinge pins with shaking hands as the canines closed in, the moment she realized she'd mounted it wrong.

She exhaled slowly. A giggle escaped her throat. She'd need to find time to fix the door. The wild canines wouldn't forget the Huntsman so easily. They'd come back.

Kicking the chair aside, she crept forward and gave the door a cautious push. It groaned open an inch. She leaned into the gap and scanned the yard. Sparse underbrush, open ground. Nothing obvious for a predator to hide behind. Li-ara scanned to the left. The barn loomed quiet and still, the perfect place for an animal to conceal themselves. And then there was the back of the house. She was blind to anything hiding there, waiting for her to make a mistake.

"What do you think, Kii?" she whispered. "Are they gone? Is it safe?"

Kii glanced up at her, ears perked. Then a single sharp bark. His tail wagged like a flag in the wind.

She gave a wry smile. "I'll take that as a yes."

The door creaked wider. Kii shot through it like a loosed arrow, Beta bounding after him, both tails high.

"Don't go far," she called. "And Kii, catch me a bird, will you? A broth might do our friend some good."

Opening the top section of the door, a cool breeze stirred the cabin's stillness, washing away the smell of blood. Li-ara filled a basin with warm water. Gathering the few clean towels that remained, she carried them and the water to the bedside table. She removed another shirt from her closet and ripped it into long strips of cloth for bandages. Moving with quiet purpose, she sat down beside the stranger, her eyes fixed on the figure lying motionless in the bed. It was time to tend his wounds.

Lifting his left arm, Li-ara carefully unwrapped the bandages. The bruises had faded from black to a deep, angry purple, stretching down to a dull yellow at the edges. She ran her fingers lightly along the muscles. They were probably still tender, but healing. She laid the arm down on the bed. For now, she'd leave it unwrapped and wrap it after she attended to the rest of his wounds. Another day of compression would help with the swelling.

Li-ara looked at the broken arm. The bone needed time, immobility, patience, and quiet. Best to leave it alone. She studied the swelling, the deep bruising that crept from beneath the wrapping. With a breath she didn't realize she'd been holding, she draped the edge of the blanket over it.

She folded the covers down to his waist. Dipping a towel in the water, she wrung out a cloth, steam rising faintly from the basin. Slowly, carefully, she bathed him.

The cloth glided across his neck, beneath the helmet, catching flakes of dried black blood. It peeled away in brittle flakes, some of it caught in the stubble along his jaw. She kept her strokes gentle.

His chest was a battlefield of claw marks. The bear must have been enormous, its power immense, to tear through a Huntsman's defense like it did. His breastplate, though battered and splintered, had done its job - barely. It had absorbed just enough of the assault to keep him alive. Just enough to give her a chance to save him.

Li-ara noted that two of the new wounds would leave marks of their own, permanent souvenirs. But the surrounding tissue was clean. No redness. No swelling. No smell. He was healing.

She moved lower, across his abdomen, her cloth tracing along the ridges of muscles beneath. Something stirred deep within her. Despite the wounds, his body was still strong, firm, masculine. Even at rest, she could feel his power.

With a slow breath, she pulled the covers off his legs.

Each cut, each bruise, each scab she examined as she ran the warm cloth across them. Most were superficial. Scratches. But just above the knee, where his shin armor had ended, she spotted two cuts she'd missed the night before. Swollen. Red. Oozing at the edges.

"Damn it," she muttered.

She dipped the cloth again, then hesitated, listening for any sound that he was awake. He didn't stir. Her hands moved with practiced care, pressing the warm cloth to the inflamed skin.

33

He flinched, barely. A twitch. Then stillness.

She scrubbed gently until the scabs lifted and bled anew. She wiped away the fresh blood and, hopefully, the infection. Li-ara dipped the cloth again, continuing her work.

"That hurts," came the masculine voice.

"I'm sorry. I missed two cuts last night. They're red, so I wanted to clean them well."

"Leave them open. They will heal faster."

"I thought that same thing. How do you feel?"

"Like a bear tried to eat me."

Li-ara laughed. "I'll let you in on a secret. One did. Do you need something for the pain?"

"Perhaps after you're done. How are the side bites?"

"I haven't checked them yet. I planned on doing them last."

She gently lifted the bandages. The bright blue thread she used to stitch the wounds was visible against the swollen red skin. Dried, crusted blood covered the bites. "They appear to be healing. A clear liquid is draining from them, which is an excellent sign. I will wash them, apply medicine, and re-wrap them. We must keep them covered until they stop draining."

He shifted, a groan slipping from his throat as he instinctively tried to move his right arm.

Li-ara reached out fast, her fingers landing gently on his bare shoulder. "No, don't," she said, her voice low but firm.

His muscles tensed beneath her touch. He flinched as if even her light contact sent shockwaves through the battered nerves.

"It's broken," she added softly, her hand not pulling away. "You'll only make it worse."

For a moment, he said nothing. He lay there, breathing hard beneath the helmet. But the arm stayed still.

Her fingers lingered on his skin a heartbeat longer before retreating. "You don't like being touched, do you?"

"No. How bad is the arm?"

"You broke it in two places. I set the bones, and they are mending. As for touching you, I am afraid there's no way around that. You can only use your left hand, and its strength is weak. If you are going to become better, I need to doctor you. And that involves touching your skin."

"Just don't remove the helmet."

"The helmet," Li-ara said in unison. "I know. It stays on no matter what."

"That is the Huntsmen's tradition. To protect the Hunter and his clan, his or her face must remain hidden from outsiders."

"Even in life and death situations?"

"Yes."

"Pretty dumb tradition, if you ask me."

"I didn't. Where is my weapon?" The Hunter raised his head in search of his gun. As he did, he saw he was naked. "Please cover my body."

"What, no one may look at your body either?" She asked, lying the sheet across his mid-section. "I can't cover your entire body until I finish tending to your wounds and re-wrap them."

"I know of no rule stating my body cannot be seen. I feel..."

Li-ara continued dressing his wounds as she waited for the Hunter to finish his sentence. He remained silent. Had he fallen asleep?

"You feel what?"

Beneath the helmet, the Hunter drew in a long breath, then exhaled. "I am not accustomed to being helpless and at the mercy of another, especially someone I don't know. Lying here with no clothes makes me feel, well, awkward and vulnerable. Plus, you're a female."

"I thought we established the fact that we're not female and male. I'm your nurse, and you're my patient."

"So, we did. I need my weapons and my clothes."

Li-ara tilted her head towards a pile of material and hardware on the chair. "Your knife and gun is lying on the chair along with what's left of your clothes."

"Only one gun? I have two."

"You only had one with you when I found you. As for your clothes, the bear shredded them to pieces. What remained I had to cut off to dress your wounds. I didn't have a way of saving them." She placed three layers of cloth over the bear bite and taped the bandage in place. "But you will need clothes, eventually. When you're better, I'll go to town and buy material to make you a new shirt and pants."

"I'm to remain naked until then?"

"You can wear one of my lacey nightshirts." Li-ara laughed. "A nightie is the only thing I have that might fit you." She wished she could witness the look on his face.

"Naked will be fine. What of my armor? How much damage did the bear do to it?"

"Most of it is okay. Your breastplate took the brunt of the bear's attack. It's pretty bent up and torn. I thought a Huntsman's armor could withstand anything."

"Normally, that's true. Our armor can withstand a strike force up to a hundred and fifty *glancs* without damage. But that bear was enormous. I've never encountered one of that strength and fierceness."

Li-ara reached up and felt the teeth indentations on the side of the Huntsman's helmet. "Most fanged bears are, but even I haven't heard of one large enough to do this much damage. He must be very old. He even left new marks on your helmet as well."

"I'd say more like one in the prime of his life." Using his uninjured arm, the Hunter reached up, his fingertips falling inside the teeth indentations. "He did his best to sink his teeth into my skull. At least these can be hammered out with no problem. Had he succeeded in penetrating the metal, we wouldn't be speaking." He paused for a second, the realization of how close he had come to death reverberating in his mind. "Would you bring my gun and knife over and place it beside my left hand?"

"You think you'll be needing weapons?"

"A Hunter is never without his weapon."

She tried to imagine how she would feel if their roles were reversed and asked no further questions. "Do you want your gun in or out of the holster?"

"Out."

Li-ara retrieved his weapons and placed them beside his uninjured hand. She took his fingers and wrapped them around the gun's handle. "Here you are."

Grasping the handle, the Hunter lifted the gun two inches above the bed before his hand crashed. "I don't even have any strength in my good arm."

36

"Give yourself some time. Your body's been through a lot. I'm sure by tomorrow, you'll be able to raise your weapon."

"Perhaps. I will take that pain medication now."

Li-ara walked into the kitchen and mixed the bitter tonic. Repeating the procedure from the previous night, she blindfolded herself with the scarf and lifted his helmet just enough for him to drink.

"In case you're wondering," she said softly, "my name is Li-ara."

A pause. Then a sound so soft, so sincere, "Thank you, Li-ara, for saving my life."

"You're welcome. Remember, your gun is at your side. Try not to shoot me or the canines."

"I thought I remembered dogs."

"They're *Gloxdirian* Canines."

He turned slightly. "That breed's extinct."

"Apparently not. I've got two."

"Ferocious man-eaters, aren't they?"

"Only when I'm in a bad mood."

He chuckled. She liked his laugh. Warm. Real.

"Where are they now?"

"Getting us breakfast."

"Are they good shots?"

She grinned. "Better than you, I think."

A pause. Then, unexpectedly, "You have a beautiful smile."

Her heart skipped. "Thank you. Do you have a name? Something I can call you?"

"I am known as Hunter."

"Not very original."

"It is sufficient."

"That it is. Do you need anything, Hunter?"

"Just more rest." Li-ara covered him with the sheet and blanket, tucking both around his body. She heard a yawn, followed by a soft snore.

Li-ara eyed the chair beside the Huntsman, her body aching for rest. But the moment passed. Too much to do.

With the town out of reach, she wondered if any of Kal's old clothes remained. The thought of the Huntsman's bare, sculpted torso flickered in her mind. Her cheeks flushed hotly. *Focus,* she scolded herself, grinning despite it.

She crossed to the closet and dragged out the marriage trunk. Dust puffed into the air as she lifted the lid. Her wedding dress lay on top. Beneath it, old photos of her parents, her brother, a flash of smiles, and long-ago days. She paused, thumbing through the images. It had been five years since she'd left for a new life. Kal had died four days into it, killed by a fanged bear. She had no photos of him, only fading memories.

She reached deeper and uncovered a pair of dark trousers and a neatly folded blue shirt. She gave the shirt a shake. It looked like it might fit. The pants were definitely too short. Maybe enough fabric resided in the cuffs to fix that.

A sudden scratching at the door jolted her. She shoved everything back into the trunk, except for the clothes, and hurried to the door. She opened it to find Kii on the porch, tail wagging like mad, a fat wild chicken dangling from his mouth. His eyes sparkled with pride. He'd done his part.

"Where's Beta, Kii?" Li-ara asked. The female never missed a meal when Kii brought something home. "Beta? Girl, where are you?"

A sharp bark pulled her gaze to the barn. Beta stood guard by the door, alert and tense. On the other side, Li-ara heard Fillo baying.

"Oh no," Li-ara said. "Fillo, I never put you in your stall or fed you last night."

She shoved her feet into her boots, grabbed her weapon, and sprinted across the yard.

"I'm so sorry, girl. I meant to put you inside and give you food and water, "Li-ara said as she pulled the barn door open." Fillo stood just inside. "I just got occupied with the Huntsman." Fillo huffed, clearly unimpressed. "You're right. That's no excuse."

Li-ara reached for Fillo's reins and turned to lead him forward. But stopped cold. Kii's low growl rumbled through the air behind her,

Kii stood beside the barn door, his back hairs raised, nose to the ground, growling low and steady. Li-ara dropped to one knee and studied the earth. Tracks. Wild canine tracks. And they were fresh.

Her stomach turned. Beta hadn't just been loitering. She'd been protecting Fillo. But why hadn't they attacked? The door wasn't secured. Her pack animal had been easy prey. She glanced toward the mountains. Was it the stranger? Were they still hunting the Huntsman?

Why?

Li-ara looked between her two loyal companions. "We need to get rid of his scent. All of it."

Both tails thumped in agreement.

"We'll burn the bloody bandages and clothing. Anything soaked through. The rest of the sheets and towels I'll wash. And the lock. I need to put it on the inside of the door. But that upside-down door won't stop them if they're determined to get him."

She watered and fed Fillo quickly, gave her a rub between the ears, then raced back to the house.

Water pans hit the stovetop in rapid succession. As the heat rose, she moved through the house in a blur, gathering anything touched by blood. Bedding and towels landed by the sink. Bandages, shredded clothes, anything ruined, were tossed into the stretcher still lying on the floor. The blanket that carried him home would have to be burned along with the stretcher bars. She'd have to remember to scrub the floor beneath the blanket.

There was no time to waste. Every second counted. Somewhere out there, the wild canines were waiting, plotting.

Kii eyed the bird he had caught hanging on the kitchen wall hook. "Sorry, Boy. I don't have time right now to dress the chicken. We must rid the house of his blood, or the wild canines will think the Hunter is weak and an easy target."

Li-ara dragged the step stool to the sink and climbed up, fingers groping through the cluttered upper cupboard. Her hand brushed cold metal. *Got it.* She hopped down, cradling a small, dented tin in her palm. Inside were thirty wooden matches, worn but dry. Precious. She rarely used them, saving each for when a fire couldn't wait.

Today, one couldn't wait.

Clutching the tin, Li-ara shoved it deep into her pocket and jumped down. She untied the blood-soaked blanket from the stretcher bars, wrapping its stained edges tightly around the items that she had to burn. She disassembled the stretcher, tucking the wooden poles under her arm alongside four sticks of kindling.

Juggling the awkward load, she leapt from the porch and sprinted to the fire pit. She dumped everything - the blanket bundle, the poles, the kindling - onto the blackened earth. Breath ragged, she darted around the yard, snatching up sticks and brittle branches, throwing them onto the growing pile. Then she dropped to her knees, pulled out the match tin, and flipped the lid open.

She struck the first match. A flare, brief, bright, then nothing.

She cursed under her breath and lit another.

It sparked… then fizzled, useless.

She dashed to the side of the porch and ripped up two fistfuls of brittle, dead flowers. Back at the pit, she stuffed them into the pile. One more match. Flame ignited. She eased it into the nest of dried blooms, and for a heartbeat, it flickered uncertainly.

"Come on, damn it. Burn. I don't have time for games." The flame caught, leaping up, hungry and alive.

Li-ara crouched low and blew gently, coaxing the flames until heat licked her face and the bloodied remnants curled into ash.

"Beta, stay here and monitor the fire. Bark if you need me." She ran back to the cabin, sweat now covering her body. The day was too hot for so much running around.

The water on the stove was starting to boil. She pumped chilly water into the kitchen sink and added a pan of boiling water and soap. She pushed the bedding down into the water, using the bar soap to scrub areas covered in dried blood. Leaving the wash to soak, she grabbed the chicken. Seeing it was time, Kii ran in a tight circle, barking for his treat.

"Shh, you'll wake him." She tiptoed toward the bedroom to learn if her visitor was still asleep. He groaned. "I'm sorry if Kii woke you. He's been waiting for me to dress a bird. Do you need more pain medication?"

"No, I have a different problem."

"What kind of problem?"

"I desperately need to urinate."

"Oh," was all Li-ara said.

"Where are your facilities?"

"Facilities?"

"Your toilet?"

"It's outside."

"I need you to help me reach it."

"You can't get out of bed. You'll fall flat on your face. And I can't lift you back into bed."

"What do you propose I do? Urinate right here in the bed?"

Li-ara thought for a moment. "I have an idea. Wait right there."

"I wasn't planning on leaving quite yet."

Li-ara dashed into the kitchen and grabbed a glass jar from the cupboard filled with nails. She dumped the contents onto the table, rinsed the bottle out, and brought the container to the Hunter.

"Here, you can go in this. When you're done, I'll dump the contents outside. Urine is an excellent way to keep critters away." She hoped the liquid would also deter the wild canines.

"And how am I supposed to use that? I only have one good hand. I can't hold it and the bottle. You must hold it for me."

"Hold it?"

"The bottle."

"Oh."

"You didn't think I meant?"

"Oh, no. I realized you meant the bottle." Her face bright red, and her hand shaking, Li-ara held the bottle out.

"I can't pull back the blanket and sheet. You must do that."

"Oh, right." Taking the bedding, she pulled the covers to the side, revealing his private parts once more. Li-ara closed her eyes and held out the bottle.

"Open your damn eyes. I can't get anything inside with the bottle shaking like that. You've already seen everything I have. You didn't care I was naked earlier when you bathed me and dressed my wounds. Why are you modest now?"

She giggled in embarrassment. "I don't know. Nursing you was one thing. This is different."

"Just pretend this is another part of nursing. Can you help me sit up a little?"

Sitting the bottle down, Li-ara slipped her arms under his shoulder and lifted him forward to a semi-sitting position. A groan escaped his throat. The odor of his body filled her nostrils. The smell was powerful, a mixture of body odor and blood intermingled with the pleasing scent of the lavender soap she used to wash his body. Unconsciously, she breathed in his aroma deeply. She sensed him staring at her. At least she thought he was under the helmet.

"Sorry. Stay forward, and I'll put the pillows behind you." After the pillows were in position, she retrieved the bottle and held it near his groin. "Ready when you are." She wondered if he was as embarrassed as she was. Her hand shook. It didn't matter what the Hunter said, this was different. She kept her eyes on the bottle.

Sighing with relief, the Hunter directed his stream into the bottle. The liquid rose inside the container, and Li-ara feared it would overflow. The urine stopped just beneath the rim. Exhausted, he lay back on the pillows.

"Thank you." She held the bottle up to the light, inspecting the contents. "What are you doing now?"

"Checking for blood. Any redness in the urine would mean you are bleeding internally."

"Do you detect any?" Li-ara noted a tone of concern in his voice.

"No, your urine is a nice clear yellow. No internal bleeding."

"That's good." Within seconds, he was asleep once more.

5 TIGRINE EPIDOL

"Hmm, something smells good," the Hunter announced as the odor of cooking chicken soup tantalized his nose. He wasn't hungry, but if he wanted to regain his strength and heal, he needed substance.

"My specialty. Chicken and vegetable soup," Li-ara shouted from the kitchen. She walked into the bedroom carrying a stein of homemade soup, a glass of water, two towels, and her scarf. "I remembered my husband had this stein up in the cupboard that you can use. I cut the vegetables and meat up really small so you can drink the soup." She placed the items on the nearby table. "Ready to be lifted again?" Li-ara placed her arms under his shoulders while he hugged her neck. "Once I bring you forward, I'll rearrange the pillows behind you again. They slid down while you were sleeping." As she lifted the injured Hunter, she thought he was a little weaker. "Doing okay?" she asked as she stuffed the two pillows behind his back.

"Yes. My right arm needs to come down some."

"Don't you try to move it," Li-ara stated as she hurried around the bed. She lifted the splinted arm and laid the appendage across his lap. "How's that?"

"Better."

"Still no chance of removing the helmet?"

"You may ask me a thousand times, and each time my answer will be the same. My helmet cannot be removed as long as you are in the room."

"Unless I'm blindfolded." She tucked one towel beneath his chin.

"Not even then. But I foresee no alternative except to starve to death. I cannot grow stronger without nourishment."

At least he realized that much, Li-ara thought. "I won't be able to determine where your mouth is with the blindfold on. May I use my hand to locate your mouth?"

"That should be tolerable."

"You really don't enjoy being touched, do you?"

"I'm … I'm … It's just that no one has touched me for many decades. I am no longer accustomed to anyone's skin touching mine."

"Decades? How long have you worn the helmet?"

"Since the day I entered Bounty Hunter training. I was eighteen."

"And you haven't taken it off since you were eighteen?"

"I take the helmet off all the time. Just not in the presence of others. It is …"

"Your custom, I remember. Okay, let's try this."

Li-ara tied the scarf firmly over her eyes, plunging herself into darkness. Her hands moved with practiced care as she reached up and gently lifted the Hunter's helmet free. She stretched out her right hand until it found the stein of soup. With her left, she reached blindly toward him, fingertips brushing his face. She hit his nose. A quiet giggle escaped her lips, unexpected, soft.

Adjusting, she slid her hand to the side, tracing down the curve of his cheek until her fingers found his mouth. She paused there, surprised by the warmth of his breath, and the softness of his lips. With slow precision, she lifted the stein, guiding it to meet her other hand.

"Open up." She dipped the stein forward, dropping a small amount of soup inside. "Tell me when you want another sip."

Li-ara distinguished no sound. Was he chewing, or had he swallowed the broth?

"Another."

Feeling for his lips again, she poured more inside. They repeated the process four more times.

"No more."

"You need to eat, Hunter."

44

"Maybe later. After you put my helmet back on, go to my supply belt. In the third compartment to the right of the buckle, you will find a small bottle. Bring it here and pour a third of the bottle in my mouth."

Sitting the stein down on the table, Li-ara replaced his helmet, then retrieved the bottle. No label specified what was inside. She unscrewed the lid and smelled it, but it was odorless.

"What is this?"

"Something that will help me heal better and help with the pain," Hunter said, evading her question.

"But what is it?"

"*Tigrine Epidol.*"

"*Tigrine Epidol?*" Are you crazy? That's a powerful narcotic. Plus, that medication is meant to be taken as an injection, not poured into your mouth."

"Do you have something to inject the liquid with?"

"No."

"Then why are you questioning my request?"

"Because taking it orally is dangerous."

"So is me being in this condition. I am a Bounty Hunter. Just as I hunt others, others hunt me for revenge and retribution. And I fear the canine pack may return."

"They already did. I found fresh prints out by the barn."

"I must heal, and the *Tigrine Epidol* will aid me in my recovery. Plus, it will combat any infection. With all these cuts and wounds, at least one will become infected. In my present condition, such an infection will kill me." She still hesitated. "I cannot protect you or myself like this. I must take the *Tigrine Epidol.* This is my choice. If something goes wrong, you have no blame."

"Have you ever taken this stuff before?"

"Yes. Twice."

"And nothing went wrong?"

"I am here, aren't I?"

His answer didn't comfort her. But he was right. "How will I determine how much to pour in? Remember, I won't be able to see when I do this."

"True. And the bottle contains enough medication to kill me." The Hunter looked around the room. "Pour out the water in the drinking glass and pour a third of the bottle into it. You will be able to give me the appropriate amount."

Li-ara poured out the water and measured the dose into the glass. She hesitated, then covered her eyes and removed the helmet again. Feeling for his lips, she poured the bitter liquid into his mouth, whispering a silent prayer it would help.

Within seconds, his body convulsed violently as a savage tremor seized him. His back arched, his eyes rolled back in his head, and his breath rasped through gritted teeth.

"Hunter, what's wrong?" Li-ara screamed. "I said this was an awful idea. I don't know what to do." She reached up to remove her blindfold.

His hand shot out, closing around her arm with a sudden, rigid grip.

"Don't remove the blindfold," he said. "My face is still exposed. I'm fine." The words came out tight and gritty, like they were being ground between his molars.

"Your damn face!" Li-ara shouted, stomping her foot as she backed away, trembling. "You'll let me poison you! But heaven forbid I see that damn face of yours while I do it!"

Her voice cracked, the last word choked by rising sobs. Tears spilled freely, blinding her. Her body shook as grief overtook her. "I thought I killed you."

"I'm sorry. Please don't cry. This is often a side effect of the medication."

"You didn't think you should tell me that before I gave that medication to you?"

"Would you have given it to me?"

"No."

"That's why I didn't tell you."

Li-ara's tears stopped. She stared at him in disbelief. "To hell with you." She stormed out of the room, her footsteps echoing across the silent space.

"Can you please replace my helmet?"

"Do it your damn self!"

Li-ara muttered under her breath, her jaw tight. Her hands worked fast, removing the front door lock and reinstalling it on the inside. When it finally clicked into place, she stepped back, breathing hard. "Well, it'll have to do."

A chorus of howls traveled across the wind, emanating from the distant forest. The wild canines were awake and active. She needed to hang the laundry on the back porch and bring the canines inside.

She darted out the back door, crossing the yard to the barn. Fillo stood quietly in her stall, watching her with tired eyes. Li-ara gave her fresh water and grain, then closed and locked the windows. She slid the wooden bolt across the door, then wedged two large stones against it for extra peace of mind.

"Kii! Beta!" she called. "Inside. Now."

Both canines came trotting into the house, ears perked, tails high. They spotted the bowls of chicken innards swimming in broth by the door and picked up speed. Their tails thumped the floor as they dug in, content.

Li-ara turned back to the laundry. After rinsing out the blood-stained bedding, she draped it over the porch rails. The towels she hung from the wall hooks by the door. The clothesline out by the trees was too risky this late in the day.

As the last of the light faded, she caught a whiff of the strong soap in the air and muttered, "Let's hope they hate the smell." With any luck, it would keep the wild ones at bay, at least until morning.

One more thing to do, and she could rest. The Hunter's wounds needed cleaning and re-bandaging. As she redressed each wound, Li-ara saw how much better they looked. There was no infection, and each had good scabbing covering them. Perhaps the Hunter was right - the *Tigrine Epidol* did his body good. He just might make a full recovery.

"No!" Li-ara said as she lifted the bandages over the two missed leg wounds that had shown a slight infection earlier. Pus seeped out of the claw marks. The skin was an ugly, bluish-red, and a foul odor drifted up to her nose. Touching his leg, she detected heat radiating from the infection. "This is not good."

Li-ara dashed into the back room and yanked open the drawer where she kept her small stash of medicines. Bottles clinked as she rifled through them, scanning faded labels with shaking fingers. Nothing. Nothing. Still nothing.

The fourth bottle stopped her cold.

A murky liquid inside, thick and bitter-smelling. She remembered it instantly - something the town doctor had given her months ago when Kii tangled with a *glindore*. He had lost a toe during the skirmish. An infection had set in, black and angry. The stuff in this bottle had pulled him back from the brink.

She turned it in her hand, weighing the memory against the risk. If it worked on Kii, maybe it would work on him.

There was no time to second-guess.

Back in the kitchen, she filled a basin with warm water and tossed in crushed garlic and a pinch of cinnamon. From the back porch, she grabbed clean towels and a roll of bandages still warm from the sun.

All she needed now was the *myjigor* flower. Its pale petals were known to pull infection from deep within the flesh. But outside, the light was fading fast. Shadows stretched long across the ground. The night stalkers would soon be on the move.

Li-ara glanced toward the horizon, then back at the door. He needed those flowers. She snatched her weapon, squared her shoulders, and slipped out onto the porch. No time for fear.

She listened astutely. She tried to sort out the various night-time noises. Several howls filled the night air, but they came from the distant hills. A crunching sound caught her ear. Turning, she barely distinguished the shapes of three razorbacks rustling through the harvested corn stalks, rooting for dropped kernels. If they were out, the dark contained no danger from hunters.

"Come, Beta. I believe it's safe. You be my eyes and ears in the dark. Kii, you stay and keep an eye on the Hunter."

Li-ara sucked in a breath and vaulted from the porch, boots slamming against the ground as she tore toward the garden. Beta bolted beside her, every muscle coiled, her nose slicing through the air. A low growl rippled from the dog's throat. The scent of predators was thick. The fur along her spine stood up like a warning.

Almost there.

Li-ara didn't stop. Couldn't. She dropped into a crouch mid-stride, hand sweeping through the garden bed. Her fingers closed around a clump of *myjigor* blooms. Then she was moving again, legs pumping, lungs on fire. The house rose ahead like salvation. The porch steps were only feet away.

Then, a blur in the dimming light.

A *Gloxdirian* canine exploded from the shadows, its massive form slamming into her side. Jaws snapped. Hot breath. Snarling teeth. Li-ara twisted just in time, but not enough. Razor fangs ripped across her arm, slicing through flesh and cloth in one brutal swipe. Pain flared white-hot. Blood soaked her sleeve.

The impact sent her reeling. She stumbled, losing her footing.

Her hand shot out, fingers grazing wood, then catching. The porch railing. With a strangled cry, she dragged herself up and lunged up the steps, taking them two at a time on adrenaline alone.

Beta dashed through the door just as Li-ara pulled it shut behind them.

But before she could completely close it - *BOOM*.

The entire frame shook. The flowers flew from her hand, scattering across the floor. A snarl tore through the crack in the door. A gnarled paw wedged in. Foam-flecked jaws snapped.

Li-ara pulled, her muscles screaming, breath ragged. The creature was winning, pushing the door open, inch by inch.

"No, I won't let you in. You can't have him."

With a roar, she lifted her boot and stomped on the exposed paw with all her weight. A yelp shattered the air. The beast recoiled, limb and muzzle vanishing in retreat.

Li-ara pulled the door shut and rammed the bolt into place.

Silence.

She sank against the door, chest heaving, sweat pouring down her face. Blood trickled from her arm, but she didn't move.

Beta whined softly and nudged her leg.

Li-ara let out a shaky laugh, her voice raw. "Let's never do that again."

Beta barked once in firm agreement

Li-ara scooped up the scattered *myjigor* blooms and carried them to the kitchen table. Blood still trickled from her arm, warm against cooling skin. She yanked back her sleeve and grimaced. The teeth hadn't sunk deep - just long, angry gashes. But they burned like fire.

She moved to the sink, pumped the handle, and let the stream rinse away the blood. Crimson swirled down the drain. She hissed through her teeth as cold water hit raw flesh. Grabbing a clean towel, she wrapped it tight around the wound and tied it off with a jerk.

The Hunter came first.

She turned back to the table, jaw set, eyes locked on the flowers.

Time to save him.

"Hunter, I don't know if you can hear me. The leg wounds are infected. I need to open, drain them, and apply a poultice. I am afraid this will hurt." No response. She hoped he would remain asleep while she did the procedure.

Li-ara dipped the cloth in hot water and wiped away the fresh swellings of pus. A sickly yellow fluid oozed from beneath his skin. The infection was spreading. She swallowed hard and reached for her filleting knife.

"I'm sorry," she whispered, voice barely audible, more for herself than him. With a steadying breath, she pressed the blade to the wound and cut.

The Hunter's body arched. A guttural moan tore from his throat. His legs jerked. Blood spilled from the opened flesh, followed by thick, rotting pus that clung to the air with its sour stench.

Li-ara wiped fast. She could see more festering beneath the surface. Bracing herself, she gripped his leg with both hands and forced the wound open, pressing her fingers deep into the surrounding muscle.

The Hunter screamed, the sound ripped through the cabin, pure, animal pain.

"I know," she said, pressing harder. "I know it hurts. Just hold on."

More blood. More infection. But it was leaving him now. Finally. And she was still standing. Just barely.

Outside, the pack leader prowled the cabin's perimeter like a phantom - silent, calculating, lethal. Her glowing eyes cut through the dark, scanning every board, every seam, every flaw waiting to be torn open. Each step was deliberate. Each breath a test of the air. The scent of blood, fear, sweat. It was all there, thick and ripe.

Behind her, the pack waited, pacing in the gloom, growls rumbling low like distant thunder, barely restrained.

Then, a cry. Sharp. Fragile. Full of pain.

The leader froze, ears snapping forward.

Another cry, high-pitched and desperate sounding. This one emanated from the barn.

The leader's lips curled, exposing long, wet fangs. Her body dropped low as she turned, eyes locked on the barn door. She moved first, her shoulders rippling, paws soundless on the earth. The others followed. Toward the barn. Toward the helpless prey inside.

The hunt had begun.

6 A BATH

Li-ara woke to the sound of a loud thump. She snatched the Hunter's gun from where it rested on the bed, rose to a crouch, and aimed into the shadows. The room was dim, still, silent. She listened, daring not to breathe.

"Kii? Beta?"

A soft shuffle answered from beneath the bed. Two sets of eyes stared back, calm and unbothered. No tension in their bodies. No warning growls.

She exhaled sharply and turned her gaze toward the bed. It was empty. She bolted into a standing position. Fear pumping through her veins, she scoured the room. Her eyes detected a mass on the floor. The Hunter.

A groan of fatigue escaped her lips. He must've rolled too far in his sleep. She let the quilt fall away and stood, stretching her stiff muscles until her back popped.

Yawning, she shuffled toward him, the gun still in hand.

"You just couldn't stay put, could you?" she muttered, already dreading the weight of lifting him.

"I hope you can stand a little because I'm way too tired to lift you into bed." No reply. "Hunter, are you awake?" She now hurried to his side. Why wasn't he answering her? Surely, the fall should have woken him.

She dropped to her knees beside him. He was mumbling soft, unintelligible sounds in a language she didn't recognize. His skin gleamed with sweat, the bedding beneath him soaked through. Her fingers brushed his arm. Searing heat radiated off him. She touched his abdomen, his thigh. Every inch burned.

Fever. A bad one.

She dragged the lamp closer and peeled back the bandages. The wound was bleeding, likely from the fall, but the flesh didn't show signs of a new infection. So why the fever? Fanged bears weren't venomous. At least, not that she knew.

A hundred possibilities thundered through her mind as she tried to pull him off the floor. Dead weight. He was too big, too limp, too far gone. Still, she struggled to lift him.

Li-ara laid the Hunter back on the floor. She shoved her bed across the floor, knocking over a side table. The lamp toppled, clattering to the floor. She didn't stop. She ripped off the sweat-soaked sheets, hauled the feather mattress to the floor, then bent to drag him on.

Her breath came in gasps. Her arms screamed. But somehow, inch by inch, she got him on. His body trembled with fever, uncontrollable shivers wracking him despite the heat blazing inside.

She paused only to listen for his heart. It was there, but faint. His breathing was shallow. Too shallow.

She slid a pillow beneath his head, fingers hesitating near the helmet.

"If that doesn't help," she whispered, "I'm taking it off. I don't care what rules you made. Hate me if you choose. I'll take the consequences for removing it."

Then she bolted through the house, grabbing towels, coats, anything dry. She layered him in fabric, but the shivering didn't stop.

Not enough. She needed more to cover him with. Then she remembered. The closet. The box. The *afghan*.

She nearly ripped the closet door off its hinges getting to it. On the top shelf, tied with a purple ribbon, was the wedding afghan, a gift she had never used. After Kal's death, she couldn't bear to touch it.

Her hands hovered over it.

Then she untied the ribbon and flung the afghan over him, tucking it around his body like it might hold in his soul.

Still cold. Still shivering.

Li-ara dropped beside him. "I'm not letting you die," she whispered hoarsely. "You hear me? Not after everything. Not here. Not tonight."

Her hand closed around his. More was needed. Maybe a warmer room was the answer.

Li-ara spun on her heel and rushed to the back room, aiming for the firewood bin. Three logs. That was it. She'd forgotten to bring in the day's supply from the back porch. How could she forget something so simple? Her mind was too scattered, her body too tired, and now the Hunter was paying for it.

She stared at the pitiful stack of wood. Burn them now and risk the fire dying before dawn, or find another way to warm him. Her gaze shifted toward the bedroom, to the shivering figure beneath layers of mismatched cloth and memories. Body heat. That was all she had left - her canines and herself.

It would have to be enough.

She exhaled and turned to the next, more terrifying problem: his fever.

He was too far gone to take liquid medicine. Delirious. Unresponsive. If she poured medicine into his mouth, he might choke. And that damned helmet. Even if she had something stronger, there was no way to get it past his lips.

She paced, running her hands through her hair.

"Think, Li-ara. Think."

Li-ara stopped, staring at him. She ran over and dropped to her knees beside him, her hands resting inches from the helmet.

"You said this thing couldn't be removed," she whispered, "but I see no other option. You'll die if I don't. Is that what you want? Is death better than letting me see your face?"

She brushed her fingers against the edge of the helmet, hesitant, desperate.

"Hunter, please. What should I do?"

He mumbled, incoherent, lost in fever dreams.

Li-ara's eyes widened.

Tigrine Epidol.

Last time, the medication helped. But it had nearly killed him, too. Could he survive another dose?

"Maybe just a drop or two," she murmured. "Diluted. I can blindfold myself. I won't look. I promise."

She moved to retrieve the liquid, then remembered the crash. The bottle had been on the table when she shoved the bed. It had fallen somewhere. She dropped to her knees, running her hands frantically over the floorboards.

"Come on, come on. Where are you?"

Her fingers closed around the familiar shape. The bottle.

She poured a glass of water and stared at the dark liquid. One part Tigrine Epidol. Three parts water. Enough to help. Hopefully, not enough to kill.

"Hang on," she whispered.

Kneeling beside the fallen Hunter once again, she covered her eyes with the scarf and removed the helmet. With diluted medicine in hand, she prepared to give him a small dose.

"No, this won't work. I can't see how much I'm giving him. If I give him too much, he'll choke. What if it runs out of his mouth and he doesn't get enough?"

Running her fingers around on the floor for something to cover his features, she grabbed the soaked sheet and draped it across his face. She removed the scarf and sat back on her legs.

"I'm sorry, Hunter, but the helmet must stay off. I can't help you if I am blindfolded. You will die if I leave it on, and I can't allow that. Please don't hate me for this."

Li-ara blinked through a vale of tears. She reached out and lifted the edge of the sheet and revealed his lips. Her heart thudded with a mix of dread and determination. As her fingers brushed the fabric, a thought struck her - simple, brilliant.

"You don't need the helmet," she whispered. "You just need something to *hide* your face. It doesn't have to be metal. Cloth will do just fine. And I have the perfect compromise. My Sunday bonnet."

She leapt to her feet, startling both canines. Kii gave a low whuff. Beta tilted her head.

Rushing to the closet, Li-ara grabbed the bonnet Kal had once given her for church. A soft thing, wide-brimmed and decorated with delicate frills. Without hesitation, she ripped the lace from its edges.

"I don't think frills suit you," she said with a watery chuckle. "Unless you want them. Should I ask the experts?" She turned to the dogs. "What do you two think?"

Kii blinked. Beta yawned.

"Exactly what I thought."

She returned to the Hunter's side, voice softening. "Okay, here's the deal. I'll keep my eyes shut while I swap the sheet for the bonnet. Once it's secure, I'll peek. Just enough to adjust it and tie it in place. I'll leave a little space under your chin so I can give you the medicine."

She took a breath to steady herself.

"All right, here we go."

Keeping her eyes closed, she gently pulled the sheet away. Her hands moved carefully, learning the shape of his face by touch alone. She placed the back of the bonnet over his forehead, smoothing it down to conceal his features. When she was sure nothing above his chin was visible, she opened her eyes.

"There," she said softly. "Not bad for a bonnet emergency." She flipped up the bottom edge slightly. "Just enough so you can breathe."

As the fabric shifted, she noticed the coarse texture of several days' beard growth. "You need a shave. Or is stubble your thing?"

Cradling his head, she tied the bonnet behind it, securing the makeshift mask in place. Then she pulled a small spoon from her shirt pocket, filled it with a diluted dose of the medicine, and knelt beside him.

"All right, Hunter," she whispered. "Just a few drops."

Gently, she eased his mouth open and let the liquid fall slowly onto his tongue, one careful drop at a time.

"Please," she breathed, "Let this work."

Once the medicine was gone, Li-ara returned to the task of warming Hunter's body. She patted a spot on the mattress above Hunter. "Kii, I need you to lie down here, above the Hunter. Beta, you lie beside Hunter's

57

right arm. Be careful. That's the broken one." Both canines did as requested.

"Hunter, Kii, and Beta are lying beside you," Li-ara whispered. Their body heat will help keep you warm and hopefully sweat out that fever. I will lie along your good side with my body curled up over yours. Don't be startled if you wake up and find yourself in an awkward arrangement."

Li-ara slid beneath the quilt and layer of clothing, aligning her body next to his. Wrapping her arm around the Hunter, she rested her head on his chest. The heat radiating from his body was almost unbearable, but she remained beside him. She listened to his heart. The beats sounded slower, and his breathing wasn't as labored. As she dozed off, she did not hear him call out her name.

Two hours later, Hunter coughed, waking Li-ara and the canines. She listened intently to his breathing. "Your breathing is better, and your heartbeat is normal." She touched his body. "Your temperature seems to have come down too. I think the *Tigrine Epidol* is working. You've sweated through your bedding again. After I change it, I'll give you some more medicine. Don't worry. I'll make sure your face stays covered."

She had no way of knowing if he heard her or not, but somehow, talking to the Hunter eased her worry. She switched the soaked bedding, laying the sweat-filled sheets out to dry. Climbing back onto the mattress, she curled up beside him.

The sun was up the next time she woke to the sounds of the Hunter speaking in the strange language. Upon her rising, both canines made a mad dash to the front door, desperately needing to relieve themselves. Li-ara peeked through a crack in the door to ensure the wild canines were gone. She opened the front door, and both canines zoomed outside, spraying everything in sight.

The bedding contained little dampness, but Li-ara changed it, anyway. Kneeling beside the Hunter, she carefully redressed his wounds. She placed small drops of the diluted medicine onto his tongue, ensuring he swallowed before giving him more. His condition was improving.

Li-ara hauled armfuls of firewood into the house, stacking the logs neatly in the bin in the back room and across the wall in the living room. With the possibility of wild canines being nearby, she opted to use the house pump to fill a bucket of water for Fillo. She quickly carried the water to the barn.

As she neared the door, she noticed the bottom of the door and the outer wall had been chewed and broken. Had they got inside? She rushed forward, water splashing from the bucket.

She pushed the rocks aside and removed the wooden security bar. Dreading the worst, she burst inside. Fillo neighed, glad to see a friendly face.

"They didn't get inside," Li-ara said, wrapping her arms around the pack animal. "The door held." Wiping away a tear, she emptied the bucket of water into the trough. She remained alert, straining her ears for any sound of wolves beyond the barn walls. She poured a generous portion of grain into the feeder. Using a hay hook, she pulled a heavy hay bale into Fillo's stall.

Slicing through the ties, she allowed the compact bale to fall apart into thick, fragrant portions. Normally, she would spread the hay out in the stall, but not today. "Now, don't you eat this all at once. This hay needs to last a couple of days in case I can't make it out here. Do you understand?" Fillo neighed. "I'd bring you inside if I could. But the house is too small. Besides, the barn is strong. It will keep you safe." Patting the pack animal's side, Li-ara turned and hurried back to the house. Her eyes darted across the yard.

Li-ara sighed when she reached the back porch and witnessed the aftermath of the night's chaos. Her clean laundry lay torn and scattered across the yard, remnants of the wolves' attack. Beta and Kii stayed close, keeping their mistress protected as she retrieved the shredded bedding. She paused at the garden, her fingers plucking more *myjigor* flowers, a handful of mint for tea, and the last of the vegetables untouched by hungry critters.

"Kii, your turn," Li-ara said, stroking the younger canine's head. His sharp gaze met hers, eager to act. "Find us dinner." She sent him off with a quick pat, watching as he darted away into the underbrush. Beta remained by her side, her growl low and constant, a warning to any would-be threats. Thirty minutes later, Kii returned with two freshly caught rabbits hanging from his jaws.

In between the endless tasks, Li-ara checked on the Hunter. Sitting at his bedside for a moment's rest, she explained her actions softly, updating him on his condition even though he remained asleep. His breathing was even now, his fever reduced to a faint warmth.

"You're getting better," she murmured, smoothing the blanket over him before rising again. There was still much to do, but with each small victory, hope flickered brighter in the quiet corners of the cabin.

With the outside chores done, Li-ara began the inside ones. She dressed both rabbits. With one, she made a rabbit stew with half of the vegetables. The other rabbit she fried up for later. The rabbit scraps she fed to the canines, then ate a small bowl of stew. There were more chores to do, but Li-ara decided to lie down again with the Hunter. Crawling beneath the covers, she rested her head on his chest and drifted off.

"Why is my vision blurred?" Hunter shouted. He brushed his finger across his face. "What is over my eyes, and where is my helmet?" He tried to move but seemed pinned down by something lying on his chest. He lifted the cover of the bonnet and looked around. "Why are you lying on me? And why are we on the floor?"

"Hmm?" Li-ara asked, stirring slightly.

"Where is my helmet?" came a thunderous, angry voice.

Li-ara bolted into being awake, surprised the sun was up again. The two canines exited the room. "What? Oh, you're awake."

"I told you my helmet could not be removed. What have you done with it?

Li-ara grabbed his arm before he could yank the flimsy covering off his face. "Don't take it off. I have your helmet right here. Give me your hand." She placed the helmet in his palm. "You can remove the cloth covering and put on the helmet while I let the canines out." Once the canines were outside, Li-ara returned and knelt beside the angry Hunter. His helmet covered his face again. "I made sure I never saw your face. I swear. I kept my eyes closed. But you got so sick and were running such a high fever." Tears filled her eyes. "Oh, Hunter. You couldn't breathe, and your heart was beating so fast. I was so afraid you would die."

"We prefer dying to removing the helmet."

"But I saw nothing. I made sure your face remained covered, but this time with a cloth helmet. That's why I didn't put any eyes in it because I thought it was forbidden to look upon them. Hunter, please understand. You were burning up. I had to find a way to place medicine in you. I'm sorry. I didn't know what to do. I, I ..." Tears flowed from Li-ara's eyes. "I was so scared. Please don't hate me."

Hunter realized what his host had gone through and how close he came to death. Instinctively, he reached out with his good arm and brought her to his chest, holding her tenderly. This action went against everything he practiced, yet he did not question it. "Forgive me. I was wrong to yell. I became frightened because I didn't understand. But I believe you when you say you didn't see my face." Li-ara's tears did not subside. "Please stop crying. You did the right thing. You kept me faithful to my creed while saving my life. I cannot fault you for that." Hoping to shift the subject, he asked, "Is there anything to eat? I'm famished."

"That's because you haven't eaten in two days."

"Two days? Did you forget you fed me soup yesterday?"

Li-ara sat up and looked into the eye band of the helmet. "Hunter, you ate that soup the day before yesterday. You've been unresponsive for two days. That's why I had to . . ."

"Please don't." Tears had never bothered him before. How many bounties cried while begging for their lives? Why did her tears bother him? "What can I do or say to make you understand I'm not mad?"

"I don't know."

"I wasn't kidding when I said I was hungry. Can you help me stand and walk to the chair?"

"You're just trying to make me busy, so I'll stop crying."

"Is it working?"

"Yes." She sat up and stood, offering him a brief smile.

"There's that beautiful smile I remember."

She ignored the comment. "How do you propose we stand you up?

The Hunter looked around the room. "Why are we on the floor?"

"You were delirious and fell out of bed," Li-ara explained. "I didn't have the strength to put you back in bed. So, I brought the bed to you."

"And why were you lying on my naked body?" he teased.

Hunter smiled beneath the helmet when he noticed her face flush red.

"Because I needed to warm you. Your body was freezing from the fever. I covered you with everything I could find. But you were still freezing. Using my body heat was the only thing I could think of to use."

"Sounds like a suitable explanation."

"It's the truth," Li-ara stammered. "You don't think I enjoyed laying with you being naked, do you?"

"Oh, no." Hunter chuckled. Li-ara didn't smile. "I'm still weak, but if you bend down and I put my good arm around you to steady myself, I think I can use my good leg to push myself up."

"Wait. Let me wrap the blanket around you before you try to rise."

"Are you tired of my naked body already?" Li-ara gave him an irritated look. "I guess at the moment, this is not a suitable topic of discussion. But I will need clothes to wear at some point."

"I agree," Li-ara stated. "You were too sick to leave to go into town. But I found some of my husband's clothes that might fit you. But for now, I'm afraid the blanket will have to do."

Once the blanket was securely in place, they tried Hunter's suggestion. To their surprise, it worked. He took a step with his bad leg and grimaced in pain. "Oh, can't do that yet. Way too painful."

Li-ara slipped her arm around his waist. "Lean on me and try hopping on your good leg."

It was only a few hops to the nearby chair. Hunter grabbed the arm, pivoted on his good leg, and plopped into the chair.

"Doing okay?"

"A little exhausted, but okay otherwise."

"Good. I'll bring you some tea and food." When she returned with both, Hunter had dozed off. "Hunter, wake up."

"Just resting my eyes. That trip to the chair took more out of me than I thought. I must be as weak as a newborn baby."

"I added some *faxtip* seeds to your stew. They'll help you replenish your blood supply and strengthen your muscles. Do you need me to feed you?"

"No, I think I can manage."

"I'll close the door so you can take your helmet off and eat."

Once she left, Hunter removed his helmet and took a sip of tea. The warm liquid felt good trickling down his throat.

Li-ara left the door open a crack so she could hear if the Huntsman needed something. Through the opening, Hunter thought he heard her crying again. Had he upset her that much by his statement about removing his helmet?

"Li-ara, may I have some water to drink?"

Hunter searched her face when she brought the water, but he could not determine if she had been crying or not. "I'm not as strong as I thought I was. I don't think I can feed myself after all. Might I accept your offer to feed me?" Before she said anything, he added, "I think I tossed the cloth helmet somewhere over there. I can wear it so you can reach my mouth."

Li-ara quickly retrieved the bonnet and handed it to him. "If you turn around, I'll switch the helmets."

"I can just close my eyes like I always do." A tinge of anger resonated in her voice.

"One of these times, you *will* peak."

"Not today. Now, do you want me to feed you or not?" She closed her eyes.

Hunter switched the helmets as fast as one hand allowed him. He tried balancing the metal helmet on his knee, but it tumbled to the floor, startling her.

"What was that?"

"I dropped the helmet. You can open your eyes now. I'm covered."

"Are you sure?"

"Yes. It won't help us much if neither of us can see." Hunter chuckled, but he heard no response from Li-ara. Still upset. "Do you have any tinted, see-through material around here that can be bent?"

"Nothing that I remember."

"What about tinted eyewear?"

"Never needed such things. Why do you ask?"

"I thought if we found something to put over my eyes while in the cloth helmet, we might eat our meals together. In a few days, I might be well enough to eat with you at the kitchen table."

"Open." Li-ara placed a small spoonful of stew inside his mouth. "I would like that." Hunter noted a softer voice. Perhaps her anger was subsiding.

"If I had my haversack with me, I'd have the exact thing we need inside. You didn't bring a bag with me, did you?"

"No, you didn't have one when I discovered you."

"Probably thrown when the fanged bear attacked, along with my long rifle and second weapon. When I'm a little stronger, we will need to go out to where the attack occurred and retrieve both. That is, if they're still there."

"Few people pass that area. And I comprehend no reason an animal would take your bag unless it contained food. Open."

Hunter chewed and swallowed. "Nope, just some shackles, some extra ammunition, and a change of clothes."

"Open."

"You mentioned your husband's clothes earlier. Is he currently off-world?"

"No. A fanged bear killed him shortly after we moved into this cabin. Open."

Hunter wondered if that was why she had fought so hard to keep him alive. "I am sorry. My encounter must have brought back dreadful memories. How long ago did he die?"

"Open. He died just a little over three years ago. It was his idea to domesticate the *Gloxdirian* canines. He purchased this place for the sole purpose of breeding them. He thought it would make us rich."

"And when he died, you carried on his plan?"

"Open. We had already gotten Beta. She was a young pup he purchased from a nearby farmer. I raised and trained her myself. One day, she came home pregnant and had Kii. Being by myself, I never thought I could breed or train more. Last bite. You were hungry. Here's your helmet. You can switch them again while I take your dish out to the kitchen."

"Thank you."

"I have some work to do in the barn, and I need to clean Fillo's stall. Would you like me to help you back into bed before I go outside?"

Hunter grabbed her hand as she reached for the bowl. "Li-ara, I don't think it's a good idea for you to go out to the barn. It's too dangerous."

"I have to take care of my pack animal."

"When was the last time you fed her?"

"This morning."

"Then she should be okay until tomorrow. Please remain inside where you are safe. Hopefully, I will be stronger tomorrow and I can sit on the porch and keep watch over you." He saw her hesitation. "Please grant me this request."

"I guess she can wait until tomorrow to get her stall cleaned."

"Thank you."

––––––––––––

The sound of clattering pans in the kitchen woke Hunter. "Li-ara, is that you?"

"Did I wake you?" she called from the kitchen.

"No, I was already awake," he lied. "Is it getting dark out there already?"

"Yes."

"How long did I sleep?"

"A few hours. You needed the rest." Li-ara walked into the room, carrying a tall, rounded piece of wood about three inches thick and sixty-four inches long. The top was shaved into an upside-down curve in which sat something resembling an armchair rest. "I made you something to help you walk. You can place the curved part under your right arm, and it can act as an extra leg. I still need to add some padding on the top and a place for your broken arm. Since your right hand isn't strong enough to control it, I thought connecting your board to the outside of the stick would give the needed support you require."

"Can I try it out?"

"Okay, but be careful. You won't have any way to hold on." Li-ara helped Hunter to a standing position, then slipped the crutch into the cradle of his armpit. "Height seems good."

"Yes. Let's see if I can walk with it." Before Li-ara objected, Hunter grabbed hold of the stick with his broken arm and tried to move forward. His hand could not take the stress, and he fell forward. Li-ara caught him just before he went down. "Guess you were right," he stated as she plopped him into the chair.

"Once your arm gets stronger, and I put the straps on, you'll manage better. Now for the next thing on your agenda. Clothes. Although, I must confess, having you naked under that blanket has some appeal."

"I knew you liked me naked." Hunter chuckled, a rare occurrence.

She smiled. Her eyes twinkled. Then, she scrunched her nose. "But you need a bath. You really stink."

"I thought I smelled something. I think I can do my own sponge bath this time."

"No sponge bath. I mean, a proper bath in a real tub."

"You're kidding me."

"Nope, have the water heating as we speak. I have a large trough at the end of my sink customized for taking baths. You, dear sir, will sit inside, soak that bad leg, and wash your body, face, and hair. I even have my husband's shaving equipment so you can shave off that stubble underneath your helmet."

"I thought you didn't look."

Li-ara walked right up to him and stared into his eye visor, an argumentative look in her eyes. "I glimpsed your chin when I pulled up the cloth helmet to give you the medicine when you were unconscious. So, shoot me. Plus, you're a man. I've been with you for four days, and I have first-hand knowledge that you have not shaved, nor have I been able to shave you. You have stubble."

He could not argue with that. She was right. "How do you expect me to reach the kitchen? I haven't been able to take over two steps without falling."

"Already have that figured out. I will strap your bad arm to the pole. Then, after you're clean, I'll help you dress, and we'll have supper. Then you are off to bed."

"What if I'm not tired?"

"Trust me, you will be. I'll be right back." Li-ara returned several moments later with three belts and some rope. "Let's stand you up. If we place the crutch beneath your shoulder, it will give you some needed leverage." Using the crutch, Hunter stood with minor difficulty. Li-ara strapped the broken arm to the crutch. "Try that."

Hunter took a step forward, then another. "Hey, it works."

With Li-ara's arm around his waist for support, he slowly walked into the kitchen. There, as promised, was a large trough filled with warm water.

"I'll need to take off the blanket and help you in," Li-ara shyly stated.

"I swear, you'll use any excuse to see my cute butt."

Ignoring his tease, Li-ara removed the crutch and blanket and helped him into the tub. The tub was long enough to stretch out his injured leg as he sat down.

"The soaking will do that leg good. And you were right. You have a cute, small, rounded butt."

"I only said it was cute, not round and small. I knew you looked at it."

She gave him a warm smile. "Guilty as charged. But at least I didn't see your face." She grabbed a new washcloth. "Sit forward. I'll wash your back and neck. Then I'll remove the splits and bandages from your broken arm and wash it, too. After that, I believe you can handle the rest."

"You're not going to wash all my body?" Li-ara couldn't comprehend if he was serious or teasing her again. Damn that helmet.

Hunter leaned back in the trough. "I must admit, this feels wonderful. I haven't replaced my filth for at least a good two months."

Li-ara placed a small table beside the trough. "Here's a bucket of water you can pour over your head to wash your hair and face. I put the shaving equipment on the table, too. I didn't find any shaving cream, though."

Hunter picked up the razor. "I'm liable to cut my head off with this thing. If you can retrieve the knife from inside my boot, that will be sufficient. That's what I normally use. That and a little soap and water."

When she returned with the knife, Li-ara stopped and burst into a full belly laugh. She laughed so hard she had to sit down at the table.

"What is so funny?" Hunter asked.

It took Li-ara a few minutes to stop laughing. "I wish you could see what I'm seeing. A man sitting in a tub naked except for a metal helmet on his head. Now, if that's not funny, I don't know what is."

Although he tried to hide it, Li-ara heard him snickering beneath his helmet. "Just wash my back."

Li-ara unbuttoned her shirt and laid it on the nearby chair. The garment was her last clean shirt, and she didn't want to get it wet. With his eyes hidden, he couldn't help but look at her breasts resting in what he assumed was a bra. As he averted his stare, he noticed her bandaged arm and several spots of blood. As she reached for the washcloth, he gently grasped her arm at the wrist.

"Why is your arm bandaged?"

"Just a silly accident from the other day."

"This is a new injury. You have fresh blood marks on the cloth."

"One of the wild canines caught me by surprise on the back porch when I went outside."

"A canine attacked you during the day?"

"No. I needed some *myjigor* flowers for your poultice. I didn't realize any of the canines were so close to the house."

"You should not have done that. How bad is the wound?"

"Just a scrape."

"Scrapes don't bleed that much. I want to look at your injury."

"Okay, perhaps it's a little worse than a scrape, but not much. There's nothing to see. Now, do you want me to wash your back or not?"

Hunter wanted to inspect her injury, but her face was flushed with anger. He did not want to upset her with his current line of discussion. She had a temper. He'd wait until later and try to talk her into letting him examine the arm.

Li-ara dipped a cloth into the water, then ran the bar of soap over it several times, working up a lather of soap. She washed his back, carefully wiping the cloth across the many scars his back held.

"Does my washing your back hurt you?"

Realizing his hostess' concern about the marks crisscrossing his back, he answered, "No. The scars are old. They haven't hurt for a long time."

"May I ask how you got them?"

Hunter paused for a moment. "When I was four, three *Rogarian* Traders took me and sold me into slavery. One of my keepers had a fondness for beating those under his care."

"You have so many. How often did he beat you?" She softly ran her fingers across the hundreds of marks on his back. Hunter closed his eyes, taking joy at her soft touch. He silenced the sigh building in his throat.

"At least once a day," Hunter replied, forcing his voice to remain emotionless. "More if he was in a pleasant mood."

"A pleasant mood?"

"If one did something he especially liked, he rewarded you with a beating."

"That's horrible."

"Not really. The alternative was worse."

"What was the alternative?" Li-ara couldn't imagine anything any worse.

"A trip to the sex dens."

Li-ara paused for a moment, unable to say anything. Although the Hunter did not elaborate, she understood what he meant. Wishing to alter the subject, she stated, "I need to remove the wooden spoons from around your arm so I can wash it." Cautiously, she removed the temporary splints and rested his arm on the nearby table. Re-lathering the washcloth, she swabbed the injured arm. "The majority of the swelling has gone down. And most of the black-and-blue markings are fading."

"That's good to hear."

Li-ara continued washing beneath his armpit and down his side. Halfway down his side, he winced.

"Is that sore?" She feared possible broken ribs.

"No."

"Oh, that's right. You don't like to be touched."

"I don't mind your touch anymore." In fact, he almost craved it. Now that he re-experienced the touch of another's flesh on his, would he accept others? Would they bring him enjoyment? Or just hers?

"Then what?"

"If you must know, I'm ticklish."

"Ticklish? Really? Where?"

He blocked her hand as she reached out to find the soft spot. "Please, don't."

Li-ara quickly withdrew her hand. "I'm sorry. I forgot myself and became too familiar with you. Please accept my apology." She stood and handed him the washcloth. "You should be able to wash the rest yourself. If you need anything, I'll be in the bedroom. Call me when you're ready to get out, then I'll help you dry off and dress." Slipping her shirt back on, she left the room in silence. Once inside the bedroom, she closed the door.

He heard the sound of items being pushed around the bedroom. What was she doing? Had he upset her again? It wasn't his fault he was ticklish. Maybe she thought he was mad. He wasn't. Just uneasy.

Once his body was washed, he removed his helmet. With the edge of his knife, he removed the stubble from his face. In the mirror, he spotted several severe bruises and cuts across his nose. Because of his helmet, Li-ara had not tended to them. He wished he had thought to ask her for some healing ointment to put on them. Maybe later. Carefully, he ran the washcloth around the bruises. After applying soap to his hair, he dumped the bucket of water over his head. He took another look at himself in the mirror - an enormous improvement.

Taking the towel Li-ara had left him, he tossed his hair until it was dry. He looked around for a brush or comb but did not see one. To flatten his thick hair, he ran his fingers through his lock and noticed he needed a haircut. Replacing his helmet, Hunter called out, "Li-ara, I'm done."

"Be right there," she shouted from the bedroom. The sound of wood scraping on the floor reached his ears. When she returned, she did not have a cheerful look on her face. He thought it better not to ask questions.

It surprised Hunter how weak he was. After so much inactivity, the simple act of bathing and shaving had exhausted him. Li-ara had to help lift his legs over the trough's sides because he didn't have enough energy. He quickly sat at the nearby table. He shivered. Li-ara wrapped a blanket around him and then quickly dried him with a towel. After re-splinting the broken arm, she helped him dress.

"Do you think you can walk to the bedroom?"

"I don't think I can go that far. Perhaps to the chair in the living room."

"The clothes seem to fit you well. I thought you were about the same size as Kal. You're just a little smaller in the waist. I will alter them to fit."

"That was your husband's name? Kal?"

"Yes. I thought I told you."

"Not that I remember."

Halfway across the room, Hunter's legs started to give out, and his grip around her was lessening. "Hold on, Big Guy. Just a few more steps."

"Too weak. Can't make it."

Li-ara reached out with her foot and pulled the closest chair forward. As the Hunter went down, she spun him around. He landed in the chair and not on the floor. She retrieved a blanket from the bedroom and tucked it around him. He was already sound asleep.

"Not even the willpower and determination of a Huntsman can overcome the power of the body when it is exhausted." Although she had never met one in person before, she knew the stories of the mighty Huntsmen. They were legendary.

"How did I ever end up with such a being in my chair?"

7 J'DAR JEN

A deep, powerful growl emanated from Kii's throat. Hunter opened his eyes, surveying the room. Kii stood alert two feet away, facing the door.

"What do you hear, Boy?" Hunter patted the top of the canine's head. "Are the canines back?"

A chill ran through him as he recalled Li-ara's injured arm. He surveyed the room for her and Beta but detected neither. Had the two gone out to pick some vegetables for dinner or to feed the pack animal? No, she wouldn't go out at dusk. But where was she?

The full moon climbed into the night sky, its brilliance filling the kitchen with a faint light. Its beams revealed a sleeping Li-ara at the table, her head down.

The sound of nails running across wooden blanks broke the quietness. Kii bolted to the door and barked menacingly when a flash of fur sped across the window of the upside-down door. Beta, who was asleep beneath the kitchen table, rushed forward and remained beside Kii. Both canines gnashed their teeth, scratching at the windowpanes to get what was outside the door.

"Kii, Beta, *kata que jara*," Li-ara said, rising and turning on the light at the end of the table. Both canines lay down in front of the door, reluctant to withdraw farther. "They can't breach the door."

"They hear the wild canines. It appears they have returned."

Li-ara walked around the cabin, turning on lamps and supplying the rooms with their soft creamy-white gleam. "They normally don't come near the house. They've changed their habits."

"They've never tried to break in before?"

"No. The one that attacked me did try to come in through the door before I closed it," Li-ara admitted. "But I assume he did that because he was after me. He tried nothing once I sealed the door. I'm confident they'll soon go back into the Highlands."

"No, they are bred hunters. They smelled death and presumed easy prey rested behind these walls. They will continue until they detect a way in."

"I've never known wild canines to break into a residence."

"As long as their leader lives, she will require they obtain her selected prey."

"And who is her selected prey?"

"For some reason, I believe it's me." Hunter paused, listening. "Nothing will deflect them. Nothing is too complicated, too exhausting, too time-consuming to keep them from their objective."

"Like a Bounty Hunter."

"Yes. Both are raised from a young age to battle, engage the opposition, and defend the pack. Defeat is not a term in either vocabulary. Only death will stop them. Have you seen the leader?"

"No. I haven't gotten an adequate look at them in the sunlight."

"Do you have weapons?"

"Yes, two pistols and a rifle."

"I require my gun. From now on, neither one of us must be without at least one weapon. I would also suggest we each carry one or two knives. If we cannot make a shot before an assault, we can defend ourselves with a knife."

"Do you really believe they will attack us? They're animals. They will become tired of waiting and leave."

"No, they are preparing for battle, and we must equip ourselves. Tomorrow, we fortify this camp. Until we can take down their leader, none of us are safe."

The bottom glass pane of the door exploded with a deafening crash, shattering the fragile calm. Shards rained across the floor like jagged confetti, slicing through the air and showering Kii and Beta with glittering debris.

A split second later, a massive wild canine rammed its head through the opening, saliva flying, jaws gnashing, guttural snarls ripping from its throat.

Beta lunged first, closest to the breach. Her teeth sank deep into the beast's muzzle as it fought to wedge its bulk through the narrow gap. Blood splattered across the floor.

Kii charged, desperate to reach the intruder. He shoved against Beta's side, squeezing through just enough to get his teeth into the attacker's ear. With a vicious twist, he tore a chunk from the tip.

The creature howled in pain, jerking back with a roar of rage and retreat. Kii lurched forward, preparing to leap through the shattered frame after it. Hunte stretched out his leg, blocking Kii like a barrier of steel.

Kii snarled in frustration but didn't push past.

"My weapon," Hunter yelled as he ripped off the cutting board from his arm. Slamming the board across the opening, he used his foot to hold the wooden rectangle in place. With his other foot, he continued to keep Kii from reaching the opening. The wild canine pressed against the piece of wood, pushing Hunter's foot back. "Hurry. I can't hold this beast at bay much longer. He's too strong."

Li-ara dashed into the bedroom and grabbed Hunter's gun. From the bedroom doorway, she tossed the weapon.

"Keep your canines back," Hunter exclaimed, reaching up and catching the gun in midair. "I'm going to take the board away so I can have a clear shot."

"Won't the wild canine come through the broken window?"

"That's what I want. The only way to stop their attack is to plug the hole from the outside. They're too strong for this small board to keep them out."

Li-ara lunged forward and grabbed both guardians by their collars, yanking them back just as Hunter raised his weapon. His eyes locked on the shattered door. Without hesitation, he kicked the board aside.

A wild canine was waiting. It surged forward, jaws snapping, eyes wild with bloodlust. Then, BANG.

The gun roared.

The bullet struck clean between its eyes. The beast dropped instantly, its lifeless body slamming into the frame, plugging the opening with dead weight.

Snarls erupted outside. The pack descended on their fallen companion, teeth tearing into its flesh, desperate to drag the body free. But it was jammed tight, wedged in the frame like a broken cork in a bottle.

Another howl pierced the night.

The wild canines vanished, melting into the shadows, leaving only silence … and a dead companion.

"I think their attack is over," Hunter said. "But predators can be sly. Can you bring me my walking stick? I need it to push the beast's head back outside. And something to seal this opening. Now that the leader realizes a broken window means a way inside, they may try to break another window. I suggest we cover all the windows. Is there anything in the cabin we could use?"

"No. Any long boards I have are out in the barn."

"We can't go outside until daylight. Don't you have anything wood inside, like a long drawer or a shelf? Even an ironing board or some long cutting boards will do."

Li-ara thought for a moment. "I think I have something in the bedroom that might suffice. Kii, Beta, sit." Both canines sat, watching the dead beast apprehensively, ready to strike if the body moved at all. "Guard Hunter." Releasing her hold on her protectors, she grabbed the Hunter's walking stick and slid the wooden pole over to him, then dashed into the bedroom.

The sound of things falling to the floor filled the room. Several moments later, Li-ara emerged with three wooden shelves she had torn from the closet. "Will these do?"

"Perfect. Now, please tell me your hammer and nails are not out in the barn."

Li-ara smiled. "While most of the nails are, Kal always insisted we keep a hammer and a small jar of nails in the house. He said you could never anticipate when an emergency might occur. They're under the kitchen sink. I'll retrieve them."

"Sounds like your Kal had a bit of Hunter in him, thinking of the possible."

"Not really. He was a practical man and a bit on the lazy side. I think the actual reason he kept the hammer, nails, and a few other tools in the house is because he didn't want to have to go to the barn each time he needed something." She sat down beside Hunter on the floor.

"Hold Kii and Beta again. I will push this dead, wild canine back outside with the walking stick. When I do, any mutts still lingering will probably try to break through. Don't let either Kii or Beta free." Once Li-ara had a hold, Hunter pushed the dead beast's head outside. The moment the corpse was through, two wild canines grabbed the cane. "Quick, a board."

Li-ara kicked a board over to Hunter. He slammed the piece of wood across the opening and on top of the shaking cane. Kii and Beta barked at the attackers outside.

"You were right," Li-ara said. "They were waiting for us to do something."

"Always helps to think like an animal that wants to eat you."

The wild canines tugged at the stick. Hunter tried pulling the walking stick back through, but the canines outside had a firm grip on his crutch. "Dang, these animals are powerful. I can barely hold on to it. Guess it's their walking stick now." He let go, and the crutch shot forward. A loud thud sounded when the armrest hit the window frame, its width preventing the crutch from being pulled entirely outside. "Well, it looks like they don't get it either." The cane shook erratically as the canines fought to pull the long stick through. "For now, we'll leave the cane where it is and nail the board across it. Tomorrow, when the sun's up, we can remove their toy. I'll hold the board while you nail."

Kneeling, Li-ara pounded nails through the shelf and into the door. After five nails, she stopped, the hammer held in mid-air. A sober look came over her face. "I'm not even sure I loved him."

"Who?"

"Kal."

"Then why did you marry him?"

"I don't know. It's a question I've asked myself many times. I think I liked the idea of going to a new world, someplace with adventure, somewhere different from the life on my homeworld. Back home, the girls grew up, married, had a ton of kids, cooked, cleaned, did laundry, and other domestic chores. I wanted more."

"Isn't that what you do now? Cook, clean, and do laundry?"

She smiled. A twinkle glistened in her eyes. "Yes, but here I have so much more. I have freedom. And the opportunity to train wild *Gloxdirians*. I can go for lengthy walks, take pleasure in the gold and pink clouds of sundown, and view this world's beauty through Kii and Beta's eyes. Plus, when I don't feel like cooking or cleaning, I don't. With you being a wanderer, you must understand the sense of freedom."

"Yes. Was he kind to you?"

"Oh, yes. Exceedingly kind. He never argued with me, even when I was mad at him or did something idiotic. He, too, had the privilege of experiencing my temper several times."

"So, I'm not the only one to experience its sting?"

"No." Li-ara laughed. "My temper comes from the *Crowdian* side of me. It gets me into trouble at times."

"Have you ever thought of returning home?"

"Never. I love living here. On this world, I am my own boss. I go and come as I, or the canines, please." She tugged on the nailed board. "There, I think that should hold."

"I agree."

"Let me help you up. By the way, how did you get over here without help?"

"I guess I just reacted to the danger and forgot I wasn't supposed to be able to walk."

"Your pants are covered in blood. I best check your leg and determine whose blood this is. Any idea of how we can stand you up without the walking stick?"

Hunter pulled on the long cane. It slid through the opening with no problem. "Guess they're done trying to drag the stick outside." With the crutch and his hostess's help, he stood. He put a negligible weight on his bad leg. "Doesn't feel bad. A little sore, but not like before." With his arm around Li-ara and her arm around his waist, he hobbled over to a kitchen chair.

"I need to wash your pants right away if I want to wash most of this blood out," Li-ara said as she helped the Hunter slip off his trousers. "If I hang them by the fire, they might dry in time for bed tonight." She felt his smile. "And no, I'm not trying to get you naked again."

"Did I say anything?"

"No, but I can feel you thinking it."

Hunter leaned close to her and whispered. "I'll never admit if I did or didn't think it."

Li-ara laughed.

She filled a basin with water and placed the blood-soaked pants inside to soak. She brought a second pan of water over to the Hunter and knelt at his feet. Slowly, she ran a wet cloth down his leg, washing off the blood on his legs. She then removed his bandages.

"Marvelous news. The blood on your pants wasn't yours. It was all canine blood. The cuts on your leg are healing nicely."

"I believe the soaking in the bathtub is to thank."

"We'll do that again. The water definitely sped up your healing process."

Hunter thought of teasing her about getting him naked again, but she was in a jovial mood. And he didn't want to spoil it. "Any of that rabbit stew left?"

"No, I gave the canines the last while you were sleeping. But we have the other rabbit meat I cooked up. And I baked some fresh bread. I can fry up some *pittabrit* to go with it."

"*Pittabrit?* What's *pittabrit?*"

"Um, *pittabrit* is ground cornmeal with potatoes and peppers."

"You mean mush."

"I don't understand that term, mush."

"Trust me. It's mush."

"You don't like mush?" Li-ara lifted the Hunter's pants that had been soaking in the tub. She applied a layer of soap over the blood-soaked areas, then scoured them with a scrub brush.

"No, to the contrary. My mother used to fix me mush each morning. It is one of my favorite memories of her."

"You had a mother?"

The Hunter tilted his head in amusement. "I would not be here if I didn't have a mother. No one made me in a test tube on some remote asteroid."

"I meant, I didn't think Huntsmen parents raised their children." Li-ara dumped out the red-colored water, refilled the tub with fresh, clean water, and rinsed the pants.

"Few Huntsmen become Hunters. Although we live by the same creed, some never put on the armor. As for families, most children remain with their parents and siblings until they reach the consenting age of ten. Then, they train to learn what being a Huntsman is. After a few years, those who wish to may enter the school of combat and eventually Bounty Hunter training."

"So, Huntsmen take mates and produce children?"

"A species cannot continue if they do not propagate. The Huntsmen have existed for hundreds of thousands of years. That fact alone answers your question."

Li-ara again dumped the water, although this time, the liquid was pink instead of red. The blood was coming out. "Is that how old you were? Ten?"

"I was a little older. The Traders held me captive for over two years, so I missed some fundamental teachings. When I returned home, I needed an additional two years before starting my schooling."

"You said *Rogarian* Traders took you?"

"That's what my father told me."

"How were you lucky enough to be rescued?"

"A cruel, foul Kentite bought me at auction. Me and two others. An older Huntsman child named Sooh Rey, and a Biiloot kid named Hag. He used us as rentable servants for his high-paying clients."

"He's the one who gave you all those scars?"

"No. He beat us sometimes, with his bare hands. The scars came later from the whip of a male who ran the sex dens. Our master often rented us to him."

"We were on that ship together for two years and five months. Then, the Rogarian Traders made a mistake. They took five more Biiloot children. Their Hunters tracked them back to the auction house."

His eyes darkened.

"Our master brought me along that day. Sooh Rey should've gone with him, but he pretended to be sick so I could go instead. I hadn't eaten in days and they fed us well at auction houses. Fat, cheerful kids made better merchandise."

Hunter's voice dropped to a whisper. "Sooh Rey saved my life."

"Was Sooh Rey rescued too?"

"No. When the *Biiloot* attacked and defeated the Traders, they discovered me. Hag had taught me his language, so I was able to speak with their Hunters. I told them of Hag and Sooh Rey's imprisonment on the *Kentite* ship. They tried to rescue both boys, but in their attempt, the *Kentite* ship was destroyed. All aboard died, including Hag and Sooh Rey."

"I'm sorry your friends died."

"Why? Their deaths were not your fault?"

"I know. But they were your friends." Her words touched the Huntsman's heart. She was like no female he had ever met - caring, empathetic, someone who not only understood but experienced his pain.

"I was so young when taken that I didn't remember where I was from. All I knew was my name - J'Dar Jen. And that my father was a Huntsman Bounty Hunter."

"J'Dar Jen. Is that your name?" Li-ara wrung the water out of the pants and placed them before the fire to dry.

"That was my childish name. I go by my father's clan's name. I am called BiiJun D'Kolor, son of Kolor whom the *Biiloot* returned."

"If you didn't remember where your home planet was, how did the *Biiloot* discern where to take you??" Li-ara asked.

"My father was not only a Bounty Hunter but a well-known one, a member of an elite club of Hunters from various nations. Several of my *Biiloot* rescuers had worked with him during the *Permise* War. I remained with the *Biiloot* for a few weeks until they located my parents and reunited us."

"Are your parents still alive?"

"Yes. They remained on Kolora and still live there today." Hunter reached over and tried to scratch a persistent itch beneath the broken arm's binding.

"How's your arm doing?" Li-ara asked. "Can you move your fingers?"

"Good, except for this constant itch." Hunter raised his fingers and flexed them. "Fingers work. And the pain is pretty much gone. I think we should leave the board off."

"I agree." Li-ara looked at the bloodied cutting board lying by the front door. "But the arm needs to remain splinted for another three weeks to ensure the bones knit properly."

"Another three weeks of itching." He handed Li-ara a piece of paper. "Here's a list of things we should try to do tomorrow to prepare for the wild canine attack."

"Read it to me while I wash the dishes." Li-ara listened to her protector's suggestions on what they needed to do and what the canine leader would probably do. When she finished drying and putting away the dishes, she made some fresh biscuits for the morning, giving Kii, Beta, and Hunter one when finished.

"Your pants are still damp," Li-ara stated as she felt the cloth.

"I have slept this long without them. I don't think another night will matter. I suggest we retire early since we have a busy day tomorrow."

With the help of Li-ara and his chewed-up walking stick, Hunter hobbled to the bedroom. He was surprised to discover that she had dragged the mattress back onto the bed frame along with the bedding.

"I thought it would be easier for you to stand from an elevated position rather than from the floor," she said.

Hunter slowly lowered himself onto the bed. He realized his leg was getting stronger because he didn't plop down this time but sat. Placing his weapon beneath the pillow, he swung his legs up and lay down, pulling the bedding up over his body.

"Aren't you going to sleep in the bed?" Hunter asked when Li-ara crawled into her regular sleeping chair.

"Your fever's gone. You do not need my body warmth."

"You need a good night's rest, and you cannot receive one in that chair. Plus, it is not right that I am the only one in comfort. This bed is big enough for both of us. If you do not wish to share it, I can sleep on the floor, and you can lie here."

"No, your body still needs the bed."

"Then lie beside me. Please. I cannot protect you on the chair."

Grasping her quilt, Li-ara climbed in. But this time, she lay on top of the bedding, not beneath. She pulled her cover over both. Both canines came running, ready to hop in the bed, too.

"Kii, Beta, No. Lie down." Kii looked at her with sorrowful eyes. "I said, lie down." Snorting a sneeze in protest, Kii curled up on the floor.

"If you lay as you did when I was ill, we will have more room," Hunter softly said. "I also think you should lie beneath the covers in case my fever comes back during the night."

Li-ara was going to protest, but she enjoyed lying beside him. Nervously smiling, she slipped beneath the bedding, scooting against Hunter's side and resting her shoulder and head on his bare chest. Hunter wrapped his arm around her body and held her firmly in place.

"Good night, Hunter. And thank you again for saving us."

"As is my duty. Good night, Li-ara."

Unable to reach their quarry, the pack of wild canines ran down a large deer and devoured the animal. The leader pulled off a massive chunk of flank and carried the meat to a nearby hill. Biting off a considerable piece, she lifted her head and swallowed it. She stared at the quiet cabin below. There had to be a way inside, and she would discover what it was.

8 KII GOES MISSING

A thin blade of light pierced the darkness, slipping over the jagged mountaintops and casting a faint golden slash across the bedroom window. Dawn was still an hour away, yet the first hint of morning stirred Hunter from his uneasy rest. Li-ara lay curled beside him, her breath warm against his chest, unaware of the storm gathering in his thoughts.

By sunrise, the wild canines would vanish into whatever shadows birthed them, if they followed the rules of nature. But these beasts weren't adhering to normal behavior. One had attacked Li-ara in broad daylight. A fluke? A rogue acting alone? Or the first sign of something worse?

Hunter didn't trust the quiet. These creatures weren't just hungry. They were calculating, erratic, too bold for comfort. The old patterns no longer applied. And with each broken rule, the danger edged closer to her. He couldn't afford to wait for the next attack. He had to act before the canines made her their next lesson in unpredictability.

The Huntsman slipped out from beneath the sleeping female. He swung his legs over the side of the bed. Seizing his weapon and sliding the walking stick beneath his armpit, he pushed himself into a standing position. He took a step forward on his uninjured leg, then one on the bad one. Surprisingly, he was still upright.

"Don't fall and break your leg," came a soft voice from behind him.

"The injury feels much better today. I believe I can walk finally on my own."

"Good, but don't overdo it. I had planned for you to soak in the tub tonight before dinner, but since the hour is early, I think we should do it now. Perhaps tonight as well. The water definitely is making a difference."

"You need not rise so early. Sleep until the sun rises above the mountains."

"No, I'm ready for the day. I'll fill the tub with water, and you can soak while I prepare breakfast. Do you drink coffee?"

"Occasionally, when I am in port. I don't take the time to make it when piloting my aircraft."

"Speaking of your aircraft, aren't you afraid someone or something will discover your ship and ransack it while you're here with me?"

"She is well hidden in the forest. A security field ensures nothing can touch my craft. Plus, anyone would have a hard time seeing her because she is cloaked and invisible."

"Really? You can make something as big as an aircraft invisible?"

"Yes, as long as you possess the necessary equipment."

Kii and Beta ran to the front door. "Sorry, guys, it's too dangerous to go outside yet," Li-ara said, rising from beneath the covers and stretching. "You'll need to use the backroom this morning."

"Will the canines urinate where you designate?" Hunter asked.

"Mostly."

"If you ask them, will they urinate on the front door? Their spray should be strong enough to mask the scent of blood and death that still lingers in here. It might deter the wild canines."

"They've never been allowed to urinate inside the house. I can try." Li-ara called the dogs to the front door. "Kii, Beta, go here." She pounded on the boarded-up door. Kii sniffed the door, then turned to her. "He doesn't understand what I want him to do."

A strange sound reached Li-ara's ears - soft, rhythmic splashing against the wooden door. She turned and saw Hunter standing with his back to her, his healing arm braced against the wall, the other held low in front of him, just out of her line of sight. A pale stream arced from him, striking the bottom of the door and darkening the wood in uneven trails. For a moment, she just stared, trying to make sense of what she was seeing.

Was he?

He was.

Her lips parted, stunned. "He's marking the door!" she chuckled under her breath, half in disbelief, half in awe.

Kii trotted forward, nose twitching. He gave the wet patch a long, deliberate sniff. Then, as if understanding his part in the ritual, he lifted his leg and added his own contribution, right over Hunter's.

Li-ara clapped a hand over her mouth to stifle the laugh that bubbled up. This was territory-marking, plain and wild. The kind of behavior she expected from wolves, not men. And certainly not the stoic, calculated warrior in her house.

"Sometimes, you just have to show them what to do," Hunter said, snapping shut his fly. "Okay, Beta, it's your turn." The female canine sniffed, then spun and went into the backroom to relieve herself.

"Ladies need privacy," Li-ara said. "I'll try to persuade her to urinate on the door, but I doubt she will. She realizes where her spot is."

Li-ara filled the bathtub halfway full of lukewarm water. After helping Hunter into the tub to submerge his leg, she stepped into the backroom and removed a slab of breakfast meat from the wall hook. She sliced off two chunks and set them aside for the canine's breakfast.

"We're running low on food. I need to have Kii do some hunting. Do you think it's safe for him to wander out?"

"As long as he doesn't go out too far."

"I cannot control that. I can't explain it to him. Maybe we can hold out for another day. I might be able to flush out some *gurrnies* from the backwoods. They're not the best tasting, but in a stew, they're palatable."

Hunter soaked in the warm water, watching Li-ara scurry around the kitchen preparing breakfast. She filled an old coffee pot with water, then ground some fresh coffee beans, adding them to the pot's basket. Before long, the aroma of coffee filled the room.

Hunter breathed in deeply. "I forgot how pleasing the aroma of fresh brewing coffee is."

"It does stimulate the taste buds."

"By any chance, do you have any ion batteries?"

"Only those that run the lamps."

"They're too small. What about in the barn?"

"Again, only those in lamps."

"Do you own any speeders, tractors, or other farm equipment?"

"Kal's old tractor is out in the field behind the barn. It broke down the second day we were here. He never got a chance to fix it. I never got around to doing the work either, probably because I didn't have any use for the machine. I don't farm."

"But your fields are planted."

"One of the farmers from town rents the land. He pays me a percentage of the harvest."

"Is his equipment nearby?"

"No, he never leaves his equipment here. I'm too remote, and he fears someone may strip it or, worse yet, steal it."

"Then, let's hope the tractor's batteries are still usable. How far is the field?"

"Too far for you to walk. Perhaps in a couple of days, you might be able to."

"We don't have a couple of days," Hunter said.

Seeing that the breakfast was almost ready, the Hunter stood and exited the tub with only the walking stick as added support. He dried himself off and then walked over to detect if his trousers were dry. "Stop looking at my ass," he said in a slightly annoyed tone.

"Sorry." Li-ara's cheeks blushed, and a small nervous giggle escaped her throat. "I couldn't help myself. It's just so dang cute. Are your pants dried?"

"Yes." Beneath his helmet, the Huntsman smiled. Somehow, it was comforting knowing she enjoyed viewing his body despite all the cuts and scars. He grabbed his pants and struggled to thread his foot through the leg. Balancing awkwardly on one side, he used his good hand to guide the fabric. But it twisted, buckled, and refused to cooperate. With only one hand, the task felt impossibly clumsy. After the third failed attempt, a growl of frustration escaped his throat.

"Let me help you," Li-ara said softly, stepping beside him.

Hunter rested his arm on her shoulder for balance as she knelt and guided each leg through the pant legs. She pulled the fabric up over his hips and fastened the snaps at his waist. Next, she picked up the shirt and carefully slid it over his broken arm, eased it across his shoulders, and slipped his good arm into the second sleeve. She began buttoning it from the bottom up, her fingers moving slowly, deliberately, as if each button deserved her full attention. The fabric shifted slightly with each motion, brushing against his skin.

She paused at the third button, adjusting the collar to sit just right before continuing. Her knuckles grazed his chest now and then, sending a subtle warmth through the space between them. When she reached the last button near his throat, she hesitated for the briefest second, then fastened it gently, smoothing the fabric with both hands.

Then, with the same quiet care, she tucked the hem into his pants, her touch steady, unhurried. The intimacy of the gesture lingered in the air, unspoken but unmistakable.

Hunter sat down at the table. Li-ara poured him a cup of coffee and sat a plate of breakfast meat, sliced tubers, and several biscuits before him.

"I'll dress in the bedroom and make the bed while you remove your helmet and eat."

"What about your meal?"

"I'll eat after you." She threw each canine a biscuit.

"I wish you didn't have to leave. Maybe you can locate something in the barn that will suffice as a visor so that we can eat together."

"I'll look. Call me when you're done."

"Don't forget your weapon. You need to keep it with you at all times." Li-ara grabbed her gun and strolled into the bedroom.

Everything Hunter needed was back at his ship or lying in his satchel somewhere on the road - goggles, large ion batteries, and his long gun. If he only had a way to reach it. What he wouldn't give for a speeder.

"I forgot to ask you, what do you need ion batteries for?" Li-ara shouted from the bedroom.

"I want to electrify the front porch. After the wild canines are shocked a few times, they won't attempt to breach the door. If the battery is massive enough, I can connect the windows as well. It won't take the leader long to figure out that if they burst through one of the larger windows, we won't be able to stop her pack from coming inside after us."

"Makes sense. We barely kept them from entering through a small window. I can't imagine what would happen if they broke a bedroom pane."

That thought haunted Hunter. He finished breakfast and replaced his helmet. "You can come in. My helmet's on."

Li-ara stepped back into the room. She wore a delicate pink shirt that hugged her frame gently, the collar embroidered with tiny green flowers like spring clinging to her skin. A pair of well-worn khaki pants that fit her just right flowed over her legs, each rolled slightly at the ankles, revealing her bare feet as they padded softly against the wooden floor.

Hunter's gaze lingered longer than he meant it to, drawn to the way the color warmed her complexion, the way the loose strands of her hair framed her face. There was a grace to her movements, quiet, unassuming, but impossible to ignore.

A strange unease stirred in his chest. He didn't usually notice things like this. Beauty wasn't something he had time for. Not in his world. Not in his line of work.

And yet, here he was - noticing.

Li-ara cleared Hunter's plate and carried the slab of breakfast meat back to its hook. Her voice drifted from the back room. "Hunter, you might want to come back here and take a look at this."

A beat passed.

"Want me to help you get up?"

"No, I think I can walk on my own." With the walking stick as his crutch, he pushed himself up and hobbled across the floor. "What's wrong?"

"That!" Hunter followed Li-ara's finger and spied what had her concerned. At the edge of the door was a four-inch hole that had been gnawed by wild canine teeth.

"So that's why they attacked the front door. They weren't trying to breach the entrance; they were trying to sneak in through the back. The broken window was a distraction, so we didn't realize their true intent. You said these canines were smart. You understated their ability. They are problem solvers beyond anything I've ever witnessed in an animal. And I fear each failure makes them smarter, more capable of accomplishing their goal."

Li-ara turned and stared at her two trained canines. "That's why Beta and Kii sometimes seem to know what I want before I even ask them."

"I wouldn't be surprised if they can understand your words."

"How do we defend ourselves against such animals?"

"You said you've lived here for four years? And canines have never been a problem before this?"

"Never."

"Perhaps this is a new pack that recently arrived. Or a new leader. Our number one objective is to eliminate the leader. Once he is dead, the others should retreat."

"She, not he. *Gloxdirian* canines are a matriarchal rule. A female leads the group."

"No wonder you like them so much," the Hunter teased. Bending down, he ran his fingers across the chewed opening. "The wood is damp." He stood and walked over to Beta, rubbing her head. "Good, Girl. That's why you urinated back here. You understood what the leader was doing. You were marking this territory as your own. Is there any chance Beta and the canine leader are related?"

"I don't think so. Why do you ask?"

"Kii is her only offspring?"

"She gave birth to three pups two-and-a-half years ago. The smallest pup died at birth, one mysteriously disappeared, and Kii is the third."

"Why do you say the pup mysteriously disappeared?"

"One day, it was just gone. I never found its body. I presumed it wandered off and died or was killed and eaten."

"And you're sure she had no other litters."

"Kal bought her as a pup, and I raised her. She's never been away from me. I'm positive. Why?"

"I think the leader is related to Beta, possibly her daughter or granddaughter. Beta recognized her scent. It's possible that the leader may be here to fight Beta for dominance. It is the hunter's way."

"You think the lost pup became the leader?"

"Possibly."

"Hello, in the house," came a voice from outside. "Anyone home?"

"Callers? At this time of the morning?" Hunter clicked off his weapon guard.

"It must be important. I never have callers. I'll go find out what they want."

"No."

"I must. If I don't, they'll think something's wrong. If I stop them before they reach the house, they won't try to come inside. I won't say anything about you being here."

"I am not worried about me."

Li-ara softly touched his arm. "It's okay. I recognize the voice. It belongs to the farmer who plants my land."

"Keep your weapon with you. And don't step off the porch." Hunter didn't like the idea, but he knew she was right.

Li-ara walked to the front door and opened it. Kii and Beta followed, standing at her side. The site of three men on quillbacks greeted her. "Hi, Duu. You're out awfully early this morning."

"We wanted to check on you. A pack of wild canines came down from the mountains and are causing some trouble. Last night, they attacked Ji-nob and almost ripped his arm completely off. We're checking on all the families to determine if anyone else has been attacked." The males eyed her front door.

"Something wrong with your door, Li-ara?" one of the males asked.

"It warped from all that rain we had last week," Li-ara lied. "I took the door down to shave off one side. I guess I was so tired last night I put the dang thing back on upside down. I didn't have the strength to take it back off and put it on right."

"Want us to help you?" the third male asked, preparing to dismount.

Hunter drew closer to the window, being careful to remain in the shadows. He raised his gun.

"Thanks, Brin, but the door is fine for now," Li-ara quickly responded. "I need to shave off more. Plus, as you see, I broke the window. I need to go into town and buy a new piece of glass. I'll let you know when I purchase the window, and you and Haven can help me fix it."

"Will do." The male settled back into his saddle. "Just give me a holler."

"You said Ji-nob was attacked?" Li-ara tried to change the subject. "Is he alive?"

"Barely," Duu replied. "Since you are the expert on their kind, we were hoping you might know something about them, why they attacked without being provoked. Canines have never attacked us before. Any ideas?"

90

"Nope. They were howling something fierce last night, but I never saw them."

"A big forest fire is burning in the mountains," Duu said. "Speculation is that the flames drove them down here."

"Those canines were definitely by your place last night, Li-ara," Brin added. "The road running past your house is full of canine tracks. Make sure your pack animal is secured before it gets dark. And stay inside."

"Will do."

A fourth man emerged from behind a small clump of trees. Li-ara immediately raised and cocked her weapon. "Get off my property, Ting. I swore I'd kill you if you ever stepped foot on my grounds again."

"Notice, I am not on your property," the man announced, swaying both arms out to show what part of the land he was on. Hunter listened intently. She called him Ting.

"Easy, Li-ara," Brin cautioned. "We understand you two had some trouble. Ting is here on our invite. He is helping us warn the neighbors and encourage those in the outer areas to move into town where they are safer."

"Warn them or find new victims?"

"He was never convicted of any offense," the second man said. "You seem to be the only one who has a problem with him."

"Double check with your daughter. Just because he's your best friend doesn't mean your women are safe. You never found out how Anishe got pregnant. Unless you fathered your own grandchild."

"You *notrill galop!*" the man said, reining his quillback closer.

Li-ara fired into the ground several feet in front of the animal. "I wouldn't come any closer."

"I told you that you misunderstood my intentions," the man behind the tree shouted.

"The hell I did. You raped me."

Hunter's muscles tensed. He brought the man standing behind the trees into his weapon's sight. One bullet to the head would eliminate the threat.

"Li-ara, you never offered proof that happened," Duu stated. "Ting willingly testified as to what happened. We found no guilt."

"**I** found guilt," she shouted.

"Look, we're not here to discuss the past or cause trouble," Brin interjected. "We just wanted to tell you of the threat and offer you sanctuary in town. The wife and I feel it's too dangerous for you to be out here by yourself. You're welcome to stay with us if you don't want to stay in town."

"I'm not by myself. I have Kii and Beta for protection. Now get the hell off my property before I turn MY canines on you." Without another word, the four men left. Ting looked back at her when he was out of firing range and smiled. Ordering the canines inside, Li-ara closed and locked the door.

"That man raped you?" Hunter stepped from behind the door and in front of Li-ara, preventing her from retreating into the kitchen. His weapon was still in his hand, cocked and ready to fire.

"I don't want to discuss it.".

Hunter grabbed her arm and spun her around. "Did he rape you?"

"Yes."

"You called him Ting. Might his full name be Ting D'ton?" Hunter asked as he opened the door a crack, watching the men trot away.

"I think so." Hunter slipped his weapon's barrel through the opening. Li-ara pulled on his shoulder. "Hunter, you can't. Shooting him is murder."

"Ting D'ton is wanted on three planets for rape. I am a Bounty Hunter. Shooting him is not murder."

"Then they will discover you are hiding in here and have all kinds of questions. I thought you didn't want anyone to know you were here."

Hunter lowered his weapon. "Why are you protecting him?"

"I'm not. I'm protecting you. They won't care if you're a Bounty Hunter. They will execute you for killing their friend."

Before Li-ara could react, Hunter pulled the trigger. She tore open the door, fearing she would discover Ting lying dead on the ground. Instead, she observed his quillback bucking the daylights out of him. Laughing, Li-ara closed the door before anyone saw the Bounty Hunter.

"A sting to the right of the tail makes any quillback buck until he throws his rider."

"I must remember that trick," Li-ara laughed. "At least we now know the wild canines are attacking others besides us."

"Or there is more than one pack," Hunter stated. "We should start fortifying this place as soon as you eat breakfast. I think I'm strong enough to go out to the barn and help bring in the wood and nails."

"I don't want you even thinking about going out there. You're still too weak." Li-ara's tone left no room for argument. "I'll grab what we need from the shed. You stay inside and focus on what you *can* do. Start with the closet. Take down those last two shelves. Just toss the contents on the floor. I'll deal with the mess later. Do you think it's okay to take the canines with me?"

"I won't let you go without them. They will protect you as I would." He paused a moment. "Do you think those men will be back?"

"No. They are heading towards the Coray's place. They'll stop at the three cabins to the east, then circle back to town. They won't be back this way anymore today. Should I send Kii out to catch food?"

"I would wait until the sun is high in the sky. The wild canines should be in their den for sure during the hottest part of the day. Plus, with the men out hunting them, they may stay down longer. Do you have any conducting wire?"

"There's a spool … out in the barn."

"Out in the barn," Hunter said at the same time. "Do you keep nothing in this house?"

"Only the things I need. I have no use for conducting wire." She sensed Hunter pause for a moment as if he wanted to say something. "What?"

"I was wondering if I might impose upon you for a favor?"

"You only need to ask."

"Can you help me put my boots on before you go out?"

Li-ara purposely sighed loudly.

"What?" Hunter asked, wondering why the display of irritation.

"I don't think I will like you in clothes."

"Just help me with the boots." His helmet hid the enormous smile on his face.

———————————

93

With the two canines beside her, Li-ara brought Fillo out into the corral for some needed air and sunshine. The animal neighed and ran around the yard, kicking her hind legs and tossing her head.

Li-ara rummaged through the barn, eyes scanning the dim interior until she spotted five large boards stacked along the back wall, a rusted bucket of nails beside them, and a spool of conducting wire tangled like a sleeping snake. The boards were heavier than they looked. She had to drag them one at a time, the ends kicking up dust as she hauled each one up to the porch.

On her final trip, she ducked into the smokehouse and unhooked the last chunk of cured deer meat. Slinging it over her shoulder, she made a quick stop at the side garden, yanking up whatever vegetables her hands could reach - carrots, turnips, a few tired onions - before heading back inside.

Hunter worked methodically, unloading the cluttered shelves in the closet and yanking the two boards free. Bracing himself, he used his good foot to slide the planks across the floor to the back door. Once there, he coated each board with a thick layer of bitter soap, spreading it edge to edge. Then, gripping the hammer awkwardly in one hand, he nailed the planks in place, stacked one above the other, to cover the jagged hole the canines had gnawed through. If the wild beasts came back for another bite, he hoped the foul taste would stop them cold.

Li-ara carried the nails and wire into the kitchen and placed them on the kitchen table. "The meat is a few months old, but I think it'll be okay in a stew," she said as she hung the deer on the meat hook. "It will feed us for a few days if Kii catches nothing. I also found the fishing net and the spool of wire. I don't know if the wire is the kind you want. How are you doing?"

"A little tired, but okay. How about you? You look like you need a rest."

"No, I'm okay as well."

Hunter sensed she wasn't. The days and nights of caring for him had taken a toll on her. He was glad she had at least gotten a decent night's sleep.

"The sun is straight up, so you can send Kii off hunting if you like."

"Do you think we should?" Li-ara walked to the door and peered outside. She searched the visible landscape for any signs of danger, man or beast.

"I cannot make that call. Kii is your canine. There is a chance he will be injured or killed. You must decide."

Li-ara knelt and called Kii to her. "What do you think, Boy? Can you run us down some rabbits, wild birds, or even a young razorback without encountering those wild canines? Can you keep yourself safe?" Kii panted and wagged his tail. He loved hunting. "What if I send him out, and he doesn't come back?"

"Then he died a warrior's death, the kind any Hunter wants." Hunter's words gave her no solace. "I'm afraid I can offer you little comfort in your choice. But I believe going today is safer than going tomorrow will be. And tomorrow will be safer than the next day. Each new day will bring more danger to your canines as the others learn. We have the slab of meat in the back room. And, with luck, we will catch some fish. We can make do with these items, plus the vegetables you collected."

"What happens after a few days? What do we do then?"

"This battle will be over before the food runs out. Either the canines will be gone, or we will be in their bellies."

Li-ara sighed. "Okay, Kii, fetch us some dinner. Hunt." The canine ran out the door and down the walkway. He disappeared down the road.

"Can you show me how to operate your stove?" Hunter asked.

"Why?"

"Tonight, I make supper. I can do wonders with scraps and leftovers."

"No, I can cook you something."

"It is my turn to let you rest."

"I'd rather keep busy. Otherwise, I will dwell on Kii being out there."

She was right. Busy minds were distracted thoughts. "Then why don't you pull the boards in and place two in front of the living room window and two at the bedroom window? By the time you do that, the meal should be ready."

Li-ara did as Hunter asked. Her body was drenched in sweat when she returned to the kitchen. With the sun at its peak, the cabin was stifling. Usually, Li-ara kept the windows and doors open during the day, allowing the cool breeze outside to flow through the house. But with the danger of an attack, it was too dangerous to leave them open. Turning on the cold water, she stuck her head underneath, allowing the liquid to cool her body and wash away the sweat from her face. She then plopped in the nearby chair. Hunter sat a plate of fried mash cakes and biscuits in front of her

95

with two pieces of breakfast meat and a cup of coffee. He threw Beta a round mash cake, which she quickly devoured.

"Where's your plate?"

"Right here," Hunter replied, lifting his plate into the air. "I'll take my meal into the bedroom and eat it."

"This is ridiculous, Hunter. Why can't we eat together? Why does one of us always have to leave the room?"

"I need not tell you the answer you already know."

"You can't let me see your face. Well, I won't look. We can turn our backs to each other. You must realize by now that you can trust me."

"I trust you with my life. But that is not our tradition."

"I'm sick and tired of your traditions," Li-ara screamed, grabbing her plate and throwing it against the wall, shattering the china. Beta cowered, too afraid to eat the scraps on the floor. "I'm tired of being afraid. I'm tired of tiptoeing around your traditions. I hate this." She stormed into the bedroom and slammed the door shut.

Hunter crouched and gathered the shards of broken china, setting them on the cupboard. Beta padded over and sniffed at the spilled food. With a nod, Hunter encouraged her to eat the scraps.

The Huntsman understood. Li-ara was scared, frustrated, drained from trying to connect with someone who kept himself hidden behind cold *kolomite*. And he couldn't blame her. But the law was clear. The helmet wasn't a choice. It was a mandate. One he couldn't break, no matter how much he wanted to ease her pain.

His gaze drifted toward the bedroom, where she'd disappeared in silence. Should he follow her? Say something?

Women, their tears, their emotions. All were unfamiliar territory. As a Bounty Hunter, most of his interactions with females had ended in shackles or worse. The ones he'd known were cold, cunning, dangerous, often more lethal than the men.

"What do I do, Beta?" he asked.

The canine trotted to the door and scratched it softly with one paw.

"You think I should go in?"

Another scratch. She looked back at him, ears pricked with expectation.

Hunter reached for the handle, then paused. Faint, muffled sobs drifted through the door, raw and unfiltered. He drew his hand back, unsure. Beta gave a soft, encouraging bark. Taking a breath, he turned the handle and stepped inside.

Li-ara lay curled on the bed, shoulders shaking, her face buried in the pillow. The sound of her crying struck something in him, something unfamiliar.

Unsure of what else to do, he sat beside her. His thoughts drifted back to his childhood. His mother had held him when he cried, when the pain became too much. Maybe that's what Li-ara needed. Not words. Not explanations. Just someone to hold her.

Gently, he lifted her trembling form into his arms. She melted against him, arms sliding around his neck, sobs tearing from her throat. Her body shook violently, each breath a struggle, her grief overwhelming. Hunter held her tight, feeling her anguish crash into him like a tidal wave.

"Everything will be okay," he murmured, though he wasn't sure it would. Her sobs only grew louder, the pain in them carving into his chest. "Kii will be fine," he tried again. No change. "I'm sorry I can't take the helmet off. I'm sorry I'm … the way I am." She cried harder.

Could he say nothing right? He stopped speaking and simply held her, letting silence wrap around them like a fragile shield. At some point, without realizing it, his fingers began stroking her hair. Slow. Rhythmic. Comforting.

The strangeness of her in his arms began to shift. No longer strange but wanted. Familiar. Too familiar. Was he feeling something deeper for her? He couldn't afford that. Not here. Not now.

Her breathing evened out. Her grip on him loosened. She'd fallen asleep.

Hunter laid her down and pulled a blanket over her. He lingered for a moment, then turned and slipped into the kitchen.

"Thanks, Beta," he said quietly, stroking the canine's head. "You knew what she needed. Stay with her till she wakes, all right?" Beta padded back to the bedroom without hesitation.

Hunter turned to the door, needing something, anything, to keep his mind from spiraling. He began wiring the front porch. As he worked, he discovered an old lithium cargo battery tucked away in a forgotten corner of the back room. A quick test showed it still held a charge. If he could rig it to the other ion batteries, he might generate just enough power to electrify the porch and create a shock field to ward off anything that tried to cross it.

Maybe tomorrow, once Kii was back, Li-ara could help him retrieve the larger tractor battery.

Hunter threw himself into the work, hoping the motion would be enough to drown out the thoughts clawing at him. He hammered harder than necessary, forced boards into place with too much force, moved with the sharp efficiency of a soldier trying not to feel. But no matter how hard he pushed, his focus kept slipping.

Her voice echoed in his mind, cracked with hurt. Her tears lingered in his memory like shadows. And her anger? That cut the deepest.

Guilt wormed its way beneath the armor he wore because deep down, a part of him wished he could break that vow. Just for her.

And if he did, what then? Was there a compromise? A way to make a cloth mask work, one that honored the vow but gave her the comfort she needed?

He abandoned the wires and stormed into the back room, tearing through every drawer, shelf, and storage bin. Nothing. The kitchen next. Every cabinet. Every dusty corner.

Still nothing.

He looked out the kitchen window, eyes falling on the barn. If something useful existed, it was probably there. But, could he make it? One wrong step outside, and the wild canines could be on him in seconds. In his weakened state, he wouldn't stand a chance. And if he collapsed out there, she might never know where to find him.

No. Not yet.

Soon. When he was stronger.

"I'm sorry," came a soft voice. He turned to see Li-ara standing in the bedroom doorway. "Can you forgive me?"

"For what?"

"My outburst. I had no right to be angry at your oath to remain faceless."

"You warned me you had a temper."

"That was more than a temper tantrum." She opened the front door and peered outside. "Has Kii returned yet?"

He hesitated for a moment. "No."

She turned and gave him a worried smile. "It will be dark soon. I need to put Fillo back in the barn and feed her. Come, Beta."

"Wait. Take your weapon with you."

"I have it in my belt." She walked outside, Beta beside her. Fearing the canines were close, Hunter kept watch from the front porch, weapon in hand. Switching to heat vision, he combed the landscape for Kii's body signature. He was nowhere to be seen.

With Fillo housed and fed, Li-ara returned to the house. In silence, she helped Hunter cover the windows. She pounded the nails while he held the boards, but both kept their attention on the setting sun and the road.

"Where is he?" Li-ara asked as the shadows of night filled the rooms. She opened the door and whistled for the canine. No response. As she passed by, Hunter noticed the tears in her eyes.

As Li-ara chopped vegetables with rhythmic precision, the scent of garlic and herbs filled the kitchen. Nearby, Hunter sliced several thin strips from the aged deer meat. The moment his blade parted the flesh, the stench hit him, even through the helmet.

He flinched. Spoiled. But worse than the smell was the dilemma it stirred.

He glanced at Li-ara, humming softly as she stirred the pot. If he didn't eat with her, she'd be hurt again. He knew that much. And he didn't want to cause her more pain. But how could he eat? The helmet made it impossible.

The cloth mask? Maybe. But even that had limits.

He stood up abruptly. It was too fast. His leg buckled under him with a jolt of pain.

"Slow down," he muttered, catching himself on the edge of the table. "Still healing, remember?"

Limping to the bedroom, he retrieved the cloth mask and pulled it over his head. Sitting on the bed, he tugged at the front, trying to gauge how much space he had to slip food inside.

Too tight.

What if he cut the sides? No. Too risky. It could shift. Expose him.

He stared at his reflection in the small mirror on the wall. But, if he added material, created a drop flap beneath the chin. That could work. He put the helmet back on and scanned the room. A scrap of cloth lay crumpled on the floor inside the closet, soft, neutral, thick enough. Perfect.

Then he spotted Li-ara's sewing kit tucked into a nearby drawer. He opened it. A needle, thread, even a thimble still inside. Exactly what he needed.

With as much speed as his leg allowed, Hunter returned to the kitchen, the cloth and kit in hand. He sat down and began stitching, every movement driven by a single, unspoken thought: *She deserves to eat beside someone. Not a mask.*

"What are you doing?" Li-ara asked, wiping away a tear.

"I have an idea. I think I know of a way I can wear the cloth helmet without eyes and still be able to eat."

Wiping her hands on a towel, Li-ara watched in interest. Hunter cut two triangles from the cloth he brought, then cut the sides of the cloth helmet up two inches. Threading a needle, he placed a triangle inside the cut with the tip pointing up and stitched it to each side of the fabric. Holding up his achievement, he announced, "I believe this will do. We can eat together in the same room."

Li-ara placed a plate on the table before the Huntsman, then took a seat across from him. The meal consisted of only a few vegetables and biscuits. "I'm sorry. With the deer meat spoiled, and Kii not returning, supper's a little sparse."

"Where is your plate?"

"I'm not hungry," Li-ara said.

"No, Li-ara. You don't eat, I don't eat."

"You need it more than me."

"We both eat, or I don't." He pushed the plate towards her. She knew Hunter was a man of his word. Plus, it was important for him to eat if he wanted to gain his strength. Li-ara took a piece of tuber root and chewed it, swallowing. Within seconds, a wave of nausea surged up her throat as her gut twisted violently. Clutching her abdomen, she lurched toward the sink. The root came up in a sour flood, her stomach heaving.

"Where is he?"

This time, Hunter did not hesitate. He walked over and brought her into his arms. "I'm worried, too."

9 PREPARING FOR BATTLE

"Don't turn the electrical field on yet," Li-ara requested when it was time to retire for the night. "Kii might still come home. He won't be able to scratch at the door if the porch is booby-trapped."

"All right." Hunter flipped the toggle switch off. He left the wire attached to the battery in case he needed to turn the current on in a hurry. The charge wasn't much, but the voltage would give a nosy critter an unwelcome shock.

Hunter took her hand, his rough fingers folding gently around hers, and together they walked in silence toward the bedroom. No words were needed. None could hold the weight of what they both carried.

Li-ara curled beside him, her head finding its place on his chest as though it had always belonged there. She rested across his arm, her breath soft, trembling, but steady. She told herself she wouldn't cry again. She had no more tears left to give.

Hunter tightened his hold around her, drawing her in closer than he ever had before, as if by sheer force he could shield her from everything. From pain. From fear. From himself.

He closed his eyes and silently recited the Huntsman's code, the mantras drilled into him from boyhood. Cold *kolomite* metal. Clear mind. No attachment. No weakness. But the words were just whispers now, fading beneath the steady beat of her heart against his ribs.

Where was his stamina, his ability to remain aloof, his lack of emotion, his resolve? Li-ara had slipped past all of it. Past the training, the armor, the years of discipline. She had found the cracks and planted something warm, something alive.

It terrified him.

He wasn't built for this. He was a Huntsman. A ghost in the dark. A weapon forged in silence. The son of a legend. A top-tier assassin. A man who had survived by needing no one, feeling nothing.

And yet, here she was, in his arms. And for the first time in his life, he didn't want to let go.

———————

Growls emerging from Beta's throat broke the night's stillness. Hunter opened his eyes. He remained motionless, listening. He watched Beta's body for signs of danger. She just stood beside the bed, staring at the door, her ears up, her body crouched low.

"Are the wild canines back?" Li-ara whispered.

"I'm not sure." Hunter slowly rose to a sitting position, his gun in his hand. Then Beta's ears relaxed, and her tail wagged widely as she ran to the front door. The sound of nails scraping against the bottom of the door reached her ears.

"It's Kii," Li-ara yelled as she sprinted, preparing to open the door.

"No, wait," Hunted cried out as he hobbled to catch her. "It might be a trick."

"Beta would know the difference." Li-ara removed the chair propped against the door. She flicked the lock and pulled the door open. Hunter held his breath as he waited for several wild canines to enter, but it was only Kii. He was covered in blood and holding a large bird in his mouth. "He's hurt."

Finally reaching the door, Hunter looked out into the darkness. "Quick, bring him inside. We are vulnerable with the door open and the voltage off. This is the opportunity they've been waiting for."

Beta also stared into the night. Within seconds her tail dropped, and she pulled back her lips, revealing her teeth. A menacing growl rose from her throat.

"Hurry," Hunter screamed as Li-ara grabbed Kii's collar and pulled him inside. Hunter slammed the door closed just as two wild canines hit the door, almost knocking him over. Li-ara rushed forward and helped Hunter push the door shut. As she held the structure in place, Hunter turned the lock and replaced the chair brace. "That was close."

"Why did they let him through?" Li-ara asked. "They could have easily killed him out on the road. And with the dead fowl in his mouth, the smell must have been alluring for them."

"This time, Kii was the distraction. They anticipated we would open the door for him and give them the opportunity to breach the door."

"They can do that? Rationalize?"

"Oh, yes. After what just happened, I'd say their intelligence is almost equal to ours. Let's put Kii on the table and determine how badly he's hurt."

Too heavy to lift, Li-ara led Kii into the kitchen and coaxed him to jump onto the table. His tail wagged excessively. A trail of blood dripped behind him.

Li-ara removed the bird from his mouth. "What a good catch." She ruffled the hair on the top of his head. "This will feed us for several days." The sound of his tail happily hitting the wooden table echoed across the room, drowning out the sound of wild canines sniffing and scratching at the door.

Hunter connected the batteries to the wiring for the front porch. The moment the wire made contact, a massive cry filled the night sky. Kii sat up and looked. Beta ran to the front door, sniffing the scent of burned canine hair. The sound of howling canines faded into the night.

"Stay back from the door," Hunter warned, grabbing Beta's collar and pulling her back. "Too dangerous." The canine snorted, then lay down under the table where Kii lay.

"I can't find any cuts or wounds," Li-ara stated. Using a wet cloth, she washed the blood from Kii's fur.

Hunter ran his hand over the canine's coat, separating the strands to analyze the skin. "I don't find any bite marks or teeth wounds either. Only scratches. If I were to guess, I'd say Kii chased that bird into a thicket. The thorns did a job of grating his skin and making small punctures."

103

"Then what took him so long to come home?"

"He may have sensed the wild canines and remained hidden until he was certain returning home was safe," Hunter answered. "Or he got trapped in the thicket and couldn't find a way out. Crawling into an area of thorns is much easier than trying to get out. Believe me. I've done it."

"Is that what happened?" Li-ara inquired as she placed her face close to her canine. Kii happily licked her face, his tail hitting the table again in joy. "You had me so worried. I thought the wild canines got you. But you were too smart for them, weren't you?"

Hunter inspected Kii's paws and his snout. "I can find no major injuries. After a good washing, he should be as good as new. While you do that, I'll clean the bird."

"Be sure to set the heart and gizzard aside for Kii. He deserves them. And he probably hasn't eaten all day."

The Huntsman agreed. As a hunter and provider, Kii would eat nothing until he took his kill back to the pack. That was Li-ara and Beta.

"We never ate anything for dinner. Are you hungry? I can cut and cook some of this meat and mix it in the leftover mush."

"I am hungry. Are there any biscuits left?"

"No, I'm afraid Beta ate the last of them when they fell on the floor."

"You mean when I threw them on the floor. I apologize again for my outburst. I normally am not this emotional. Would you like me to make some fresh biscuits?"

"No, this should be sufficient," Hunter said. He lit the stove, the flame flickering to life, and placed a skillet on the burner. Working with quiet focus, he stripped the meat from the bone, then added chopped vegetables to the pan. The savory scent of simmering broth and spices soon filled the cabin, wrapping around them like a blanket.

To his quiet satisfaction, the modification he'd made to the bottom of his cloth helmet worked. He could finally eat at the table with Li-ara. They ate slowly, savoring the moment. No alarms. No shadows at the door. Just warmth, food, and the silent gratitude of being whole again.

Once the dishes were rinsed and set to dry, Li-ara extinguished the lamp. With full stomachs and lighter hearts, they slipped beneath the blankets. Kii stretched out beside the bed, while Beta settled near the door. Kii was home. He was safe.

And for the first time in days, peace reigned inside the cabin. But outside, she was watching.

From the shadows beyond the trees, a pair of yellow eyes pierced the dark, low to the ground, unblinking. The wild canine leader crept forward, her movements silent, practiced. She paused at the edge of the clearing, her gaze fixed on the cabin. Then she moved closer. Like a ghost, she reached the porch, lifting her muzzle to the wind. The scent was strong. Blood, fire, and something strange.

She stepped forward and stopped.

A sudden twitch of static pulled at the fur along her snout. The wood beneath her paws crackled with blue light, faint but dangerous. Her mate lay sprawled near the porch rail, his body stiff and lifeless, small arcs of energy still flickering around the metal nails beneath him.

She whined low in her throat, calling to him. No answer. He was cold. Gone. This was no natural barrier. No ordinary trap.

The seasoned alpha stepped back, eyes narrowing. This two-legged male had power. Unseen. Deadly. She would not attack again. Not tonight. But she would return. And next time, she would not come blindly.

The sun's rays covered the bed with its brilliance and warmth. Li-ara, Hunter, and the canines stirred. Both were surprised to discover the sun was already halfway to its pinnacle.

"Do you think it safe to let the canines out?" Li-ara asked.

"Let me look first." Hunter walked toward the front door, Beta and Kii eagerly following behind him. "Stay." He opened the door enough to peek outside. A dead wild canine lay at the threshold. He closed the door to Kii's disappointment. "I see nothing except a dead canine on the porch. It must have taken the full brunt of the charge last night." He turned off the current, then walked over to where his armor rested and sorted through the pieces until he found his left metal wristband. "Just a few more minutes, Boy. I need to double-check for hidden enemies." Pushing a few buttons, the heat-detecting vision surfaced in his helmet. He looked from right to left, but he only detected a few birds and small animals. He identified no wild canines within two miles. "Okay, go out." The moment the door opened, Kii and Beta bolted out, happily urinating across the porch, marking the wood as their territory.

"Do you have any rope out in the barn?" Hunter asked.

"Yes."

"Can you bring me a shank thirty *junkles* long?"

"*Junkles*? I don't know that term."

Hunter wasn't familiar with the planet's form of measurement. "What about *glicks*?" *Glick* was an Imperial measurement. Many worlds were familiar with their terms.

"Don't know that one either."

"Hmm. See that tree in the front yard?"

"Yes."

"I need a piece of rope from which I can hang that dead canine from the second bottom branch."

"I can get it right after breakfast."

"No, I need for you to retrieve it now, before breakfast. We need to make a statement the leader cannot misinterpret."

"Okay." Kii followed Li-ara out to the barn while Beta returned to the porch. She sniffed the carcass and bit its hind leg.

"No, Beta. Don't touch the animal. I don't want your scent on the body. Otherwise, the female will think you killed it." Beta sat, intently watching the body.

Li-ara emerged from the barn with a large coil of rope over her shoulder and Fillo. After placing the animal in the corral, she ran back inside and returned with an armful of hay. She threw it in the fenced area and then ran back to the cabin.

Hunter shaded his eyes with his hand and looked up. Not a cloud in the sky. "Looks like today will be a warm one. That's good. The heat will keep the wild canines below for most of the day."

Tossing the dead canine onto his good shoulder, Hunter carried the body to the tree. Lying the animal on the ground, he constructed a noose and tossed it over the second branch. Pulling the knot taut around the dead canine's neck, he lifted the body to eye level.

He removed a hunting blade from his boot. In one clean motion, he drove the tip into the windpipe and sliced down the length of the belly to the tail. The skin parted, and entrails spilled out in clumps onto the earth

"Do you have something I can put some of these inners in?"

While Li-ara fetched a pan, Hunter tossed each of her canines a kidney. He then sliced the heart and liver in half, throwing a part to each animal.

With Li-ara's help, he scooped up the remaining innards. "We need to burn this and spread the ashes around the house."

"What are you going to do with the body?" Li-ara questioned.

"I'll raise the carcass high enough so that neither the wild nor domesticated canines can reach it. When the leader returns with her pack, she will understand that we are dominant. The canine's demise might even make a few of her followers question her ability to lead."

Li-ara watched as Hunter cut off the animal's testicles and penis and dropped them to the ground before lifting the carcass. Once at the appropriate height, he swirled the end and closed his knot. No animal would reach the body unless they climbed up the tree.

"Where did you learn to do that?" Li-ara asked.

"As a Huntsman, they train us in animal behavior. We learn how they think, what makes them think you are easy prey, and what makes them fear you. Although these are canines of a different species, all dogs think alike. The leader will see we gutted her pack member, and its innards are missing. She will believe we ate the insides out of spite and that we are well enough fed that we didn't need to eat the flesh. Our actions will make her fear we are too strong to defeat."

"And why did you cut off his private parts and leave them on the ground?"

"It's not uncommon for some animals to castrate their opponents. The act eliminates the competition for mating rights. The penis and testicles will show her we plan on wiping out her clan, I mean pack."

"And Kii or Beta won't bother them?"

"No. They understand the gesture and will not challenge the alpha's decision."

"And who is the alpha?" Li-ara asked, a smile on her face. This Hunter was full of himself.

"For now, I am. When I leave, you will be once again." Without another word, he walked towards the house.

Li-ara hesitated and watched him walk away. When he leaves - those words tore at her heart. That time was drawing near. His leg and side were almost healed. The broken arm was the only thing that held him there. Once the bones finished knitting, he would fly away in his aircraft, and she would never see him again. Her life would return to the way it had been, alone and single. Kii looked up at her sad face and whimpered. "I know, Kii. I will miss him, too."

While Li-ara prepared breakfast, Hunter lit a small fire in the outdoor fire pit and burned the dead canine's innards. Kii stared into the flames with immense interest. Once cooled, Hunter used a piece of bark and scooped them into a jar.

Li-ara knocked on the kitchen window to catch Hunter's attention. "Breakfast is ready," she shouted.

"Be right there," Hunter yelled back. With Kii at his side, Hunter hobbled along the side and back of the house, sprinkling the canine's ashes. Kii sniffed the flakes. "What do you think, Boy? Will his ashes discourage your relatives from wanting to enter the house?" Kii snorted as several ashes drifted up into his nose.

After breakfast, Hunter loaded the guns and stuffed bullet casings with powder while Li-ara washed the dishes and mixed up bread for rising. She placed a towel over the bowl and pushed it to the back of the counter.

"I think we should try catching some fish today," Hunter suggested.

"Do you think you're strong enough?"

"Probably not, but we need to stock up on food and prepare for the leader's assault. Once the battle begins, we won't be able to leave the cabin for several days."

"I'll take a few baskets with us. We can pick the wild strawberries and blueberries that grow along the stream edge. Some tubers and beans should be ready in the back garden, too. The beans flowered several weeks ago, so some of them might be ready for picking." Li-ara remembered Hunter's broken arm. "You're kind of limited on what you can carry. I think we should bring Fillo with us, too. I can string the baskets over her back to carry our supplies. Plus, I am sure the change in scenery will do her good."

"Excellent idea."

Hunter waited on the back porch with a gun in hand while Li-ara and the canines retrieved Fillo. Kii and Beta ran around the pack animal in excitement, the prospect of an outing delighting them.

"Doing okay?" Li-ara asked when they reached the stream bank. Hunter's breathing had increased, and his face looked clammy.

"A little winded," Hunter confessed. "I appear to still have a way to go until I'm fully recovered."

"Why don't you rest and stand guard for a bit? I'll set the fishing net and gather some berries."

Annoyed by his body's weakness, Hunter sat down on a nearby rock with his gun resting on his knee. Puckering his lips and grinding his teeth in frustration, he watched his hostess fill two baskets with fresh berries. It wasn't long before an eruption of the stream's waters at the net caught his attention.

"Hey, I think you caught something."

Li-ara scurried over to the net and peered inside. "Hunter, come and see this."

Using his crutch to stand, Hunter hobbled over to the stream. Inside the net was enough food for days. With Fillo's help, they pulled the net from the water. Sorting its contents, they had caught one turtle, a freshwater eel four feet long, three frogs, and eight fish. The turtle decided he didn't want to be dinner and meandered away. Kii flipped the turtle with his nose, then bit its head off.

Once their catch was bagged, the small expedition started back towards the house. They stopped long enough in the back garden to pick the beans and tubers.

Hunter helped unload their supplies onto the porch, but he was too exhausted to do more. He stood guard once again while Li-ara took them inside, and Beta put Fillo in the corral.

"Let's get you inside to rest," Li-ara stated when she finished, slipping her arm around Hunter's waist. He didn't say a word but was thankful for her support. The couch let out a disgruntled gasp of air as he plopped down on the cushions.

"Hunter, it's getting awfully warm in here. Do you think I can crack the doors and bring in some fresh air?"

No answer.

Li-ara turned. He was already asleep, his chest rising and falling beneath a shirt darkened with sweat. Kii and Beta lay sprawled on the floor nearby, panting heavily. The air was thick, stiflingly hot. Every breath clung to her lungs like a wet cloth.

She pressed her palms to the kitchen table and weighed the danger. If she opened the door and the wild canines came back, she and Hunter wouldn't stand a chance. But if the heat didn't break soon, they'd dehydrate. They would die either way.

Her eyes scanned the room, searching for an answer. The front door offered the best airflow, but it was a known vulnerability. She couldn't risk it, not unless she reinforced it.

Her gaze landed on the tangled fishing net thrown in the corner. She darted from room to room, gathering scraps of wood - broken chair legs, shelving, anything she could use to make a frame. With arms full and jaw set, she hurried to the front door. Outside, the sun had begun its slow descent, shadows lengthening across the clearing. Time was running short.

She paused on the porch, scanning the open fields beyond. Were the canines hiding out there, waiting for her to turn her back? Even with Kii and Beta standing guard, there was no guarantee she'd have enough warning to close the door. She glanced back into the room. Should she wake him? No. He needed rest.

Hands trembling slightly, she began anchoring the net. She hooked it on the rough edges of the wood siding, leaving the excess to reinforce the seal. Rolling each strip of wood into the netting, she nailed the thick net to the door frame. Every few strikes, she froze, listening. She heard no approaching danger.

The breeze caught the back window and swept through the house, cool and sweet like a whispered promise. It carried through the kitchen and into the bedroom, rustling the edge of the quilt on the bed. Already, the air inside was shifting. Breathing became easier.

For the next hour, she worked. Nail. Pause. Listen. Repeat. Sweat dripped from her brow, but she didn't stop. When the last nail was hammered in, she tugged at the netting, testing its strength. It held. It was not perfect, but it was enough to buy time if an attack came.

She gathered the remaining supplies and returned to the kitchen. The cabin was cooler now. The oppressive heat had broken. She glanced at the snoring Huntsman. The dark patch on his shirt had begun to fade. His breathing was deeper, calmer. At peace, for now.

Li-ara exhaled, finally, and leaned against the doorframe, letting the breeze wash over her skin like relief. Setting the turtle aside for dinner, she processed their catch. She had just finished gutting the turtle when Hunter stirred.

"Hey, Sleepyhead. Still doing okay?"

"How long have I been asleep?"

"About two hours. That fishing trip wore you out."

He clenched his jaw. How could he mount a proper defense if the slightest activity tired him out? When the leader attacked, he would not have the luxury of needing a nap.

"Why is the upper portion of the front door open?"

"Don't worry. Nothing can enter." Li-ara walked over and placed her hand on the net. "I strung the net across the opening and nailed it to the frame outside."

Hunter rose and walked to the door, inspecting her work. He closed the upper section and noted no interference with it shutting. Reopening the door, he examined how the net was attached. "Did you do this while I slept?" Li-ara sensed the anger in his voice.

"Yes. It was so hot inside I had to find some way to push fresh air through. But don't worry, I was careful. Kii and Beta stood guard. And I kept my weapon with me at all times."

"That was very foolish, Li-ara. You might have been attacked and killed. You are never to do anything like that again. Do you understand?"

Her face red, Li-ara walked up to the Bounty Hunter. She jabbed her finger into his helmet. "Listen here, you arrogant Huntsman. I have lived on my own for almost four years with no help from you. And I am none the worse for it. I can take care of myself."

"Except when Ting raped you." A flood of regret filled Hunter's heart the moment his ears perceived his words. Why did he say such a horrible thing? Li-ara's facial muscles dropped. The color from her cheeks drained and her chin quivered. Once more, his lack of decorum caused her sorrow.

Li-ara turned and stormed out the back door, grabbing the basket that hung on the wall. She didn't even call the canines to accompany her.

"Kii, Beta, guard Li-ara," Hunter shouted. "Where are you going?"

"I need some rosemary and garlic for the turtle." Her tone was controlled, emotionless.

"Li-ara, this is too dangerous. Nightfall is coming. You must come back inside." Grabbing his weapon and crutch, he hobbled after her.

"Don't tell me what to do."

"Please, Li-ara. You're an easy target. The wild canines might attack."

"Then you won't have to worry about my stupid actions."

"Don't say that. I was wrong to say what I did about Ting. I was scared and angry at myself, not you. If you had been hurt while I slept, I would

111

never forgive myself. I've never been vulnerable like this before. Forgive me. I don't always say the correct thing."

"I can protect myself."

"Yes, you can. But while I'm here, it is *my* job to protect you. At least let me help you so we can go inside sooner." He knelt and hunted for the needed herbs.

She pushed him away. "Now, who's being stupid? If the wild canines attacked, you could never stand fast enough. If you want to be helpful, stand guard with Kii and Beta."

Switching on his heat-seeking vision, Hunter surveyed the area. He detected no threat. As he swung his head to the south, Li-ara crossed his path of vision. "Now, where are you going?" Hunter screamed, trying to hold in his anger as he chased her. Were all women this much trouble?

"I need to put Fillo away for the night and feed her. Or do you want me to leave her outside as dinner for the wild canines?"

"Of course not." His hobbling now progressing to limping, he followed her to the barn. He kept an astute eye on the two canines for a sign of approaching danger. Glancing to determine Li-ara's progression, he noticed a square box on a table - a large ion battery. Beside it, leaning against the barn wall, was an old rusty long rifle. "I can't believe our luck. These are just what we need. Is there any more wire out here?"

"There's a roll behind the door."

Slinging the rifle over his shoulder and grabbing the spool of wire, he stared at the battery and his broken arm.

"I'll carry the battery," Li-ara said in a rough voice. "Don't think I didn't notice you were limping. You probably re-injured your leg chasing me. And you call my actions stupid."

"I didn't call them stupid. I said foolish."

Li-ara stopped and looked at him. "What's the difference?" Deciding it was better to say nothing, he remained silent. "Well? Now you have nothing to say?" Oh, he had lots to say, but doing so would only make matters worse.

"Can we please go back inside?"

Li-ara reached out and grabbed the roll of wire and the cumbersome battery. "You'll have enough trouble getting back without this weighing you down." She turned and stomped towards the house, then purposely slowed down to allow Hunter time to catch up. Neither said a word.

Placing the battery and wire inside the backroom, Li-ara helped Hunter up the back steps. His eyes scrunched close with each painful step. As she led him to a kitchen chair, a horrified gasp escaped his throat.

"What's wrong?" Li-ara asked. "Are you in severe pain?"

"Look," Hunter said, pointing towards the front door. The bottom part of the door lay open. Beyond the net, the canine carcass was gone.

"Where's the body?" she inquired.

"Impossible," Hunter replied. "There is no way she could take that body down." Fearing she or another wild canine was inside, Hunter grabbed Li-ara's arm, stopping her from moving. He held his finger to his mouth, instructing her to remain quiet. Using his heat vision, he surveyed the rooms. Once convinced no assailants were present, he let go of her arm. "Close the door." Without hesitation, Li-ara quickly shut and bolted both sections of the door.

A worried bark from Beta drew their attention to the bedroom. There, lying on their bed, was a scene more horrifying than the first. The head of a long-eared hopper rested in the middle of their bed. The rest of its body was nowhere to be seen. Blotches of fresh red blood dotted the bedding, and a single bloody canine print glistened on the floor.

"She was in the house," Li-ara said in terror.

"Yes."

"How did she open the door?"

"It wasn't locked. She might have been able to push it open."

"Why would she do this? Why here in the bedroom?"

"In response to what I did to the dead canine. She is showing me that this is your future. I killed her mate, and she will kill mine. And she will do it as we sleep."

Li-ara looked at him in bewilderment. "But I'm not your mate."

"She doesn't understand that. She only sees the two of us working together to defeat her. In her eyes, you are."

"When will she attack?"

"Soon, when she thinks our guard is down. We must finish fortifying this place. Help me push that cabinet up against the door." Resting his back against its side, Hunter pushed the heavy wooden china cabinet as Li-ara pulled from the front. Its position in front of the door nullified Li-ara's hard work of stringing the net.

"As of this moment, no one goes outside. She's bringing the war to us."

"What about Fillo?"

"She must manage the best she can until we can go back out to her. The canines need to keep urinating on the front and back doors." He walked into the back room and closed the partially opened window.

"We can't stay cooped up inside all day. We'll die from heat exhaustion."

"We have no choice. We'll sleep by day and remain vigilant at night. With any luck, the winds will bring clouds and rain to help cool us."

"That's your solution? Clouds and rain?"

"Best I got at the moment." He pulled out a length of wire and pushed the end into the small window casing. "Maybe you can finish dinner while I connect this wiring to the kitchen window. After dinner, you and I can wire the remaining windows. If she tries to breach the house, I'll fry her like a hot bug on a firestick."

Li-ara did not question Hunter's request. Her life was in his hands now, no matter if she wanted it to be or not.

.

10 THE ATTACK

In the flickering glow of the lantern, Hunter sat hunched over the forgotten long rifle, hands steady as he stripped it down to its aged bones. The weapon hadn't been fired in years, but he intended to change that. With patience and purpose, he worked the grime from the metal, turning rust and time into something deadly.

Beside him, Li-ara sat curled in her chair, the half-finished afghan draped across her lap. Her fingers moved through the familiar rhythm of crocheting, though her mind wasn't fully in it.

Spark.

The wire around the window sparked again, a sharp flash of blue against the shadows. Kii and Beta barked in alarm, rising from the floor in perfect sync, ears perked and teeth bared.

Li-ara lost her count. Again. She sighed, setting the yarn aside, her hands trembling just enough to betray her nerves.

"Can I help?"

Hunter didn't look up. He simply slid the small container of gun grease toward her, then offered a section of the barrel, a scrub brush, and a torn cloth.

"Think you can clean out the carbon inside?"

"It doesn't look too difficult," she said, squinting at the task, eager for distraction. She pressed the brush into the metal.

"Not so hard," Hunter said, catching her wrist before she shoved the scrubber in again. His grip was firm but gentle. He moved to her side, placed a second cloth across her lap, and guided the end of the barrel onto it.

"You want to coax it out," he murmured, "Not gouge the chamber. Scratch it, and the barrel won't fire straight."

He bent closer to demonstrate, his hand guiding hers with practiced ease. Her skin was warm against his. Then he caught it - a breath of lavender and honey. Her scent drifted up, subtle and warm, disarming. He closed his eyes for a moment longer than necessary, letting it settle deep inside him before catching himself.

"Focus," he thought.

"What do I do next?" she asked softly, her voice pulling him back.

Embarrassed by the pause, he gently took her hand again and guided the brush in smooth, circular motions. "Like this. Slow, steady. Let the tool do the work." Black soot drifted onto the cloth between them like ash. "When it's clean, coat the other cloth with grease and polish the chamber."

She nodded, fully absorbed now. Her eyes sparkled, not just with focus, but with something deeper. Despite the fear of what waited beyond the walls, she looked content. Hunter watched her a moment longer. She wasn't like anyone else. Not even close.

The sound came without warning. A scream, long, high-pitched, filled with raw, primal terror.

Fillo.

Li-ara dropped the rifle barrel with a clatter and bolted to the kitchen window. Her fingers clawed at the glass, trying to see through the blackness, but the moon was swallowed by thick clouds, and outside, only darkness pressed back at her.

"What's happening?!" she gasped. "What's happening out there?!"

Hunter appeared behind her, his voice low, urgent. "It's the leader. She's baiting us."

"We have to help Fillo, Hunter, we can't just let her die!"

"That's exactly what the leader wants. The second we open that door, they'll strike."

"She's *screaming*, Hunter!" Li-ara spun, panic wild in her eyes. "She's out there alone!"

"We have no other choice," Hunter said, quiet but firm. "We stay inside, or we all die."

She couldn't listen anymore. Li-ara turned her back to the window, hands pressed tight over her ears, trying to block out Fillo's terrified cries.

Kii and Beta whimpered beneath the table, tails curled tight, eyes wide and unblinking.

Hunter moved quickly. He grabbed the two small pillows from the chair and pressed them over Li-ara's ears, covering her hands with his own. His grip was strong but gentle.

"This'll help," he said quietly.

For fifteen minutes, he stood like that. Holding her, shielding her, while outside, the nightmare unfolded. He switched his visor to night vision.

And saw hell.

The barn door had been dragged open. Inside, Fillo was surrounded. Hunter counted at least ten canines. Fillo reared and kicked, her strength surprising, her will to live astonishing. But it wasn't enough.

Hunter watched in grim silence as they swarmed her, teeth flashing, claws ripping. One clamped its jaws around her hind leg and yanked. Another tore into her belly. Her intestines spilled out in coils, steam rising from the gore.

Fillo screamed.

One of the canines latched onto her throat. With a sudden twist, her trachea snapped.

The sound ended.

Fillo collapsed into the dirt. And the pack fed.

Tears blurred Hunter's vision - hot, sudden, and unwelcome. He blinked hard, furious at himself. She was just a pack animal. But still, the ache twisted in his chest. Is this what caring feels like? Is this what Li-ara has done to him?

Movement caught his eye.

Down the road, just beyond the reach of the cabin's light, the female leader appeared.

Blood smeared her muzzle. Bits of flesh hung from her jowls. She stepped forward, slow and deliberate, her eyes locked on his. She made no sound. No growl. No snarl.

Just stared.

Right through the visor. Right into him.

He felt it. Not just in his head, but in his bones.

Her voice.

"This is what awaits your canines … and you. The woman dies last."

Hunter's jaw clenched. "Not on my watch."

The female turned and disappeared into the blackness.

Hunter turned back to Li-ara, removed the pillows, and gently pulled her hands away from her ears. "It's over," he whispered.

She collapsed into his arms, trembling, broken by the silence that followed. Her sobs came hard, body-wracking, grief too large to hold in. He wrapped his arms around her without hesitation, drawing her close, letting her fall apart against him. He shouldn't have. He knew that.

But he did.

He held her.

Not out of duty. Not out of strategy. But because he *needed* to.

And that terrified him more than anything outside. But as she wept against his chest, he didn't let go.

––––––––––––

Morning came slowly and gray. The first light revealed the aftermath - shattered wood, streaks of brown-red smeared across the earth. The barn door hung from one hinge, barely clinging to the frame.

Fillo was no longer an animal, only fragments. A foreleg, a strip of hide, parts of her spine, a pool of drying blood already crusted by dirt and dust.

Hunter didn't stop Li-ara from looking. She needed to see. To understand. To carry this truth, like he did now.

The female wild canine wasn't just dangerous. This was personal. And she would return.

"I've never seen canines devour an entire *packtoo* in one night. How many were there?"

"I counted ten.

"There's no way ten canines could eat so much. Not even a fanged male bear could gobble down that amount of food."

"I believe they carried off a good portion of the kill," Hunter remarked. "The female must have pups back at the den. If I possessed my long rifle, I would have ended her reign last night."

Li-ara thought for a moment, then turned to Hunter. "Canines, especially wild ones, won't offer a vulnerable side. Yet you said she stood beyond the fence and almost taunted you. Why would she do that? She had to understand she was placing herself in danger."

"Somehow, she calculated what our firing distance is. Plus, without the moon's light, she perceived her position as safe. I don't believe she realizes I can see in the dark or detect body heat. That advantage may make the difference in our victory or death." He returned to the table and continued putting together the new weapon. "With so much food consumed, the pack should remain underground for at least a day. With this new gun, I could try to return to where the fanged bear attacked me and find my long gun. I can take her out with no problem if I have my weapon."

"No," Li-ara shouted. "I won't let you."

"Li-ara, it might be our only chance. I don't think I can defeat her without it."

"No. Promise me you will not try to go out."

"Li-ara."

"Promise me on your honor as a Huntsman."

"You'll die."

"Then we'll die together. Promise."

Her conclusion was wrong, based on emotions. But after last night, Hunter did not wish to add to her grief. "I promise."

After a small breakfast, Li-ara curled up in Hunter's arms and slept. A light rain drizzled outside, making the cabin cool. After the killing of Fillo, not even an inch of a window could be left open for ventilation.

A mournful, "Help" startled Hunter awake. Bolting upright, he listened intently. Kii and Beta let out a single bark as they tried to determine where the sound originated from.

"Did you hear someone?" Li-ara asked.

"I thought I heard someone calling for help."

The cry came again. Li-ara ran to the window and peered in between the nailed boards. "Oh no, it's the farmer."

Hunter darted to the window, heart pounding as he pressed his hands against the cold wood and stared down the road. The dogs swarmed around his legs, whining anxiously, scrambling for a view. Kii bumped the Huntsman's knee, nearly knocking him off balance. But Hunter barely noticed. His eyes were locked on the figure in the distance.

Blood covered the farmer from head to toe. He dragged his left foot as he hobbled towards the cabin. Hunter could see that a good section of his right arm was missing.

"What's he doing out there?" Hunter asked,

"Oh, no, what's today?" Li-ara asked in horror.

"I don't know."

Li-ara calculated the number of days since finding Hunter. "Today is the 11th. The farmer planned on stopping by my house today to discuss the new planting of the field. I completely forgot. We must help him." She ran towards the door.

This time, Hunter moved fast enough to reach the door seconds before she did. He slammed the door shut. "You can't save him."

"We can't let him die."

"Li-ara, he's already dead."

A blood-curdling scream filled the air as four canines attacked the farmer, sinking their teeth into his flesh. Their weight pulled him down onto his knees. A pool of red blood filled the ground below him. "Help me."

"We have to do something," Li-ara screamed as she covered her ears, once more trying to block out the sounds of death.

This time, Hunter could do something. He went to the front door and cracked it open. The fish netting was shredded, torn to pieces during the night or while they slept, giving him no shield from the blood-thirsty carnivores outside. Fearing an attack, Hunter closed the door and then reopened the top section. Aiming his gun, he fired, hitting the farmer in the heart. The farmer's eyes widened in disbelief and he toppled forward. The canines let go and yipped, uncertain of what had happened.

"Hunter, what did you do?" Li-ara yelled.

"I ended his suffering," Hunter said.

Before Hunter could shut the door, a blur of fur and fury exploded from the shadows. The wild canine leapt through the opening. It crashed into his chest, knocking him backward. His weapon flew from his grip, skidding across the floor. Before he could recover, the beast was on Li-ara. It slammed into her with bone-rattling force, and she went down hard, screaming as its teeth tore into her arm.

"KII! BETA!" Li-area screamed.

The guardians didn't hesitate. Snarling with fury, they lunged at the attacker, jaws snapping, claws ripping. Kii clamped onto the canine's hind leg. Beta tore into its shoulder, dragging it away from Li-ara.

Then, another beast came through the door. It hit Hunter like a battering ram, slamming him to the floor. His helmet cracked the wood beneath him. Fangs lunged for his throat. He caught the creature's head in both hands, barely holding it back, its hot breath washing over his face.

"Connect the battery to the window wiring!" Hunter roared. The canine's claws raked down his chest, slicing through cloth and flesh. Blood gushed. "Or the whole pack's coming through!"

From the corner of his eye, he saw Li-ara stagger up, bleeding, barely able to stand. She stumbled toward the wall and grabbed the switch.

Another canine leapt onto the porch. She slammed the lever back. The creature's body seized midair.

Blue lightning shot from the metal wiring into the wooden porch boards, lighting the scene in a hellish glow. The canine convulsed violently, jaws snapping in the air, then collapsed in a smoking heap. The scent of burnt fur and seared flesh filled the cabin.

The alpha barked, a sharp, clipped command. The remaining pack froze, then vanished into the dark like ghosts.

But the two canines inside the house still remained. One on Hunter, one fighting Li-ara's canines.

Hunter needed his knife. But to reach it, he had to let go of the beast. With a roar, he opened his hand and shoved his splinted arm forward. The canine lunged and bit, sinking its teeth into the makeshift brace. Wood splintered.

Hunter's hand shot down, fingers finding the hilt of his boot knife. In one fluid motion, he ripped it free and drove it into the canine's heart. The beast shrieked, spasmed, and fell still.

Hunter shoved the carcass aside, gasping, blood flowing from new wounds.

Across the room, Li-ara swayed on her feet, trying to aim Hunter's fallen weapon. Kii and Beta were still locked in battle with the third canine. Fur and blood flew. The wild canine darted, avoided Kii's jaws, and latched onto Beta's stomach.

She yelped in pain and collapsed, whimpering.

"NO!" Li-ara screamed, taking aim. But the creature broke away, bolting for the door. Kii gave chase.

Li-ara jerked the weapon upward, her finger froze on the trigger. She couldn't shoot. Kii was too close.

The wild canine leapt across the porch, narrowly avoiding the still-glowing trap. And to Li-ara's horror, Kii followed.

"KII, NO!" Hunter lunged, his hand outstretched, fingers grasping for Kii. But he caught only empty air. The space where the canine had existed a heartbeat ago was already gone. Kii vanished into the darkness, chasing the retreating beast.

Hunter slammed the door shut with a bang, his chest heaving. He threw his weight against it and locked it just as Li-ara crashed into him, trying to wrench it open.

"Let me out! He's still out there. He's …"

"You can't go after him!" Hunter shouted, grabbing her shoulders, holding her back.

She froze, staring into his visor. "But he'll die." Hunter remained silent. Li-ara turned, her gaze shifting to the wounded canine on the floor.

Beta lay in a twisted heap near the table, her once-proud body broken and bloodied. One ear was nearly torn off. Her front paw mangled. Deep gashes crisscrossed her stomach, blood pooling fast, soaking into the floor. Her chest rose and fell in shallow, ragged gasps.

Li-ara knelt beside Beta, her hands trembling as they hovered over the wounded canine. Hunter moved in quietly, crouching beside her without a word. Beta's brown eyes fluttered open, dull and glassy, yet still searching their faces. Her tail gave a faint, almost imperceptible thump against the floor. Li-ara glanced up, her eyes meeting the dark visor of Hunter's helmet, searching for answers she wasn't sure he could give.

"Please, Hunter, at least save her for me."

"I'll do my best," he said.

He grabbed the leftover rope and cut it cleanly in half. Without hesitation, he flung each piece over the thick kitchen rafter, looping them around and tying off the ends. Then he grabbed two clean towels, threading them through the hanging ropes and securing them tightly to form a makeshift stretcher.

"Bring Beta here," he said, voice soft but firm. "Lay her in the sling."

Li-ara moved like a ghost, bloodied, dazed. She sucked in a breath, ragged and trembling as she cradled her beloved canine. Carefully, reverently, she placed Beta into the sling. The towels cupped her broken body, suspending her just above the floor.

Almost instantly, Beta's breathing eased.

Hunter turned and guided Li-ara to a chair. Her knees buckled the moment she sat. He wrapped her arm with a clean towel to help with the bleeding, gently pressing it against the bites on her arm. She barely reacted.

Their wounds could wait. Beta couldn't.

With hands stained red and ignoring his own pain, Hunter returned to the canine. He stitched the torn ear first, steady, his own blood dripping quietly onto the floorboards. He set the shattered paw with a tight splint, wiped the worst of the wounds, and applied a small amount of the antiseptic ointment. He cursed under his breath. The bottle was almost empty. He'd have to save the rest for Li-ara.

He turned to Li-ara. She sat in the chair, unmoving, staring at nothing. Her skin was pale, her eyes glassy, her breath shallow. She didn't even flinch as he approached.

Hunter knelt beside her, dipped a fresh cloth in the basin, and wiped the blood from her forehead. Her arm trembled as he unwrapped the soiled cloth, revealing deep punctures. Four crescent wounds from canine teeth. Raw. Angry. Swollen. He pressed his fingers gently to her wrist, rotating it slowly. No fractures. Just torn flesh.

"Li-ara," he said softly, but she didn't answer.

He poured the last of the medicine over her arm. She didn't flinch. He bandaged her carefully, wrapping the fabric tight but not enough to cut off circulation.

Hunter ignored the throbbing of his own wounds, the torn flesh across his chest, the new bruising on his arm. He slipped one arm behind her legs and lifted her into his arms.

She didn't resist. She didn't speak. She simply leaned into him.

Holding her close, he sank into the chair. Her weight was light against him, but the emotions she carried - grief, fear, exhaustion - were crushing. His arm screamed with pain. His chest bled freely into his shirt.

Still, he didn't let go.

He reached for a nearby quilt, pulling it over them both, cocooning her against his chest. She trembled once. Then went still.

Keeping her warm. Keeping her safe. It was all he could do to keep the shock at bay - for her and for himself.

Outside, the wind howled. But inside, Hunter held her like she was the last real thing left in the world.

"Kii," Li-ara shouted as she jumped out of his arms, startling Hunter.

"Li-ara, Kii's gone."

"No, I hear him. Listen."

Hunter prepared to tell her she imagined the sound when he, too, caught the sweet sound of the canine's bark. He was alive. Standing Li-ara on her feet, Hunter rose and bolted to the window. He saw Kii loping towards the house as fast as his legs would carry him, dragging something in his mouth. What was Kii up to? Behind him ran six canines and the leader.

Hoping Li-ara was coherent enough to understand, he shouted, "Li-ara, when I tell you, cut the power. Then turn it right back on the moment I tell you to."

Hunter opened the door and viewed the pack closing the distance. "Come on, Boy, you can do it. Run as you've never run before." Kii reached the front yard, the lead dog closing the gap and almost within striking range. Taking aim, Hunter fired over Kii's head, striking and killing the lead dog. When it went down, the canine tripped the second dog, giving Kii the needed time to reach the porch.

"Now," Hunter shouted as Kii leapt into Hunter's arms. "Turn it back on." As he closed the front door, two of the wild canines did not stop in time and jumped on the porch, dying instantaneously.

"You crazy, wonderful canine," Hunter said as he realized what Kii brought. He hugged the dog. "How did you know this was our only hope?"

Kii licked Hunter's helmet, then trotted over to Li-ara, panting and wagging his tail. She dropped to her knees, hugging the large canine. "Is that what I think it is?"

"My long gun and satchel." He stared at Kii. "I said his species was intelligent, but I never thought this was possible. How did he ever comprehend what to look for?"

After licking Li-ara's face, Kii walked over to Beta. He sniffed her bandaged paw, then licked the cloth. He let out a small whimper.

"Is he all right?" Li-ara asked.

Hunter walked over and ran his hands across Kii's body. "I don't find any bruises, any cuts, or any blood. Somehow, he got through their line, found my stuff, and ran it back here without a single scratch." Li-ara walked over and knelt beside her protector. Hunter was still concerned about her condition. "Are you okay?"

"Yes. You're hurt," Li-ara stated when she saw the bites and scratches on Hunter's arm and chest. When she reached out, she identified her own bandaged arm. "I'm hurt as well. When was I hurt?"

"Don't you remember the canine attacking you? Or Kii and Beta fighting the canine off?"

"Not really."

"What do you remember?"

"I vaguely remember you being attacked and Kii running out the door. That's about it. Why can't I remember the rest?"

"You were in shock. But I think you're okay now."

"Come over to the table," Li-ara motioned Hunter into the kitchen. "Slip your shirt off. It appears the canine did some new damage to your chest." He pulled out a chair and sat, removing his garment. She filled a basin with water and washed his cuts, carefully checking his bear claw wounds on his side. "Thankfully, the canine did not reopen the side teeth marks."

"That's excellent news," Hunter stated.

Li-ara held up Hunter's bloodied and torn shirt. "Well, so much for this. I'll try soaking it overnight. I should be able to get most of the stains out, but not all. Plus, the canine's nails ripped it pretty badly."

"Stained and stitched-together shirts are a normal part of my life. To tell you the truth, in its former pristine condition, I felt a little awkward. The newness of the shirt was a little too high society for me."

Li-ara smiled. She imagined Hal's shirt was probably the first new garment the Huntsman had received in a long time. She wished it had remained nice for more than a day.

Grabbing a nearby towel, Li-ara carefully dried Hunter's body. Once dried, she grabbed the bottle of antiseptic ointment. Feeling its weightlessness, she peered inside.

"I used the last on you," Hunter said nonchalantly. "But throw me my satchel. I should have some inside." He searched through the jumbled contents and brought out a bottle of medicine. "Catch. We'll need to put some on Beta's wounds, too." Hunter tossed the bottle.

Li-ara poured a small amount of ointment into her palm. Slowly, she spread it across Hunter's chest, her touch gentle and deliberate. Her fingertips glided over the contours of his muscles, tracing the rise and fall of each breath. His skin was warm beneath her hand, firm despite the many scars it contained. The sensation sent a flutter through her core. A rush of heat bloomed in her cheeks as unfamiliar feelings stirred - uninvited, but not unwelcome. Butterflies fluttered in her stomach.

Hunter sat still, mesmerized, his breath snagging with every slow circle of her fingertips across his skin. Just days before, he would've recoiled from her touch - guarded, distant. But now, each gentle stroke sent a ripple of warmth through him, unraveling walls he thought unbreakable. He closed his eyes for a moment, letting himself feel, really feel, the quiet pleasure of her hands and the tenderness he never expected to miss.

The canine leader's howl brought the two back to reality. Her pack cried in response. Hunter jumped up and ran to the kitchen window. Atop the hill just out of the old weapon's range stood the she canine, possessed, calculating. Her pack circled around her, yipping in excitement.

"She's getting ready for the last assault." Hunter silently unlatched the window and pushed it open just enough to slide the barrel of his long gun through. The air was cold, brushing against his skin as he steadied the rifle. He raised it, sighting down the scope, his finger resting on the trigger. But the angle was off. He couldn't see enough of the target. The side of a tree blocked part of his view, and shadows danced across the figure, making it impossible to be sure. No matter how he adjusted, there was no clear, clean shot. His jaw tightened as he drew the rifle back.

"Can you make that long of a shot?"

"This weapon can reach a distance twice that length. And the best part is, she does not understand what Kii brought us. But I need to stand where I can get a decent shot. I'll only get one chance."

Gun in hand, Hunter rushed to the front door. He unlocked the top section and opened it. His eyes narrowed. The view was almost perfect. Almost. But the doorframe clipped his line of sight.

"I'll need to shoot from the porch," he muttered.

The blood drained from Li-ara's face, but she didn't speak. She simply nodded, lips pressed into a tight, pale line.

Hunter shut the door, latched the halves together, and opened it fully. "Kill the current."

Li-ara threw the switch. The hum of electricity faded instantly.

Hunter stepped out, his boots thumping against the wood. He moved to the edge of the porch. Still not enough. Gritting his teeth, he stepped down onto the top step.

The hill came into view.

He raised the long gun.

A flash of movement.

The leader stood, her golden eyes fixed on him. Hunter adjusted, heart hammering. He had her. Then, another canine lumbered in front of her, blocking the shot.

Hunter cursed under his breath, his finger twitching on the trigger. "Move … move, damn you…"

The leader barked a deep, commanding sound that echoed off the trees. And the pack charged. The ground rumbled beneath their paws, a wall of snarling fur and teeth thundering down the road straight for Hunter.

He didn't flinch. But his hands tightened on the rifle.

Too fast.

Too many.

His shot gone.

"HEY! YOU OUT THERE!" Li-ara's voice rang out, sharp and desperate. She had stepped onto the porch beside him, waving her arms like a madwoman. "OVER HERE!"

The leader snapped her head up. Hunter didn't hesitate.

Crack.

The first bullet struck the leader cleanly between the eyes. Her body hit the ground with a sickening thud.

Crack.

The second canine fell before it even registered what had happened.

The charging pack faltered instantly. They skidded to a halt at the edge of the yard, tails between their legs, eyes darting. Whimpers filled the air. Confused. Lost. They turned, circled once, twice. Panic rippled through them. Their leader was gone.

Hunter stepped forward. One by one, he pulled the trigger. Bodies dropped to the ground.

Li-ara reached up and lowered his long gun. "Don't kill them all. They have pups back at the den that will starve to death without someone to feed them."

"You're kidding."

"Everything has a right to live."

"Those animals were going to kill you."

"True. But what did we do to them first to make them hate us so much? For me, let the rest of them live."

Hunter slung his long gun over his shoulder and watched the last three canines trot away, not even stopping to look at their dead leader. Perhaps the war was not their idea.

The next morning, Li-ara and Hunter woke to the sounds of people. Through the boarded windows, they witnessed a gathering around the half-eaten body of the farmer. Further down the road, a second group inspected the dead leader. Several boys poked long sticks at the dead canines lying at the edge of the front yard. People pointed towards the cabin. A small group walked towards it.

"Hurry, go inside the bedroom," Li-ara shouted. "I won't let them in."

She hurried to the door, Kii beside her. Holding his collar, she opened the door. "Don't step on the porch unless you want to die."

"Did you kill the leader?" Rey Fin asked. He kept his eyes on the growling Kii.

"Yes. They attacked last night. I got off a lucky shot."

"Lucky? I don't know any man who can make that distance of a shot," Binn stated.

Li-ara asked, "Is someone dead on the road?"

"Looks like Duu Envine. His wife said he left to visit you. You never heard him?"

"No," Li-ara lied. "The canines were barking a lot with all the commotion outside. You said the wild canines killed him?"

"Appears so. They ate his major organs: liver, kidneys, and heart." Li-ara exhaled, relieved to learn the canine took the heart, along with the bullet.

"Do you need anything?" a woman called out. Li-ara didn't remember her name. "You are welcome to come and stay at my home for a while."

"Thanks, but I'm fine here. I need to stay and take care of my canines. My female was injured in the attack."

"I noticed they got your pack animal," Rey commented. "I can bring you a new one in a few weeks. I'm getting a new shipment in."

"Thanks. I'll need a new one. We'll get together in a few weeks and discuss the price."

"You're sure you're all right? You don't need anything?"

"I'm a bit shaken up, but okay. Thanks for checking on me. Give Duu's wife my sympathy."

"Will do."

Li-ara watched several men load Duu's remains into a cart. She remained at the door with Kii until they were out of sight, then closed and locked it. "They're gone."

"It's reassuring knowing your neighbors care about you," Hunter stated, exiting the bedroom.

"Did you know the canines would eat his heart?"

"That's why I shot him there. If I had shot him in the head, there would have been questions. No heart, no questions."

"I must remember that."

11 THE LAST NIGHT

Hunter threw the ball outside for Kii to chase. Beta watched from a lying position on the back porch, still recuperating from her attack.

"Your arm is getting its strength back," Li-ara shouted through the kitchen window as she pounded the bread dough.

Hunter flexed his fingers. "Almost as good as new, which means time to move on. I have three prisoners in cryosleep aboard my ship whom I should have delivered to Gladius three or four weeks ago."

"Any idea when you will leave? I'll bake some extra bread, biscuits, and muffins you can take with you."

"I planned on early tomorrow morning."

Li-ara kept her back to the Huntsman. "That doesn't give me much time to bake."

"That's why I didn't tell you beforehand. I assumed you'd make a fuss over my leaving. Are you sure you don't want me to drop you off somewhere a little more civilized or closer to town?"

"I'll be fine out here. The wild canines have retreated into the mountains. They'll stay in the forest until another fire drives them out, which might be never. As for the town, I'd rather take my chances with the wild animals than those people."

"And what if that Ting person comes around?"

"Don't worry. I'll keep a weapon with me. If he steps foot on this property, I'll put a bullet in his heart and feed him to the razorbacks."

Hunter laughed. "I like the sound of that. I should go pack my things."

As the sun slipped behind the mountains, the two once-strangers shared their last supper together. Neither said much, dreading the subject of Hunter's upcoming departure. Finally, Li-ara spoke up. "I thought you should take Kii with you when you return to your ship. You can fly over and drop him back off when you leave."

"No, you need him."

"The journey to your vessel is still a dangerous one. Kii can protect you. I'd feel better if you'd take him. Besides, he is fond of you. He and Beta will miss you." She fought back the tears.

"I will miss them too. Li-ara, I want to thank you for all you did for me. I would never have survived if . . ."

"Don't," Li-ara said. Her bowl in hand, she went and stood in front of the sink, keeping her back to Hunter. She could not stop the tears from streaming down her face as she rinsed her dish. "I did what anyone would have done. You were injured, and I nursed you back to health."

His appetite gone, Hunter placed his bowl in the sink. "I'm not hungry tonight. I think I'll turn in early. Join me?"

"I'll be there shortly," Li-ara said, keeping her back to him. "I've still got muffins in the oven."

As Hunter stepped into the bedroom, a rush of memory surged through him, raw, intimate, unrelenting. This was where he had clung to life, where every breath had been a battle, and where Li-ara's arms had become his anchor. He remembered her warmth, the sound of her voice in the dark, the way her fingers had threaded through his as he drifted on the edge of death. Nothing physical had passed between them, yet he had never felt more whole. She had touched something in him no one ever had. He didn't want to forget any of it. And yet, remembering now, letting it in, was dangerous. Those memories stirred something too deep, too fragile. He couldn't afford that. Bounty Hunters didn't get to keep heaven. They just visited it briefly before returning to hell.

With a quiet breath, he gathered his armor from the corner and placed it on the chair. The metal glinted in the moonlight. It was cold, merciless, unfeeling, just like the man he was supposed to be.

A sour wave rose in his throat as he stared at it. It felt heavier now. Uglier. Something inside him recoiled at the thought of wearing it again.

He turned back the blankets and slipped beneath them for the last time. He hoped she wouldn't be long.

Sleep claimed him quickly, but it was shallow, uneasy. The comfort of the bed only reminded him of what he was about to leave behind.

A clatter in the distance yanked him from slumber. His body snapped upright, instincts flaring. An enemy? Movement. His eyes darted to Li-ara's side of the bed. She wasn't there. Where was she? Li-ara wasn't beside him.

Hunter bolted out of bed. He rushed into the kitchen, searching the rooms.

The soft glow of moonlight filtered through the window, cutting through the shadows like a blade of silver. It fell across the bathtub and Li-ara rose. Slowly, deliberately, as if summoned by the light itself. Water clung to her skin, catching the moon's glow. Her bare shoulders shimmered, ethereal, almost unearthly. Wet strands of hair draped over her collarbone and down her back, glistening like ink dipped in starlight. For a moment, time forgot to move. She was a vision torn from a dream he never dared have. And he couldn't look away. Hunter just stood, watching. Not in desire, but reverence.

Li-ara turned, her eyes locking onto his helmet.

"I'm sorry. I detected noise and thought the canines were back." Hunter turned his head.

"Not this time. Tonight's my bath night, so I figured I might as well get back into the routine since you're leaving. You may look if you like. After all, I've seen what you have numerous times."

"I wouldn't say numerous times."

"More than you know," she chuckled, her cheeks blushing slightly.

The light reflected off his helmet. She sensed he was looking directly at her. "Your body is so beautiful."

She stepped out of the tub, grabbed a sheet, and wrapped it around her naked body. As she walked towards Hunter, she seized a kitchen towel from the chair. Standing before the Hunter, she tied the cloth around her eyes. "I want you to kiss me at least once."

"Li-ara, I don't think kissing you is a good idea."

"If you want to thank me for what I did, remove your helmet and kiss me. My eyes are closed, and I'm blindfolded. I can't see you." She waited.

Silence.

No kiss.

No movement.

Was he still there? Was he hesitating? Wrestling with his traditions or with his heart?

Seconds stretched like lifetimes.

She could feel her pulse in her throat, her chest, her fingertips. The silence wrapped around her, too loud, too still. Hope bloomed, and with it, fear.

"Are you still there?" she whispered, her voice breaking with the weight of not knowing.

"Yes," came the reply. Low and raw. She could feel the heat of his breath on her lips - soft, humid, and startlingly intimate. It stole the air from her lungs, catching her off guard. She hadn't realized how near he'd gotten until the warmth of him brushed against her mouth, not quite a touch, but close enough to blur the line. Her lips parted slightly, instinctively, as if answering a question he hadn't asked. The world narrowed to that fragile space between them, charged, quiet, and impossibly still.

"I'm right here," Hunter said, his voice barely steady. "My heart's beating so loud, I was afraid you'd hear it."

The air between them pulsed. Fragile. Electrified. Demanding.

A tingling swept through her, curling through her limbs as she waited. Every second stretched into eternity, her senses heightened, aware of nothing but his nearness. She didn't move, barely dared to breathe, afraid the moment would vanish if she did. All she could do was hope, hope that he would close the distance, that his lips would find hers and silence the storm inside her heart.

His lips met hers. Tentative at first, tasting, exploring, then deepening with a hunger that stole the breath from her lungs. Time fractured. He cupped her face in his hands, fingers trembling against her skin as he pulled her closer, as if the space between them had become unbearable.

The kiss grew wild, raw and desperate, fueled by weeks of denial, longing, and emotions neither had dared voice. A flame ignited, devouring hesitation. Li-ara parted her lips wider, letting her tongue slip into his mouth, seeking him with a need that left her dizzy. He answered her with a low, guttural sound, his tongue finding hers, dancing in slow, burning strokes that sent heat crashing through her.

His kiss became everything: consuming, claiming, promising. It wasn't just a kiss. It was a breaking point. A surrender. It lasted a long time before he broke it.

"I've never been with a woman," Hunter whispered as he rested his forehead against hers. "I'm not sure what to do."

"Never?"

"Such intimacy is not our tradition."

"I was only with Kal twice, so I'm new to this too. I think we can figure it out." He kissed her neck. Her body ached for him.

"Tell me what to do," Hunter whispered as his tongue caressed her ear. She moaned softly.

"Use your hands to explore my body. Listen to my breathing. You'll know what I like by it and the sounds I make."

Bringing her lips to his again, he ran his hands over her shoulders, dropping the sheet to the floor. He glided his fingers down her arms, then back up, his fingertips lightly stimulating her. Her back instinctively arched as his hands continued down her backside, stopping at her buttocks. Her soft moans and rapid breathing excited him. Any movement that brought her pleasure, he repeated. Bringing his fingers up over her shoulders, he skimmed down her sides, across her abdomen, rising until his hands cupped her breasts. She let out a sound of joy as he squeezed them. Following her cleavage line down beyond her chest, he continued to the area between her legs.

"Oh," he moaned. "It's so soft, warm, and wet. Never did I imagine it would be like this."

"It's warm and wet so you can slide in," she whispered.

Li-ara removed his shirt, running her hands across the scars on his body. She placed her lips on his chest, kissing it, delighting in the sounds he made. He brought her face up and wildly kissed her, entwining his fingers in her hair. Remembering the sensation when Hunter ran his fingertips down her back, she did the same to Hunter, stopping at his buttocks. She squeezed each through the cloth. As he gasped, she slipped her thumbs inside his waistband and followed the band around to the front. She took his belt and tried to unbuckle the clasp, but with her eyes shielded, she couldn't find the catch. Hunter's fingers swept over hers, unhooking the stubborn hook and dropping his pants to the floor. After stepping out of them, he pulled her as close as possible to his body. His hardness pressed against her abdomen as he kissed her with as much passion as he possessed. Guiding her backward, he led her to the bed.

"Use your tongue and mouth to explore my body," Li-ara whispered in his ear.

Hunter moved his mouth to her neck and down her body, tasting her, exciting her. She did the same, her hunger for this man growing more profound. For twenty minutes, the two explored each other's body, caressing every inch, delighting in the sounds escaping the other's throat.

"I want you," Hunter whispered, his desire about to reach its pinnacle.

"Sit with your back against the headboard," Li-ara breathed.

Li-ara lifted her right leg over his thighs and lowered her body down on top of him. A cry from the depths of Hunter's soul escaped his mouth as he experienced the warm wetness inside her. Locked in ecstasy, they consummated their love for each other as only two beings can.

"That was unbelievable," Hunter murmured as Li-ara rested her head on his chest. "I never dreamt anything could be so beautiful, so intense, so consuming." He held her tightly, not wanting the moment to end. Craving the taste of her lips, he raised her chin until their lips met again. Their kisses rose in passion and desire until neither could deny their need for the other. Once more, they consummated their love, two separate halves now joined as one. They pleased each other throughout the night until their bodies were too exhausted to do more. In the happiest rest of their lives, they both slept, unaware of what tomorrow would bring.

The next morning, Li-ara woke to find her bed empty. Hearing clattering in the kitchen, she walked out to view Hunter sitting at the table, dressed in his full armor, his long rifle, and satchel by the front door.

"Were you going to leave without saying goodbye?" Li-ara asked.

"Never," Hunter said, remaining on the side of the table away from her. "I wanted you to get as much sleep as possible."

Suddenly self-conscious, she grabbed the quilt and wrapped the covering around her naked body. Walking over to the counter, she covered two of the baked loaves of bread in brown paper. "Don't forget to take these with you."

"Thank you." Hunter placed the loaves inside his satchel. "I left the old long gun for you. I finished cleaning and oiling it. She shoots fairly well now." Sensing her quietness, he walked over and took Li-ara's hand, pressing it to where his lips would be beneath the helmet.

"Can't you stay a little longer?"

"Another day would not alter the outcome. I must leave. I believe it is best if I left this morning."

"Why?"

"Please understand what I am about to say. Last night will remain in my heart until my body is dust. I will never share with another what I shared with you. But, last night was a mistake. It should never have happened. Once more, I allowed my actions to put your life in terrible danger. As I've told you several times, a Bounty Hunter is both Hunter and hunted. If anyone knew of my feelings for you, they would use you as a pawn to get to me, to make me release them, or track an innocent. They would torture you to make me suffer."

"So last night meant nothing to you?"

Hunter froze, his chest rising and falling with the weight of everything he couldn't say fast enough. "How can you even ask that, Li-ara? It meant everything to me. Every second. Every breath. Every wonderful kiss. But I am a Bounty Hunter. I cannot allow myself to have feelings. The Huntsmen's creed I am bound to allows me no other life."

Li-ara pulled her hand away from his. "The almighty creed." She walked to the front door, issuing Kii outside. "Remember to drop him off."

Hunter hated the look of pain and disappointment covering her face, emotions he created. What could he do, what could he say to help her comprehend that a life together was not possible? He had to try.

"No matter how much I may want a life with you, it cannot be mine. Each day with me would put you in terrible danger. Therefore, I will not offer you the life you want with me. Can't you understand?"

Li-ara walked to the cabinet and removed a coin on which she had carved a likeness of Kii and Beta. She opened the side pocket on his left sleeve and placed it inside. "Something to remember us by."

"I will never forget you, Li-ara. A part of you now lives in me." She sensed his gaze on her face.

"May I ask a favor of you before you leave?"

"Anything."

"One last kiss." He did not object but took a step backward.

She closed her eyes and waited.

And waited.

A faint sound of metal scraping stirred before her, and for a moment, hope flared in her chest. He was removing his helmet. He was staying. But the silence stretched.

Another minute passed. Then another.

Li-ara opened her eyes. The room was empty, the front door shut. He was gone.

The weight of it slammed into her. She wanted to run, to rip the door open, to chase after him, to scream his name. But it was useless. He was a Huntsman. A Bounty Hunter. Bound by oath, by duty, by a code she could never compete with. Even if he had feelings for her, even if last night had shaken him to his core, it wouldn't change the path he was sworn to walk.

Her legs gave out beneath her. She collapsed to the floor, the sobs tearing from her chest raw and unfiltered. Tears soaked her hands as she buried her face in them, mourning not just the man, but the part of herself he had taken with him. The part that had opened, bloomed, and now would never feel his kiss again.

―――――――

Three miles before his ship reached Li-ara's cabin to drop Kii off, a finder beeped loudly. Searching his flight console, he located the *doc* blinking red. The name flashing was *Ting D'ton*, the reason he had come to Proxima Prime and the scoundrel who raped Li-ara. What was he doing so close to her home? His Hunter instincts activated, he turned the craft around and followed the beeping. Within seconds, he spotted a lone rider on a quillback meandering down a path leading to Li-ara's house. Zooming in low, he purposely spooked the animal. Bucking, it threw Ting off. He hit the ground hard, swearing and cursing as his ride trotted away. Hunter set his craft down, lowered the ramp, and walked outside.

"Hey, you *kadoo perdane*, you almost killed me," Ting shouted as he dusted himself off, trying to act strong and brave. When he stood, he witnessed his perpetrator dressed in Huntsmen armor - a Bounty Hunter.

"I see your foul mouth is not only for women." Hunter walked forward, his fingers releasing his weapon's lock.

"You owe me a new mount."

"Ting D'ton, you are wanted for rape on Regulus Three, Nigel Eight, and Rhodedron, besides the rape of Kal Veerde's wife. Authorized by the Guild, I am placing you under arrest."

"Yeah? You and what army?"

Ting drew his weapon, but Hunter was faster. Streaks of electricity spread across Ting's body as the stun ray hit his chest. Robbed of his muscle control, Ting collapsed, his body convulsing on the ground. Hunter stood over his capture, waiting for the spasms to subside. Aiming his weapon at the male's heart, the Bounty Hunter contemplated pulling the trigger. No, death was too good for this piece of scum who raped Li-ara and the other women. He would allow the perpetrator to live the rest of his life in prison, where he would be the victim. Rolling Ting to the side with his foot, Hunter handcuffed him, yanked him to his feet, and dragged him up the ramp.

"Hey, man, you're making a mistake. I never touched those women. I don't care what they claim. As for that Veerde woman, I was just trying to comfort her after her husband died. She misunderstood my intentions."

"Misunderstand this." Hunter pulled back his left arm and hit Ting in the jaw, knocking him out cold. "A present from Li-ara." He threw the unconscious criminal into the cryo-chamber and encased him in carbonite.

The sound of a ship grew near. Hunter was bringing Kii back. Walking to the front door, she allowed herself a moment to believe he would change his mind and come to her, to the life he desired. She'd dash into his arms.

As she opened the door, she chastised herself, for that future did not exist. His ship rested yards away in the field across the road. The door was open, and Hunter stood at the top. Kii was walking down the ramp. Li-ara whistled. Kii ran down but stopped at the ramp's end, turned, and looked at Hunter, waiting for him to exit. He gave the Huntsman a sharp bark as an inquiry about why he wasn't following. Li-ara sensed Hunter's eyes on her. He waved. She did not respond but whistled for Kii again.

Kii bounded towards the cabin. Once he was inside, Li-ara closed the door without glancing at Hunter. She embraced the canine, tears, and sorrow consuming her body again.

"What's this?" Li-ara asked when she noticed a piece of paper under Kii's collar. She opened it and read:

Li-ara

Ting D'ton will never hurt you again. I have fulfilled the mission I came here to execute - his arrest. He will live out his days on a prison planet where it will be his turn to be raped each day.

BiiJun D'Kolor

II

You cannot love one thing when your heart has been given to another. You must find and face Li-ara and ascertain where your heart lives.

The Dominee

12 RIGEL THREE

"You summoned me, my Lady?" Hunter's voice was low as he stepped into the Dominee's shadowed chambers. She was more than the ruler of his clan. She was the unseen hand behind all Kolora's Huntsmen. Alchemist. Truth-seer. Keeper of secrets no man dared speak aloud.

"Please, be seated."

Before him stood a thick wooden table, its surface swirling with veins of red and brown. A single chair waited on his side, its back to the door. Hunter sat, spine straight, every sense alert.

"Hornsmier tells me you are not sleeping well," the Dominee stated. She kept her back to Hunter while searching through her alchemist bottles on the shelf. "Is this true?"

"As of late, sleep does not come easily to me."

"Does she still fill your dreams?" Hunter did not answer. "When I ask a question, I expect an answer, BiiJun." She turned to face him. Even though her eyes were hidden behind her metal helmet, Hunter sensed her disapproval.

"Yes, My Lady."

"Yes, what?" The Dominee returned to looking over her bottles.

"She still haunts my dreams."

The Dominee reached for a slender vial filled with yellow powder. She tapped a small amount into a nearby glass of water, stirred until the liquid shimmered, then set it aside.

From a high shelf, she laid out a sheet of white parchment and measured a third of the yellow powder onto it. In silence, she uncorked a second vial. This one held granules the color of storm-lit skies. She let the blue powder cascade gently over the yellow. Pinching a few of the blue grains between her fingers, she dropped them into the waiting glass. The mixture hissed, bubbled, and turned an eerie shade of green.

She folded the parchment over the remaining powders, each crease sharp and deliberate, sealing the mixture within. With a final press of her fingers, she laid the packet on the table.

At last, she turned to Hunter and extended the glass. "Drink this. The liquid will not remove her from your dreams, but it can hide her and allow you to sleep."

She pushed the envelope towards him. "Each night before you lie down, place a *tabernot* of powder in a glass of water and drink the solution. The envelope contains enough for three nights."

Not questioning his Dominee, he drank the liquid. A bitter, chalky taste filled his mouth, but Hunter said nothing. "Thank you, My Lady." He stood and turned toward the door.

"I do not recall giving you permission to leave." Hunter sat back down. The Dominee pulled out the only other chair in the room and sat across from him. "I also received reports that you have not gone on a hunt for over six months. Is this true?"

"Yes. My ship is in need of repair."

"Is your vessel still in need of repair because you cannot obtain the necessary parts or because you have no desire to fix it?"

"An interest in repairing the ship has not been part of me lately." His voice was quiet, scraped raw by something deeper than exhaustion. He didn't look at her. He couldn't. The words tasted like defeat, and the silence that followed felt like it might swallow him whole.

"Has your desire to hunt also left you? *Renaw* informs me that even before your ship needed repair, you did not ask for any Bounty Hunter assignments from him or the Guild. Is this correct?"

"Yes."

"And when bounties were offered to you, you turned them down. Is this also correct?"

"Yes."

"Understand, BiiJun, neither *Hornsmier* nor *Renaw* openly told me these things. They only conveyed to me such details after I questioned them about you. How long since Li-ara tended to your wounds?"

"Four years, eight months, and fourteen days."

A precise calculation, the Dominee thought. This Li-ara not only possessed his dreams but also lived in his soul. "BiiJun, you told me of your time with her and her canines, how she saved your life, and how you fought side-by-side against the wild dogs. But you have never revealed the most important part of your story."

"She never saw my face."

"I do not care if your face was revealed or not. If I removed my helmet here, at this moment, would I stop being your Dominee?"

"No."

"A Hunter hides his or her face from the world to protect their identity, not because our law demands it."

Hunter raised his head. "Isn't that one of our most sacred rules?"

"Only because several males, long dead, declared it so," the Dominee said, her tone steady. "Other sects may see unmasking as a betrayal of their oath, but the Kolora Huntsmen do not. There is no law forbidding the removal of your helmet, especially when survival demands it. If no Huntsman had ever set aside his mask, our kind would have vanished ages ago."

She paused, letting the truth settle before her voice softened, grew heavier. "BiiJun, I never asked why you left her. But I'm asking now."

Her voice gave no command, only quiet insistence.

"What happened that final night on Proxima Prime?" His shoulders tensed. A tremor passed through his fingers, barely noticeable unless one was looking. He lowered his head, gaze fixed on the grain of the table as if it might save him.

"What made you run?" the Dominee pressed gently. "You've buried it, sealed it behind iron walls. But it lives there still, clawing. Face it, BiiJun. Tell me. Did you give yourself to her? Did you consummate that love?"

For a long breath, there was silence. Then came a sound the Dominee would never forget - raw, broken, the soul of grief torn loose from a man who no longer knew how to carry it.

"Yes," he whispered. And in that single word, everything he'd lost came spilling out.

"I feared as much," the Dominee sighed, her voice a whisper wrapped in sorrow. "When the Biiloot rescued you from the Traders and returned you to your father, I saw the fracture in you, the way you flinched at the light, recoiled from touch. You struggled to reclaim the rhythm of your Huntsmen's life. But you did not yield. You trained until your hands bled. You relearned the disciplines, the rites, the very breath of our creed. And when you came of age, you stood before the sacred flame and pledged your love and loyalty to our people … and to me."

She closed her eyes, and though she could not see his tears behind the metal mask, she *felt* them. Silent rivers carved through the ruins of his soul.

The Hunter remained still, as if movement itself might shatter what little strength he had left.

"You were not born on Kolora," she said quietly. "But your spirit, your fire, is no less Kolorian than any warrior born beneath its twin suns."

She stepped closer, her gaze gentle but unrelenting.

"But…"

Her voice trembled on that single word, not from weakness, but from the weight of what she was about to say.

"You left something behind on Proxima Prime. Or someone. And I fear what you left is what keeps breaking you."

She waited, giving him space to breathe, or fall, or speak.

"Do you wish me to turn in my Hunter's designation?"

"That is not for me to decide," the Dominee said gently, her eyes never diverting from his mask. "Only you can make that choice. That burden, that freedom is yours alone."

She rose and circled the table slowly, each step echoing like a heartbeat in the stillness. "But understand this, BiiJun: you cannot love one thing while your heart still belongs to another. Divided hearts do not endure. They fracture. They rot from the inside."

She stopped behind him, close enough to feel the pain radiating off him like heat.

"You must find her," she said softly. "Find Li-ara. Not for duty. Not for penance. But because the wound refuses to close. And until you stand before her and truly see her and not the memory, you will never know where your heart lives. Or if it can live at all."

The Hunter remained motionless, but his breathing faltered - once. It was enough. She laid a hand on his shoulder, her touch light and supportive.

"I went back," Hunter spoke, each word splintered with the weight of memories he had long tried to forget. "Remember? She was gone. I couldn't find her."

"You must search."

His head lifted slowly. "I searched. For over four years."

A long silence stretched between them, thick with what had never been spoken.

The Dominee's composure shifted. No longer the commanding Mistress of the Huntsmen, but something softer. Older. Wiser.

"So that's why your hunting expeditions took so long," she said quietly. "You weren't just tracking prey." She stepped around to face him fully. "You were chasing ghosts."

His shoulders sagged under the weight of the truth. "I thought … maybe she had returned to her family. Or moved to another city. Or worse." His voice faltered, and something dark flickered in his voice. "Each lead ended in ash. Every trail faded into silence."

"And still you searched."

"I had to. I told myself it was to find answers. Closure. But …" He exhaled sharply. "But it was always her. Even now, it's still her."

"Then your heart has spoken. It is time to follow where it leads. Not with weapons or duty, but with truth."

The Dominee returned to her seat, her heart aching for the Huntsman sitting across from her.

"Does your mother cover her face with a helmet?"

"No."

"Does your father?"

"Not anymore. When his age and injuries prevented him from hunting, he removed his armor and had it melted down and reshaped into armor for a new Hunter."

"And where do they live?"

"My Lady, why are you asking me questions that you know the answer to?"

"In your remorse and sorrow, do you feel the need to challenge my right to ask such questions?"

"No."

"Then what is the answer? Where do your parents live?"

"Here on Kolora."

"Neither are banished, outcast, or diminished for choosing to live with their faces revealed," the Dominee said, her voice quiet but unwavering. "If you chose a different path, one that no longer bore the title of Hunter, your worth would remain. You would still be BiiJun, the revered Huntsman. That does not change."

She paused, letting her words settle.

"If you choose to remain a Huntsman, you may do so without the covering. Though I will not lie. Your life would likely be short. The path of the Hunter is cruel and cold. Most die young, their names whispered in fading winds. But some - some stray far enough to find something else. A companion. A family. Joy. They were Huntsmen, too. The difference between them and you, BiiJun, is not in their choices. It is that they made them. And you? You have not." The Dominee paused. "Love is not common. It is not easily earned. When it comes, it is a gift few are wise enough to recognize. You saw it. And rather than embrace it, you ran."

The Hunter's hands clenched on the table's edge, knuckles white.

"You were wrong to leave her," she said gently. "And now, you must find a way to make it right."

He looked up, lost, hollow. "But how?"

"That is for you to discover."

She circled around, each step calculated, deliberate, the hem of her robe whispering across the stone.

"Perhaps the only path forward is to take responsibility. To speak the truth you've buried. Admit your wrong. Grieve what you've lost. And then choose. Hunter, or something else."

She stopped.

"You may one day cross paths with her, only to find she no longer remembers you. Or worse, she does but belongs to another. That pain, too, you must be prepared to bear."

Hunter swallowed hard, jaw clenched, but said nothing.

"Or, you may meet another. Someone new. Someone who reaches into the broken places and teaches you how to breathe again. Life is not a single path. There are many forks. Many turns." The Dominee returned to her seat. "Remember this, BiiJun. No matter where you go, what choices you make, you will always be one of us, a Huntsman. Only you can choose if you are a Huntsman *and* a Hunter. Do you understand?"

"Yes."

The Dominee reached into her breast pocket and removed a piece of paper. She handed the note to Hunter. "I have an assignment for you during which time you must decide if you are a Hunter and decide about Li-ara."

Hunter read the paper. "Rigel Three?"

"You told me of the great intelligence of the canines, both Li-ara's two and the wild pack. Their talent to problem solve, their innate instinct to determine what you needed, and their talent to think as we do defies explanation. Ever since I heard about them, I have dreamt of them joining our forces, fighting beside us in battle, being companions to our Hunters, and guarding our families. Are you familiar with the old legends?"

"I believe I know most of them. My parents spent many evenings telling me the stories, as did my teachers."

"Do you remember hearing of the Great Huntsmen walking beside canines?"

"Yes. Those were always my favorite stories. The Huntsmen and their canines were inseparable. The Bounty Hunters used them to hunt down the most ruthless criminals. Because of these canines, the Huntsmen became known as the greatest warriors in the galaxy."

"Do you know why our people stop using them?"

Hunter thought. "No, My Lady. My parents never told me that part of the story."

"They did not tell you because no one knows why. One day, they simply stopped. I believe the reason is buried somewhere in the Great Library amongst the recordings of our history."

"Why would they bury it?"

"That, I do not know. But one day, I hope to discover the answer, especially after what you told me about Kii and Beta."

"They were extraordinary canines."

"I wish to restore that lost history and have our Huntsmen fight beside canines again, BiiJun. I have learned of a trainer who lives on Rigel Three who breeds and sells these canines. I want you to travel to Rigel and discover if these canines are as smart as Kii and Beta. If so, bring me four female pups and four males. That will be enough to start our own pack. Learn all you can on how they are trained so you can teach us." She laid fifty Rigel coins on the table. "This should be enough to buy the pups and fix your ship. You start your repairs tomorrow and will depart in three days."

"Yes, My Lady."

"You may go now."

The Hunter slowly rose and left her abode. The Dominee wondered which life he would choose.

With purpose finally steady in his chest, Hunter set to work on his ship. In just two days, he had it fully repaired. Each bolt tightened, each system calibrated with care. At night, he followed the Dominee's instruction and drank the sleeping potion.

The Dominee was right. If Li-ara's face visited his dreams, he no longer remembered. The weight that once crushed him as he slept had lifted. Each morning, he rose clear-headed, steady, ready to move forward.

On the third day, just as the last stars blinked into place, the Dominee summoned him once more.

"Are the repairs done?"

"Yes. I leave tomorrow."

"What were the costs of the repairs?"

"Just under twenty-two *clegg*."

She placed another fifty coins on the table - Tibian jubels this time, their glint unmistakable. A universal currency accepted on nearly every planet in the galaxy. Once Hunter witnessed them, the Dominee swept them into a small leather purse and tied it shut.

"Take these as well," she said, handing him the pouch. "Spend them as needed. Inside the bag, you will also find a sealed note. You are not to read it until you have the pups and are safely en route back to Kolora. No sooner. Do you understand?"

"Yes, My Lady."

With the coins secured and the trainer's coordinates in hand, Hunter launched from Kolora at first light. It felt strangely good to be back behind the control stick, to hear the hum of the engines beneath him, feel the quiet response of the ship to his touch. Something familiar. Something with purpose.

He slipped a hand into the narrow pocket sewn inside his left sleeve and brushed the cool surface of the coin Li-ara had made him. Drawing it out, he let his gaze fall on the etched faces of the two canines. It was her gift, her memory, pressed into metal. If he truly meant to confront his feelings, perhaps it was time to let go.

With a sharp flick, he tossed the coin aside. But silence settled too quickly. After a few heartbeats, he reached down, retrieved it, and returned it to the safety of his sleeve. There would be plenty of time to decide what to do with the past later.

As his fingers withdrew, they brushed something else, something he'd long forgotten. He pulled it free and stared.

His marriage bracelet, the one he had forged for Li-ara. It consisted of twisted strands of metal shaved from his armor and woven together in a delicate rope. At either end, polished metal spheres sealed the clasp. Suspended in the center, a small glass bead, its fluid faintly aglow, held a single fleck of his helmet and a drop of his blood.

His pledge. His promise. One she had never heard. One he doubted she ever would.

Thanks to the modifications he'd made to his craft, the journey to Rigel Three took only forty-two days. Half the time it would have taken before. As the stars thinned and the curve of the planet filled his viewport, Hunter keyed in the final coordinates. A digital map flickered to life across his screen, glowing blue against the black.

Within seconds, he found the name the Dominee had written - *Cashmere*. It was a small town, almost forgettable, nestled between endless fields and modest clusters of industry. Hunter landed his ship on the landing field two miles east of the city's edge. Functional and isolated.

He didn't expect much in the way of entertainment here, and with luck, he wouldn't need any. If the trainer had pups available, his business would be swift. But if not, he suspected he'd be stuck in this dusty outpost longer than he liked.

His boots crunched against dry soil as he strolled into town, every sense alert beneath his calm exterior. The air held the scent of machine grease and sun-warmed grain, and the breeze carried the low hum of a world too busy surviving to bother with strangers. Still, he watched them. All of them.

Rigel Three was unfamiliar terrain, and he had no idea how its people might respond to a Huntsman walking their streets. Yet, no one stared. No one whispered. Eyes passed over him with idle disinterest as if his presence barely registered. Odd. Were bounty hunters common here? Or had they simply never seen one of his kind and didn't recognize what he was?

"I was wondering if you might help me," he asked a man who was sweeping the porch of his food shop. "I'm looking for this address." He handed the man the note.

"You must be here to buy some canines. She raises the best ones in this quadrant. Possibly in the entire galaxy. Top-notch, they are."

"She? I thought the trainer was a man."

"No, the trainer is a female. And a pretty one."

"Can you tell me how to find the trainer?"

"Her house is out in the country. A ferocious canine guards her property, so you must be diligent when approaching. But wait. I see her son across the street leaving school. He can take you to meet his mother. I'll call him over." The man raised his hand and waved. "Hey, J'Dar. J'Dar Jen, this Hunter wants to buy some of your mom's canines."

Hunter staggered, his hand shooting out to grip a nearby hitching post as his knees threatened to buckle beneath him. His gloved fingers screamed in pain as he forced them into the wooden post. His world tilted. The air seemed to vanish from his lungs. He had heard the name, clear and unmistakable.

Not the Hunter's name he'd worn for years. Not the code name etched into bounty records, or the name his enemies whispered in the dark.

His *real* name.

Panic surged like wildfire in his chest. No one knew that name. No one except the Dominee and his parents ...

And Li-ara.

Hunter turned as if drawn by some invisible tether. Crossing the street beside a woman he didn't recognize was a boy. Laughing. Alive. Free.

The child walking toward him wasn't just familiar, he was *him*. Not a resemblance or a trick of memory but a living, breathing reflection of Hunter. Same eyes, same stride, same face - the one he used to see staring back at him from the still waters before the weight of duty, bounties, and loss carved it into something harder.

Hunter's heart pounded so hard it hurt. Here was a memory he'd never made. And for the first time since leaving Li-ara, Hunter felt fear as his past walked toward him. Should he reach for it or run?

"Are you a Hunter?" the boy blurted, eyes wide and sparkling. He leaned forward on his toes, practically vibrating with excitement. "A real Huntsman?"

Hunter's entire body locked. The boy's question struck like a blade, cleaving through years of silence, discipline, and hidden truth. His throat burned, refusing to release a single word. His chest heaved, but no breath came easy. He stared at the child. Those eyes, that voice. A storm rose inside him, wild and undeniable. He managed a nod, stiff and jerking, praying his knees wouldn't give out and expose the trembling truth beneath his armor. Because if he spoke, if he moved, he might lose control.

"You wish to purchase canines?" the woman asked.

"This is Tallie," the store owner explained. "She's J'Dar's watcher."

"Look at his armor, Tallie," J'Dar shouted in excitement. "Can I touch it? Can I look at your weapon?"

"J'Dar, don't bother the man," the watcher said. "You ask too many questions."

"Is that your name? J'Dar?" The words burst out of Hunter, too fast, too loud. His voice cracked with urgency, the name leaping from his mouth before he could rein it in. His fingers pressed harder into the hitchboard, white-knuckled and shaking. He remained frozen, eyes locked on the boy, caught between disbelief and desperation.

"Yep." The boy grinned. "J'Dar Jen. I'm named after my dad. He was a soldier in the Correllian Skirmish. He died in the war. It's just my mom and me." The boy noticed the gun across Hunter's back. "Do you shoot people with that long gun across your back?"

"Sometimes," Hunter said. His voice had returned, shaky but intact. "How old are you, J'Dar?" The question slipped out softer, more controlled, but the tension in his jaw remained.

The boy looked up at Tallie for the answer. She held up four fingers, after which he proclaimed, "I'm four. I'll be five in…How long, Tallie?

"Ten weeks."

"Ten weeks," J'Dar repeated.

Hunter didn't move. The words "Yep, J'Dar Jen. I'm named after my dad. I'm four," played over and over in his mind. Was this boy Li-ara's son? Was he *HIS* son?

The child continued watching him, eyes curious, unaware of the storm unraveling just feet away. How could he not feel it? The ground was cracking open beneath Hunter's feet.

Hunter blinked, and for a moment, he wasn't standing in the street anymore. He was back on Proxima Prime, in the clearing where he last saw her. She was standing in the doorway. Alone. Vulnerable.

He'd left her.

He'd left *them*.

Hunter flinched as he felt something warm in his hand. He looked down, startled, unprepared, to find the boy's small fingers curled around his own, firm and trusting as if they'd always been there. As if they *belonged* there.

"Come on," the boy said cheerfully, giving his hand a tug. "We'll take you to my mom. She'll be surprised a Hunter wants to buy her canines."

Hunter opened his mouth to respond, but his words stuck again. A lump had taken their place, swelling up from his very soul. The boy tugged again, and this time, Hunter moved.

He didn't think. Didn't resist. His legs simply obeyed. One step. Then another. And then he was walking, *following*, drawn forward not by duty or mission or command but by the quiet gravity of a child's hand wrapped around his own.

"Can you take that helmet off?" the boy asked, glancing up with wide, curious eyes.

Hunter swallowed, forcing his throat to open. "No," he murmured. "We never remove our helmets when someone is near."

"Boy, I bet that gets boring. Is it hot under there?"

"Sometimes."

"Tallie, don't you think his helmet is great? Do you think your husband would make me one like his?"

"Perhaps. You must ask him," Tallie said. "My husband is a blacksmith if you need any repairs. The house is about five miles down the road."

The boy's hand remained in his, pulling him forward. Light. Warm. Steady. Each step brought Hunter closer to the unspoken questions screaming in his chest. What if Li-ara waited down the road? What would he say to her? What *could* he say to her?

"Up ahead, around that bend, J'Dar's canine waits for him," Tallie said, interrupting Hunter's thoughts. "He doesn't like strangers and might act aggressively. He won't hurt you. If he moves or comes toward you, remain still. Let him sniff your clothes, and it should be okay. "

"Understood."

Hunter's eyes stayed locked on the winding road ahead, every muscle coiled beneath the armor. The dirt lane curved in the distance, shrouded by trees and shadows, and he watched it like a soldier anticipating gunfire.

Then, movement.

A massive black blur surged around the bend, pounding down the road like a storm unleashed. Ears pinned back. Paws striking the dirt like thunder. A deep, menacing growl rolled ahead of it.

It was Kii.

"Stop, Kii!" Tallie shouted. "He won't hurt us!"

Hunter smiled beneath the helmet. A quiet, aching smile no one could see. Kii had recognized him. Even after all this time, the canine hadn't forgotten. He wasn't charging to attack. He was coming home.

"I'll catch him!" J'Dar shouted, laughing as he sprinted toward the oncoming blur, arms stretched wide.

Hunter's legs moved before thought could catch them. He reached out instinctively. "J'Dar!". But the boy was already in motion, fearless, joyful. Kii didn't slow.

He barreled past the boy in a blur of fur and muscle, brushing J'Dar's shoulder with his flank and knocking him clean off his feet. The boy tumbled into the dust with a surprised grunt. Kii barely paused, bounding right past Tallie and lunging straight for the man in armor.

Hunter braced himself as the canine rose onto his hind legs, placing massive front paws on his chest with joyful weight. His tail wagged furiously, and he let out a high-pitched yip before licking Hunter's helmet with frantic affection. The helmet fogged with the warmth of breath and slobber, but Hunter couldn't stop the wave of emotion crashing through him. He dropped to one knee, letting the familiar weight of Kii lean into him, his hand rising instinctively to press against the canine's thick fur.

Hunter scratched the canine's head. "Hello, Kii. I'm so happy to see you."

"I thought you were a goner," J'Dar said as he picked himself up from the ground. "He seems to like you."

"Down, Kii. I sometimes have a way with animals, especially canines. He may sense I've dealt with his kind before."

"I agree with J'Dar," Tallie said. "When Kii came around that bend full force, I thought you didn't have a chance. I've never seen him act that way around a stranger."

J'Dar gave the Hunter a suspicious glance. "How did you know his name was Kii?"

"I heard Tallie call him by his name," Hunter replied. This explanation was acceptable to the boy.

Kii remained at Hunter's side, wagging his tail profusely as they continued. When they cleared a small grove of trees, Hunter got his first view of J'Dar's home. It reminded him of the cabin he had shared with Liara.

"Mom, wait till you see who came to buy some of your pups," J'Dar shouted as he rushed into the house. "You won't believe who came to meet you."

"Won't you come in?" Tallie invited.

Hunter stepped into the kitchen. He moved to the counter and gripped the edge with both hands, grounding himself. If she was here, really here, he needed something solid to hold onto. Something to keep him from falling apart.

"Who's here?" came a feminine voice from the other room.

A woman's voice.

Soft. Familiar.

Unmistakable.

Hunter shuddered.

He had no doubt. It was Li-ara's voice. After so long, he had at last found her.

"Come, Mom. See who's here," J'Dar shouted in excitement.

Hunter's vision blurred, the edges of the room melting into formless shapes. The tears burned hot against his eyes, collecting beneath the seal of his helmet. He blinked rapidly, desperate to clear them, but it only made them fall faster. He stood unmoving, waiting, unable to breathe or hope - a silent monolith in steel.

Then, movement.

J'Dar reappeared, tugging gently on someone's hand, guiding them from the shadows of the adjoining room.

A single syllable whispered through Hunter's mind. *Please.*

Hunter's gaze clung to that hand, delicate fingers wrapped in the boy's. A wrist followed. Then a forearm, pale and slender. The slope of an elbow. A shoulder framed in the pink fabric of a woman's blouse.

And then her neck. Her jaw. And finally, her face.

Her face.

Li-ara.

Real. Alive.

Hunter could only watch her emerge from the shadows like something sacred, something stolen and suddenly returned. The breath he'd been holding escaped in a jagged gasp. He pressed harder into the counter just to stay upright.

Li-ara turned her head slightly, speaking softly to J'Dar. Her eyes scanned casually at first, her mind still on whatever task she'd been pulled from. It brushed past him, then stopped.

She stared. Blinked. Took half a step forward.

Her mouth parted slightly, lips forming a breathless sound that didn't come. She stared at the man standing in her kitchen - tall, armored, silent. She couldn't understand what she was seeing for a moment. Her knees went weak.

No. He wasn't real.

Then he lifted his head just slightly, and something in his posture shattered the last of her denial. He hadn't changed.

Her hand flew to her mouth. "Hunter..."

How many nights had she imagined this moment? How many times had she dreamed of him returning, only to wake with tears drying on her face? But this wasn't a dream.

She wanted to run to him.

She wanted to slap him.

She wanted to feel something solid, to know he was real.

Instead, she stood there, trembling, breathless.

"Aren't you surprised, Mom? He's a real Hunter."

Li-ara gave a small nod, slow and uncertain, unsure what to say.

Hunter took a shallow breath. "Is there somewhere we could speak privately?" Hunter asked.

His eyes didn't leave her face. He stood perfectly still, as if even breathing too loudly might shatter whatever fragile thread still tied them together.

"Oh no, J'Dar, we forgot to purchase the peppers from the store," Tallie said, breaking the stillness. "I'm sorry, Ms. Li-ara. I got involved with this Bounty Hunter and forgot about the peppers. J'Dar and I will go back to the store and purchase them."

"You go," J'Dar shouted. "I want to stay with the Hunter. I've got lots more questions to ask him."

Li-ara's gaze shifted to J'Dar, who stood nearby, watching them both with wide, curious eyes. She couldn't let him see what this moment truly was, what this man truly meant. Not yet.

"Go with Tallie, Sweetheart," she said, reaching to brush a hand over his hair, her fingers lingering a moment too long. "I need to speak with this Hunter... about canine business."

The lie stung her lips.

"Do I have to?"

"Yes and take Kii with you."

Hunter turned toward the boy, his fingers aching, stiff from clenching the counter like a lifeline. He hadn't realized how tightly he'd been holding on. "After I've discussed matters with your mom, you and I can sit down, and I'll answer your questions."

"Promise?"

"Promise."

J'Dar hesitated, but Tallie touched his shoulder and gently guided him away. He grabbed Kii's collar, dragging the canine outside. "What's wrong with you, Kii? Let's go!" He cast one last look over his shoulder before disappearing through the doorway.

Li-ara stepped forward, clicking the door shut behind them, the sound final. She stood motionless, her eyes fixed on the doorknob. She didn't turn right away. She knew who stood behind her. And she knew what waited in his silence.

She had no escape. For the first time in years, she was alone with her past. Face to face with the man it belonged to. And the truth she'd buried.

Slowly, deliberately, she turned.

Hunter stood like a ghost made solid - unmoving, armored, real. There was no anger in his stance. No blame in his posture. But that only made it worse. Because his silence wasn't empty. It was filled with all the questions she'd spent a lifetime avoiding.

"We can talk in my bedroom," Li-ara whispered. She walked past him, not touching, not looking, only brushing the air between them as she opened the door to her bedroom.

Hunter followed in silence. He turned the lock with trembling fingers, the soft click echoing in his ears with devastating finality. The world outside ceased to exist. There was only this room. Only this moment. Only her. He took a step. Another.

"Why does your son bear my true name?" Hunter blurted.

Li-ara flinched at the words. At first, she only stared, unable to speak. Then from somewhere deep inside of her, came the words. "I think you know the answer, Hunter."

"Is he my son?"

Li-ara's lips parted. She wanted to say yes. She wanted to scream it, cry it, tell him after all these years. But her voice refused to obey. The truth was too big. Too frightful. Too painful.

Behind her, Hunter waited. Not moving. Not breathing. Waiting for the answer he already knew.

"LI-ARA, IS J'DAR MY SON?"

"Yes."

"I have a son," Hunter whispered. The words escaped before he could stop them, barely more than breath, yet they struck like thunder inside his chest. He had said the words out loud. And they were real.

A child who walked the world without knowing his father's name, his father's voice, his arms. A boy who laughed, ran, and lived. He hadn't been there to protect him, to teach him, to love him.

"I have a son," he said again, softer this time. Hunter collapsed into the chair behind him, the strength gone from his legs, his armor suddenly too heavy to bear. "Why didn't you tell me?"

"I didn't find out until two months after you left."

"You should have contacted me."

"How?" Li-ara screamed, turning to face her former lover. "How was I supposed to contact you, Hunter? I didn't know where you were or how to get in touch with you. I didn't even know what name to search for. Besides, you made your desires clear when you left that you wanted no other life other than a Hunter's."

"I came back," Hunter quickly whispered. "I came back for you."

"You came back? Why?"

"I wasn't gone an hour before I realized I made the biggest mistake of my life. A mistake that has haunted me every day since I left you. It is with me the moment I wake each morning; it remains with me each minute throughout the day, and then it haunts my dreams at night."

Summoning what strength he had, Hunter pushed himself up from the chair. He stepped closer, carefully, like she might vanish if he moved too fast.

"I realized I didn't want a life as a Hunter anymore. I only wanted a life with you. I arranged for another Bounty Hunter to take my prisoners back for processing. He paid me a fraction of what they were worth, but I didn't care. I was going back to you. But on the way, I ran into some smugglers. They shot my ship up pretty bad. I had to put down at the nearest station for repairs. Seven weeks waiting for parts. Two more to make the journey."

He swallowed hard. "When I finally got back to Proxima Prime, you were gone." He swallowed again, locking his jaw tight, refusing to let the storm of emotions break free. "I searched, Li-ara. For over four years. Every outpost. Every whisper of your name. And you were just … gone. Why did you leave? Why didn't you tell someone where you were going?"

"When I found out I was pregnant, I remembered what you said about Bounty Hunters not only hunt, but they are hunted. And if someone found out about us, they would use me as a ploy. I feared what they would do if they realized my son was yours. So, I left and came here to Rigel Three and started a fresh life where no one knew me. I put Kal's ring back on my finger and made up the story he was killed in the war. No one questioned me."

Determined not to lose her, not now, not after everything, Hunter closed the distance between them in two purposeful steps. His hands reached out and gently took hold of her arms. His touch was soft, reverent, as if he were afraid she might shatter.

"Li-ara, I want you to be my wife."

Disbelief hit her like a jolt. Her eyes went wide, and her body seized with a tension that stole her breath. "Are you crazy?" she asked, backing away from his grip. "I can't be your wife, Hunter."

"Yes," he said, holding her gaze on her face as if it was the only thing anchoring him to the world. "Yes, you can."

Li-ara's fear deepened. No longer just fear of what was, but of what *might be*.

And then, he reached for his helmet.

"No," she whispered, her voice small and sharp.

But he was already lifting it, revealing his face, his armor parting from his skin for the first time in her presence since that night.

"No, Hunter. Stop," she said, panic overtaking fear. "Don't do this. Don't."

The helmet came away, revealing the man beneath.

Li-ara pressed her eyes shut, her hands rising as if to shield herself from a blow that would never come. "Put it back on," she said, urgency in her voice. "Please, don't do this. I beg you." Tears slipped down her cheeks, silent and relentless.

Hunter gently took her hands in his and lowered them. He rested his forehead against hers. "Marry me."

"No."

"Be my wife.

"I won't open my eyes."

"I love you, Li-ara. Please look at me."

She pushed him away, forcing her eyes to remain closed. "You love me? Why? Because you found out we have a son together? Is that why you love me now?"

"I've always loved you. Ever since that first day you saved my life, brought me to your cottage, and nursed me back to health."

"You couldn't even kiss me goodbye that day," she screamed, her voice filled with the despair caused by his actions long ago. "Why didn't you kiss me?"

"I was afraid."

"I don't believe you. You're never afraid."

"I was then."

"Why?"

"Li-ara, open your eyes."

"No. Tell me why you were afraid."

"I feared to have you love me," Hunter shouted as he turned and walked several steps away from her, trying to come to grips with his own failings. "And for me to love you back. Hidden deep inside me is still that little boy who was stolen from his parents, from his life. I couldn't take the chance of losing you someday. Plus, I was a Bounty Hunter who had killed hundreds of people. How could anyone as beautiful as you ever love someone like me?"

"I did love you."

"And I loved you. I still do. Please, tell me my stupidity hasn't caused me to lose you. Tell me you love me."

Li-ara stepped back, turning her back to him. She reached for the back of a nearby chair, clutching it with white-knuckled fingers.

Her voice, when it came, was little more than a whisper - thin, strained, breaking under its own weight. "No," she said, though it didn't sound like a command. It sounded like a plea to herself. "You … you need to go."

She tightened her grip on the chair, her body trembling. She could feel her resolve slipping through her fingers like sand. Because the truth was, she didn't want him to go. She wanted him to be in her life, to be a father to their son. But it was a statement she could not voice.

She kept her back to him. She knew that if she turned around, she couldn't ask him to leave again.

"Don't do this, Li-ara." Hunter walked over and grasped her upper arms. "I know you still love me. Why else would you name our son after me?"

"As I said, I loved you then, but not now."

"Prove it."

"How?"

"Turn around, open your eyes, and look into mine. If you can do that and still say you don't love me, I'll find a way to live with it. I'll leave. You'll never see me again."

"Hunter, just go."

"No. Tell me to my face."

"You said I could never see your face. What has changed? Why is it okay now?"

"Because I love you. Husbands do not hide their faces from their wives."

"I won't be your wife."

"When I returned to Kolora, my Dominee told me I had been taught wrong. A Hunter doesn't have to hide his face. It's a choice, not a decree."

"You mean I could have removed your helmet the moment I found you dying? I didn't have to tiptoe around that stupid helmet? Struggle to keep you alive?"

"Yes, I'm sorry to say."

Li-ara remained silent, thinking. "It doesn't change anything. You need to go."

"Do you know how I found you?"

"How?"

"My Dominee. She sent me here to purchase canines." A smile spread across his face as he realized the truth. "I don't know how, but she knew you were here. She told me I could not love one thing when my heart belonged to another, that I had to face you and my past. Somehow, she realized that when I witnessed my son and saw your face, my life would return to me."

He gently turned her towards him. Her eyes clenched shut, he took her face in his hands. "I've been so lost without you. I have no desire to live if you're not part of my life. Don't you understand, Li-ara? We were meant to meet and fall in love, to become part of each other. Open your eyes and tell me you will be my wife. Or say you no longer love me."

Li-ara said nothing, using all her strength to keep her eyes shut.

"LOOK AT ME."

"ALL RIGHT!" Li-ara opened her eyes, determined to tell the person before her she no longer loved him. But the moment she looked upon his face, she had no words. His face was worn and scarred, but beautiful. Tears flowed from his soft blue eyes onto his cheeks. Her expression transformed from anger to one of pure love as she raised her hands and touched his temple.

"You have blue eyes. J'Dar has your eyes."

"Yes, he does. Tell me you love me."

He leaned in, brushing his lips against hers. Softly. Reverently. A kiss that asked rather than took. There was no hunger in it, only devotion. A quiet promise. A longing held too long.

His forehead rested gently against hers, her breath mingling with his. "Please," he murmured. "Tell me."

She crumbled into his arms. "What if you leave again?"

"I won't. Be my wife."

"What if two months or three years from now, you realize you want your Bounty Hunter life back? I can't lose you again, Hunter. I can't."

"I won't. You and J'Dar are the only things I want. Marry me."

"I'm scared. Aren't you?"

"No, because this is what the fates deemed for us. If we are together, nothing can happen to us. Not even the wild canines on Proxima Prime defeated us. Say you love me." He raised her chin and stared into her eyes. "Say you will be my wife."

Unable to deny her love, Li-ara answered, "I love you, Hunter. I will be your wife."

She reached for him, pulling him into her arms, her lips finding him in a kiss that mirrored the one they shared that first night - fierce, tender, and overflowing with everything left unsaid. In that moment, time unraveled.

She was no longer the woman who had fled. He was no longer the man who had been lost. They were simply two souls colliding back into one.

Hunter let go of the silence, the sorrow, the ache he had carried for years. Every breath, every touch poured his love into her, and in her embrace, he found the peace he'd been denied for so long.

Their reunion was more than physical. It was a binding of what had been broken, a rejoining of halves torn apart by fear and fate. And as they gave themselves to each other fully, completely, there was no separation between them. No past. No future. Only now.

All they knew was this: they loved. And as long as they faced the universe side by side, nothing could defeat them. Nothing could break them. Not this time.

.

13 A NEW FUTURE

"What do we do now?" Li-ara asked as she rested against his body. "How do we tell J'Dar the truth of who you are?"

"We'll figure it out." Hunter reached into his left sleeve pocket and removed its contents. He laid the coin on the table.

"You kept the coin?"

"It has never left me since the day you gave it to me."

He reached into his pocket and removed the bracelet he had made so many years before. "In our custom, a man weaves a bracelet from something that represents who he is. This bracelet is made from shavings of my armor. The droplet contains my blood. It is my promise to you. It tells the world I am yours. And you are mine."

Taking Li-ara's arm, he placed the marriage bracelet around her wrist. "*Ti gwen to revenue, ti vignow to began, ti glob to beyan, ti wix du corrin to antip daa brokit. Havendare ni dorant ni indotute linldou en Kolor.* To you, I give my sword as protection, my arm as strength, my heart as love, and my soul as my commitment. I declare you to be a member of House Kolor. From this moment on, you are my wife, and I am your husband." For the first time, he kissed her as his wife.

The sound of the door handle jiggling interrupted their kiss. "Mom, are you still inside?" J'Dar asked. Kii barked.

"I'll be out in a minute," Li-ara called out. "We're still talking business."

"The Hunter said he'd answer my questions when I got back."

"I will," Hunter said. "I just need a couple more minutes with your mom. She's a tough negotiator."

"All right. But no more."

"Is Tallie still here?" Li-ara asked.

"No, she went home. She said to tell you she'll take me to school tomorrow morning since you'll probably have business to conduct with the Hunter."

"Why don't you start on your homework?"

"Do I have to?"

"Yes."

"Okay, but if you're not out in ten minutes, I'm breaking the door down."

"Take Kii with you," Hunter shouted.

"He won't listen. He's acting all funny."

"Kii, go with J'Dar," Hunter ordered.

As the child went into the other room to start his schoolwork, Kii followed. "Why do you listen to him?"

"We'd better get out there," Li-ara said, her cheeks turning rosy. "If not, he'll find some way to bust in here. Besides, trying to explain to a four-year-old why his mother is lying in the arms of a naked man might be a little hard."

Hunter laughed. "I can't wait for the day when he knows that I am his father."

"Me neither. We'll talk more about how to handle the situation after he goes to sleep." Li-ara rose, quickly dressing. She looked at her face in the mirror. "Can you tell I was crying?"

"Yes, but you still look beautiful."

"He will ask why I was crying. What am I going to say?"

"Tell him the truth. They're tears of joy."

"For what?"

"His father's return."

Li-ara frowned. "But we can't tell him you're his father yet."

168

"I'm not." He kissed her, then dressed. "I am merely the Bounty Hunter who brought the news your husband and his father is alive."

"Returned? I don't understand. Where has he been?"

"In a prisoner of war camp. He was captured in the war and was just released."

"All this time?"

"He's four. He won't care." Hunter paused. "I didn't see Beta anywhere. Is she around?"

"She died about six months ago. She never fully recovered from the wild canine attack. But she lived a happy life."

"I would have liked to have seen her again."

"She often went down to the bend in the road and lay there, as if she expected someone. I often wondered if she wasn't waiting for you, that she somehow knew you'd come back into our lives one day."

"If she was waiting for me, she knew more than I did. Plus, that's a scary thought, that she could see into our future."

"That it is."

The moment Hunter stepped out of the room, Kii came running, his tail wagging, his favorite ball in his mouth.

"He sure likes you," J'Dar stated. "Normally, he doesn't like strangers. A few weeks ago, he bit a *Veegill*. Almost got Mom in trouble."

Hunter chuckled. He leaned close to the boy's ear. "Truth be told, I don't like *Veegills* either. Besides, Kii thinks I'm too enormous to bite. And he realizes I won't hurt you or your Mom."

"You're allowed to laugh?"

"Why would you think I couldn't laugh?"

"Because Hunters are all serious and stuff like that."

"All Hunters laugh."

Li-ara emerged from the bedroom. Immediately, J'Dar noticed her face. "Mom, you've been crying. Did he make you cry?"

"No, Sweetheart. These are tears of joy. The Huntsman brought me some wonderful news."

"Oh, okay." J'Dar turned his attention back to the stranger in armor. "Can I ask you my questions now?"

"Ask away."

"Why don't you two go outside with Kii and play some ball with him while I fix dinner," Li-ara suggested. "J'Dar, you can ask your questions while Kii chases the ball. Then, after dinner, we'll take the Hunter out to view the puppies."

"Okay." J'Dar slipped his hand inside Hunter's once more. "Is that your name? Hunter?"

"Yes, it is."

"Not very original."

Hunter turned to Li-ara and smiled. "So, I've been told. Would you like to know my real name?"

J'Dar's eyes opened wide.

"It's BiiJun D'Kolor."

"I like Hunter better."

"Me, too."

For the next hour, Kii chased the ball while J'Dar asked a hundred questions. When Li-ara called them inside for dinner, the young boy was disappointed to learn Hunter would not take off his helmet to eat in front of them. Instead, he took his food into another room and ate alone. The child anxiously watched the closed door, wondering what he looked like beneath the metal covering.

"Do you think he's all gross under his helmet, Mom?"

"Probably not."

"Maybe he's all bloody from his fights and battles. Or maybe he doesn't have a face at all."

"I'm sure he has a face."

"Then why do you think he hides his face?"

"It is the Huntsman's way. They hide their faces to protect their identity and keep their families safe."

"That's what he said when I asked."

"Li-ara smiled. "Finish your meal, or no going with us to the kennels."

Scrunching his face in protest, J'Dar cleaned his plate, watching the door for any movement. When the knob turned, he jumped up. "Are you ready to go see the puppies?"

"Yes."

"How many puppies are you interested in buying?" Li-ara asked.

"I would like four females and four males, all from different litters. My Dominee wishes to start her own pack."

"I have a number from which you can pick. But I can't guarantee they'll all be from different litters."

As they approached the kennels, the air erupted with noise. Sharp, echoing barks from the adult canines, followed by the eager, high-pitched whines of waiting pups.

"Are any of the pups Kii's?" Hunter asked.

"It's been several years since Kii was a father. Many of his pups carried the trait of extreme intelligence and canine ferocity. Most buyers didn't like those qualities. They wanted guard dogs, but not ones who thought for themselves, so I stopped letting him breed my females."

Hunter glanced over the canines. The kennels were arranged in orderly rows, their sturdy metal fencing worn smooth from years of pacing paws. Larger pens housed the adults. A smaller structure enclosed the nursery pens. Dozens of wide-eyed pups scrambled at the gates, their tiny claws clicking against the flooring as they climbed over one another in frenzied attempts to be seen. Their whines rose in pitch as they caught his scent - new, unfamiliar, full of possibility.

"You don't call this a lot?"

"Actually, I usually have more than this."

"I'm sure I will have no problems finding eight pups to satisfy my Dominee."

"He's finally asleep," Li-ara reported as she returned to the kitchen. "I didn't think he'd ever doze off. He's so excited about meeting a real-life Hunter."

"I never imagined a child his age could ask so many questions." Hunter removed his helmet, took his wife into his arms, and kissed her tenderly.

Li-ara broke the kiss when a noise emanated from the hallway. "He's asleep, but he might wake up for a drink of water or to use the facilities. We should go to my office to formulate our plan on what to do."

"I think your bedroom would be a more comfortable place to discuss our future together." Hunter smiled, grabbing his helmet and her hand. He led her through the door, tossing his helmet on a chair. Bringing her lips to his, he kissed her, igniting the fire burning strongly in both.

"I've been waiting for hours to kiss you again."

Li-ara reached over and unhooked his breastplate. Slowly and amorously, they removed each other's clothing, allowing the act itself to complement their desires. Earlier, their lovemaking had been one of passion, fast and furious. This time, it was an act of pure love, each desiring nothing more than to please the other.

The two lovers lay on the bed, Li-ara resting her head on Hunter's chest while he held her securely in his arms. Li-ara traced her fingers across the bear wound on his side.

"The scar from the bear attack healed nicely." She ran her hand across his ribs. "So did the one on your chest."

"That's because I had a good nurse." Li-ara smiled. "I want you and J'Dar to come with me when I take the pups back to Kolora.".

"Is that allowed?"

"I'm never going anywhere without you again." He rested his lips on the top of her head, breathing in the aroma of her hair. "You are my wife. My Dominee will welcome you with open arms, as will my people."

"Will we come back here to live?"

"No. For J'Dar's and your protection, we must leave this place. I will ask the Dominee for permission for you two to remain on Kolora. You can help me train the pups and establish the Huntsmen canine team. Kolora is a beautiful planet, filled with rolling purple hills and golden lakes."

Hunter sensed Li-ara's uneasiness. "This does not please you?"

"I am sure Kolora is gorgeous and, for Huntsmen, a perfect place to live. But your ways are not ours."

"And you fear the possibility of J'Dar following in his father's footsteps and taking on the life of a Bounty Hunter."

"Yes. Is that wrong?"

"No mother or father wants their child to endure a hard life or die at a young age. Both are genuine possibilities for a Huntsman. Many Hunters do not live past the age of twenty-six. I am proud to call myself a Huntsman and Bounty Hunter, but I do not necessarily wish such a life for my sons or daughters."

"Then why don't the Huntsmen modify their way of life?"

"This has been our way for hundreds of thousands of years. Our lifestyle goes back to when endless wars plagued the galaxy. To survive, we adopted a warrior's life and became the Huntsmen we are today. We exist because of that decision. Many other cultures, including some factions of Kolorians, were wiped out of existence."

"Aren't all Kolorians Huntsmen?"

"No. Once, many divisions existed. Today, only four remain. Each has unique philosophies and creeds, but all are of Kolora. But we don't need to decide now. We can discuss a place to live on the way. For now, we need to agree on a story to explain to J'Dar why his father has miraculously returned."

The two spent the next three hours discussing options and making plans for their future. After one more act of love, they fell asleep. For the first time in over four years, neither haunted the other's dreams.

———

The next morning when J'Dar woke extra early, he jumped out of bed and ran straight into the guest room to discover if Hunters slept with their helmet on. To his disappointment, the bed was empty. He walked into the kitchen, where Hunter was sitting at the kitchen table.

"Good morning, J'Dar," Hunter greeted. "You appear disappointed this morning."

"I was hoping you were still sleeping. I wanted to see if you really slept in your helmet."

"As I explained yesterday, when I am around others, I never take my helmet off. When I am alone, I seldom wear it."

"Mom, do I have to go to school today?" J'Dar asked as his mother placed a plate of mush before him. "Can't I stay home and go with Hunter to his ship?"

"Did I offer to show you my ship?" Hunter teased.

"No, but I was hoping you would." J'Dar smiled.

"I'm glad you mentioned his aircraft," Li-ara stated. "Hunter invited us to accompany him to his home planet to deliver the pups. I will help train them and show the Huntsmen how to proceed when I leave. If you would rather stay here, I can arrange for you to remain with Tallie and her family."

"No way," J'Dar shouted. "When do we leave?"

"I was waiting for you to rise and dress," Hunter said. "I thought you might want to go with me to bring the ship over to the house. Once we load the puppies and the items your mom wants to take with her, we'll lift off."

"I'm ready now," J'Dar announced, jumping off the chair and running towards the back door.

"J'Dar, aren't you forgetting something?" Li-ara asked. "Your outside clothes?"

The child looked down and realized he was still wearing his nightclothes. "Don't leave without me." He ran from the room.

"Even with the pups in cryosleep, there won't be much room for things. My cargo space is limited," Hunter explained.

"I possess few items that mean anything to me," Li-ara said as she washed the morning dishes. "A few remembrances, J'Dar's toys, our clothes, the weapon you left me."

"You kept the long rifle?"

"Yes. As you kept the coin, I kept the gun."

Hunter walked up behind her and wrapped his arms around her. "I could make love to you right here, right now."

"J'Dar won't be gone that long."

Hunter removed his arms and took a step back upon hearing J'Dar's footsteps.

"I'm ready," the child announced as he ran into the room. "Take me to your ship."

"J'Dar, when you return, you need to go through your things and decide what you want to take with you on the trip."

"Everything."

"No, not everything. You can pick out three things to take."

"Ten."

"Three."

"Eight."

"Three."

"Why don't you settle on five. I think I can make room for two more," Hunter suggested.

Li-ara gave him a disapproving expression. "Don't encourage him."

"It's a lengthy trip and a small aircraft. He will get bored with only three items to play with."

"Very well. Five items and no more."

"Can we *PLEASE* go now?" the impatient child asked. J'Dar ran out the door, Kii right behind him, his tail happily wagging.

"Be back shortly." Hunter briefly touched her hand so his son would observe nothing.

"I'll have everything ready to go."

Kii eagerly ran around the two as they walked to the airfield. Hunter said little because J'Dar never stopped talking. Unlike yesterday when he was full of questions, today he was a never-ending summation of what the trip would be like, what they'd do if they ran into rogues, and much more. He did, however, have one question: How do you go to the bathroom in space?

J'Dar's eyes opened wide as he stared in awe at Hunter's ship. "Wow, you call this small?" J'Dar asked. "It has to be the biggest and best ship in the universe."

"Although bigger than most single-pilot ships, she is considered small. When we arrive at Kolora, you'll understand what I mean by a big craft."

"I bet yours is still better."

"I think so." Hunter pressed the command buttons on his wrist guards and released the ramp, which slid open.

Unable to contain his curiosity and eagerness, J'Dar jumped up on the ramp before it touched the ground. Kii followed, as did Hunter. J'Dar ran from one area to the other, trying to take in everything at once. As he passed Hunter, the Huntsman grabbed his energized son.

"Slow down, J'Dar, and listen to me for a minute. You must never enter a ship until you are given permission by the captain to do so. He or she will tell you when it is safe to board. The ship belongs to the captain, and you are there as his or her guest. Understand?"

"Yes."

"And we never jump on the ramp until it is completely on the ground."

"Okay. Can I look around some more?"

"How about I give you a quick tour, and then you can help me fly her to your mom." Hunter showed J'Dar the limited amount there was to see of the bottom cargo area.

"Where are we going to sleep?" J'Dar asked as he surveyed the area. "You have a lot of junk down here."

"Needed junk," Hunter chuckled. "I usually sleep in my navigator's chair. But I do have a sleeping berth. That's where you and your mom will sleep. I'll show it to you when we climb the ladder to the cockpit." J'Dar walked over to the metal ladder and tried to lift his leg onto the first rung but was unable to. His legs were too short.

"You'll need to grow a bit more before you can climb on your own. I'll help you up." The Huntsman lifted the boy into the air, surprised at how light he was. Were all children this weight? He'd have to ask Li-ara. A warm sensation filled his heart as the boy grabbed the second rung.

J'Dar glanced down at the floor. Kii was sitting beside the ladder, looking up. "What if I fall?"

"You won't," Hunter assured his son. "I'll be over you. We'll climb together. That way, if you slip, I'll be here to prevent you from falling."

"Can Kii come up?"

"No, he must stay on the cargo deck. Now climb up till I tell you to stop."

J'Dar lifted his leg and barely reached the next rung. Grasping the back of his pants, Hunter lifted the boy and helped him climb. A few more rungs would need to be added so J'Dar could climb up and down, a necessity since the bathroom facilities were on the bottom deck.

Keeping close to the boy, the two climbed. "Okay, stop."

J'Dar saw a half-oval compartment with a dimension of eight feet long, five feet high, and ten feet across. Nine narrow windows encircled the outside wall. A makeshift bed of several pillows and blankets lay on the floor. A trunk rested in the right corner. J'Dar wondered what treasures were hidden inside.

"This is where you and your mom will sleep."

"But how do I go inside?" J'Dar looked down at the floor again, which was farther away.

"Swing your leg over and step in."

"I don't think I can do that. My legs are too short. I'll fall for sure."

Hunter realized the boy was right. Until he reached a greater height, trying to climb in and out of the sleeping area was an accident waiting to happen. "Now that I think of it, I don't think Kii will enjoy sleeping down below by himself. He will be scared by all the unfamiliar sounds and being alone. How about you and I clear a section in the cargo area where you and your mom can sleep until Kii isn't afraid?"

"I'd like that."

"Ready to see the cockpit?"

"Yes."

They ascended the final rungs of the ladder, the metal cool beneath their fingers. At the top, Hunter reached down, gripping J'Dar under the arms to swing him effortlessly onto the navigation floor. The security door sensed their presence and whispered open, revealing the heart of the ship.

The cockpit stretched before them, encircled by a massive curved viewport that bathed the entire space in golden sunlight. J'Dar's eyes widened, a gasp escaping his lips as he bolted toward the towering navigational chair positioned before the panoramic view.

"Is this where you sit?" J'Dar asked, his small face illuminated by the constellation of indicator lights that pulsed across the console.

"Yes," Hunter confirmed, watching the child with a mixture of amusement and caution. "That is the navigator's chair."

"Wow!" J'Dar breathed, his fingers hovering reverently over the command console. "Look at all the buttons, switches, and lights!" Before Hunter could intervene, the boy's hands darted forward, flicking switches and turning knobs with reckless abandon.

Hunter moved with the reflexes of a seasoned pilot, gripping the nape of J'Dar's shirt and yanking him back mid-reach. The ship gave a warning beep as several systems momentarily activated. With his free hand, Hunter flicked off the glowing switches, silencing the alarm with practiced precision. He deposited the squirming child into the passenger seat recessed against the back wall, just right of the doorway.

"This is where you and your mother will sit during our journey," Hunter said firmly. He crouched down, bringing himself eye-level with the boy. "And J'Dar?"

The child looked up, still vibrating with excitement. "Yes?"

"Until you learn what each of those switches and knobs controls, it's vital that you don't touch them." Hunter's voice softened but remained serious. "They aren't toys. They're how I fly the ship, how I keep us alive. Moving the wrong lever could have detrimental consequences."

J'Dar's forehead wrinkled in confusion. "Huh?"

Hunter smiled, realizing his error. He placed a hand on the boy's shoulder. "What I mean is, if you push the wrong buttons, we could blow up or crash."

J'Dar's eyes grew round. "Oh," he whispered, suddenly sitting very still in his seat, hands clasped tightly in his lap.

"Ready to take off?"

J'Dar nodded vigorously, fear and excitement rendering him speechless. His small hands gripped the edges of the seat as Hunter strode back to the ladder, checking the deck below for Kii.

Kii looked up, his tail pounding against the metal floor. "Lay down, Boy. We'll be back home in a few minutes."

Hunter punched the ramp control. The hydraulics hissed as the massive entry platform sealed with a resounding thud that reverberated through the ship's hull.

His footsteps were barely audible on the metal flooring as he returned to the cockpit. He slid into the pilot's chair, his fingers danced across the control panel. Hunter flicked a yellow lever, the action so fluid, so natural, it seemed the ship was merely an extension of his will.

The massive right engine awoke. A deep, thunderous rumble vibrated across J'Dar's chest. He watched as the propulsion chamber glowed, first a pale yellow, then a brilliant molten gold. The vibration intensified, and J'Dar clutched his seat tighter, his eyes never leaving Hunter's silhouette.

"Are we going to blow up?"

"No. We need the engines to lift us." Hunter repeated the process with the left engine. After several more pushed buttons and moved dials, Hunter turned to J'Dar, holding out his hand.

"Come here and sit in my lap." J'Dar looked at the masked male, hesitating. "It's okay. If you want to fly us home, you need to sit on me."

A huge smile spread across the young boy's face, the biggest Hunter had ever seen, as he jumped down and ran to the Huntsman. Using both hands this time, Hunter lifted J-Dar up and sat him in his lap.

"Put your hands here on the steering wheel, but don't move it until I advise you to. Once we rise, I need to retract the landing gear before we can proceed."

J'Dar hung onto the wheel with enthusiasm as the turbos turned downward, pushing the spacecraft up. The sound was deafening. J'Dar lifted his hands and covered his ears. Hunter quickly grabbed the wheel.

"You mustn't let go of the steering handle, J'Dar, or we'll smash into something."

"She sure is noisy," J'Dar said loudly.

"I guess she is. I'm so used to her sounds, I don't realize how loud she is. Once we're out in space, she won't be as noisy." Hunter searched the console. "I have some dampeners around here somewhere you can wear."

Reaching into a small cubbyhole, Hunter withdrew a small box and opened it, revealing two plugs. "Here we are."

"Does your ship have a name?" J'Dar asked.

"Yes, she does. She's called the Li-ara."

"Just like my mom's name?"

"Yes, just like your mom's name."

Hunter placed the earplugs inside J'Dar's ears. "Is that better?"

"What?" J'Dar screamed.

Hunter lifted one of the plugs. "Retake the driving handle. I'll give her some fuel, and you can fly us to your house. Remember, tell me BEFORE you let go again."

"I won't forget."

"When I retract the landing gear, the ship will shake. Don't be afraid. It's just a normal part of the landing gear fitting into its housing."

"Okay."

Hunter reached over and flicked the landing gear control. Massive gears ground against one another, each tooth catching and releasing with mechanical precision as the hydraulic system strained against years of use. The braces lifted slowly, folding inward and retracting into the belly of the ship. Small vibrations rippled through the deck plates, traveling up through J'Dar's feet and into his spine. The boy's eyes widened as he gripped the wheel, feeling the ship becoming truly airborne. He looked up at Hunter's masked face, wondering if the shaking made him afraid, too.

Hunter slowly pushed the throttle forward. Placing his hands over J'Dar's, he turned the ship northward, then slid the steering wheel forward. Once in flight, Hunter removed his hands, keeping the speed slow so his son could maneuver the airship with little help.

"Hey, look." J'Dar pointed to his house, remembering this time to keep one hand on the steering handle. His mom was standing outside with Tallie. She waved, to which J'Dar waved back. As they drew closer, Hunter took back control of the ship and landed the craft two plots away.

"Mom, I got to fly Hunter's ship," J'Dar shouted. Remembering what Hunter told him, the child waited until the ramp touched the ground before running down with Kii. He ran right into his mom's arms. "Hunter owns the best ship in the entire galaxy."

"Did you remember to thank him?"

"What?"

Hunter pointed to his ear. "He has plugs in his ears. The ship's sounds were a little too intense."

Li-ara chuckled. She reached down and removed the earplugs. "I said, did you remember to thank him?"

"I forgot." J'Dar broke his embrace of his mom and ran to Hunter. He threw his arms around the Bounty Hunter's legs, squeezing them tightly with fierce sincerity.

Hunter stood there, staring down at the top of his son's head, willing himself to remember this moment, brand it into memory. He wanted to drop to his knees. To wrap the boy in his arms. To hold him until time rewound and gave them back the years that had been stolen.

But he didn't. He couldn't. Not yet.

So, Hunter stood perfectly still, his heart thundering behind the cold steel, letting the moment wash over him like fire and rain. He closed his eyes for just a second.

"Thank you, Hunter, for letting me fly The Li-ara."

"Li-ara? Your ship's named Li-ara?" An enormous smile spread across Li-ara's face.

"Yeah, Mom, just like your name. Isn't that funny?"

"Yes, it is." Li-ara turned her back to Tallie, hiding dampness in her eyes and the look of love on her face.

"Ready to pick out your pups?" Li-ara asked, turning towards the kennel.

"The sooner the better."

Under Li-ara's recommendations, Hunter chose eight pups: five females and three males from four different litters. He brought them onboard and placed them in cryosleep for the journey to Kolora.

"What about the other pups and canines?" J'Dar asked. "Can't we take them too?"

"There's no room for more canines," Li-ara said. "But don't worry. Tallie offered to care for them while we're gone. She'll take good care of them like always."

"How long do you expect to be gone?" Tallie asked.

"At least six to twelve months," Hunter said. "Possibly longer." Lifting several of Li-ara's possessions into his arms, he shouted, "Li-ara, bring some extra blankets and pillows for you and J'Dar. The temperature gets chilly in the cargo area and sometimes in the sleeping chamber."

"Okay. J'Dar, grab what you want to bring, or it stays behind."

With everything loaded, Li-ara and J'Dar said their goodbyes. Both hugged Tallie repeatedly.

"Don't forget to take care of the canines," J'Dar shouted from inside the ship as the ramp closed. "And don't forget to feed my turtle."

Sitting behind Hunter in the cockpit, Li-ara and J'Dar waved goodbye as the aircraft lifted into the air. Punching in Kolora's coordinates, Hunter set course for his homeworld and an unknown life as father and husband.

14 THE LETTER

As Hunter had feared, the airship proved to be far from ideal for a four-year-old. The tight corridors and exposed panels were an irresistible playground for curious hands. J'Dar had a knack for squeezing into narrow compartments, discovering hidden levers, or twisting valves that had no business being touched.

Despite both parents' repeated warnings - calm explanations from Li-ara and more stern ones from Hunter - the boy's sense of adventure always won. To keep him safe and to prevent any accidental disasters, Li-ara took on the role of shadow and sentinel. She followed him through the compact vessel, guiding, distracting, intercepting tiny fingers just seconds before they flipped a crucial switch or tugged at a cable that could have grounded them mid-flight.

It was exhausting, but necessary.

J'Dar was not the only problem. Kii, unaccustomed to being left alone for long stretches, made his displeasure known in increasingly destructive ways. He tore into sealed containers, shredded bedding, and, worst of all, chewed through delicate wiring.

After the third repair in twenty-four hours, Hunter had no choice. For Kii's safety, and the ship's, he placed the canine in cryosleep.

J'Dar was not pleased. He glared, crossed his arms, then marched over and kicked Hunter square in the shin. "You're mean!" he shouted with all the outrage a four-year-old could muster.

Hunter barely flinched at the blow, but the guilt stung. He'd survived war zones, assassins, beings intent on ending his life, but none of that prepared him for the heartbreak of disappointing his son. In that moment, he understood that he had a *lot* to learn about being a father.

Thankfully, there was one small advantage. J'Dar couldn't climb the ladder without help, which meant he was confined to whatever section of the ship he was in. It wasn't ideal, but it gave them brief moments of order, especially when he was tucked safely asleep.

Hunter used the time to slip off his helmet and eat without fear of his face being seen. And occasionally, those moments offered something rarer: intimate time alone with Li-ara.

A stolen breath in the middle of chaos.

But such moments came with challenges. Trying to maintain course coordinates and please his wife in a cockpit barely wider than his outstretched arms took a level of multitasking he'd never been trained for.

Two weeks into their journey, two blinking red dots appeared on Hunter's radar. "Li-ara, bring J'Dar up and strap both yourselves in the passenger chairs."

She looked over his shoulder at the blinking dots. "What is it?"

"I'm not positive. Their craft signatures indicate *Urocnik* vessels."

"Are they dangerous?"

"It depends."

"On what?"

"If I ever arrested or killed one of their family members." The ships alter their course on his display. They were coming to intercept Hunter. "Yep, they know me."

"Can we outrun them?"

"No. Their ships are too fast."

"Can we jump to hyperspace?"

"Not right away. I'll make the calculations, but the canine's cryosleep is draining a lot of power from the system. I need at least ten minutes for the hyperdrive to mass enough power to make the jump."

"What about the cloak?"

"It's offline. I needed its power also for the cryo-unit. I can try diverting some of the cryo's power to the cloaking program without endangering the canines, but, again, the process will take time."

Li-ara leaned over and kissed him on the cheek. "Don't forget to put your helmet back on." She hurried down below and brought their son back, strapping him in a chair with herself.

"J'Dar, did you ever ride a sled down that big hill behind your house in the winter?" Hunter asked as he scrutinized the two glowing blimps growing closer. He hoped he could outmaneuver them.

"Sure, lots of times."

"Did you go fast?"

"My sled went faster than anyone else's."

"Two ships are coming to play with us. We will zoom around each other like sledding down your hill. We might zoom sideways or upside down, but if you stay strapped in with your mom, you won't get hurt. Okay?"

"Mom?" J'Dar looked up into his mother's face, fear visible in his eyes.

"It will be okay, Darling. Hunter won't let anything happen to us."

Setting his shields and arming his weapons, Hunter prepared for battle.

"*Urocnik* vessels, state your business," Hunter stated into his communications mike.

"To rid the universe of *stheiew weothee* like you," came a deep, rough voice. "Today, we stop your heart from beating like you ended our mother's life."

"If she wanted to live, she shouldn't have resisted arrest. If she had served her time for her crimes, she'd be alive today."

"You gave her no chance to surrender."

"I gave her the same chance I give all my bounties. She chose not to take me up on my offer."

"And for that, you will die."

"It will be you who dies today." Hunter's voice had focus, determination. Li-ara witnessed the mild male she loved turn into the cunning Bounty Hunter.

The ship shook as the *Urocnik* mercenaries opened fire on Hunter. He swerved, swinging sideways, racing up and dropping fast to avoid their weaponry. Alarms sounded as a bullet hit the side of the right engine. Flames shot out through the small hole. Hunter turned off the affected gas line, and the fire died. Had they struck the main line, the entire ship would have blown.

Li-ara wrapped J'Dar tighter in her arms and buried her face against his neck.

"All right, enough being Mr. Nice Guy," Hunter said, his eyebrows furrowed. "If a war's what you want, a war's what you'll get."

Restarting the engine and loading his laser cannons, he pushed the throttle forward while simultaneously moving the steering wheel. The ship rose straight up into space, catching the *Urocniks* off guard. They tried to follow, but the design of their ships did not allow such a maneuver. Hunter climbed, taking a curved trajectory until he had come full circle.

Ten more blinking dots appeared on the screen as the Li-ara swung around behind the two *Urocniks*. He couldn't fight another ten fighters. He needed to get them out of there. Firing, he destroyed the ship on the left, blowing it into pieces. As the remaining craft tried to turn, Hunter fired again, cutting its hull in half. He witnessed the pilot eject before the plane erupted into a ball of fire. Hunter drew a bead on his attacker and fired one bullet. The projectile entered the *Urocnik's* helmet, breaking the pressure seal, and causing the alien's suit to compress, killing her instantly.

Hunter glanced at his gages. Thirty-seconds to hyperdrive. "Come on. They will be on us soon." Rechecking his calculations, he anxiously watched the needle rise on the hyperdrive.

Five more seconds

The sound of bullets ricocheting off the shield filled the cockpit. Hunter needed more time. Hoping for a miracle, he released three space bombs to destroy his pursuers. Through the rear camera, he saw the closest ships come within range of the devices. He pulled the trigger and hit the middle bomb. The massive explosion destroyed the first two flyers. The remaining *Urocnik* ships slowed and circled the two remaining bombs.

Two seconds left.

Three of the *Urocnik* vessels opened fire on the floating bombs while the other five pursued him, drawing closer. A massive ball of fire emerged from the two bombs, wiping out the three ships firing upon it. A cloud of extreme force and temperature sped toward Hunter and the five vessels pursuing him. The instant the hyperdrive showed ready, Hunter pushed the lever forward. The blast reached the ships behind him in seconds, vaporizing them into dust. As the cataclysmic cloud reached his ship, they slipped into hyperspace.

Hunter sighed and sat back in his chair. "That was too damn close." Hunter swirled his chair around. "Are you both okay?"

"That was fun. Can we do it again?" J'Dar asked.

"How about you, Li-ara?" Hunter inquired. He noted her tense facial muscles and the firmness of her lips. She was not happy. Plus, her skin had a tinge of green color. Before Hunter inquired further, she leaned over and vomited.

"Space flying can be hard on the stomach without erratic flying. In the cabinet by the food cupboard are bottles of medicine," Hunter said. "Take the one with the *Duberry* leaf on the label. It will help settle your stomach."

"Come, J'Dar, we're going downstairs."

"I want to stay with Hunter."

"You're coming with me." She grabbed her son's hand and led him through the security doors and down the ladder.

Li-ara had witnessed the actual life of a Bounty Hunter. Not just the title, not just the armor, but the raw, unfiltered reality of a Bounty Hunter's life. She had witnessed what he was capable of. The precision. The violence. The cold efficiency that had kept him alive all these years.

Hunter watched her leave. He wondered what bothered her more: what he had done or how easily he'd done it.

They needed to talk. Badly. But with the ship locked in hyperdrive, he couldn't leave the cockpit. Not yet. Not until they cleared enough distance between them and the Urocnik. Not until Li-ara and J'Dar were safe.

So, he waited.

Two hours of silence, broken only by the steady hum of the engines and the faint ticking of the nav system. Li-ara stayed below deck - silent, unreachable. He told himself to be patient. To give her space. But with every passing minute, doubt crept into his heart. Was she rethinking everything? Did she regret telling him the truth about J'Dar? Did she regret letting him back in?

His chest ached with questions he couldn't ask and answers he wasn't sure he could bear. And the longer she stayed away, the more certain he became that whatever bridge had begun to form between them might already be burning.

When the nav display finally signaled they were safe, he eased the ship from hyperdrive, set it to autopilot, and pushed back from the controls. His legs were tense as he stood. He walked through the door and descended, his mind focused on the conversation ahead.

He found her below, seated on the floor with her back to the wall. J'Dar slept soundly beside her, one hand still clutching the edge of her coat. She looked up as Hunter approached.

Hunter stood before her, unmoving. His gaze locked on her face. He searched for signs: a flinch in her brow, a tremble in her mouth, a shift in her posture. But she gave him nothing. No condemnation. No relief.

Just silence.

"Li-ara," Hunter said softly, his voice carrying the weight of everything left unsaid. "We need to talk about what happened."

She didn't answer. Just stared at him with a fire in her eyes that burned his soul.

He swallowed hard and took a step closer. "If we're going to move forward and exist as man and wife, we have to talk about this. Otherwise, we have no future."

He extended his hand to her. She slapped it away without hesitation and stood. She turned sharply, climbing the ladder to the sleeping berth with sharp, silent purpose. She disappeared without a word.

Hunter stood there for a heartbeat, then followed. He found her seated on a nest of pillows, her arms wrapped tightly around herself, her back straight as a blade.

"I'm listening," she said flatly.

"You're angry with me," he said, though the words felt pitifully small against the weight of the moment.

"Of course I'm angry with you," she hissed. "You killed a helpless being. That pilot was floating in open space, his ship destroyed, his weapons gone. He was defenseless, Hunter."

"No," he said, his tone cold, certain. "She wasn't."

Li-ara stared at him, her mouth slightly open. "She?" she whispered. "You … you killed a woman?"

Hunter's eyes darkened. "They were all women. The *Urocnik* are a matriarchal species. Nearly every soldier and every pilot is female."

He stepped closer, his voice steady but low. "You must understand, Li-ara, that as a *Urocnik*, she would never stop. Not until I was dead. And once she found me, she would have found you. And our son. I couldn't risk that. I didn't kill her out of vengeance. I killed her because I had to. Because letting her live would've meant condemning all of us."

Li-ara sank into the pillows as if the weight of what he'd said stole some of the strength from her spine, some of the innocence from her heart.

Hunter dropped to his knees before her, reaching for her hand. She tried to pull away, but he held it firmly, gently. "Li-ara, this is who I am. I am a Bounty Hunter. I don't get to hesitate. I can't hope they'll show mercy."

His fingers tightened just slightly.

"I don't have the luxury of choosing peace when survival demands war."

"You're not a Hunter anymore."

"Part of me will always be a Hunter. I've told you a Hunter not only hunts but is hunted. They were hunting me, and I had to protect us. Others from my past may arise. If they do, I will become a Hunter again. Like I did on Proxima Prime. Like I did back there. I will always protect you and J'Dar. Can you understand and live with the truth?"

"I was so scared."

Hunter pulled her into his arms, removed his helmet, and kissed her tenderly. "I was scared, too. The only one who wasn't was J'Dar."

"He thought it was the best ride of his life." They laughed.

"Can you accept me for the Hunter I am?"

"You will only kill to protect us?"

"Yes. I give you my word."

"Then, I can accept you as a Huntsman, Hunter."

He placed his hand on her cheek. "Know that I have never harmed an innocent, and I never will." He kissed her again. "I need to return topside."

"I'll make you something to eat." When Li-ara finished preparing the meal, she carried a bowl up to Hunter in the cockpit. Before placing the food on his console, she moved a small bag of coins. An envelope fell out and drifted to the floor. Li-ara picked up the note and saw Hunter's name written on the front. "I believe this is for you."

"Why do you say that?"

"It has your name on it." She handed the envelope to her husband.

"I forgot all about this. The Dominee gave it to me with some coins when I left and said I wasn't to open it until I was on my way back with the pups." He tore the envelope open and removed a single piece of paper. Reading the words, he collapsed into his chair. "No. It can't be true."

"What's wrong?" Li-ara asked. She had never seen such a look of loss, of disbelief on Hunter's face. Unable to speak, he handed her the letter.

> *BiiJun D'Kolor,*
>
> *If you are reading this letter, you are on your way back to Kolora with the eight canines I requested. This also means you faced your past. You witnessed the results of your love for Li-ara and have chosen your future. To ensure you continue to make the correct one, as of this date, you are removed from the order of Hunter and banned from Kolora until I, or my predecessor, say you may return. This is my wish. This is my command.*
>
> *I have one last assignment for you. Take the canines and find a quiet home where Li-ara and you can train the canines. Their potential is far greater than anything I can contemplate. They may be the salvation of us all.*
>
> *Raise your son with Li-ara at your side. He is destined for greatness, but it never can be achieved without your teachings. Train him in the Ritual of Combat, in the scripts of Kolora, and the wisdom of the Catsmere. Trust me on this, BiiJun.*
>
> *Use the coins I gave you and the rubels hidden beneath the floorboard in your sleeping compartment to buy a farm somewhere, have many children, and enjoy that beautiful woman who loves you deeply and your son.*
>
> *Ordered and executed: 352-58329-2085*
>
> *Dominee, Chancellor of Kolora*
>
> *Ruler of the Triibone Clan.*

"Hunter, I'm so sorry. Is there a chance she will change her mind?"

"No, this is final. She has issued an official decree." A perplexed expression passed over his face. "She never doubted what choice I would make. The Dominee planned the entire thing."

"She mentioned your son in her letter. How did she know about J'Dar or that you were his father? I've never told anyone."

A smile of understanding spread across Hunter's face. "The Dominee possesses many talents, including the gift of foresight and conversing with others, both living and dead, in the spirit world. Before she even called me into her office, she knew of J'Dar and my need to know of him, to welcome him into my life."

"So, what do we do if we can't go to Kolora?"

"Do as she ordered; find somewhere where we can breed your canines and raise our family." He turned on his maps and thumped through the screens. "I've been a Hunter on most of the planets, moons, and asteroids in this sector of the galaxy. I am well known. We could try to go farther in, but the farther one goes, the more corruption and politics one encounters." He flipped more screens. "Here." Hunter pointed to a small planet on the Outer Rim. "Orallia."

"Orallia? I've never heard of it."

"Few have. Orallia is a minor planet with no major port or industry regions, with agriculture as their chief source of income. They pretty much keep to themselves and have almost no trading with off-world nations. It's perfect."

"Have you been there before?"

"Yes. I had to land once to make repairs. The inhabitants were warm and friendly. And, Li-ara, they have an indigenous species of canine, I believe, that is as smart as Kii is."

"Did you encounter them?"

"No, but the village where I stayed had many legends about the canine's intelligence and cunning. I think Orallia is the perfect place for us. Quiet, out of the way, with children ours can play with, and a wonderful life."

"Our children? Might I ask how many you're planning on?"

Hunter smiled. "Fourteen. More, if the girls are as beautiful as you."

Li-ara laughed. "Tell you what. I'll have five, and you can have the rest."

"Deal."

––––––––––––

After the brutal encounter with the *Urocniks*, Hunter altered his ship's transponder signal. If the *Urocniks* were tracking his ship, he needed to hide their location. He also changed their course, taking a longer, less-traveled route to Orallia. It added three weeks to their journey, but the detour gave them distance and safety.

Several days from their destination, they came across a drifting junk barge, its hull patched and weather-worn, held together by ingenuity and luck. Hunter hailed the crew and stepped aboard, bartering for supplies he knew they'd need to begin their new life. Among the salvaged goods, he found several intact panes of glass, a rare treasure in the Outer Rim. He secured them quickly, already imagining the sunlight pouring through their future windows.

Then, on a whim, or perhaps something more tender, he spotted a ruby-red water pitcher, its surface glinting like flame, and beside it, a delicate crocheted doily, fraying slightly at the edges but still beautiful in its craftsmanship. He purchased both, tucking them away as quiet gifts for Liara. A housewarming token. A peace offering. A promise. He hoped he could keep them hidden until the moment was right.

After eight weeks in deep space, the ship descended through Orallia's atmosphere, the familiar patchwork of green fields and rust-colored roofs appearing like a long-lost memory. Hunter landed in the open field behind the village, the same place he had touched down years ago.

As the ramp lowered and his boots met the earth, a breeze swept through the grasses. One by one, villagers began to emerge, and before long, a small crowd had gathered at the base of the ship. He wasn't a stranger here. They remembered him.

"Engine problems again?" Searra, the head member of the Ruling Council, asked.

"No, the ship is fine. I come to ask a favor of you and the Council."

"We owe you much. What can we do to repay you for helping us?"

"Inside my ship is a woman and her son. For the past four years, she thought her husband was dead, but he is alive. He was a prisoner in the Correlian War. Once he was free, he placed a bounty on his wife and son's whereabouts. I found them. He is still far away and asked if I would find them a quiet place to live. I thought of your village. Might there be land he can purchase for himself and his family to live on? He offers fifteen rubels."

"Fifteen rubels?" Searra asked, surprised at the excessive amount. "Fifteen rubels for land?"

"I ask for the section up on the third hill, the one beside the clear stream."

"That is a prime location, but not worth so many rubels. We *Genubites* live as a community, and our homes lie in a circle around the Great Hall. We do not need possessions. This, you know. We have no use for the land. Five rubels is sufficient."

"He instructed me to give you fifteen. He also hopes you will build for his family a home on the hill."

"When will he arrive?" Jasmere, her husband, and the second member of the Ruling Council asked.

"Four to five weeks."

"That is not much time to build a home."

"No, it is not," Hunter replied. "That is why I am to offer you the fifteen. Some of your farming will need to be left undone, and he did not want your food supply to dwindle because of him. He offers an excessive amount so you may hire helpers to harvest. Plus, for your help, kindness, and sacrifice. What say you?"

Searra and Jasmere took several steps away from the Hunter and discussed the proposition. "We will accept fourteen rubels. No more. This amount will allow us to bring workers from my sister's village to help cut trees and build the hut."

"No, this is not a hut," Hunter quickly corrected. "A home, a house."

"Are not our huts homes?"

"Yes, but this woman needs a place with solid walls, doors, and windows made of glass. She has a diagram of what she desires."

"Glass? What is glass?"

"Glass is hard and transparent, like the water in the mountain lake when it freezes."

"Won't the glass melt in our sun?"

"It's not the same thing." Hunter wasn't sure how to explain what glass was. "I brought the glass windows with me, so you needn't worry about them."

Searra studied the Hunter's body language and listened to his voice. This female was important to him. They would do as he asked. "We will build her home starting tomorrow. Jasmere, send runners out to my sister's village and your brother's. Ask for males to do the work and females to help feed them. Until we complete her home, I offer her shelter in one of our huts. You may sleep in the barn if you so wish."

"I will remain on my ship. The lady needs one more thing. She raises animals and needs pens to keep them in."

"What kind of animals? We cannot have her bringing beasts which will eat our crops."

Hunter worried about the next part of his plan. Although the *Genubite* legends were filled with canine stories, the people feared them and killed them on sight. Would they accept Kii and the pups? He took a deep breath. "She brings with her a full-grown tamed canine and eight additional pups."

"Canines?" Jasmere's eyebrows lowered in disapproval." No. She may not stay if she brings canines."

"Searra, Jasmere, I give you my word as a Huntsman and a Bounty Hunter, her canines will not harm you. In fact, they will improve your life. They will keep the animals that eat your plants out of your gardens. And protect the village and your children."

"They will eat our children," Searra shouted.

"No, they are good canines. And all but one are babies."

"Wait, Searra," Jasmere said, laying his hand on his wife's arm. "Let's not judge before we look at the truth. Our ancient stories tell of how our people and the noble canines lived in peace together. Maybe the time has arrived for us to do so again." He turned to Hunter. "Do you trust them?"

"With my life."

"Then show us."

Hunter waved to Li-ara. Seeing the signal, Li-ara brought J'Dar and Kii out of the shadows. The moment Kii stepped into view, the air filled with screams and yelling.

"No. The canine will not hurt you," Hunter shouted. "He is my friend."

Jasmere walked in front of the crowd. "This Bounty Hunter has always spoken the truth. We will allow this canine to come to us and show us he is our friend." He nodded to Hunter.

Hunter lifted his arm, palm open in a steadying gesture, signaling to Li-ara that all was well. She gave a faint nod and stepped forward, guiding J'Dar down the ramp. The boy held tightly to Kii's leash, the big black canine trotting obediently at his side.

Everything was going smoothly until Kii saw Hunter. In an instant, the dog froze, ears pricking forward. Recognition flared in his eyes, and with a joyful bark, he surged forward.

The leash tore from J'Dar's small hand.

The massive canine barreled down the ramp, paws pounding the metal, tail whipping like a banner behind him. He ran straight for Hunter, overcome with excitement after weeks in hypersleep and separation from his closest companion.

Gasps erupted from the villagers. Shouts of warning rang out, and within seconds, panic spread like wildfire. Men reached for sticks and tools, prepared to defend themselves, mistaking the loyal creature's charge for an attack. An alarm call pierced the air.

Hunter saw it all happening in a blink; Kii's joyful sprint, the misunderstanding on the villagers' faces, the weapons rising. He knew he had only seconds to stop what was coming.

Hunter raised his hands in the air, "Don't hurt him. He's just excited."

The Huntsman strode forward, closing the distance with swift, unrelenting steps. He halted twenty feet from the stunned villagers.

They froze in fear, eyes wide, as the massive black canine came barreling toward the Huntsman, his ears back, muscles coiled, paws pounding the dirt. Several villagers recoiled, certain the beast would kill their visitor.

The canine reached the Huntsman at full speed and leapt.

Gasps rang out. A few turned away. But instead of tearing him down, the creature reared up, planting its massive front paws against the Huntsman's armored chest. Then, his tail wagging like mad, Kii licked his helmet, whining with joy.

The villagers stared, mouths open, as the terrifying scene twisted into something almost tender. The beast wasn't attacking. He was greeting him.

"Down, Boy," Hunter said, petting the canine's head. Kii immediately sat, his tail wagging excessively as he looked over the new faces. "See, the animal is loving. He is not dangerous."

Jasmere inched forward. "May I pet him?"

"Yes. Hold out your hand and allow him to sniff you. Once he gets your scent, you can pet him."

Kii sniffed the male's hand, then licked it, still wagging his tail. "This is no wild animal," Jasmere announced loudly. "Does he have a name?"

"His name is Kii," Hunter said.

Jasmere held out his hand to his wife. "Come beside me, Searra. Come meet Kii."

Searra approached with small steps, keeping an eye on the canine's movements. She held out her hand, allowing the canine to investigate her scent. Kii eagerly licked her hand as well. The leader giggled.

"Never have I witnessed such a thing before. Come, everyone, come and meet this amazing animal." Those who were brave enough to meet the canine came forward, permitting the canine to investigate their scent.

"He is as you said, Hunter," Searra said. "He will be the fifteenth rubel."

Word of the newcomers spread quickly, drawing helpers from across the countryside. Not just to lend a hand in building the lady's home, but to catch a glimpse of the legendary canines she had brought with her.

At the center of it all was Kii - majestic, watchful, and utterly devoted. Though his size alone could stop a man in his tracks, he won the hearts of the villagers with his gentle nature. Children clung to his thick fur without fear, and he greeted every visitor with a wagging tail and a warm nuzzle. By night, he patrolled the outer fields, driving off the wild creatures that had once decimated crops. Farmers soon noticed the change - fewer losses, fuller baskets.

The eight young pups, all wiggling energy and soft paws, became constant companions to J'Dar and the village children. From dawn to dusk, they played, tumbled, and grew under watchful eyes. Li-ara began training the two eldest to fetch firewood, carry dinner satchels, and haul small buckets of water from the spring.

During this time, Hunter had to find innovative ways to find time to be alone with Li-ara. Every few days, he'd secretly whisk her away to a secluded section of the forest, behind secluded bushes, or hidden aboard his ship.

"Someone is going to see us," Li-ara always said. "If they do, it will destroy our story about J'Dar's father coming. We can't keep doing this."

"If we're discovered, so be it," was always Hunter's reply. "I cannot go another moment without making love to my beautiful wife."

Two weeks after their arrival, a nearby farmer arrived with a half-starved wild canine pup cradled in his arms. Its ribs showed through its matted coat, and its eyes were dull with exhaustion. Without hesitation, Li-ara took the pup in. She cleaned and fed it, whispering softly as she introduced it to the others. She nestled it among the domesticated puppies, determined to show the villagers that even their native wild canines, creatures once feared, could be shaped into companions, protectors, family.

With so many willing hands, the house rose quickly. Sturdy walls, a sloped roof, and a chimney that smelled of sweet smoke. Just two days shy of five weeks, it was finished, complete with hand-carved doors and three precious windows: one overlooking the bed where dreams might return, one above the kitchen sink to catch the morning light, and one in the living room that framed the distant mountains like a painting.

With a bright blue sky and two shining suns overhead, Li-ara stepped inside for the first time, the scent of fresh wood still clinging to the walls. She paused as her eyes fell on the kitchen table. There, in the center, sat a ruby-red water pitcher, its glass catching the light like a flame held in still water. Beneath it, resting like lace spun from memory, was a delicately crocheted doily.

She didn't have to ask where they came from. She only smiled and let her fingers linger on the gift, knowing exactly who had placed it there.

"Welcome home," Hunter said as he stepped out of the shadows.

"Thank you. But my home won't be complete until my husband arrives."

"His presence will truly make this building a home."

"Thank you, Hunter, for doing this for us."

"No thanks are needed." Hunter spread his arms. "All of this was possible because of your ability to train the canines. You enticed the villagers to build this for you. I was simply the man holding the purse strings."

"Will you be leaving soon?"

"In a few minutes."

"No, Hunter," J'Dar shouted, running into the room and locking his arms around the Huntsman's legs. "I don't want you to go."

"I must."

"Why?"

"Your father will be here soon. I have fulfilled my contract."

"I don't want him. I want you."

"He loves you," Hunter said softly, noticing the tears streaming down the young boy's face. "I promise, when you finally meet your father, you'll like him."

The boy wiped his eyes with a trembling hand. "But if he loved me, where has he been all these years?"

Hunter knelt down, meeting the child's gaze. "Sometimes the people who love us most are kept from us by circumstances beyond their control. Trust me. He's dreamed of this day as long as you have."

"Don't you love me?"

Hunter's heart was breaking. If only he could tell him the truth. "Oh, J'Dar. Of course, I love you. My leaving has nothing to do with whether I love you or not."

"Will you come back?"

"One day, when you are older."

J'Dar turned to his mom. "Make him stay."

"I can't, Sweetheart. Hunter has sacrificed enough time for us. He must be on his way."

"How about you walk with me to my ship?" Hunter held his hand out to the small boy.

Clenching the Hunter's hand tightly, J'Dar walked beside the Huntsman. Li-ara followed close behind. Standing before the ship was Searra waiting to say her goodbyes.

Hunter raised his hand to his forehead and bowed. "Thank you, Searra. And thank the villagers for me. You've made her very happy."

"It was a debt we owed you. And now that debt is paid, along with fifteen rubels." She laughed. "May the stars guide you back to us soon, Hunter of Kolora."

Hunter lifted J'Dar into his arms, giving the boy one last hug. "You take good care of your mom." He extended his hand to Li-ara. "May your home be filled with nothing but happiness and the laughter of children. I take my leave." Thankful his helmet hid his tears, Hunter turned and walked up the ramp.

Kii bounded across the grass, his powerful legs eating up the distance with ease, ears perked and tongue lolling in excitement as he chased after his closest companion, unwilling to be left behind.

"No, Kii," Hunter said firmly. "Not this time. You must stay and protect Li-ara and J'Dar."

The canine skidded to a stop, ears twitching, gaze locked on Hunter.

"Go to Li-ara."

Kii hesitated, taking a few reluctant steps back. He turned again, unwilling to leave.

"All the way down," Hunter urged.

With his tail lowered and head hung, Kii retreated to Li-ara and settled beside her.

The ramp groaned under the strain of thick cables pulling it upward, the sound echoing like a final farewell. A soft hiss followed as the seal locked into place. Beside her, J'Dar clung to his mother's leg and buried his face against it, his small body trembling with sobs he no longer held back.

Hunter appeared in the cockpit window waving. This time, Li-ara waved back. Her beloved Hunter was leaving and would return as her husband and genuine love – BiiJun D'Kolor AND J'Dar Jen.

The ship rose, then slowly guided forward before zooming away, its presence gone within seconds.

"Come, J'Dar, let's go inside," Li-ara said. "We need to prepare for your father's arrival."

J'Dar looked into his mother's eyes, his stare cold and filled with anger. Then, without a word, he turned and bolted toward the house, choked sobs escaping him as he ran.

"When he returns as your husband, will you tell him?" Searra asked as she walked beside Li-ara.

Li-ara stopped. "What did you say?"

"Did you and Hunter believe you would fool me? Or hide your many secret, intimate excursions? I saw the deep love in your eyes whenever you looked at him. And his helmet did not hide his feelings either. And the way he fussed over the details of your home, making sure everything was just the way you wanted it. Those are not the actions of a Bounty Hunter but the behaviors of a male in love. The truth was visible for anyone with eyes to see. I realized the day you arrived that it would be he who would live there, not a male you haven't seen in years. But do not worry, his and your secret is safe with me. Even Jasmere will not learn the truth."

"Thank you."

"So, will you tell him tonight?"

"Tell him what?"

"That his daughter grows inside you."

Li-ara blinked, stunned, the words hanging in the air like a thunderclap. Her mouth parted slightly. "My daughter?" she echoed, barely above a whisper. "How could you possibly know that?"

Searra smiled at the pregnant woman beside her. "My child, I have birthed many babies. I am familiar with the subtle physical transformations and walk of a pregnant woman."

"I thought I might be, but I wasn't sure."

"It will bring me joy to see the Huntsman I call a friend without the covering that hides his face from the world," Searra said. "And the joy in his eyes when he learns he will be a father once more." She smiled. "J'Dar has his voice and his mannerisms."

"Is there nothing you don't know?"

"Come, you and J'Dar will eat with Jasmere and me tonight. You need nourishment for the baby to grow."

15 BLACK SHE CANINE

Hunter piloted his ship low over the rugged terrain, scanning the landscape for a place to hide the vessel. Truly hide it. Somewhere remote, somewhere no curious traveler or wandering child might stumble upon it. Even cloaked, he knew that, over time, discovery was inevitable.

Ten miles south of Li-ara's home, Hunter saw his answer. Below was a quiet lake nestled beside a forested hill, fed by a silver-threaded waterfall. Isolated. Untouched. Ideal.

Setting her down on a grassy clearing, he lowered the ramp and stepped onto the platform, breathing in the crisp, earthy air. The silence was absolute. Good. It would have to be. Whatever he left here might never be retrieved.

He scurried around the ship, gathering anything he might have forgotten to hide beneath the cabin. The walk back was long, so only essentials would be carried.

His biggest problem was his armor. It practically needed a guardian of its own. He couldn't bring it with him; it was far too bulky to carry, and leaving it in the house or an outbuilding was too risky. Someone might stumble across it and learn his true identity. Plus, *kolorite* brought a hefty price on the black market. Just having it around might put Li-ara and J'Dar in danger. Stowing it inside the submerged ship wasn't an option either, not because it wasn't safe, but because it would be too far out of reach if he needed it quickly. Enemies had a way of resurfacing when least expected, and if that day came, he had to be ready.

Hunter scouted the surrounding hillside and discovered a cave hidden beneath a tangled outcrop of roots and moss. A sharp, foul stench hit him as he approached - the unmistakable musk of *grittzlebores*. Nasty herbivores with the temper of horned demons.

Cautiously, he peered inside.

Droppings littered the floor, and tusk marks gouged the stone walls. A sanctuary for the nasty beasts, no doubt. And perfect. No one in their right mind would enter this place willingly with *grittzlebores* hanging about.

He returned to the ship, spread a blanket across the grass, and began removing the pieces of his armor, one by one. He removed the helmet, trailing his fingers across the smooth, silver surface. It reflected his face, though it was not the one he remembered. The man staring back at him was older, sharper around the edges. Worn by time. Hardened by survival.

For over two decades, the armor had shielded him. From bullets. From enemies. From the world. From himself.

And now, he was burying it.

Leaving out one wristband, he rolled the armor carefully into the blanket and carried it into the cave. With his hands, he dug into the dry, gritty soil, forming a hollow deep enough to swallow the last pieces of his old life. He placed the bundle inside, covered it with sand and rocks, and rolled a large, blue-speckled stone over the top. A marker. A silent grave.

Hunter couldn't return his armor to the furnaces on Kolora, but he could give it a proper burial. Bowing his head, he recited the Kolorian creed. Upon completion, he rose and stepped outside.

Certain that there were people who would recognize his long rifle, he disassembled it. He wrapped the pieces in his bedding and strapped the bundle to the top of his pack. Like his armor, it needed to be close in case it was needed again.

Stripping off his clothing and hiding it below a bush along with his pack and wristband, Hunter scrambled up the ramp into his ship, then continued to climb to the cockpit. His heart skipped as he sat in the navigator's chair, knowing this might be the last time he ever flew her. But a life with Li-ara and J-Dar was worth the sacrifice.

Hunter lifted the vessel into the air and inched her forward until she hovered over the glassy lake. The water below was crystal clear and impossibly deep. The perfect hiding place. Suspending silently above the surface, he activated the emergency escape protocol. A hissing sound filled the air as the escape hatch opened. Lifting his body through the narrow opening, he looked around. Assured no one was watching, he took a deep breath and dove into the frigid water. Slicing to the surface, he swam hard toward the shore.

Cold, wet, and slightly breathless, he hauled himself onto the rocky shoreline. Water streamed from his body as he sprinted up a narrow, winding trail that led to higher ground. At the top, he retrieved his wristband, slid it over his forearm, and tapped in a precise sequence of commands. The device chirped in response, soft beeps followed by a flicker of blinking lights.

Below, he heard the faint hum of the escape hatch sealing shut. The Li-ara responded instantly, enclosing herself in a nearly silent, airtight cocoon. Slowly, she began her descent, gliding down until her hull kissed the water's surface, then slipping beneath it. The lake accepted her without resistance, rippling gently as the ship vanished into the depths, the last glint of her metal form swallowed by the dark.

"Goodbye, my dear friend," Hunter whispered.

He dressed quickly, buried the wristband deep in his pack, and turned toward home, toward Li-ara, toward J'Dar, toward a life he never believed he'd be allowed to live. But as he stepped past the cave, a sharp twinge in his gut stopped him cold. Someone, or something, was watching. Were the *grittzlebores* back? Had someone seen him hide his ship? He didn't know how he knew, he just did. That primal instinct, the one that had saved him more times than he could count, screamed through every nerve in his body.

His hand dropped to his sidearm. With a flick of his thumb, the safety clicked off. The forest held its breath. No birdsong. No rustling leaves. Just an unnatural silence that pressed in around him like a closing fist.

Hunter moved forward in slow, measured steps, each one deliberate, each muscle coiled tight. His eyes swept the trees, the underbrush, the shadows that seemed too deep for the midday light.

He cursed under his breath. He needed his helmet. The sensors, the thermal scans, the enemy-tracking software. He was blind without them. And somewhere out there, hidden in the silence, something watched him.

A twig snapped above him. He spun around, following the sound to a rim above the cave. Standing at the edge was a wild canine. Black as midnight. Motionless. Massive. Her powerful frame rippled with quiet strength, muscles tense beneath her sleek coat. She didn't move. Didn't growl. Just watched. Judging.

Eyes like polished obsidian locked onto his, unblinking. Calculating.

Female. Alpha.

Hunter raised his weapon, steady and sure, but didn't fire. He held his breath, studying her closely. Every line of her body. Every twitch of muscle. The angle of her ears. The set of her jaw.

This wasn't a predator about to strike. She could have leapt down and torn into him. She had the size, the muscle, the advantage. But she didn't.

Without a sound, three more canines emerged from the shadows beside her. Their eyes gleamed with primal intent, and each step was deliberate, predatory. Lips curled back to reveal rows of sharp, yellowed teeth. A low, unified growl rumbled from their throats, deep, guttural, and unmistakably territorial.

"Not good," Hunter muttered, tightening his grip on his weapon.

The black one snapped her jaws - just once, sharp and commanding. Instantly, the growls ceased. The others dropped into sitting positions at her sides, their bodies still, their eyes alert but no longer hostile. The transformation was immediate - feral chaos replaced by disciplined silence.

Hunter remained still. The black canine took one step forward, then lowered her front leg and bowed. Hunter blinked. Slowly, cautiously, he bowed in return. Without another sound, the she canine turned and slipped back into the forest. The others followed.

Hunter exhaled. "Li-ara's never going to believe this," he said. "That's one for the books."

He shouldered his pack and began the long walk home. But when he reached the open plains, his gut tightened again. On his left, the black female and her trio flanked him at a distance. On his right, five more wild canines emerged, matching his pace with eerie precision.

He stopped. So did they.

He started again, and they followed.

An escort?

Testing the theory, he picked up his pace to a trot. The packs mirrored him, keeping rhythm, forming a protective arc. Hunter allowed himself a rare, private smile. They were guarding him.

"So, where is your husband going to sleep?" J'Dar asked as his mom removed the bread from the oven.

"I told you. With me in my bed."

"Are you going to kiss him?"

Li-ara laughed. "Of course, Silly. He's my husband. I love him. Husbands and wives kiss and share a bed."

"I thought you loved Hunter."

"I did, but as a friend."

"Why is loving a friend different from loving a husband?"

"It just is. You'll understand when you're older and like girls."

"I'm never liking girls," J'Dar said with conviction. "Do I have to call him Dad?"

"He is your father, but you can decide if you call him Dad or not."

"What if I never want to call him Dad?"

"That is your choice, but I think once you know him, you'll want to. Now, sit on the front porch and keep watch. Tell me when you see him walking toward the house."

"Do I have to?"

"Yes. Scoot. And don't go running off with Kii or anyone else."

Dragging his feet along the floor, J'Dar headed towards the front door. "Come on, Kii."

Li-ara noted the sun was sinking in the west, its brilliance rapidly descending into the mountain peaks. Would Hunter arrive home before dark? Or would he wait until tomorrow? She cooked a celebration dinner to celebrate his first night without his armor and officially welcome him home.

She took a step back and surveyed the table. It looked beautiful. The ruby-red pitcher and doily that Hunter gave her rested in the center of the table. Hunter! She must remember not to call him that anymore. Hunter was the Bounty Hunter's name, as was BiiJun. Nor could she call him J'Dar because their son went by that name. Jen was a possibility, but Hunter didn't feel like a Jen. In the end, the couple decided on a shorter version of J'Dar - JD.

"Mom, I think he's here," J'Dar called out from the front porch.

Her heart pounding, Li-ara raced to the porch and scanned down the hill. "Where? I don't see him?" A head emerged, then a chest, then legs. She dashed towards him.

As the sun set, its fleeting glow lit the last few steps of Hunter's journey. Walking up the hill, he saw Li-ara running towards him. He dropped his pack and ran to her, swooping her in his arms and kissing her repeatedly. He was home, really home.

"Come, it's time for you to meet your son," Li-ara said. After retrieving his pack and knapsack, the two walked hand-in-hand to the porch where their son waited. "J'Dar, I want you to meet your father."

Hunter held out his hand. "I am happy to meet you at last. The Hunter told me impressive things about you."

J'Dar's eyes lit up as he accepted the stranger's hand. "Did he come back with you?"

"No. He said he had business waiting for him." J'Dar huffed, kicking the grass. He turned and walked into the house.

"You must be starving," Li-ara stated. "Dinner is ready."

Hunter walked into the kitchen. His eyes opened wide in surprise. Before him was a dinner the Dominee would be impressed with.

"This looks delicious. You shouldn't have gone to all this trouble."

"Nothing is too much trouble if it's for my husband."

J'Dar said little during the meal. His lack of words, and the expression of annoyance on his face, stated he did not want this male sitting at the table. He wanted the male he loved - Hunter. The moment dinner ended, he dashed from the table.

"Come on, Kii, let's go," J'Dar grumbled when the canine didn't follow. "Kii, I said come."

"Kii, go in J'Dar's room," Hunter said. Immediately, the canine did as instructed.

"Why did Kii do what you said?" J'Dar asked. "He doesn't know you. And why didn't he attack you when you arrived? The only other person he never attacked was Hunter."

"He does know me," Hunter said. "We spent time together before I left for the war. He still remembers me. Now, off to bed. I'll answer all your questions tomorrow." J'Dar gave a puzzled look. He remembered when Hunter said almost those exact same words.

Taking her hand in his, Hunter led Li-ara to their bedroom. Locking the door behind him, Hunter grabbed her and kissed her passionately.

"Oh, Hunter, dinner was so incredible. You actually ate with us, your face uncovered," Li-ara said.

"I cannot believe I sat at the table, eating with my wife and son. I barely ate. I don't believe J'Dar enjoyed dinner. It will take him time to accept me. He genuinely loves Hunter."

"Why wouldn't he? You are Hunter."

"Technically, yes. But J'Dar doesn't know I am."

"Pretending you're not Hunter will be harder than I thought. I caught myself calling you by your name twice at the dinner table."

"It will become easier with time. Remember, keeping the truth of my identity from our son will keep both him and you safe. We should turn in. I'm sure J'Dar will be up early tomorrow."

"Wait, I have a welcome home present for you." Li-ara ran over to the small trunk she had brought from Rigel Three. Digging down deep, she pulled up a small cloth package wrapped with a ribbon. "Here. This is for you. I made it today, waiting for you to return home."

"You didn't need to give me anything. Just being with you and J'Dar is the only present I need."

She kissed him. "Open it." Her eyes twinkled with anticipation as he untied the ribbon.

Hunter stared at the contents. Inside the package lay the bonnet he altered and wore on Proxima Prime. "Why are you giving me the cloth helmet back?"

"I made some alterations. It's not your helmet."

"You took the extra material out and stitched the sides back together. What do you want me to do with it? I can't wear it like this."

Filling a million pin pricks stinging her body, Li-ara answered, "I thought you might give the bonnet to your daughter."

"Daughter?" he echoed, confusion flickering in his eyes. "I … I don't have a daughter."

Then he saw the way her eyes shimmered, saw the tears gathering, unspoken words trembling on her lips.

His voice dropped, barely more than a whisper. "Are you … are you telling me …" He took a breath that didn't quite reach his lungs. "I'm going to be a father?"

"Is that okay?"

"Okay? That's the best news I've heard since the moment I laid eyes on J'Dar and discovered I had a son." He grabbed Li-ara into his arms and spun her around. He stopped, setting her feet back on the floor. "Oh, I shouldn't lift you."

"It's okay. You can't hurt her. Are you sure you're okay with this?"

Hunter kissed her, a slow, gentle, loving kiss. "You made me the happiest male in this universe. How do you know the baby is a girl?"

"Searra told me."

Hunter froze, the smile disappearing from his face. "What does Searra have to do with this? How does she know?"

"I don't know how, but when you left in your ship, she told me your daughter was growing inside me."

"JD's daughter?"

"No, Hunter's daughter. She knows the truth. She also knows that J'Dar is Hunter's son."

"Li-ara, we need to leave this place. She might tell others."

"No, Hunter. She promised not to say a word to anyone, not even Jasmere. You brought us here because you trust her, right?"

"Yes, I found her to be an honorable woman."

"Then trust her. I don't want to leave, Hunter."

"I'm not happy about this, Li-ara. Every instinct I have tells me to take you and J'Dar away. But, at your request, I'll give Searra the benefit of the doubt. But at the first sign my identity is compromised, we leave."

"Okay. But it won't come to that."

Hunter dropped to his knees, eyes wide with wonder, the weight of what he'd just heard was only now truly settling in. With trembling hands, he gently lifted the hem of Li-ara's shirt, revealing the soft swell of her belly - small but unmistakable. He leaned forward and pressed a kiss just above her navel, his lips lingering.

"Hello, Little One," he whispered, his voice thick with emotion. "I'm your father. And I can't even begin to tell you how happy I am to know you're coming into this world."

He rested his cheek against her skin, his eyes closing, a quiet smile pulling at his lips. "I already love you more than I ever thought possible. I love your mother beyond words and your brother, too. You'll like him. He's brave and kind and has a heart big enough to hold the stars. He's going to be the best big brother."

Li-ara's hand moved to the side of his face, her fingers sliding into his hair as she cradled him close.

Hunter stayed there, silent, soaking in the moment, his heart full to the brim. "Imagine that," he murmured, his voice no more than a breath. "Me, the father of a daughter."

"How do you think J'Dar will accept the news? He hasn't adjusted to you being here yet. And how did I become pregnant in one day? He will think I cheated on his father. With Hunter, his father. Oh, this is impossible."

Hunter rose and took her in his arms. "We'll think of something. We always do." He paused. "Can we still make love? Because right now, that's the only thing I want to do."

"Yes."

The instant Li-ara's eyes opened, a sour wave churned in her stomach. She bolted from the bed, one hand clamped over her mouth, the other fumbling for the wall to steady herself. Her bare feet slapped the floor as she staggered to the sink. Morning sickness had arrived.

"Li-ara, what's wrong?" Hunter asked, bolting out of bed and chasing after her.

"I'm okay," she replied. Another wave of nausea hit her, and she vomited again. "It's just morning sickness, a normal part of being pregnant. The nausea will go away after a few months."

"A few months?"

"Don't Kolorian females experience morning sickness?"

"I don't know. I was never around pregnant females before. Were you sick with J'Dar?"

"All eight months."

"Eight months? That is not acceptable.

"Hunter, this is part of bringing a child into the world."

"Then tell me what to do to help," Hunter shouted, his voice a little too strong, too loud.

"Some tea would be nice." She looked up at him, eyes shining with quiet gratitude. "Just don't hover."

"I can't promise that," he muttered. "But I'll try."

The next morning, the scenario repeated itself.

Li-ara jolted upright, one hand pressed to her mouth as she bolted from the bed. Hunter was right behind her. He'd fought off raiders in the Barron Dunes. Survived missions no one was meant to return from. There had been only a handful of times in his life when he'd faced something he couldn't control, couldn't fix with strategy, strength, or firepower.

This was one of them. There was no fight to win. No enemy to strike. Just her, suffering.

Hunter fetched a glass of water and silently placed it beside her. When she turned and gave him a faint smile, he forced one in return. "I'm fine," she whispered, her voice hoarse.

He nodded, unsure what else to do. He wanted to lift her, wrap her in blankets, track down some cure, do something. But instead, he stood there trying not to hover, trying not to make her feel worse, failing at both.

But she never complained.

After two weeks, the cruel pattern worsened. What had begun as morning sickness crept into the afternoons … and then, to Hunter's growing alarm, into the evenings. The clock didn't seem to matter anymore. Whether the sun was rising or sinking, Li-ara would suddenly bolt from wherever she was - bed, chair, even mid-sentence - and rush to the sink. Sometimes she didn't make it in time.

Hunter tried everything. Herbal teas. Dry roots. Broths he made himself, even though cooking had never been part of his skill set. Nothing stayed down.

In desperation, he went to Searra for help.

Searra spotted the father walking up the path, his steps uneven, his gaze flicking anxiously toward the hut. She didn't need to ask. His worry clung to him like a second skin. Searra invited him inside.

"She says she's fine," Hunter muttered. "But she's not keeping anything down. I ...I don't know what else to do."

Searra placed a steady hand on his arm. "Then let me see her for myself."

Before heading up the path, Searra stepped into the herb garden and plucked a handful of dried *trillium* leaves, placing them in a leather pouch. She added a tuber of moonroot. On the way, she spotted a patch of blue-spiked *korra* blossoms pushing up between the rocks. She clipped three and nestled them among the herbs. A few wild chamomile petals followed.

"I think we have everything we'll need," Searra said, tying the pouch to her belt. "Hunter, I've been wanting to talk with you, but our responsibilities have kept us apart."

"I've been needing to talk to you ever since Li-ara said what you told her - that you believe I'm the Hunter who came to your village all those years ago. And that J'Dar is his son."

"I did not need to observe the face hidden behind your helmet to determine it was you. Do you deny you are the same Hunter?"

Hunter looked into Searra's eyes, weighing his options. Could he really trust her? After a moment, he said, "No. I am he. But how did you know? We hid my identity."

"My family has not only been members of the High Council for centuries, but many were also truth-seers. I don't understand why I can foresee some things and not others, but I have been aware of you ever since your birth on *Tallus*."

"*Tallus?* Why do you say that? I was born on the Huntsmen's world of *Ribos*."

"Being born on *Ribos* is what your parents told you. Your parents stopped on *Tallus* on their way home to *Ribos,* and you shocked them with your early birth. Your arrival was the first of many surprises, the most dramatic being when the *Rogarian* Traders stole you. Thankfully, the *Biiloot* rescued you and returned you to Kolora, where you learned the art of the Bounty Hunter. But your Dominee foresaw a different future for you."

"You are familiar with the Dominee? I thought you never left this planet."

"I never leave this world, nor does the Dominee leave Kolora. But we converse in the spiritual world. She is the one who told me you were J'Dar's father and your love for Li-ara. When you faltered on your path to your destiny, I told her where they lived."

"You know what my destiny is?"

"You will unite the worlds of Kolora and Orallia, *Tallus* and Rigel Three, Proxima Prime and *Glodtuc,* and many more worlds."

"How can I unite worlds? I am not a diplomat or a leader."

"You will show the others through your teachings. Li-ara's gift will be the training of the wild canines, which will transform many lives." Searra stopped. "But I must warn you, Hunter, your road contains many pitfalls. You must never break the bond you and Li-ara share. Your love for her is both your doom and your salvation."

Searra pressed one hand to her lower back, the other gripping a sapling trunk for balance as she trudged up the narrow, uneven path. Her breath came in short, wheezing huffs, and her knees protested with every step. She muttered something under her breath and straightened, face flushed.

"I'm going to ask Jasmere to build proper steps up this cursed hill," she grumbled, puffing between words. "This climb is downright cruel on an old woman's bones."

"What do you mean by my love for Li-ara is both my doom and salvation?"

"I've told you all I know. At last, we have arrived."

Searra knocked and entered. Li-ara was leaning over the kitchen sink and vomiting. "Child, why did you wait so long to send for me?"

"I didn't." Searra glanced at Hunter.

"I came on my own, Searra. Li-ara didn't know."

The elder smiled. "Thankfully, when one lives to be as old as I, you've helped many women with their sickness. Bring me a bowl of hot water."

"There is some on the stove," Li-ara stated, sitting down in a nearby chair, the nausea abated for the moment. "I thought some tea might help with my sickness."

Hunter poured hot water from the kettle into a small wooden bowl, steam curling into the air as he passed it to Searra. The elder accepted it with a nod, then reached into her worn pouch.

"Repeat this process each morning and evening before bed." She pulled off the eight petals from the chamomile flowers and dropped them in the boiling water. Next, she rolled the center of the *korra* flowers in her fingers, releasing tiny seeds. The rest of the centers she threw away. A pinch of moonroot followed. Lastly, she placed six *trillium* leaves in the mixture. She stirred the ingredients and handed the bowl to Li-ara. "Drink this. You will feel better before the sun reaches high in the sky."

"Is my mom going to die?" a sorrowful J'Dar asked as he silently slipped into the room.

"No, why would you ask such a thing?" Hunter scolded.

"Why do you think that, J'Dar?" Searra asked, sensing the fear bubbling inside the child.

"Because she is always sick. Back home, one of our canines got sick, and she died."

Searra gave both parents a chastising look. "You need to tell him why his mother is ill." Saying no more, she turned, walked out of the kitchen, and down the hill.

"J'Dar, can you come over and sit beside me? Daddy and I have wonderful news to tell you." Hesitantly, the young child approached his mother and sat down. "The reason I am sick is because I'm going to have a baby like Tallie did last year. Remember?"

"You will be a big brother," Hunter added. "Isn't that wonderful?"

His face red, J'Dar jumped up and faced his parents. "No. I don't want to be a big brother. I don't want a sister. I hate you both."

Li-ara grabbed her son's arm. "You do not speak to me or your father that way."

"He's not my father." J'Dar glared at Hunter. His eyes burned with contempt, hate etched across his face. "Why did you come back? Mom and I were fine without you." Yanking his arm free, he ran out the door and down the steps, his sobs audible. Kii followed.

"I'm sorry, Hunter," Li-ara said. "He had no right to say such things to you."

"Yes, he did. You two were doing fine until I showed up. I turned his world upside down because I was too afraid of kissing you that day. Had I, he would have been born with his father in the house to love and cherish him."

"Your absence is as much my fault as it is yours."

He gave her a slight smile. "You bear no blame, Li-ara. My blame is double. Not only did I abandon him, but when J'Dar met a man he wanted to call father, I took him away too."

"Are you sure we shouldn't tell him the truth of who you are? He is so torn between you and Hunter."

"His age prohibits knowing. If he were ten or twelve, possibly, but not at four. The knowledge would not only put you and him in danger but all Hunters and Huntsmen. No, for now, I must be the one to bear this sorrow." Was this one of the burdens Searra told him about? "I'll try to talk with him."

Hunter stepped outside, expecting to find J'Dar sulking on the porch, arms crossed, maybe kicking at the dirt the way he did when he didn't get his way. But the porch was empty.

He scanned the yard. "J'Dar?" he called out, trying to keep his voice calm. Still no answer.

Maybe he'd gone to play with the pups. He often retreated there when he needed space. Hunter took off at a brisk pace toward the kennels, the first threads of worry tightening in his chest. But when he reached the pens, only Canines greeted him.

No child.

No Kii.

His heart gave a hard, painful thud. Hunter brought two fingers to his lips and let out a sharp whistle, the kind Kii always responded to.

Silence.

He waited ... ten seconds, twenty. Still nothing.

His throat tightened. Something was wrong. He could feel it now. Not just the silence, but the stillness of the air, the absence of sound that screamed louder than any alarm.

Whistling again, this time more urgently, Hunter's gaze swept the horizon.

"Where are you, J'Dar? Kii, where did you take him?"

His mind raced through possibilities - rational ones, terrible ones, all twisted with fear. The kind of fear he hadn't felt since the days he'd lived under constant threat. But this was worse. Because this time, it was his son.

Huffing from running up the hill, Hunter burst into the kitchen. "Li-ara, I can't find J'Dar or Kii anywhere."

Li-ara bolted outside. She screamed both J'Dar and Kii's names. Nothing. She whistled. No Kii. "Did you check the stream?"

"Kii would never let him go near the water. It's too dangerous."

"Unless Kii's not with him. Go check the stream, Hunter. I'll check behind the house." For two hours, the worried parents searched everywhere to no avail. It would soon be dark.

"I'll go into the village and recruit some men," Hunter said. "We'll search through the night if we need to."

"Wait. Is that him?" Li-ara asked as a figure appeared in the darkening shadows on the road.

"No, it's someone from the village." When the man came closer, Hunter called out, "Did you see my son on your journey here? We can't find him."

"Searra asked me to tell you he and his canine are enjoying dinner in her hut. Since the time is late, they will spend the night. You may retrieve them tomorrow."

"Hunter, go get him now. Please."

Hunter glanced up at the night sky. Clouds danced across the night, blocking out the stars and the moon. "It will be pitch black tonight. The large predators will be out. J'Dar is safer remaining with Searra than on the road on such an evening. I will go at first daylight tomorrow and bring him home."

Early the next morning, before the sun's light appeared in the east, Hunter walked to the village. He kept repeating over and over in his head what he would say to his son, changing the wording to go with whatever scenario he imagined.

"He still sleeps," Searra said as she waited in the doorway for Hunter.

"Thank you, Searra, for watching over him. He had us worried. Did he mention why he was so upset? Is he really afraid Li-ara will die?"

"That thought crossed his mind, especially since the canine he spoke of yesterday was a female. She died giving birth to her puppies."

"I did not know that."

"But mostly, he fears to lose his father."

"Lose me? He can't lose me."

"He is four and can only judge the world by what he sees and has experienced," Searra said. "All he knows is that he lost you when you went off to war. Now, you've returned, and the possibility you will leave again haunts his thoughts. Plus, a new baby is coming. A girl. She represents someone who can take you from him. He fears there will not be enough love in yours or Li-ara's heart to love both."

"Why would he think such a thing?"

"Do you remember when you lost your parents?"

Hunter never forgot the day the raiders stole him. It was the worst day of his life. And when the *Büloot* returned him, he was afraid to love them again, afraid they would go away like before. "I remember."

"He loves you, Hunter, very much. He doesn't understand how to process all of this. Remember, he's only a small boy."

"So, he is. If okay, I'll take him home now." Hunter entered the sleeping area. His son lay asleep on the floor, Kii curled up beside him. He appeared so innocent, so small. Kii stood and stretched while the Huntsman lifted the sleeping child up and over his shoulder. In silence, he walked out and down the path to home.

Halfway home, Hunter heard, "Are you mad at me?"

"No, Son. I am happy you are okay. I was afraid you might be hurt.

"Is Mom mad?"

"No, she's glad you're safe too."

"I don't hate you."

"I know you don't."

"I need to pee."

Hunter lifted the child down and sat on a nearby rock while J'Dar attended to business. When he finished, Hunter invited him to sit with him.

"Do you still not want to be a big brother?"

"Why does Mom have to have another baby?"

"Because your mother and I love each other, and our love made a baby that's growing inside her. It's the same way you came into the world." Hunter leaned closer to the young boy. "Can I tell you a secret?"

"I suppose so."

"When I was your age, I became a big brother. I didn't want to, either."

"Really? Why?"

"My mom had another son. I didn't like him. In fact, I hated him. He was so tiny and helpless, and took all of Mom's time. I didn't think she loved me anymore. But she explained to me that parents possess so much love for their children that there's enough for all. She said a parent's love is like a spring. You can take out as much water as you want, and there will always be more. It will never be empty. A father's and a mother's love is the same. Neither your mother nor I will ever stop loving you."

"You promise?"

"I promise. Nothing could ever make me stop loving you."

"Then why did you leave us?"

"I was stupid and thought I had to take part in this other life."

"You were stupid?"

Hunter laughed. "Yes, even parents can be stupid sometimes. But believe me, J'Dar, when I say this. If I had known you were growing in your mom's belly, I never, ever would have left. And the moment I learned about you, I cried with joy."

"You cried?"

"Yes. And I sent Hunter to find you so we could be together again."

"I'm hungry. Can we go home now?"

"In just a moment. I have a few more things I want to say." Hunter took the child's hand in his and peered into his eyes. "J'Dar, your sister will be tiny and helpless like my brother was. And sometimes, it may seem like she's getting all the attention. But remember this: you are my firstborn. No matter how many children I have, no one will be my firstborn again. This makes you extra special, and I will always love you in a way I will love no other son or daughter."

"Okay. Can you carry me the rest of the way home?"

"Do you want me to?"

"Yeah. My legs got really tired walking to the village yesterday."

Hunter lifted the boy and threw him across his shoulders, allowing his legs to hang on each side of his neck. This was the best part of being a father.

16 THE FIGHT

As Li-ara's belly grew larger, so did the bond between father and son. Each morning, Hunter walked J'Dar to the village for school and back home again in the afternoon. They had long talks about many topics. Sometimes, they raced to determine who reached home first. Hunter usually let J'Dar win but occasionally bested him so his son wouldn't realize the races were rigged. Other times they lay in the grass and guessed the shape of the clouds or counted the number of birds flying overhead. Each night at bedtime, Hunter ceased whatever he was doing to tuck the covers around his son, kiss him, and tell him he loved him. J'Dar would always respond, "I love you too, Daddy." Hunter cherished these times.

Hunter also continued the tradition he started the night Li-ara told him she was pregnant. Each morning and night, he got on his knees, kissed her stomach, and told the "Little One" he loved her and how he couldn't wait to meet her.

On a beautiful day, Hunter and J'Dar went down to the stream to catch some fish for dinner. Li-ara was only a few weeks away from when they thought she might give birth, and Hunter didn't want to leave her. But she insisted she wanted fish for dinner, and one of the women staying with her would notify him if the baby came.

"J'Dar, I don't understand," Hunter said. "My fishing pole is identical to yours. I use the same bait you do, yet I've caught nothing, and you just pulled in your third trout. How do you do it? Is Kii telling you where the fish are?"

"Dad, you know Kii can't talk." J'Dar laughed.

"Well, if Kii's not giving you secrets, I must be doing something wrong. Can you show me again what to do?"

J'Dar sighed. He had already shown his father how to fish at least six times. But, deep down, he liked the idea he could do something his dad couldn't. Once more, he demonstrated the correct way to string the pole, where the hook and the anchor went, and where in the stream to fish.

"Remember, don't have the sun at your back because the fish will see your shadow, Dad. And don't shake your pole. Keep it still."

"Like this?" Hunter asked. A tug pulled on Hunter's pole. "Oh my gosh, I think I caught one."

"Pull it up, Dad. Set the hook in its mouth. Don't let the fish escape."

Hunter gave a quick snap of the line, setting the hook with ease. With a few fast turns of the reel, he hauled it in, water droplets flicking off the taut string. It was the tiniest fish either of them had ever seen. When Hunter and J'Dar's eyes met, both burst into laughter.

"I don't think that would even feed the new baby," J'Dar giggled.

The sound of someone calling broke the moment. A woman walked towards them frantically waving her arms, speaking in a language Hunter didn't understand.

"I can't hear you," Hunter shouted. "Is Li-ara okay?"

"Dad, I think she's saying the baby is coming," J'Dar stated.

"The baby? Now?" Hunter took off running, then stopped. He turned. Behind him, still standing by the stream with a rod in his hands, was J'Dar. Hunter stared for a beat, the realization sinking deep. He wasn't alone anymore. He didn't run solo.

"You go," the lady said. "I take the son."

To her surprise, Hunter kissed her face and took off running. "J'Dar, bring Kii and come straight home."

He ran all the way to the cabin and up the hill, wheezing by the time he reached the top. He paused for a second to catch his breath, then sped into the house. Several women ran around the rooms doing various chores. The sound of Li-ara shrieking an agonizing cry filled Hunter's ears.

One woman tried to stop him from entering the bedroom, but he pushed right past her. The blood drained from his face as he halted, observing an unfamiliar scene. Li-ara lay on the bed in a partially sitting position, a midwife behind her supporting her back, her legs spread open. The sheets below her legs were bright red with blood.

"Hunter, you need to wait outside," Searra said. "Despite her appearance, she's fine. She is in no danger."

"There's so much blood."

"That, too, is normal. With life comes blood. Now go."

"No way. I missed my son's birth. I will not miss my daughter's." He walked over and asked the attending female to vacate her position. When she didn't move, Hunter reached over and lifted the woman up and placed her standing on the floor. Before she could react, he slid in behind Li-ara's back and took both of her hands in his. "I'm here. We'll do this together."

"Did you catch any fish?" Li-ara asked.

Hunter nervously laughed. "Yes, but in my hurry to come home to you, I left them down at the stream."

Li-ara laughed, too. As another contraction hit, her laugh turned to a haunting scream. She squeezed Hunter's hands so hard he thought the bones would break.

"Almost there," Searra said. "The baby's head is showing. We need one more firm push. Hunter, bring her forward."

Hunter's eyes widened in astonishment as he watched the most beautiful baby girl emerge from between his wife's legs. A strong cry reverberated throughout the room as the newborn drew her first breath.

"Would you like to cut your daughter's cord?" Searra asked.

"Go ahead," Li-ara encouraged. "Go meet your daughter. You've been waiting a long time to greet her." Hunter hesitated. "Go. I'm okay."

Nervously, he slid out from behind his wife and walked to the side of the bed. There, lying on the bloody sheets, was a perfect baby girl with blond curly hair.

Searra led him closer. "Tie a string around the cord here and another one about an inch away, then cut the cord between the two," she instructed. His hands shaking slightly, the new father tied the cord and cut it. Searra wrapped the newborn in a blanket and handed her to her father. Looking at the small person in his arms, a wave of joy like nothing he experienced before flowed through his body. He dropped to his knees and sobbed.

They named her Nataa-a, which meant "Little One" in Kolorian. Li-ara thought the name fitting since Hunter called her that each day throughout the pregnancy. J'Dar wanted to call her "Trouble," but he got outvoted.

The next year, Li-ara delivered twin sons. Hunter attended their delivery as well and cut their cords. To make J'Dar feel part of the celebration, they allowed him to name his new brothers. He chose Kolo and Huns after the Huntsman he missed. J'Dar often wondered if the Huntsman ever thought of him in his adventures across the galaxy.

Thirteen months after the twins were born, Li-ara felt the signs again - the nausea in the mornings, the aching fatigue, the quiet tug low in her belly. She didn't want to believe it at first, but the truth was unmistakable. She was pregnant. Again.

She sat alone on the edge of the bed, one hand pressed to her stomach, her mind spinning. She and Hunter had agreed four children were enough. Their life was already overflowing, teetering on the edge of chaos. Another child wasn't part of the plan.

She didn't know how to tell him.

These days, she rarely saw the man she'd married. Not really. He was home, yes, but more like a shadow of himself. Distant. Quiet. Frowning more often than not. He left early for the forests, claiming he was hunting, but returned with little or nothing, his boots heavy with dust and his eyes empty. And at night, he no longer reached for her. He turned his back to her in bed and fell into a silence she couldn't break.

Li-ara carried the home now, every corner of it pressing against her shoulders. The three little ones seemed to need her all at once. J'Dar was growing more independent, but still with the wide-eyed wonder and impulsiveness of a child. The twins were a whirlwind - into everything, climbing, tumbling, racing through rooms as if powered by lightning. When one was laughing, the other was crying. And when both were silent, she worried more. Nataa-a remained attached to her, nursing endlessly, her tiny hands always searching, grasping for warmth, for comfort, for home. There were moments when Li-ara couldn't even remember the last time she'd stood without someone pulling on her skirt or calling her name.

The housework never ended. Dishes reappeared the moment she washed them. Crumbs multiplied like seeds in the wind. Dirty clothes stacked themselves overnight, as if spun from the air. She moved through the hours on muscle memory alone - sweeping, stirring, rocking, folding - her body aching in places that had long stopped complaining and simply endured.

One or two kind women from the village came daily to help, bringing warm hands, kind eyes, and a little peace, but it barely dented the chaos. The moment they left, it all returned, rushing back in like a tide Li-ara could never hold back.

Li-ara missed the canines. Missed their warmth, their eager eyes, their slobbery kisses. Once, they'd been her comfort, her companions, her joy. Now, they were Hunter's responsibility, and he barely tolerated them. He fed them, trained them, maintained the motions of care, but there was no affection in his touch. No softness in his voice.

When he wasn't hunting, he brooded. Quiet and closed. His presence filled the cabin with a heaviness. He snapped more often, wandered the woods longer, came home late without explanation. He didn't smile anymore. Didn't laugh. Didn't speak to J'Dar unless necessary. And even then, his words were clipped, cold.

Li-ara felt the distance growing between them. And though he never said the words, she saw it in his eyes, that quiet accusation, the bitterness he carried like a shadow. He blamed her. She was sure of it. So, she told no one about the baby growing inside her.

Then, one morning, a ship landed in the fields outside the village. Sleek. Dark. Clearly designed for speed and pursuit.

A Bounty Hunter.

For the first time in months, Li-ara witnessed a flicker of something familiar in Hunter's eyes, something sharp and alive. Without a word, he broke into a run, boots pounding the earth as he rushed toward the ship and the figure stepping down from its ramp. From where she stood, Li-ara couldn't make out the conversation, but she didn't need to.

She saw it in the way he leaned in, rapid-fire questions spilling from his lips. The way his posture shifted, shoulders loosening, face lifted to the light like a man remembering how to breathe. His eyes gleamed with something dangerously close to hope. No, not hope. It was longing. Then, Li-ara heard him laugh. Actually laugh. It was a sound she hadn't heard in months. And a chill ran through her body.

The Bounty Hunter stayed for two days. And in those two days, Hunter barely left his side. The two walked the perimeter, talked late into the night, huddled over datapads, sketched out plans in the dirt like boys mapping dreams. Whatever bond they shared, it ran deep.

Li-ara watched from a distance, her hands busy with tasks no one offered to help with, her presence forgotten in the wake of whatever world had just stepped off that ship.

And then, just as quickly as he came, the stranger left. His ship rose into the sky and sped off on another adventure.

Hunter didn't move for a long time. Just stood there, staring into the sky. When he finally turned back toward the house, the light was gone from his eyes. In its place, an ache, a need.

And though he said nothing, Li-ara understood.

She had seen the look before - in the mirror, the day he stopped looking at her the same way.

With the Bounty Hunter's departure, Hunter grew quieter, his silences heavier, his temper shorter. He woke one morning in a foul mood. He snapped at J'Dar over nothing, barked at the twins for being too loud, and when little Nataa-a soiled her pants, he lost control.

His hand came down. For the first time ever, he swatted the bottom of his Little One.

"I can't believe you spanked her for that," Li-ara yelled, rushing into the room and scooping Nataa-a into her arms as she cried uncontrollably. "She's just a little girl."

"Well, maybe if you didn't baby her so much, she'd grow up and learn to use the facilities."

"Maybe if you stuck around the house more and helped, I could properly train her."

"Listen, I shovel enough damn canine shit around here. I will not come home and wipe her butt too. I didn't sign up for that."

"Really, Hunter? What did you sign up for?"

"Not this. I don't even feel like we're a team anymore. You told me you would help construct those new pens, but you haven't pounded one damn nail. All you do in your spare time is sleep."

Li-ara's lips puckered. Her face reddened. "I'm tired all the time because . . ."

"Because what? Unhappy? Lazy?"

Her eyes narrowed. "Because I'm five months pregnant."

Hunter's eyes grew wide. His nostrils flared. "Fantastic. Another mouth to feed. So, another two years before you start working with the canines. Do you even plan on still training and breeding them?"

"Of course I do. Raising and training the dogs is what we dreamed of doing together."

"Together? Do you know anything about my dreams?"

"I know you wanted to go with that Hunter."

"Why wouldn't I? He has no responsibilities and can go and come as he wants. And he doesn't shovel canine shit."

"Is that what you want, Hunter? To go and come as you want? Be my guest. Perhaps you can ask him to come back and take you with him."

"Don't go putting words in my mouth. I didn't say I wanted to go."

"You didn't need to. I saw the desire in your eyes. Do you remember, JD, the day you asked me to be your wife? I told you a life like this wouldn't be enough for you. And you said J'Dar and I would always be enough. But we aren't, are we? None of this is enough. Is it?" Hunter kept silent. "IS IT?"

"No," Hunter whispered.

Tears filled Li-ara's eyes. She never thought she'd hear Hunter say she and his children weren't enough. "Get out."

"Li-ara."

"GET OUT!" Li-ara yelled. "And never come back."

"Fine," Hunter screamed. Grabbing his backpack and weapons, he stormed out the door. Kii ran after him. "Kii, stay the hell away from me."

He walked towards the mountain, unsure where he was going, anywhere but home. When the night became too dark to see, he climbed up into a tree and went to sleep. The next morning, he continued his journey deep into the wilderness. For two days, he wandered, then stopped at the edge of a cliff above a deep, clear lake.

His eyes opened wide. "This is where my ship is buried," Hunter whispered, his voice barely audible over the wind. The words hung in the air like a confession. Was this his plan all along? To take his ship and disappear into the stars? To vanish the way he always had - silent, unseen, untethered?

Remembering his armor lay buried in the cave nearby, Hunter took off at a dead sprint. He stumbled into the dark hollow, unconcerned for what might be inside. His heart pounded, his breath sharp in his chest. Dropping to his knees, he slammed his palms into the ground and began clawing at the sand with frantic fingers.

The sound of an animal hissing, scampering around the cave went ignored. He dug faster, tossing fistfuls of earth behind him, sweat beading on his brow. His breath came in short, ragged gasps. Panic coiled in his gut.

"Where are you?" he screamed.

Then, his fingers brushed cloth.

A sound escaped his lips, half relief, half desperation. He yanked the bundle from the earth and unfurled it on the stone floor, dirt flying as he unwrapped the precious cloth.

He stared in disbelief. Everything was there. The helmet. The chest plate. Shoulder guards. Leg armor. And finally, the wristband.

His past. His protection. The pieces of a man who'd once belonged nowhere and liked it that way.

Slowly, he reached into his backpack and withdrew the armband he'd brought home that first day, disguised as JD. He held it for a long moment, turning it in his hands, his reflection warped in the polished surface. With a soft tap of his finger, it came alive. Lights flickered, humming like a memory awake.

He clamped the band around his forearm. A soft hiss sounded, announcing its attachment.

Hunter rose and stepped out of the cave, each footfall heavier than the last. He moved toward the cliff's edge, to the place where the lake glittered far below in the fading light. His ship was down there. Waiting. One command, one press of a few buttons, and it would rise again - break the surface like a beast returning from slumber. He could be gone before nightfall.

Free.

Free from the noise. The pain. The weight of a life he didn't know how to carry.

Li-ara had told him to go. Ordered him. She didn't want him anymore. Maybe she was right.

He stood there, the wind tugging at his sleeves, staring down into the abyss where his old life slept. Wouldn't it be easier to slip back into the man he used to be? The man who never stayed long enough to be missed?

His thumb hovered over the control pad.

Why not leave?

She'd be better off without him. Wouldn't she?

His jaw clenched, and his eyes burned.

It wasn't his fault. Was it?

"Isn't it?" came a voice inside his head. "What did you expect her to say? You haven't been a husband of late. Why?"

"I don't know."

"Do you still love her?"

"Of course. Very much."

"Do you love your children?"

"Yes, more than life itself."

"Then, what is wrong?"

"I'm just so lost. I don't feel like I'm worth anything anymore."

"Your worth lies in your left pocket."

Hunter reached inside and withdrew the coin containing the likenesses of Beta and Kii on. "You can still go back, but if you push that button and bring up your ship, your life with her and your children is over."

The voice of Searra drifted across the wind. *"You must never break the bond you and Li-ara share. Your love for her is both your doom and your salvation."*

"The life of a Hunter is lonely and hard," came the Dominee's voice. *"And most die too soon. But a few, on their travels, found a different life. They removed their coverings, joined with another, had children, and lived joyful lives. The difference between them and you is that they decided and lived by their choice. Love is precious, a gift. You must now find a way to right the wrong."*

"But how? She will never forgive me for what I said," Hunter said.

The shadow of a peasant woman materialized in the water ripples below. She seemed familiar, but someone from long ago.

"Do you no longer remember your grandmother?" came a voice rising above the crash of the waves.

Hunter gasped. "Grandmother. I have not seen your face since the *Biiloot* returned me. Many times I tried to remember your face, but your features blurred over the years."

"Is this what you want for your children? For Li-ara? A memory with no face?"

"How can I face her, Grandmother? I hurt her so badly."

"By telling her the truth. Because she loves you, she will forgive you. Go. Your family needs you."

The sound of a lone canine howling averted Hunter's attention away from the waters below. In the distance stood a black canine on top of a hill, alone and in need of her pack. Hunter turned back to the water, but his grandmother was gone.

Hunter stared into the dark, clear waters below. The canine's howl sounded again, but this time its cry was lonely, forgotten. It sounded so mournful, so unloved. And he remembered what his life had been like before Li-ara, before the children.

"What's wrong with me? I'm making the same mistake I made on Proxima Prime when I left Li-ara. I must go back. Li-ara is the only thing I ever want, ever need." Re-wrapping his armor and burying it again under sand and rock, he grabbed his belongings and darted down the mountain. The journey there took three days. Now that he knew where he was, the trip home would only take hours. He would arrive home shortly after nightfall.

Halfway down the mountain, Hunter spotted another canine. The animal waited ten yards away, blocking his path. Was this the canine he met at the cave? Were others with it? He could defeat one, perhaps two, but not more. He couldn't die before he told Li-ara how sorry he was.

The canine took one step forward and sniffed the air. Hunter drew his weapon and cocked it. He raised his knife slightly out of his boot for a more natural grasp. Bending one knee, he prepared to fight.

The canine charged straight toward him, tail whipping like a flag, barking with wild, unmistakable joy. It was Kii. Behind him, two riders thundered into view on galloping steeds. Hunter squinted through the dust. He recognized one as Piinew from the village and the other as J'Dar.

"Dad," J'Dar shouted as he leapt from his mount and ran to his father. "I was afraid we'd never find you. Mom's hurt really bad."

Hunter directed his attention to Piinew for an explanation. "We don't know what happened. J'Dar found her at the bottom of the hill, bleeding profusely. Searra fears she will lose the baby. Everyone has been out trying to find you before it's too late."

"Too late?" The words resounded in Hunter's mind, distant at first, then deafening. A suffocating weight pressed down on his ribs, and panic surged up his throat like bile. His heart thudded once, twice, and then felt as if it were gripped by something ancient and merciless. The icy hand of death clenched around it, squeezing with finality.

"She might not survive," Piinew said.

"I have to go back and tell her I was wrong, that I'm sorry."

Piinew jumped off his steed and handed Hunter the reins. "Take mine and ride as if a hellion canine chased you. I will ride with J'Dar."

"Thank you." Hunter clasped the villager's shoulder. He leapt onto the steed's back.

The ride blurred into wind and dust. At a full gallop, it took three hours, three relentless, bone-jarring hours with fear gnawing at Hunter's gut the entire way.

He didn't slow when the house came into view. Didn't breathe. He charged straight to the back door, reins slipping through his fingers as he leapt from the saddle before the steed had fully stopped. His boots hit the ground hard, body already moving.

And nearly collided with Searra. emerging from the side door. She carried a small bundle in her hands.

"I'm sorry, Hunter," Searra said, tears on her cheeks. "The child did not survive."

"Was the child a boy or a girl?"

"A girl."

"A girl? Another little one." He stepped forward; the blood drained from his face as he held out his arms. "Give her to me. I need to hold her."

"I would not advise it."

"This is my fault, Searra. I want to see the daughter who paid the price for my selfishness and ignorance."

Searra stepped forward. She placed the tiny bundle into the Huntsman's hands. He felt no weight. The child barely filled the breadth of his palm.

Hunter looked down, and with trembling fingers, he pulled back the edge of the cloth. The covering slipped away like mist, revealing a fragile, perfect form … of his daughter.

Her fingers were no longer than rice grains, delicate and still. Her toes curled like unopened flower buds, no larger than gilliander seeds. A soft, reddish fuzz crowned her tiny head like the first light of dawn. And on her lips, a smile. Small. Serene. Eternal. A smile that would never laugh.

Hunter collapsed to his knees, pulling his daughter to his chest with a gentleness born of utter devastation. A sound tore from his throat. Not a cry, but a raw, ragged scream of anguish that shattered the stillness, a sound so violent it didn't sound natural. He rocked back and forth, clutching the tiny body, over and over, as if motion might breathe life back into her. As if his love alone could will her eyes open. But her body remained still.

She was already gone.

Tears poured from his eyes, unchecked, hot and blinding, dripping onto her soft cheek. He pressed his forehead to hers. His body convulsed, wracked by sobs so violent it felt like his grief had a life of its own, clawing its way out, piece by shattered piece.

This was his daughter. The child he would never hold in the sunlight. Never teach to run. Never hear her laugh. Never hear her call him PaPa. The future he'd dreamed of was gone before it even began. And still, he rocked her, whispering broken words into her silence, holding on to the only moment he'd ever have.

Searra waited, wanting to give the Huntsman time to grieve, but knowing Li-ara's time was short. She allowed him six minutes to grieve before tapping his shoulder. "Hunter, Li-ara still lives. For how much longer, I cannot say. If you want to speak with her one last time, you need to go to her now. I'll take care of the baby."

Hunter didn't move at first. He couldn't. His arms clung to the bundle as if letting go would tear his soul from his chest. He looked down once more at his daughter's perfect face and, through the blur of tears, nodded. His fingers lingered on the cloth as Searra slowly took the baby from his arms.

He tried to stand, but his legs had no strength. Two village men dashed forward and helped him to his feet. Fearing he would collapse, they each held an arm and escorted the despondent Huntsman up the back steps. In the kitchen, blood-soaked women carried bundles of bright red bedding, rushing here and there. So much blood.

Somehow, the villagers dragged him to the bedroom, his feet barely lifting off the floor. Li-ara lay in a bed of fresh bedding. Her skin was bone-white, nearly translucent. She looked like she was already fading, already drifting somewhere far away. Her breathing came in shallow, ragged pulls. A fresh cast wrapped her left arm, splinted tight, and raised on a pillow.

Broken. Like everything else.

Like *him*.

The sight of her hit harder than any wound he'd ever endured. The room spun, and he staggered forward, legs trembling. The men rushed him to the chair beside her bed and helped him sit before he collapsed entirely. Without a word, they left, quietly closing the door behind them.

The silence wasn't empty, it was consuming, swallowing him whole, pulling him under, stripping him bare, until he couldn't feel anything but the echo of what he was losing.

Hunter reached for her hand, cold and still in his. He pressed it to his forehead, his lips, his heart. Searching for warmth. For hope. For something to hold on to.

There was nothing.

He began to rock, slow and rhythmic, the way a child does when grief is too big to name and there's no one left to make it stop. His body shook with the last of his sobs, grief spilling out of him like floodwaters breaching a dam.

"I'm sorry," he whispered hoarsely. "Please, wake up and yell at me. Tell me I was wrong, that I ruined everything."

His voice broke. "I know I did."

He clenched her hand, head resting against the edge of the bed. And there, with the weight of loss pressing down like a stone, he drifted into exhausted, grief-stained sleep.

Hunter woke two hours later. On trembling legs, he stood and kissed his beloved on the lips. Too weak to remain standing, he crashed back into the chair.

"Li-ara, I am so sorry. Please don't leave me. You are my life. I can't go on without you." His torment bursting through again, he said no more and wept uncontrollably.

For two days, Hunter remained at her side, holding her hand, refusing to eat or allow anyone to comfort him. Sometimes, his sorrow lessened enough to permit him to beg Li-ara to stay; other times, it consumed his soul.

A soft knock at the door broke the deathly silence. J'Dar poked his head in." Dad, can I come in?"

Hunter nodded. J'Dar burst through the door and ran to his father. Hunter laid Li-ara's hand on the bed and reached out, taking his precious firstborn into his arms. Together, they cried.

"Is Mom going to die?" J'Dar asked. Hunter sat him on his lap. He remembered the last time J'Dar asked the same question. He had an answer for his son then – but this time, he had none.

"I don't know, Son. I keep telling her how much we all love her and need her. I keep hoping she will hear me and come back."

"Did you tell her you were sorry? *Catoo* said females like to hear that."

"I have told her at least a million times. Are your brothers and sister okay?"

"You don't have to worry, Dad, I'm making sure everyone is being taken care of."

Searra poked her head inside the door. "J'Dar, come. Leave your father be."

J'Dar climbed off his father's lap and kissed him goodbye. Upon reaching the door, he paused. "I'm glad you told her you were sorry. I think she heard you."

Against all the odds, Li-ara hung on, fighting to remain in the land of the living. Hunter prayed to every deity he ever heard about, begging each for their help. When he had no more hope, the impossible happened - Li-ara squeezed his hand. "Hunter?"

"I'm here, Li-ara." He raised her hand to his lips again. "Come back. You can do it."

Her eyes fluttered, then opened. At first, she didn't recognize him. The man sitting at her bedside appeared hollowed, unkempt, and unmoored. His face was pale and drawn, the skin beneath his eyes dark with grief and sleeplessness. His lids were swollen, his cheeks puffy from weeping. Red veins laced his eyes. Day-old stubble shadowed his jaw, rough and patchy, making him look older than he was, tired in a way that had nothing to do with time. His hair was a tangled mess, fallen across his forehead in wild strands like he'd run his hands through it a thousand times in anguish. His clothes were wrinkled, sweat-stained, and carelessly thrown on, whatever he'd been wearing when the world fell apart.

But then she saw it. Beneath the wreckage of the man he had been was Hunter.

Her husband. Broken. And waiting. Waiting for her.

"The baby wasn't your fault, Hunter," Li-ara whispered. Hunter bit his lip and lowered his face. Li-ara reached out and placed one hand on his chin. "Look at me, Hunter." He didn't move. "Look at me." Slowly, the Huntsman raised his gaze. "This wasn't your fault."

"Yes, it was."

"No, Hunter. It wasn't, and it wasn't mine. Something was wrong with the baby. Nature has a way of taking care of sick infants."

"I am so sorry, Li-ara, for what I said. Can you ever forgive me?"

"What we said to one another is behind us and will be forgotten. All that matters is we are together."

"I thought I heard voices in here," Searra said as she came through the door. "What a joyous day today is. You are with us once more. Hunter, if you would wait in the other room, we will change her bedding and bedgown. When we're done, you can join her for a bowl of soup."

Li-ara gave him a chastising look. "You haven't eaten in days, have you?"

"I couldn't leave you." He turned to Searra. "And I won't leave her now. Tell your women they can do their work with me here."

"I thought you'd say that," Searra laughed, shuffling three village women in.

Hunter stood to the side while the woman changed Li-ara's clothing, attended to her abrasions, and brushed her hair. When they finished, he lifted her and sat with her in his arms as the women changed the bedding. He was alarmed by how light she was. Once the bed was ready, he carefully laid her inside, piling pillows behind her back so she remained in a sitting position. Being mindful of the broken arm, he tucked the sheets around her thin body.

Searra returned with two bowls of enriched soup to help both regain their strength. Without hesitation, Hunter picked up Li-ara's bowl and slipped the broth into the bowl of her spoon.

"Hunter, you don't have to feed me."

"I am simply returning the favor of when you fed me."

After three mouthfuls, Li-ara shook her head. "No more for me until you take three mouthfuls."

"I will eat after you do. Now open."

"No. I know you, BiiJun D'Kolor. You will disregard your health and take care of me."

Hunter tilted his head curiously. "You've never called me by my Huntsman name before."

"No, and I apologize for that. You are BiiJun D'Kolor, a noble and brave member of the TriiBone Clan, son of Kolor and Meg, an elite Bounty Hunter of the highest caliber. I have not recognized the true Hunter, the male I fell deeply in love with since we arrived here. Because you are my husband and the father of my children, I allowed you to hide, but no more. You are, first and foremost, a Huntsman, and I will never forget that again, nor will I allow you to. To protect us from those who may hunt you, I turned a blind eye to your hiding your true self, the Huntsman you are. No more. From this moment forward, they will know you for who and what you are. I will openly call you Hunter, and the world will know that it is your name." Hunter prepared to object. "And do not say it is too dangerous. You cannot be a whole person if half of you must be hidden from the world." Deep down, Hunter knew she was right. "And you will begin the *Gaball* starting tomorrow. You cannot be a Huntsman without the *Gaball's* exercises and training."

"You are familiar with the *Gaball?*" Hunter asked. "I have never told you about the training rituals."

"For now, just know that I know the *Gaball* and its importance." Li-ara smiled. She wondered what her husband would say if he knew the Dominee came to her in her state of unconsciousness and explained the importance of the *Gaball.*

"When and how do we tell J'Dar?" a concerned father asked.

"He must be the first one we tell," Li-ara stated. "I think we should tell him the truth before today ends. He will be excited to learn you are the Hunter he loves."

"Do you think he'll be upset that we kept the truth of who you really are from him?"

"Maybe a little. But when you explain to him we kept your secret to keep him and his siblings safe, he will understand."

"What of the villagers? How do we tell them?"

"I think we should talk to Searra," Li-ara said. "She's always known the truth of who you are. As the leader of the *Genubite* High Council, she will understand the best way to divulge your actual identity."

For three hours, the two made plans, revised them, then made more plans for their future. Hunter described in explicit detail how his training would begin and how he would teach J'Dar the disciplinary practices of a Huntsman. Already a twinkle filled his eyes, and his voice was full of excitement. For the first time in many months, Hunter felt alive.

17 THE KI-WAN

Li-ara was true to her word. She hired three villagers to clean the stalls, feed, bathe, and groom the animals, and complete everyday activities. Two women came to clean, cook, garden, and take care of the children.

She and Hunter told J'Dar the truth. J'Dar was ecstatic and gave Hunter a big kiss and several hugs. He always felt guilty for loving the Huntsman as much as he did. Now that the Huntsman was his father, his torment ceased.

"Am I a Huntsman too?" J'Dar immediately asked.

The villagers accepted the news with awe, wonder, and a bit of fear. They all recognized Hunter to be a just man, but Huntsmen had a reputation for living by a different creed, a different standard. At first, they were a little apprehensive about dealing with him, but soon they accepted his news and regarded him once again as one of their own.

One of the most significant modifications was Hunter's morning routine. Each day, he rose early and performed the Gaball. The ritual gave the Huntsmen an advantage over their competition by sharpening their self-defense movements and instincts. It strengthened their bodies and focused their minds. The teachings also instilled in the warrior a sense of compassion, empathy, and respect for all life.

Hunter had been a lost soul without the *Gaball*. Within days of engaging in the ancient practice, Li-ara witnessed a dramatic transformation in him. Once more, he had focus and direction. He became the Hunter she nursed back to health and fell in love with.

"Can you see me okay?" Hunter shouted from the side yard outside the bedroom window.

"Yes, I can see you fine. You're sure I'm allowed to watch you perform the Gaball?"

Hunter dashed to the window, leaning inside. "Most definitely. There is nothing in our laws that prohibits such an observation. Plus, by watching me, you will learn and be able to participate mentally."

"Mentally?"

"Yes. That is the beauty of the Gaball. Although meant to be performed physically, you can still reap its rewards by performing it mentally. Many Huntsmen who ascertained old age were able to remain strong by doing so."

On the second day of training, J'Dar joined his father. Hunter patiently showed his son the correct way to stand, the words to say, and how to execute the moves.

"Me too, me too," came a tiny voice on the third morning. Nataa-a came running into the yard. "Me learn with J'Dar."

"I, not me," Li-ara shouted.

Hunter smiled. Li-ara didn't think she had ever seen her husband this happy before.

"Okay, we're going to do some warm-ups first. You watch what J'Dar and I do, then repeat it with us. Don't worry about the words. Those will come later."

By the end of the week, the twins discovered the activity and created havoc. Often, in the middle of a challenging exercise, one twin would grab Hunter's legs and tumble him to the ground. He would pretend to be under attack, and all four children would pile on top of him.

Li-ara loved hearing Hunter's boisterous laughs as he rolled around with his children. When the attack subsided, Hunter stood, gave the twins a small swat on the bottom for interrupting his routine, then looked through the window and blew her a kiss. She blew one back. Silently, she thanked the Dominee for giving her the solution to Hunter's faltering.

"What, may I ask, are you doing?" Li-ara said as Hunter rushed around the room gathering pillows and a blanket. He walked over to the window and dropped them onto the porch.

"It's time for you to get some real fresh air," Hunter said." Today, you will watch from the porch."

He scurried out to the porch and arranged the pillows on the bench. He then ran back inside and lifted Li-ara into his arms and carried her to the waiting bench. Once he was sure her seating was correct, he tucked the blanket around her and handed her a hot cup of tea.

"Comfortable?"

"Yes, thank you."

Hunter leaned down and gave his wife a long, passionate kiss.

"Yuk. Gross," J'Dar and Nataa-a shouted, each tugging on their father's leg. "You don't have time for such ickiness." Their objection only made Hunter lengthen the kiss.

On rare occasions, the small group performed for thirty to forty minutes before the twins crashed their party.

"Excuse me, Hunter," one of the village women said as Hunter prepared to start his morning routine. "Piinew is asking if he might speak to you before you start."

Hunter looked at Li-ara. She shrugged her shoulders.

"Ah, sure, send him over." Hunter watched the villager walk towards him, his step happy and a little apprehensive at the same time. "What can I do for you, Piinew?"

"I have heard that you have begun practicing the Huntsman ritual of the Gaball."

"That is correct," Hunter said.

"I was wondering if you would teach me."

"You want to learn the *Gaball*? Why?"

"I want to become a better man, like you have. We've all seen the change in you, both physically and spiritually. I wish for such a transformation."

"I do not know if the *Gaball* can transform you, Piinew, but I owe you much for finding me that day Li-ara miscarried. Had you not, I don't think I would have returned in time. If you really want to learn and are willing to come each morning, I will teach you."

"I promise to be here."

"Then, please, stand behind me. Repeat what we do."

The next morning, Li-ara's eyes widened as Piinew not only returned but brought another three men with him. Each took a stance behind Hunter and the children, repeating the moves.

Li-ara grew in strength each day, as did the size of Hunter's group. Each morning, Li-ara eagerly counted how many new members joined the group. After three weeks, his tiny group of two had grown to a group of thirty-eight.

To keep the toddlers from interrupting their sessions, the caregivers kept them occupied in the house during the exercises. This allowed Li-ara to take part in the *Gaball* without the threat of an accidental fall caused by the twins.

Hunter performed a special second set in the late afternoon, one designed especially for the little ones to give them a chance to interrupt and tackle their father and J'Dar to the ground. Li-ara loved these sessions and always watched from the safety of her chair, as her husband insisted.

One day, a group of five men came up the hill from the west. Li-ara did not recognize their faces or distinctive dress. Her curiosity overflowing, she pounced on Hunter the moment he entered the house.

"Who are those strangers?"

"They are Utes. Their village lies twenty miles to the west. KyRey told me they are distant relatives to his clan, but the two have not been within fifty feet of each other for over fifty years."

"Why are they here?"

Hunter chuckled. "Believe it or not, they, too, want to learn *Gaball*."

"Why?"

"He said the same thing they all say: He knows of the Huntsmen, their ways, and disciplines. He believes his people will benefit from learning *Gaball*."

"And what did you say?"

"I said we start at six."

"They're making a twenty-mile hike back and forth every day?"

"No. The spokesman told me they are camped downstream with their families. He also said that talk about me and my exercises is spreading across the villages. More are coming from as far away as the *Tulite* Mountains."

"The *Tulite* Mountains? Hunter, they must be what, over a thousand *cams* away from here?"

"Yes."

Four days later, Hunter and Li-ara woke to the sight of six tents pitched halfway between the hill and the stream. Hunter recognized the enormous red tents embellished with one huge yellow sun painted on its side. They were Ki-Wan, a Hunting clan similar to the Huntsmen and renowned for their excellent riding of *Tyback* steeds.

"Well, I believe this will be an interesting day."

"Why? Who are they?"

"Ki-Wan, a warrior and hunting clan. I flew over their village the first time I landed here. They live past the desert. Even by steed, the journey would take at least two weeks."

"I think you will need a bigger lawn," Li-ara laughed.

"They don't like farmers."

Li-ara's eyes widened. "That might be a problem since the majority in your group are farmers."

"I thought the same. Guess I'll walk down and find out what they want." He kissed Li-ara goodbye. "Don't overdo training the pups this morning."

Taking his coffee, Hunter walked down the hill to the Ki-Wan encampment. "Do you speak *Genubite*?" Hunter asked the warrior standing at the entrance to the campsite. The male appeared to be around eighteen years of age. He was tall, taller than Hunter. His stance commanded admiration, respect, and some fear. Two impressive guns were strapped across his chest. A large hunting knife rested in his belt with a second one hidden in his boot. In his hand, he held the most beautiful spear Hunter had seen. He would have a rough time beating this opponent.

The male muttered something that sounded like *Genubite,* but Hunter didn't understand. His greeter motioned for Hunter to follow. When they reached the largest of the tents, the warrior lifted the flap and gestured for Hunter to enter. Once his eyes adjusted to the low light, he noted twelve Ki-Wan sitting in a circle. To his surprise, KyRey sat among them, talking in sign language.

"KyRey, you can speak to the Ki-Wan?" Hunter asked.

"Both of our spoken languages altered since our families split apart, but we possess the same finger language. This is *Umae.* He is the eldest son

241

of Chieftain *Omeeday*. Like the Utes and the other clans, he heard of the mighty Hunter who came to Orallia and trains in *Gaball*. He, too, wants to learn."

"Explain to him the rules and that aggression of any kind towards another clan will not be tolerated. If disagreements erupt, I will disband the group instantly, and no one will learn *Gaball*. Tell him when we train, he and his men do as I say."

KyRey translated. "Umae understands. He states he is not here to cause problems. He asks if women may train as well."

"Yes. Women are welcome. The *Gaball* does not care what your gender is." KyRey translated.

"Did he say what he hopes to learn? His people are respected for being exceptional Hunters. What can I teach his people?"

"For the past six months, *Rogarian* Traders have landed throughout their area, stealing youthful women and children."

"I thought the Huntsmen wiped out all the *Rogarian* Traders," Hunter stated, trying to keep his voice calm. He wondered if these *Rogarian* scum were related to the outlaws who kidnapped him and sold him into bondage.

"They have resurfaced," KyRey replied.

"Ask him how many."

"They counted twenty-two in their hunting parties."

"Were any of their children taken?"

"Not from their village, but three disappeared from two villages over."

"Tell him training begins in fifteen minutes."

Hunter hurried from the small encampment and jogged up the hill. When he arrived at the top, he witnessed J'Dar sitting on the steps, waiting to begin the *Gaball*. He realized that he was younger than J'Dar when the Traders stole him, which sent a chill down his spine.

———————

"I help?" Umae asked as he walked into the kennel, pointing his index finger at his chest.

"Can you train canines?" Li-ara asked. The Ki-Wan stared at her, trying to figure out what she said. She thought for a minute, then pointed at Umae. "You." She pointed to his head. "Know." She petted the young animal. "Canine?"

242

Umae touched his chest, his head, and the pup before shaking his head negatively.

"You want to learn." Li-ara did not know how to make a gesture for the word "learn," and Umae's puzzled expression confirmed he didn't understand. "You sit here and wait for me." She took his hand, led him to a chair, and gently pressed on his shoulders. "Sit."

The Ki-Wan burst into laughter, pointing at the puppy who had obediently sat at Li-ara's command. Encouraged, Li-ara dashed outside, scanning the area until she spotted KyRey. Without waiting for protest, she grabbed his arm and hauled him back toward the kennel where Umae still waited, watching the puppy stalking a beetle.

"KyRey, can you ask him if he wants to learn how to train canines?"

KyRey's fingers moved rapidly, translating Li-ara's words. Umae quickly signed back. "He says yes. Word of the great Huntsman's wife and her ability to tame the wild canine reached their village. With such canines, he can defeat those who steal their children."

"Explain to him I will teach him what I do, but the training takes many years to train a canine."

"He asks how many years."

"Two to four."

"He says having a protective canine in four years is better than no canine at all."

"That it is."

For the next hour and a half, KyRey translated as Umae and Li-ara discussed the mechanics of turning a vicious predator into a willing companion.

"So, here you both are," Hunter said as he walked into the kennel. "Umae, you and I were scheduled to practice the recent move I taught this morning. And Li-ara, Nataa-a is waiting impatiently for you to braid her hair. I tried, but she told me my fingers were too fat to fold her hair correctly."

"Just the person I need," Li-ara shouted, jumping up and running to her husband. She kissed him on the cheek and grabbed his arm, leading him over to where the other two men sat.

"Umae, you certainly put my wife in a wonderful mood," Hunter commented upon seeing the hop in his wife's step and joy on her face. "Might I inquire how you managed such a feat?"

"So you know, Hunter, I had nothing to do with this crazy plan," KyRey hastily said. "I'm only the translator."

Hunter's one brow lifted in quiet accusation. Lia-ara was up to something, and he already knew he wasn't going to like it. "What crazy plan?"

"Now, don't say anything until you listen to the entire idea," Li-ara said, pulling Hunter down to sit beside her on the crate. "Umae asked if I would show him how to train wild canines so he can take the knowledge back to his village. I said I would gladly teach him, but the minimal training takes about six months, to which he said no problem."

So far, so good, Hunter thought. Somewhere, he was sure there was a "But".

"But then I explained to him that to learn the entire process, he needed to start with newborn pups, and we don't have any. The few pups I do have are already promised, plus the youngest are at least three months old. No females are pregnant, and I wasn't planning on breeding any of the females for the next eight months. So, Umae came up with an ingenious plan, one I've wanted to try."

Hunter knew the direction the discussion was headed - the capture of wild canines. Li-ara wanted native canines to enhance their captive animals' gene pool. She also wanted to determine the extent of the wild canines' intelligence and discover if the *Genubite* stories were true.

"Umae knows where a pack of wild canines has their den. We could capture a few newborns and bring them here. It's birthing season, so they shouldn't be hard to find."

Hunter looked at Umae. "Is this really your idea, or did my beautiful wife trick you into thinking it is?"

Umae laughed when KyRey translated. "Wives do possess the ability to make us think their ideas are ours, but I assure you, Hunter, this one was mine. A breed of wild canines lives in a remote part of our forests. They possess extreme intelligence and ferocity. If she can transform one of their kind into a manageable beast like your Kii, she is as great as the winds say."

"First of all, there will be no 'we'," Hunter adamantly announced, looking directly at Li-ara. "You are still recuperating from your ordeal. And birthing season is the most dangerous time to encounter a canine. I will not allow you to go with us."

"So, you'll go?" A gigantic smile spread across his wife's face. He had fallen into her trap.

"If Umae will accompany me, I will retrieve your wild canine pups."

"Umae says it will be an honor to hunt with the great Huntsman," KyRey translated.

"There are specific rules which must be followed," Hunter said. For the next three hours, the group discussed ideas, formed and reformed plans, and agreed to leave the next day.

———————

"If you move your hook a two *damas* to the right and place it near those reeds, you'd have better luck catching something," J'Dar said to a young female standing at the stream's edge. "My name is J'Dar."

"You are the Hunter's son. You train beside him each morning. My name is Willomay. I am the daughter of Umae."

"I didn't realize any of your people spoke my language."

"My father had me learn so I can testify if he speaks the truth."

"The truth?"

"If the talker KyRey says the words correctly."

"I noticed you watching us practice the *Gaball* from behind a tree or bush sometimes. You don't have to hide. You can join us. Females can train, too."

"Oh, no, I do not believe my father would approve of such a thing."

"Are your brothers in the training group?"

"My father only has three daughters. I am the oldest."

"You should ask him. Females need to protect themselves and their families, too. If you like, I can ask my father to speak to your father about joining."

"Perhaps." Willomay's pole bent forward, almost snapping in half.

"You've caught a big one," J'Dar shouted, racing forward with his net. "I bet you caught the big eel. Dad and I have been trying to catch him for years."

Together, the two brought in the twenty-pound eel.

"I don't believe you caught him. He barely nibbles our bait, let alone takes it. What kind of bait did you use?"

"I used a special mixture we Ki-Wan make. It is a combination of rancid razorback meat with bird droppings and steed feces."

"Sounds delicious," J'Dar laughed as he helped her remove the eel from its hook.

Willomay held out the eel to J'Dar. "Here, take him to your father. If he has tried to catch him this long, the eel belongs to him."

"No, you caught him. He's yours."

"Keeping the eel would not be right. He does not belong to me."

"He doesn't belong to my father, either."

"You are right." Willomay leaned down and dropped the eel back into the stream. "He belongs to the water. He will remain in the rapids until the day your father catches him."

The journey to the Ki-Wan forest took sixteen grueling days on *Tyback* steeds. For Hunter, it was rough from the start. He'd ridden his fair share of mounts before, but nothing like these. *Tybacks* were leaner, built for endurance, more muscle than mass, and they could gallop for hours without tiring. By the end of the first day, Hunter was sore in places he didn't know existed.

It didn't take long for him to understand why the Ki-Wan were considered the best riders in the galaxy. They did everything on horseback - ate, slept, even urinated - without ever dismounting. He'd take a reliable speeder over a beast with a saddle any day.

Umae raised his hand. "We will stop here so the Hunter can water the grass." The three Ki-Wan accompanying them laughed as they dismounted their steeds.

"I can't figure out how you guys do it," Hunter said as he released his bladder. "And you say your women do it too?"

"Yes. Even our youngest can. Perhaps the mighty Huntsman is not as magnificent as we believed." Umae chuckled. "We will camp here. The first den is past the group of tall trees in the distance. We will strike tomorrow when the sun rises two *teewas*."

"So be it," Hunter replied, speaking perfect Ki-Wannsee.

He had left KyRey behind so Li-ara wouldn't be burdened with managing multiple clans, dialects, and customs alone. That choice gave him only sixteen days to learn the complex language of the Ki-Wan.

From the moment they set out, Hunter listened with fierce focus. He observed every inflection, studied their rhythm, their expressions. When he didn't understand, he used gestures. When he misspoke, he welcomed correction with humility, nodding in quiet gratitude. Words became sounds, sounds became patterns, and soon, patterns became meaning.

By the eighth day, he could hold a conversation - simple, direct, but clear. The Ki-Wan noticed.

The Huntsman's dedication especially struck Umae. Impressed by Hunter's willingness to learn their tongue, Umae offered respect in return. Without being asked, he began learning *Genubite* - slowly, carefully, sometimes laughing at his own mistakes.

The two Hunters conversed in alternating dialects: Hunter in Ki-Wannsee, Umae in *Genubite*, mirroring each other's effort with mutual pride. Their exchanges became more than communication; they became connections. By the time they reached their destination, a deep friendship had formed, tempered through language, forged through respect. For Hunter, it was more than camaraderie. It was the first true bond he had formed with another warrior since his days of training on Kolora.

And it felt like coming home.

"Shh, listen," Umae whispered as the group sat around a small fire, eating a night meal of tree jumpers and *dank* roots. The cry of a wild canine broke the stillness. "A female canine about five miles to our west. She calls to her mate, telling him to come home. She needs nourishment to make milk to feed her new pups."

"Pups?" Hunter asked. "You can tell she has pups by her howl?"

"Yes. I studied the wild canines since I was a boy. They have always fascinated me since several saved my life." Hunter gave him a curious look. "At eight, our children go off on a quest to the Bluestone Mountain. They must bring back a slice of Bluestone from which to make their first arrows."

"They go alone?"

"Yes. The journey is also a test of endurance and strength. I was on my way back, only two days away from the village, when I came across a half-grown *tumack*."

"A bear. I am very familiar with their kind."

"I was so excited about fulfilling my quest that I forgot to remain vigilant. The *tumack* was eating a steer he had killed and was startled by my sudden appearance. He attacked. Since I was surprised, the animal easily shattered my lance and grabbed me in his mouth, tossing me across the land. As I prepared to die, the barking and teeth-gnashing of wild canines filled my ears. They attacked the *tumack*, ripping open its left hump. The *tumack* ran off, abandoning me and its kill. I was certain I would now be canine food, but the leader, a beautiful black female, stood looking at me."

"She never gave the order for the others to attack. Instead, she trotted over to where my knife was thrown, picked it up, and carried the blade to where I lay. She came right up to me. Had I reached out, I could have touched her. To my disbelief, she put the knife in my lap, turned, and walked away, looking back before she disappeared into the undergrowth. Why didn't she kill me? How did she understand I needed the knife to protect myself?"

"I know of other wild canines who have displayed amazing compassion, wisdom, and intelligence," Hunter stated. "Kii often anticipates my need before I do."

"But my story doesn't end there, my friend," Umae said. "I was still two days from the village, bleeding, exhausted, with nothing but a hunk of Bluestone and a knife. I was easy prey, and every creature in that forest could smell it. But she didn't leave me. She stayed. Her pack shadowed me through the trees, silent guardians in the underbrush. Each night, I climbed into the trees to sleep, and below me, they circled and settled, forming a wall of fur and teeth between me and the dark."

"She kept me alive. And when I finally stumbled into the outskirts of the village, exhausted and half-dead, she stopped at the edge of the trees. Just once, she lifted her head and howled. Her way of saying goodbye."

"You never saw her again?"

"I spotted her many times over the years. As I grew older, so did she. One day, her reign ended when a new female defeated her and became the new dominant. I haven't seen her for the past four years. Black canines, like your Kii, are rare here on Orallia, so she was easy to identify. Our Truth-seer said I was saved because the female canine perceived in me her pack's salvation."

"Are you their salvation?"

"I don't know. But I honor her and her judgment to allow me to live. To my father's disappointment, I never hunt a canine, nor will I allow my men to. We try to avoid hunting in their territory. Whenever possible, I study them and learn their calls. But I have only studied them from afar. But, with the help of your wife, I can study them up close. I will train the wild canines in hopes of finding my connection to them and the answers I seek."

18 CANINE PUPS

Early the next morning, Hunter went over the plans with the four Ki-Wan. "As soon as the adults head out to hunt, we move in fast. We dismount, grab one or two pups, and get out. They won't leave the dens unguarded for long, and they'll be hunting close by. Expect at least one or two sentries to stay behind."

"Qua and I will tranquilize the sentries with a small arrow of sleeping juice," Umae said. "The moment they go down, move."

"Remember, an adult canine might be inside with the pups," Hunter said. "Keep alert. Inow, you take the den on the right. Umae, yours is the one on the left. I will take the one in the middle. Qua and Tamaore, you are lookouts. Whistle if any adults return. If they catch us, chances are we won't all get out alive."

"Listen for Qua's or Tamaore's alarm. The moment you hear it, stop whatever you are doing and gallop your steed out," Umae added. "Rendezvous at the big rock by the river. And remember, do not harm the adults. If they attack, use force as a last resort."

From a nearby hilltop, positioned carefully downwind from the dens, Hunter and Umae crouched low in the tall grass, spyglasses pressed to their eyes. What Hunter saw through the lens stunned him. The Ki-Wan canines had built their pupping dens unusually close together, almost as if by design. It defied the solitary nesting instincts of most wild canine species he'd studied. Umae had claimed they were as intelligent as Kii. Watching them now, Hunter began to believe it.

Two canines lingered, standing sentinel between the three dens, alert, ears twitching at every breeze. The two men watched as the rest of the pack melted into the forest, their howls fading with distance. Hunter waited until the last echo was swallowed by the trees. Then, he gave a sharp nod to Umae and Qua.

Without a word, both raised their bows. Two strings tightened. Two arrows flew. Silent. Precise.

The sentries' ears twitched at the faint whistle slicing through the still air. The darker one rose, head tilted, nostrils flaring as it tried to pinpoint the sound. Then came a sharp yip as the first arrow struck home, thudding into its flank. The second followed two heartbeats later, burying itself in the other sentry. Both collapsed into the grass, eyes fluttering shut.

With a swift motion, Hunter circled his hand through the air, signaling the team to move. The riders responded instantly, spurring their steeds down the slope.

At full speed, they reached their marks in seconds. Each rider leapt from their mount mid-stride, landing hard and sliding across the dirt. Without hesitation, they thrust their arms into the narrow tunnels, groping for the squirming pups hidden below.

Qua and Tamaore remained mounted, circling into position between the dens. From their saddles, they stood high in the stirrups, bodies tense, eyes scanning the shadows, ears tuned to the silence.

Umae was the first to reach into a den. He gently pulled out a squirming pup and set it aside. Then he reached in again, deeper this time, and emerged with a rare black newborn nestled in his gloved grip. The den's remaining pups snapped at his hands, snarling in tiny, toothless fury. But they were just out of reach, and no matter how Umae angled his arm, he couldn't reach further.

Inow, crouched at his den, grasped a pup by the tail and began dragging it up the narrow tunnel. The small black ball of fur squirmed and let out a piercing squeal that shattered the silence. Inow froze, debating. Should he continue pulling or let it go before the noise attracted unwanted attention? He released his grip, but his actions came too late. From the tree line, three adult canines burst into the clearing. They slammed into Qua and his steed, taking both down in a flurry of snarls and flashing teeth.

Hunter sprang to his feet, but a massive female crashed into him first, her jaws clamping down on his forearm. He grunted in pain, using the injured limb to hold her back just long enough to reach his belt. His fingers found the hilt of his knife. With a desperate thrust, he drove the blade into her chest, twisting until her body went limp.

He had no time to recover. Another canine hit him from behind, knocking him hard to his knees. But Hunter used the momentum. Gritting his teeth, he shifted his weight and flipped the snarling beast over his shoulder, sending it crashing across the clearing.

"Get out of here," Hunter thundered.

A chorus of blood-curdling screams tore through the clearing as five canines descended on Inow. Fur and flesh blurred in a frenzy of snarling jaws and raking claws. Blood sprayed in violent bursts, painting the trees, the dirt - everything. His body thrashed beneath them as they ripped him apart.

Hunter didn't hesitate. He vaulted onto his steed, raised his weapon, and fired. The shot rang out like a thunderclap, merciful and final. Inow's agony ended with the pull of a trigger.

Umae tried to keep hold of the black pup, but it wiggled out of his grasp. Snatching the first pup, he leapt over the back of one canine as it charged, and onto the back of his steed. With the pup in his arm, he galloped away, Inow's animal running beside him.

As Tamaore galloped past the chaos, a flash of movement caught his eye. Two pups, one black, one tawny, sat just outside their den, frozen in fear. He yanked the reins hard, wheeling his steed around. With a burst of speed, he leapt the animal clean over two canines. Mid-air, he twisted in the saddle, swung his leg around, and leaned dangerously low over the side. In one sweeping motion, he snatched both pups, one in each arm, and righted himself in the saddle.

Without breaking stride, Tamaore veered wide around the pack and surged after Umae and Hunter, hooves thundering beneath him. But the move cost him. Three canines gave chase, closing the distance fast. They lunged from the side. One clamped onto the steed's flank, another tore at Tamaore's leg, raking it open with savage claws. Blood soaked his pants.

Clenching the steed tight between his knees, he shoved the lighter pup into a sack strapped to his belt. With his free hand, he drew his stun gun and fired in rapid succession.

One. Two. Three.

The attackers fell mid-charge.

More snarls tore through the air, echoing over the wheezing breaths of the exhausted steeds. Bark after vicious bark rose in a chilling crescendo, punctuated by the gnash of teeth and the pounding of paws tearing through underbrush.

Hunter glanced back. Twelve canines were closing in, their eyes wild, jaws slick with saliva, relentless in their pursuit. "Don't these guys give up?"

"No, they'll never stop until they get their young back. Our only hope is to reach the river and cross before they can bring down our mounts. They won't cross the deep water."

"Then, let's hope these animals are faster than the canines."

They pushed forward, the thorny underbrush lacerating both the riders' and the steeds' legs. Tamaore felt his steed faltering, her stride uneven. He looked down and saw dark and thick blood streaming down his steed's legs. The canines' claws had carved deep, jagged gashes into her flesh. Each step flung crimson droplets across the ground. She wouldn't remain standing much longer.

"Hunter, catch," Tamaore called out as he threw the Huntsman the black pup. "Take Inow's horse for me. Mine will not make it. I'll slow them down and meet you on the other side."

"You'll never survive," Hunter yelled. "Just switch mounts."

"No, your steeds can't keep this pace up. If we don't slow the canines down, they will catch you a stone's throw from the riverbank." He lifted the tan pup out of the bag and held it high in the air for the chasing canines to see. "Look what I got, guys. Follow me."

Breaking away from the group, Tamaore spurred his mount towards a tree with one branch within grasping range. All but three canines followed him. With the pup held tight in his hand, he stood on his steed's back and caught the branch as his ride galloped underneath. A few feet away, another canine leapt on the path. Startled, his mount reared, giving the pursuing canines a chance to jump on her and pull her down. The front canine clenched its jaws around the steed's throat, suffocating her in seconds.

Tamaore turned to the west and saw Hunter, Umae, and Inow's mounts galloping over the hill and disappear. The sounds of growling and barks brought him back to his current situation. Eight wild canines circled the tree below, gnarling, jumping in the air, trying to reach him. But unless these canines flew, they had no way to reach him.

He held the small pup and looked into its eyes. "Well, little guy, how long do you think they'll stick around?" The small canine gave a tiny bark, then scratched his nose. "Well, that's gratitude."

Knowing he had a long wait, Tamaore tucked the pup inside his vest and climbed to a fork in the tree not far above him. The fork offered him a place where he could wedge his body in and not fall out if he slept. He debated about dropping the pup down to the adults in hopes they'd leave, but he thought they were too enraged to let him go. Better to wait until they calm down before deciding.

"You know, you guys, Hunter and Umae will not wait for me forever on the other side," Tamaore called down to the circling canines. "Are you sure you have nothing better to do?"

He surveyed the tree. "Okay, the first thing is to stay alive. Some *tangren* fruit over there. That gives me food and liquid." He stared at the overcast sky. "Those clouds will stick around, which means dew in the morning. I can collect some so the pup and I can drink. What do you think?" No sound came from the pup. Tamaore peeked inside his vest and saw the pup snuggled against his skin and fast asleep.

The three steeds raced towards the river. Their coats frothed in sweat, their breathing labored. Hunter doubted they possessed the energy to reach the riverbank in time. He drew his weapon and prepared to fire just as a mournful howl echoed across the land. The three chasing canines stopped and then retreated into the brush.

"That was sorrowful," Hunter said as his horse leapt into the river.

"Must be one of the mother canines," Umae replied as he reached out and grabbed Inow's steed's reins. Together, both animals leapt into the river and followed Hunter across to the other side.

"So, do you think he's still alive?" Hunter asked as his mount stepped onto dry land.

"He is an experienced hunter. I've seen him squeeze out of worse predicaments than this. Of course, I was with him."

Hunter dismounted. He inspected his steed's legs and flanks. Blood dripped from the crisscrossed wounds, but none of the cuts were deep. "We can't wait here long. The canines may continue their pursuit and cross farther down the river."

"Agreed. If Tamaore's not back by the time we clean the animals' cuts, I'll tie Inow's horse to a tree for him. And we'll start back."

The sound of yelping and growling jarred Tamaore awake. The canines cowered their bodies close to the ground, their tails tucked between their legs. Their ears were laid back, almost submissively. From within the forest came the sound of breaking saplings and the crunching of leaves. Two colossal male *tumacks* crashed through the underbrush, the largest Tamaore had ever seen. He estimated each weighed as much as ten men.

Drawn by the odor of the freshly killed steed, they swatted the canines aside like dried leaves. Unable to fight two such adversaries, the canines fled to their dens.

Tamaore perceived the *tumacks* as a blessing. Once they ate their fill and wandered off, he'd climb down, cross the river, and find a ride home.

One of the *tumacks* sniffed the air and directed his attention up to the meal in the tree. Witnessing the look in the bear's eyes, Tamaore wished the canines were back. The bear walked over and reared up on his hind feet, placing his paws on the tree trunk.

"You're too big to climb up here, right?"

The bear growled and showed its long, ferocious teeth. Five arrows protruded from the bear's back. Apparently, this bear had encountered Hunters before. Chances were, he didn't like two-legged beings.

Tamaore's pulse quickened as the second bear lumbered over, rising to its full height and slamming its massive weight against the tree. The impact jolted through the trunk like a lightning strike, nearly hurling him from the branches. Tamaore scrambled to stay balanced, arms wrapped tight around the shaking limbs as the first bear joined in.

Now both were attacking, slamming into the tree with bone-rattling force. Each strike was a thunderous blow, tearing bark from wood, shaking leaves loose like rain. The ground below quaked.

Hoping out of sight would be out of mind, Tamaore climbed higher as the pup in his vest clawed at his chest in fear. Higher and higher, the Ki-Wan climbed, but the *tumacks* would not give up their pursuit. Then Tamaore felt it. The tree moved. Its foothold in the earth was weakening. With each push, the tree leaned farther over.

Tamaore surveyed the surrounding area to judge where and how the tree would fall. If it went to the left, it would crash into the tree beside it. Forward, the tree would tumble down the mountain and crush him. To the right, it would land in a clearing where the *tumacks* would easily devour him. No options were survivable.

The bears slammed into the trunk with renewed fury, snarling in frustration as the tree refused to fall. Its roots clung stubbornly to the earth, groaning but holding. The trunk bent low, creaking under the relentless pressure, tilting until it hovered just shy of horizontal.

"If the tree levels out, the tumacks won't need to knock it down," Tamaore said to the pup. "They'll simply climb up, stride across the trunk like a bridge, and eat us both."

With each brutal shove, the tree dipped lower until, on the third strike, it leveled out. The smaller bear wasted no time. It leapt onto the trunk, claws sinking into the bark as it advanced, deliberate, and snarling. Foam flecked its lips. Its head swung side to side, eyes locked on Tamaore, teeth bared in a feral grin of death promised.

Tamaore had nowhere to run. No branch to climb. No time left. He closed his eyes. Drew a breath. *So this is how it ends…*

But the blow never came.

Instead, the air split with a piercing, animal scream, a sound so violent it didn't sound natural. Tamaore's eyes flew open. The bear stood frozen, just inches away. Then it staggered forward and collapsed with a thud that shook the trunk.

Prepared to strike the unseen attacker, the second bear stood on its hind legs. Two shots exploded and ripped open the *tumack*'s chest, bringing him down.

"Are you going to stay in that tree all day?" shouted a rider galloping towards him.

"Hunter. You came back."

Hunter brought Inow's steed beneath Tamaore. The hunter jumped out of the tree and onto the steed. Grabbing the reins Hunter threw him, he kneed his ride in the ribs and galloped off.

"You still got that pup?" Hunter inquired.

"It's clawing the hell out of my chest," Tamaore laughed.

Though relief flooded her when Hunter returned, Li-ara found little joy in the three wild canine pups he brought back. The price had been far too steep. Inow and Qua were dead, torn apart in the chaos, and too many canines had been killed in the process, creatures that had only been defending their own. No more, she vowed. Never again would she sanction the forced removal of pups from their packs. The cost was simply too high. And, with luck, the villagers would stumble across an orphaned pup occasionally and bring it to her.

Li-ara walked beside her husband as they made their way up the hill. But when they reached the crest, Hunter slowed, then stopped. He stood still, eyes sweeping across the valley below.

Tents covered the land in every direction, stretching for miles - red, green, blue, gold - each color a symbol of a different clan or sect. Smoke curled from campfires nestled between them. Weapons lay stacked in organized piles. And among it all moved a sea of beings, more than Hunter had ever seen gathered in one place.

It wasn't just a camp.

It was a nation - united and waiting.

"Who are all these people?" Hunter asked.

"They're from everywhere. While you were gone, they kept pouring in. I feared we'd run out of vacant land. There are even eight off-worlders who came in that ship sitting in that far field." She pointed to the north.

"Off-worlders? Why did they come?"

"They heard about your teaching of *Gaball* and came to learn. They said you are the talk of the galaxy."

"Why would all these people care about Kolorian Huntsmen's training? The *Gaball* has been around for millennia. No one ever cared before."

"Perhaps because there was never an opportunity to learn it until now." Li-ara put her arm around her hero's waist. "The Kolorian philosophy and teachings remained secluded on Kolora until you willingly shared it with the *Genubites*. For the first time in centuries, they foresaw a better future through your eyes. The hope of that future spread like wildfire, and now this is the result of your generosity."

"No, this is out of control," Hunter said, shaking his head in disbelief. "I never meant for any of this. This is too much. It must stop, Li-ara."

"And how do you propose we do that?"

"I'll stop exercising, stop showing them the way of the Huntsmen."

"No, I won't allow you to do that. Remember what happened last time you lost that part of you?"

Hunter remembered. Those days still haunted his thoughts. "Then we'll leave and go somewhere else, somewhere where they don't know us."

"I'm not moving again, Hunter. This is our home. We buried our unnamed baby here. I won't leave."

"Then we won't let any more step foot on our land."

"You can no more stop them from coming than you can stop flies from feasting on a dead deer. But I might have a solution. When my canine pups are trained and old enough to be sold, they leave and go to other places. What if your followers did the same? Some have been here since the first week you began your exercises. They know the *Gaball* almost as well as you do. Why can't they go back to their homes or villages and instruct their people? Not everyone needs to come here to learn. You do not have to train everyone personally."

Hunter smiled. She always had the answers to his problems. He lifted her into his arms and softly kissed her. "Once more, my most wondrous wife, you have the answer. I need not do this alone. Those who know *Gaball* can take its teachings back to their clans or beyond."

That night, for the first time since her miscarriage, the two lovers consummated their love for each other. Secure in Hunter's arms with her head on his chest, Li-ara decided it was the perfect time to bring up the miscarriage. "Hunter, we've never talked about the daughter we lost." She felt his muscles stiffen. "We need to talk about what happened if we are to put it behind us."

"I fear to speak of her," came a mournful reply. Hunter's emotions choked his vocal cords. "She was so perfect, so tiny. Her fingers and toes were no bigger than a grain of rice. She had your nose. It was just a minor bump on her face." He could say no more.

Li-ara pushed harder into his chest, trying to stop her tears. "We never named her."

"Meg," came a whisper.

"Meg?"

"Yes."

"Your mother's name. It's perfect." Li-ara paused for a second, choosing her words. "Hunter, I know you still blame yourself for Meg's death. As I've told you before, it was not your fault."

"I feel like it was."

"There is more that I never told you. Two days before our fight, I started bleeding. I feared saying anything because you seemed so lost and unhappy, and I didn't want to add to your burden. I was wrong. I should have told you." She propped herself up and gazed into his eyes. "When I was out at the kennel, I started bleeding heavily. I tried to make it back to the house but became faint and tumbled down the hill. Our daughter was already gone when I fell down the hill."

"But had I been a better husband, hadn't been so absorbed in my own wants, you wouldn't have had to hide the fact you were pregnant. Or that you were bleeding. No matter what you say, Li-ara, I am responsible for what happened."

"Hunter, I want you to listen to me, really listen. You are the most wonderful husband any woman could want. You make me feel so loved, so appreciated, so desired. But if I was pregnant with Meg today, she still would die. There would be nothing you could do to prevent that. Just as you couldn't stop it now, you couldn't have stopped it then. You bear no responsibility."

Tears flowed down Hunter's cheeks. He brought Li-ara's lips up to his. The last remnants of his guilt and pain were released. A new day started tomorrow.

19 CAUGHT KISSING

Hunter and Li-ara sat on the back porch, enjoying the late morning sun. A soft breeze blew from the stream, making this a most wondrous day. Today was Hunter's rest day - no training. The villagers and other "guests" respected that he needed one day every eight, and no one disturbed him. He spent the day with his wife and his children.

"This can't be good. Umae's marching up the hill with Willomay and J'Dar. He doesn't look happy."

"Oh, no. What did that boy go and do?" Li-ara asked, sliding forward in her chair for a better look. "He does appear upset."

"I would guess Umae caught them at something. Both kids appear frightened."

Umae neared the porch steps. "Hunter, what do you plan on doing about this?" He thrust J'Dar and Willomay forward.

"I am in the dark, Umae," Hunter said. "Do about what?"

"I caught these two down by the stream together."

"Yes, J'Dar told me that sometimes he and Willomay fish together. There's no harm in that."

"This time, they weren't fishing. They were KISSING!"

Hunter's eyes widened as his eyebrows raised. "Kissing? Well, this is a recent development. J'Dar, is this true?" J'Dar kept his eyes on the ground and muttered something Hunter could not hear. "I expect you to look at me when I talk to you and answer so I can hear you. Is this true?"

J'Dar raised his head and looked at his father. To Hunter's pride, the adolescent straightened his back and stood tall. In a loud voice, he said, "Yes. I kissed her."

"Did anything else occur other than a kiss?"

"No. And it was our first, and I fear, only kiss." J'Dar turned and glanced at the fuming Umae.

Hunter chuckled to himself. J'Dar was probably right. "Umae, you and I are as brothers. I have no closer friend. Therefore, I must ask, is there a reason my son cannot kiss your daughter?"

"Hunter, as you say, we are as brothers. No male is dearer to me than you. We spilled blood together, fought beside each other, laughed, and hunted together. While I would welcome your son into my family as one of my own, Willomay cannot marry him."

"Woe. Wait a minute," J'Dar quickly shouted. "I only kissed her. I didn't lay with her or ask her to be my wife."

"Do you want a wife?" Li-ara asked, unable to refrain from getting a few teases in.

"No!"

Feeling the need to explain more, Umae continued. "As you are aware, I have no sons. Only three daughters. As the oldest, Willomay will follow me as Chieftain of my clan. I made arrangements on the day of her birth for her to marry into one of three noble families. Before that day, she has years of training ahead of her and cannot be sidetracked by foolish flings of romance and kissing."

This time, Hunter couldn't hold it back. He burst into laughter. Umae responded with a dry, disapproving chuckle, shaking his head at the absurdity.

"I do not laugh at you, My Friend. Do you remember nothing of being a youthful male, your impulsive actions, and flights of fantasy?"

"I never had impulsive actions or flights of fantasy."

Hunter thought that was probably true, and the reason Umae was always so serious, so strict. "Then what of the *Gaball's* teachings? Love and understanding are the mothers of peace. But I agree these two are too young to understand the ramifications of their actions. I will talk with him." Hunter turned to his wife. "Li-ara, please take our son inside."

Li-ara grabbed her son's ear and hauled him into the house.

"Owe, Mom. Not so hard," J'Dar yelled.

Nataa-a loudly sang out in glee, "J'Dar's in trouble."

"Umae, come sit, and we will talk more," Hunter said.

"I cannot. The fault of Willomay's kiss is not hers alone. I, too, bear some responsibility. I have been busy training the canines, and I have not kept an adequate eye on her. To rectify this, I am taking my family back home. We leave within the hour."

"Leaving? Over a kiss? Can we not discuss this?"

"There is nothing to discuss."

"Are you coming back?"

"Yes. Once we are back at the village, I will arrange for Willomay to start her studies. Then I will return."

"You will miss J'Dar's birthday celebration tomorrow. He was looking forward to you showing him how to throw the Ki-Wan blades."

"I regret that I am unable to attend the celebration," Umae said. "It is getting late in the year, and the snows will soon cover the Bluestone Mountain. If I want to make it back here to continue training my pup, I must beat the snow. Tell J'Dar I will show him the technique when I return if I'm still not mad at him." This time, Umae laughed.

"Good journey, My Friend."

"Tell Li-ara I leave my black pup in her care." Umae turned and left.

The next morning, in celebration of J'Dar reaching the age of consent, Hunter woke his oldest before daylight. He had an extra special surprise; the two would venture to the clear lake in the mountains where Hunter's craft rested on the bottom. They would fish, and hopefully, J'Dar would forget his disappointment with Willomay and her family leaving.

When they reached the cliff, Hunter stepped to the edge and peered down into the calm waters below. He wondered what his son would say if he knew what rested in the water's blackness. One day he would tell him, but not today. Today, he had other plans.

"Wow, Dad, this place is spectacular," J'Dar stated as he walked up beside his father. "How did you ever find it?"

"I stumbled across it when I arrived at Orallia. Today is only the second time I have returned since the day I left as Hunter and returned as your father."

"Is the fishing good?"

"I never stayed long enough to find out. A path snakes down to the lake. Let's go find out."

Leaving most of their belongings on the cliff, the two adventurers followed the path to the plains below, their fishing poles in hand. Kii eagerly ran ahead, his tail wagging extensively in excitement. When the trail stretched across a sandy beach, J'Dar strolled along the edge, peering into the water while Kii barked and chased butterflies.

"Kii, be quiet. You will scare all the fish away with that barking." J'Dar studied the lake. "This water is so clear. It will be hard to find a spot where the fish won't see us."

"I rely upon your expertise," Hunter answered.

J'Dar sauntered over to a tree partially hanging over the water. "This tree's shadow should cover our reflections." He looked up into the sky. "The sun will be in front of us, so our shadows won't give us away. There's plenty of tall water grass for the fish to hide in." He bent down on one knee and examined the water. "Appears to contain a decent selection of minnows and water bugs. I say we fish here."

Baiting their hooks with the special bait Willomay showed J'Dar, the two placed their poles in the water. Within minutes, J'Dar caught his first fish. Five minutes later, Hunter brought an immense salmon up. An accomplishment for him because, no matter how hard he tried, Hunter was just a terrible fisherman. At the end of two hours, J'Dar claimed fourteen fish. Hunter caught four.

J'Dar gathered wood for a small fire. Hunter selected three fish - one for him, one for his son, and one for Kii. After removing their insides, which Kii gladly scarfed up, he ran a long, straight stick through their mouths and out the side gill. Hunter staked them over the fire and leaned back, allowing the sun to bathe his body. J'Dar seldom saw his father without a shirt and he was always shocked when he saw all the scars and old wounds that covered his chest, back, and arms. It was a sight he never got used to.

"Dad, did you get all those cuts from being a Bounty Hunter?"

"That's how I got a lot of them. A Hunter's job is fierce and dangerous. Someone is always trying to stab you, hit you, or shoot you. Bounties do not come willingly." Hunter rested his hand on his side. "This one is from the bear that nearly killed me and brought me to your mother." He moved his hand to his chest. "As is this one. If it hadn't been for that bear, you wouldn't be here today."

"What about the ones on your back?"

Hunter paused a moment. J'Dar was too young before to hear the truth about the markings from Hunter's childhood. Today, his son reached the age of consent. It was time he knew the truth. "No, I received them before I became a Hunter."

"Will you tell me how you got them?" J'Dar wondered why his father remained hesitant, secretive.

"You are no longer a child, so I will answer your question. Even your mother does not know all the story, but I will tell you what I told her. Then, the matter is closed. They are marks left by a toothed metal whip. I received them when I was much younger than you. *Rogarian* Traders kidnapped me when I was four and sold me into bondage."

"*Rogarian* Traders?" Willomay told him about the bloodthirsty guerrillas who stole children and sold them into servitude and sex trafficking. J'Dar had lain awake many nights thinking about them. Now seeing his father's back, he realized he hadn't worried enough. "They did that?"

"One particular Trader took immense pleasure in whipping those under his jurisdiction. They beat many worse than me. Even then, I was a fighter, and this Trader somehow admired that, so he only beat me once a day." J'Dar imagined what his father endured.

"How did you escape?"

"I was with my master the day the *Biiloot* Huntsmen attacked the auction house. They rescued me, and when they learned who my father was, they returned me to Kolora. I had trouble adjusting to my normal life because of what I endured. To help with my healing, they decided I should take my adult Hunter designation early. I was given a new name - BiiJun D'Kolor. It means 'Biiloot rescued son of Kolora'. It is the name I am now known by."

"But J'Dar was your name before that?"

"Yes. That was the name my parents gave me."

"I remember when I feared Nataa-a's birth. You told me about how you felt when your mom got pregnant with your little brother. Was he your only sibling?"

"Actually, I made that story up." Hunter laughed. "I wanted you to stop being afraid of losing me, and it sounded like a worthy story. The truth is, my parents feared other children would be taken too, so they chose to have no more children."

"But you returned. Why didn't they have more after you came home?"

"I was a mess when I came back - closed off, angry, scared of everyone and everything. I didn't know how to exist in the world anymore. My parents gave up everything to help me find my way again. They guided my heart, the Dominee guided my mind. They saved me. Both showed me what it meant to be strong, to be present, to love without conditions. Everything I know about being a parent, I learned from them. And I only hope I've done the same for you… and your siblings."

"You have, Dad. Will you tell me more about the Dominee?"

Kii let out a small bark. "Perhaps later. For now, I believe the fish is ready."

With the subject closed, father and son consumed the fish. J'Dar wanted to ask more questions, but he respected his father's wishes not to discuss it further. Perhaps he would bring up the subject later.

Hunter looked up. "The sun tells us it is time to start back. If we're late for your celebration, your mother will make me sleep on the couch for the next three months."

They doused the fire, scattered the embers, and retreated up the small trail to the top. "J'Dar, before we leave, I have one more thing to show you. Follow me." J'Dar followed his father to the cave entrance hidden behind some naturally growing bushes. "What I am about to show you is between father and son, you and me. You may tell no one what is hidden here until the day of my death. May I count on your silence?"

"Yes." J'Dar's body tingled as he imagined what might be hidden inside the cave.

"Kii, stand guard," Hunter ordered as he disappeared into the cave.

J'Dar wiped his clammy hands on his pants as he followed his father into the cave. After fifteen steps, Hunter knelt beside a large, blue-speckled rock. J'Dar overheard his father mumble some words, then remove the stone. Using the end of his hand, he brushed away several inches of sand.

J'Dar held his breath as Hunter reached inside and brought out a cloth bundle.

Almost religiously, Hunter peeled back the corners of the cloth one by one to reveal a full set of Huntsman armor, minus the arm brace hidden in his pack back home.

"J'Dar, today you reached the age of ten, the age of decision. When I turned ten, I entered the life of a Huntsman. I put this armor on and prepared for a life as a Hunter. My face remained hidden from the world behind its metal until the day I landed here and began my life with you and your mother. It is a day I have never regretted. I cannot offer you the helmet of a Huntsman, but I give you this." Hunter reached beneath the armor and withdrew a Huntsman's blade sheathed in a *Trixon* cat hide. Unsnapping the strap, he removed the knife and rested it in his hand. "She is called *D'nang do Unamae*, the bringer of a thousand cuts. She has seen many wars and battles. My Huntsman father gave her to me on my tenth birthday. He received the blade from his father on *his* tenth birthday, and so on. She has been passed down for at least ten generations, but I never thought I would have a child to pass her on to." He held out the Huntsman's knife. "It is with much pride and love that I give her to you."

J'Dar reverently took the knife, his eyes wide with awe and amazement. "Dad, this is beautiful. Is it really a Huntsman's blade?"

"Did I not just say it was?" Hunter laughed. "But with the blade comes great responsibility. Life is precious and must not be taken carelessly."

A puzzled expression crossed the younger one's face. "Dad, you were a Bounty Hunter. You killed people as your profession. How can you say life is precious?"

"The Huntsmen's philosophy teaches that all life is precious and should be preserved. That is why we hunt only to eat, we forgive those who wrong us, and we protect those who cannot protect themselves. As for the bounties, I killed only those who tried to kill me. I gave each the choice of coming in standing or dead. Many chose wrongly and paid the price."

J'Dar gazed down at his knife. "Do you think Mom will let me keep this?"

"Yes. She and I already discussed it. But you must be sure your brothers and sister never play with *D'nang*. This is not a toy, J'Dar, but a weapon that may one day save your life."

"Did it ever save yours?"

"Many times."

"When?"

"Stories for the walk home." Hunter removed the breastplate, tucked it inside his shirt, then refolded the cloth and humbly placed the bundle back in its chamber. "This we take with us for weapon practice." A solemn expression spread over the Huntsman's face. "J'Dar, never forget what I showed you this day. On the day I die, you must retrieve my armor and give it back to the Huntsmen. They will return my coverings to Kolora, where it will be melted down and made into armor for a new warrior."

"Is that why no one finds any Kolorian armor? It's all been melted down?"

"Yes, that is our tradition. My armor carries the legacy of generations of Huntsmen who lived and died in its embrace. And will continue to do so when I die. Go, make sure Kii hasn't gotten into trouble and put our gear together. If we want to reach home on time, we will have to trot part of the way."

"Kii will love that."

As J'Dar went outside, Hunter replaced the armor in its resting place, and replaced the stone marker. "You two ready?"

Silence.

"J'Dar? Kii? Where are you two? We need to leave."

Hunter stepped out of the cave. A sharp pain shot through his left side as a bullet penetrated his body, followed by another shot to the heart. Falling to his knees, he raised his head to observe a *Rogarian* Trader holding his son, his hand over his son's mouth. At the *Rogarian*'s feet lay the still body of Kii. As he crumbled to the ground, the last thing Hunter saw was the terror in his son's eyes.

———————

Willomay rode beside her father in heavy silence, her jaw clenched, eyes locked on the trail ahead. She hadn't said a word since they left Hunter and J'Dar, nor had she glanced in his direction. Every rigid line of her face radiated fury.

"Are you going to remain silent all the way back home?" Umae asked. "I was only thinking of your welfare." Willomay glared at him and gave him a hateful face. She reined her steed to a halt, then slid off and walked into the forest.

"Where are you going, Willomay? Answer me."

"She needs to relieve herself," Umae's wife said as she rode up beside him, also dismounting. "We all need a stop."

"Tamaore, Beck, go with her," Umae ordered.

"I'm not sure she will welcome protection from two males."

"Then you should have brought more female protectors," Umae replied. "These woods are filled with *tumacks*, wild canines, cats, and other animals waiting to eat us."

"She is your daughter. She knows the danger."

Umae gave his wife a disagreeing look. "In her state of mind, she is thinking of nothing besides her hatred for me."

"I would not call it hatred, but you deserve her anger." Umae scowled. "What did you expect, Umae? You embarrassed her in front of a male she likes, in front of Hunter, in front of countless others. You talked of marriage. I thought you were going to behead poor J'Dar."

"He's lucky I didn't."

"He kissed her. Don't you remember the first kiss you stole from me?"

"That was different."

"How was that different?"

"You were not my daughter."

A scream from Willomay shattered the stillness of the forest, followed by the sound of two blaster shots.

"Guard my family," Umae shouted as he and five guards raced in the scream's direction. "Willomay, where are you? Willomay, answer me."

When they reached Willomay's location, she wasn't there. Beck lay sprawled in the dirt, motionless, a smoking blaster wound burned through the center of his chest. His eyes stared skyward, unblinking, empty. A few feet away, Tamaore lay crumpled on his side. Blood soaked his sleeve, pouring from a blast high in his upper arm.

"Where is she? Where's Willomay?" Umae screamed.

"*Rogarian* Traders," Tamaore whispered, forcing the words from his mouth.

A sudden roar split the air - deep, thunderous, unmistakable. An aircraft engine.

Weapon drawn, Umae and three guards sprinted toward the sound, crashing through the thickets with reckless speed. Thorns tore at Umae's skin. Branches ripped at his clothes, slashing across his face and arms, but he didn't slow.

"Willomay!" he shouted.

The terrain grew steeper, the underbrush thicker. Vines wrapped around the Ki-Wan's ankles, roots reached for their feet, but they tore through them, lungs burning, blood trickling from fresh wounds.

They broke through the final line of trees and stopped cold at the crest of the hill. Just ahead sat a strange ship. Willomay struggled in the grip of two strangers, her body twisting, resisting, but it wasn't enough. They dragged her up the ramp.

"No!" Umae roared, stumbling forward, but the ramp had already begun to rise, sealing her inside with a metallic hiss.

Umae ran. He ran until his legs gave out, the ship lifting just beyond his reach. Dust blasted into his face as the engines roared to life.

Then it was gone, vanishing into the sky like a ghost, taking his daughter with it.

"No," Umae screamed. "Not my daughter."

––––––––––––––––

Willomay's wrists were bound, a gag shoved between her teeth before she was shoved roughly into a holding pen. She stumbled, catching herself against the cold metal bars as the gate slammed shut behind her.

Three other younglings huddled inside, their eyes wide with fear. She didn't recognize their faces, but their features were familiar—two were unmistakably Bree, with their soft, pale skin and silver-flecked eyes. The third bore the distinctive markings of a Genubite, tall, lean, a fresh laceration trailing down one cheek.

As the traders skimmed across the landscape, their eyes caught movement below. Two lone figures ascended a narrow path that wound from a shimmering lake up toward higher ground. One was clearly a man, his gait steady and purposeful. The other, smaller and slighter, kept pace beside him. Perhaps a younger man. Or a boy. The sight was unexpected and curious. Travelers this deep into the wild were unusual.

"I believe today's our lucky day. That's easy pickings."

"Five brats in one trip. We'll be celebrating tonight. And get a fat bonus."

Without a sound, the trader's vessel touched down close to the location where they had seen the two males. The underbrush barely stirred as several figures crept forward, silent and precise.

J'Dar crouched to gather their belongings. As he reached for his father's pack, a sharp whistle sliced through the air. An arrow flashed past his cheek. It struck Kii square in the chest. The loyal canine gave a startled yelp and collapsed mid-step, dead before he hit the ground.

He barely had time to process the horror when rough hands grabbed him from behind. J'Dar struggled fiercely, shoving his knife into the side pocket of his father's pack just before he was hauled upright. An arm wrapped around his throat in a crushing hold; a hand clamped over his mouth, silencing his muffled cry.

Then, Hunter appeared from the cave, unaware of the ambush. J'Dar thrashed against the grip, trying to scream. To warn him. But it was too late. One of the traders raised his weapon and fired. Twice.

The shots echoed through the clearing. Hunter staggered, his eyes wide with shock as bright red bloomed across his shirt. He dropped to his knees, then crumpled to the earth, unmoving.

"Dad," J'Dar shouted, struggling against his assailant's grip to break free. He stared at his father's still body in disbelief as the Trader dragged him away.

"Should we take their stuff?" one trader asked.

"Nah, it's just farmers' crap. Let's go. If we're late again, Rannow will have our hide." The first trader reached for the bag. "I said leave it."

The two trotted off toward their ship, catching up to J'Dar and his two captors in minutes. Dragging him aboard, they threw him into the same cage as the other four children. He clung to the bars, sobbing for the loss of his father. He didn't even realize Willomay was inside until she came over and sat beside him, laying her head on his chest.

"Ockmoo, take my family home," Umae said. "Tell my father what happened."

"Where are you going?" Umae's wife asked.

"To rescue my daughter."

She grabbed his hand. "Umae, steeds cannot fly through the sky. You cannot follow where they took her."

"I can't, but Hunter can. He has a craft hidden somewhere on this planet. I know he does. A Hunter's ship has the capability of locating where they took her." He glanced down at Tamaore as several women tended to his wounds.

"How is he?"

"I believe he will survive, but he will probably lose the arm. Little of the flesh remains."

"I will avenge you, My Friend." Tamaore nodded, too stricken with pain to say a word.

Umae chose six riders and seven of the freshest steeds. At full gallop, they raced towards the only person who might help them. They rode hard for three hours when Umae held up his hand and stopped. Up ahead, blocking their path, stood a wild canine.

"We don't have time for this," said one male as he drew his gun and prepared to eliminate the threat.

"Wait," Umae ordered. He stared at the animal. She seemed familiar, like the canine he encountered in his youth. But she was dead. Was this her offspring? The animal lifted her head and howled into the sky. Nearby, two canines answered.

"Something's wrong," Umae said, reading the body language of the canine. "She's trying to tell us something. I'm listening, Girl."

The canine ran a few yards to the south, then stopped. She looked at Umae and howled again. She ran back to her previous spot on the trail, circled twice, and then returned to her second location.

"What is she doing?"

"She wants us to follow her," Umae shouted as he kicked his steed and galloped after her.

The wild canine surged ahead, weaving through the terrain with purposeful urgency. She avoided brambles, skirted loose rock, and led them across the easiest path, as if she knew every second counted.

Up ahead, buzzards wheeled through the sky, their black wings cutting circles above the cliffs. As Umae drew closer, he saw four of the scavengers lying scattered on the ground, their bodies torn open by canine teeth - fresh kills, meant as a warning.

The lead canine didn't pause. She bounded across the cliff face and leapt onto the rocky outcrop above the cave. Her tail stiff, her body rigid, she stared downward. A low, aching howl emanated from her throat.

Umae followed her gaze. Below, sprawled in the dirt, lay Hunter's body, motionless, surrounded by six wild canines standing guard in a tight ring. Just a few feet away, Kii's body rested in a pool of silence, an arrow still lodged in his chest.

Umae pulled hard on the reins, bringing his steed to a halt. He dismounted slowly, eyes locked on the canines.

"Umae, they'll tear you to pieces. She's trying to lure us in."

"No. She's not. Her howls are cries for help, not hunting. They're protecting Hunter. Didn't you see those buzzards back there? They came down to feast on his body, and the canines fought them off. They won't hurt us."

"Is he alive?" a rider asked, watching nervously.

"Only one way to tell." Umae slowly removed his gun and knife and laid them on the ground. He proceeded forward. The canines in the circle rose. His men drew their weapons, instantaneously provoking a growl from the female. "Put your guns away. That's an order."

Against their better judgment, Umae's men obeyed, holding position as he stepped forward alone.

Every movement was deliberate. Controlled. A breath at a time. Umae moved slowly, each footfall placed with precision, the weight of a dozen eyes pressing down on him. He kept his gaze low, fixed on the dirt and rock beneath his boots, resisting every instinct to look up.

He had to appear calm. Unthreatening. Human prey that knew the rules of survival. One wrong move, and it could all unravel.

The wild canines parted and allowed Umae access to the bodies. He passed Kii first and checked the canine for signs of life. There were none. He pulled the arrow from Kii's body, examining its construction.

"*Rogarian* Traders," he said.

Umae continued to the Huntsman. Thick and dark blood pooled beneath Hunter's body, staining the earth. His shirt was soaked down one side, the fabric clinging wet and red. Over his heart was a single bullet hole, the edges of the fabric scorched from a bullet. Yet, no blood drained from the wound.

Umae leaned down and listened for a heartbeat. He could not detect one. He slipped his fingers under Hunter's neck, feeling his artery. Before he could locate Hunter's pulse, the Huntsman's hand shot up and grabbed Umae's shirt.

"They took my son," an almost inaudible voice said.

"They took Willomay, too," Umae said. "Hold on, My Friend. I will get you home to Li-ara."

Umae did his best to stop Hunter's bleeding. With all the blood on the ground, he didn't know how his friend still lived or if he would survive the trip home.

After binding his wounds tightly, the Ki-Wan lifted the Huntsman onto a hastily constructed stretcher. Unwilling to leave the loyal companion behind to be eaten by scavengers, they placed Kii's body alongside Hunter's.

The Ki-Wan began their grueling journey toward Li-ara, flanked on either side by the vigilant female canine and her loyal pack, escorting them like silent, watchful guardians.

20 HOPE ARRIVES

"Oh, where are they?" Li-ara said in an angry tone, more of a statement than a question. "He promised they'd be back hours before the celebration. Guests are already arriving, and no Hunter or J'Dar."

"Perhaps they got lost."

"No, Hunter is familiar with the area. They were probably having too much fun and lost track of time. I swear, if he's not home in the next twenty minutes, he can plan on sleeping on the couch for the next month."

A sharp, solitary howl pierced the still air. Li-ara jolted upright. She sprinted to the edge of the hill and scanned the land below. "That wasn't just a call. It was a cry for help."

"Look!" one of the caregivers cried, arm outstretched.

A swarm of people surged toward them, a wave of urgency in their steps. Li-ara stood on tiptoe, straining to see over the crowd. Among the sea of heads, she caught a glimpse of riders, steeds weaving through the masses. One rider broke into view, and for a heartbeat, she thought it was Umae. But it couldn't be. Umae had left with his family the day before.

The crowd began to part, forming a narrow path to the base of the hill. Two Ki-Wan dismounted, their faces grave and emerged from between the riders. They bore a stretcher carried between them.

273

Li-ara held her breath.

Two bodies.

One of them was Hunter.

Li-ara bolted down the hillside, her legs barely keeping pace with the terror surging through her veins. Blood. So much blood. Hunter's body lay motionless on the stretcher, his chest soaked in red, and beside him lay Kii. Lifeless.

Her eyes locked on the charred edges of the bullet holes. No teeth caused Hunter's wounds. These were made by blaster fire, accurate, purposeful, deadly.

She dropped to her knees and pressed her ear against his chest, desperate to hear the rhythm of life. But there was nothing. Just silence and blood.

Panic clawed at her throat.

"No - no, no, no," she whispered, shutting her eyes, forcing herself to still the scream rising within. She listened again, this time holding her breath, willing her pulse to silence.

A thump. Then another. Strong. Steady.

Her gaze locked on Umae.

"What happened?" she demanded. "Who did this?"

"We found him like this at the clear lake cliff," Umae explained. "I don't know what transpired."

"Kii?"

"He was already dead when we found Hunter. I speculate that whoever shot Hunter killed Kii first, so he couldn't warn Hunter. I couldn't leave him out there. He was such a magnificent canine. He deserved a hero's burial, so I brought him home too."

Terror filled her heart. Li-ara scanned through the crowd for her son's face. "Where is my son? Where is J'Dar?"

"They took our son," came Hunter's voice.

"Who took him?" Li-ara asked, looking from Hunter to Umae. His eyes were filled with tears. There was more to the story.

"We believe it was *Rogarian* Traders," Umae said, placing an arrow in Li-ara's hand. "They killed Kii with this. The design is Rogarian, but I've never seen this construction or feathering before." He paused, forcing his emotions back down his throat. "They took Willomay, too."

"Not Willomay. How?"

"Willomay went into the forest to conduct business with two guards. Somehow, they got the jump on my men. I wasn't fast enough to save her. By the time I arrived, they were hauling her into a ship and took off."

"And J'Dar?"

"I never saw him. We were on our way here to ask Hunter for help when a wild canine took us to him."

"A wild canine?"

"Li-ara, you won't believe what happened. She purposely blocked our path and had us follow her. She led us to Hunter. Canines from her pack surrounded Hunter and Kii, protecting them."

"From what?"

"Buzzards, cats, anything which might feast upon them. They kept Hunter safe until help arrived. But there's more, Li-ara. On the way here, a *tumack* caught the stench of blood and attacked. The pack fought it off."

"They followed you here?"

"No, not followed. They escorted and protected us."

"Just like they did to Hunter before. Why?"

"I don't know."

Li-ara wanted and needed more answers, but she had to stop Hunter's bleeding first. "Can we move him?"

"We need to try," Umae answered. "If the grueling trip here didn't kill him, I think we can chance moving him a few more feet."

With the reverence reserved for fallen legends, two Ki-Wan gently lifted Kii's body and laid him on a soft knoll, the grass dappled with blooming flowers. They bowed their heads in silent tribute as petals stirred in the breeze around the lifeless canine.

A small group of men stepped forward. With solemn care, they raised the stretcher and began the slow ascent to the house, Hunter's bloodied form cradled between them. Li-ara walked beside him, her hand never leaving his arm. Not once did she look away.

At the threshold, she broke away, sprinting inside. She burst into the kitchen, heart racing, eyes wild.

Without a word, she grabbed the platters of food from the table and hurled them onto the counters. Glass shattered. Bowls crashed. Then, with a cry lodged somewhere between fury and grief, she swept her arm across the table, sending every dish flying. Pans clanged. Porcelain exploded across the floor.

"Lie him here." She almost tripped over a male carrying the stretcher. "Perhaps most of you can wait outside, please. I need room to work."

"You heard the lady," a caretaker shouted. "Everyone outside. That includes you, Umae."

"No, he stays."

"As you wish, Mam."

"The gun blast went straight through his side," Umae explained as Li-ara cut away Hunter's shirt. "I briefly examined the heart wound. No blood drained from the hole, and I feared if I poked around, bleeding would begin."

"I don't think we need to worry about the heart wound." As the shirt material fell away, Umae and Li-ara were surprised to see their reflections.

"A Huntsman's breastplate. Where did he get that?" Li-ara asked.

"You don't know?" Umae asked in surprise.

"I haven't seen his armor since the day he left as a Bounty Hunter and returned as my husband. He said he hid it somewhere safe. He must have taken J'Dar to show him."

"Whatever the reason, we're lucky he put the plate on," Umae said as he scrutinized the massive blast in the breastplate. "That shot would have reduced his heart to dust." Li-ara lifted the plate. "He'll still have a hell of a bruise, though." The skin beneath the plate displayed an ugly mixture of blues, greens, and blacks.

"Do you think he has any internal injuries?" Li-ara asked, concerned about the bruising.

"No way to tell. We will need to wait and see."

"Must get my son," Hunter shouted, trying to sit up and almost falling off the table. "Must follow."

"Hunter, you can't go anywhere," Li-ara said, forcefully pushing Hunter to lie back down. He pressed against her, his strength greater than hers. His bleeding increased. "No, Hunter. Stay down. You're too badly hurt."

"No, have to rescue."

"Let us at least stitch you up before you put more holes in your body," Umae shouted as he also tried to keep Hunter on the table. But with the amount of adrenaline pumping through his body, Hunter was a bulldozer - unstoppable.

"We need some help in here," Umae shouted.

Six men stormed into the room, surrounding the table. Hunter thrashed violently, blood smearing beneath him as they fought to pin him down.

Li-ara's hands shook as she filled the syringe. She spun and crossed the room in three strides, the needle aimed for his neck. But Hunter exploded upward, ripping free of their grip with a guttural snarl. His arm lashed out, striking Li-ara hard and sending the syringe clattering to the floor.

"Hold him!" Umae barked.

Hunter bolted, shoving the others aside. He stumbled toward the door. One step. Two. On the third, his knees buckled. He crashed forward, only for Umae to catch him mid-fall, the force nearly dragging them both to the ground.

Li-ara scrambled for the syringe, snatched it up, and plunged it into Hunter's neck. His body jerked once, then went still.

"Place him back on the table," Li-ara screamed as she filled another syringe.

"Don't give him that shot," came a thunderous voice as the side door burst open, the door frame rattling from the force.

"Who are you?" Li-ara asked as she froze in both fear and amazement. In the door stood a six-foot-five, three-hundred-pound warrior covered in *kolorite* armor.

"Someone who apparently should have been here yesterday." He walked over to the table and stared at the men holding Hunter down. Without the Huntsman uttering a word, the men bowed their heads and stepped back. He leaned down to Hunter's ear. "BiiJun, it is I, Warnom. I'm here."

A fogginess coursed through Hunter's veins. His eyes weren't focusing. All he recognized was his reflection. His mind clearing, he recalled the familiar voice. "Warnom, I need my ship. They took my son."

"Stand down, BiiJun D'Kolor. You cannot go anywhere until we get your bleeding under control," Warnom said.

"No, have to go."

"That's an order, Huntsman," Warnom shouted as Hunter tried to rise again. Upon hearing his commander's voice, Hunter lay back down. The stranger injected Hunter with his own medical syringe. "This will keep him down. He'll sleep, so we can stop this bleeding and stitch him up." He turned to Li-ara. "My name is Warnom. I am the trainer for BiiJun's clan. I taught him until the day he left Kolora as a Bounty Hunter."

"What are you doing here? Other than a Bounty Hunter several months ago, no Huntsman ever visited us before."

"I'm not here to visit," Warnom said as he examined Hunter's side wound. "The Dominee sent me. She sensed something was wrong, but I don't believe this was what she expected."

"The Dominee?" Li-ara asked in surprise.

"If I must repeat myself after each sentence, this will take a long time." Li-ara comprehended why Hunter didn't enjoy repeating things. "You, there." He pointed to Umae. "Get me some water."

"I'll get it," Li-ara said.

"We are talking. He is standing there doing nothing but listening. He can fetch the water."

Umae gave the new Huntsman an expression of annoyance as he walked over to the kitchen sink and filled a pan with water.

"I want everyone except the man getting water and Hunter's wife to leave immediately," Warnom said, his voice filled with authority.

Umae carried the requested water back to Warnom. The Huntsman removed his helmet, lifted the pan high, and poured the water over his head. He thrust the pan back to Umae. "Bring another one for BiiJun's wounds." He turned to Li-ara. "I need a firestick."

"You can remove your helmet?" Li-ara asked as she retrieved a firestick from the hearth.

"Normally, no," Warnom said. "I am a teacher, not a Hunter, so I can remove it. Plus, the helmet restricts my view of BiiJun's injuries. Hellish things to see out of. If I am going to save him, I need to see what I'm doing."

Returning to the sink, Umae grumbled under his breath as he refilled the pan. He vowed if the Huntsman dumped the water over his head again, he'd punch him right through the damn armor.

Umae returned carrying the second container of water. Warnom took it from him, handed it to Li-ara, and took the firestick. "Hold this," he instructed, voice firm. "Don't pour the water until I say."

Then, with swift precision, he reached into the pouch at his waist and pulled out three vials - one empty, the other two filled with fine powders, each a different color, glinting faintly in the light.

"You." He glanced at Umae. "What's your name?"

"Umae."

"Umae, dip that towel in water and wash the blood from his wounds, so I can determine how badly he's hurt." Warnom opened the empty bottle and poured a third of the blue powder inside and two-thirds of the purple powder.

"I don't take orders from you," Umae said.

"Then he will die, and his death will be your fault."

Glaring at Warnom, Umae wetted the cloth and began wiping. "His wounds are refilling as fast as I'm wiping the blood away." Within seconds, the towel was stained a deep crimson.

Warnom walked over and examined the blast wound in Hunter's left side. In between Umae's wipes, he saw four distinct openings needing closing. "Li-ara, pour a small amount of water over the wounds as I call out their number."

"Okay."

"Umae, grab another towel. After Li-ara pours the water, I want you to push the towel down inside each wound. When I tell you to, pull it out. The one closest to you is number one. The one closest to me is number four. Leave the cloth inside each until I say to remove it. Ready?"

"Yes." Li-ara and Umae said.

"Number one." Li-ara poured the water, and Umae pushed the towel deep into Hunter's wound. The cloth turned red in seconds. "Pull it out." The moment Umae removed the cloth, Warnom filled the hole with the powder. The bleeding stopped.

"Number two." Li-ara and Umae repeated the process. The Huntsman poured the powder.

"Number three." Umae pushed his finger down again, but he did not go deep into the wound. "My finger hit bone. I can't push through."

"Push the cloth to the side," Warnom said. Umae did, and the rag slipped deeper. Warnom poured the mixture.

"Last one." Without hesitation, they did it again.

"Umae, take hold of Li-ara's shoulders as tightly as you can." Not waiting for a reply, Warnom clicked the firestick. He held the flame to the powder, which immediately ignited. Hunter rose off the table and screamed, as did Li-ara. She rushed forward, the pan dropping from her hands, but Umae held her back. Warnom caught the pan as it fell, water sloshing onto the floor.

"Are you insane? You're killing him."

For ten seconds, Hunter screamed as Warnom let the powder burn.

"Enough," Umae yelled.

Warnom poured the water over the flames. A thin veil of mist rose into the air, followed by a sharp hiss as the flames shrank and vanished.

"Umae, can you help me roll him over to his side so I can see if the burn went all the way through?"

"And if it didn't?" Li-ara asked as she shrugged off Umae's hold.

"We'll repeat the process."

"The hell you will." Li-ara grabbed Warnom's arm.

"Li-ara, I realize you think this cruel, but cauterizing the wound is the only way to stop his blood loss. If he loses much more, not even the Dominee can save him."

Li-ara held her breath as the two males rolled her husband. She breathed a sigh of relief when Warnom said, "The flame went through. The powder will now harden throughout and seal all the oozing blood vessels. Let's bandage him up."

"Thank you, Warnom," Li-ara softly said, running her hands through her husband's hair. "I never would have stopped that much bleeding."

"Come, Li-ara. Let your women cover his wounds with ointment and bind them. Can we sit somewhere in private so you can explain what happened? I arrived at the end of a tragedy; I need to understand the beginning. Might you have coffee? We don't have coffee on Kolora, so I always try to drink some when I'm off-world."

"Yes. I will ask the cook to make some immediately. We can speak in my den."

Warnom followed Li-ara. "Umae, please join us," Warnom invited. "I believe you are an important part of this tale."

"Umae is the one who found Hunter and brought him home," Li-ara said, gesturing to a chair for Warnom to sit.

"Then perhaps, Umae, you will begin." Warnom listened as Umae recounted what transpired, including the part about the wild canines.

"An interesting story." Warnom mulled over several pieces of the tale. "Were you able to identify any designations on the flyer?"

"No, I only caught a glimpse when the ship took off with Willomay. But I remember it had a unique configuration from the back and a rather unusual sail."

Warnom reached over and removed a piece of paper from one child's notebook and a pencil. "Can you draw a diagram of what you saw?"

"I think so." Umae quickly sketched a likeness of the craft he had seen.

"You're sure this is an accurate depiction?" Warnom questioned.

"Yes."

"Is there a problem?" Li-ara asked.

A knock sounded at the door. Warnom quickly slipped his helmet back on. The cook carried in a tray of three cups and a container of coffee and one of water, placing them on the desk. The moment she left, Warnom removed the helmet.

"I still don't understand why you can remove your helmet?" Li-ara said. "Hunter always said it was forbidden."

"For a Hunter, it usually is. But as I said, I am a teacher. When I am off-world, I normally hide my face, but since you are BiiJun's wife, I have no fear or shame of showing you. Since Umae is now the keeper of BiiJun's life, I may be seen by him as well." He took a sip of coffee, swished the liquid around in his mouth, then slid it down his throat. "Excellent. Now let me retake a glance at that drawing."

Umae handed him his sketch. "This is definitely a Traders' ship, but not a *Rogarian* one. A new sect of Traders called the *Bollo* has taken up residency in the sector."

"That's why the arrow that killed Kii was different," Umae said.

"They have copied many of the *Rogarian* traditions but have altered them to their own customs. We believe they are using the *Rogarians*' former hideouts, but since we never discovered where they were, these new Traders remain undetected."

"Are you saying we have no way to find our children?" Umae asked.

"No, I am not saying that."

"Then what are you saying?" Li-ara asked.

"That we need help." He pressed a button on his wristband and spoke in a strange language. Li-ara recognized a few words she overheard Hunter use over the years. It was Kolorian. Within minutes, a reply played over his wrist. "She will be here in two days."

"Two days?" Umae was horrified. "We can't wait that long. We'll lose any trail there might be."

"And how do you propose we follow them?" Warnom asked, pouring himself another cup of coffee. "Do you have a ship?"

"No. Don't you?"

"Yes, I do. Can you tell me where we should begin searching?"

"I don't know." Umae waved his hands in the air. "Somewhere out there."

"Not a very specific location. Therefore, we wait until she arrives."

"Who is coming?" Li-ara asked.

"The Dominee."

"The Dominee? I didn't think she ever left Kolora."

"She doesn't. Only one other time did she leave Kolora since becoming the Dominee. The day she brought BiiJun's mind out of hell."

"Who is this Dominee?" Umae asked.

"The Dominee is many things. She is the leader of BiiJun's sect, the TriiBone clan; she is Kolora's chancellor and our supreme ruler; she is the holder of the sacred truths and rituals, the teacher of the *Gaball*, and the enforcer of the law. But, most importantly, she is BiiJun's godmother."

"He never told me that," Li-ara said, surprised by Hunter's omission.

"I don't think he remembers."

Li-ara gave Warnom a puzzled look. "The journey from Kolora to Orallia is at least an eight-week journey. How can the Dominee be only two days away?"

"Like many before her, the Dominee is a seer. She foresaw BiiJun needing help weeks ago and launched half of the fleet."

"The fleet?"

"Yes, she brings with her many Huntsmen," Warnom added.

"If she was aware of this travesty eight weeks ago, why didn't she warn us?" an angry Umae asked. "The Traders would not have stolen my daughter and J'Dar. And Hunter would not be wounded."

"One does not question the Dominee," was all Warnom said.

21 THE DOMINEE

As Warnom stated, a fleet of Huntsmen arrived in their airships two days later. Thirty vessels landed on top of the hill surrounding the house, leaving a space for another three ships in front. Fifty landed in the airfield a mile away to the west, followed by another fifty to the east, south, and north.

Li-ara stood beside Warnom, with Umae on her other side. Three additional ships landed in front of the first thirty, almost touching the house as they landed. Beings scrambled everywhere to avoid being squashed by the ships.

"I warned them to make lots of room," Warnom snickered.

The middle ship closest to the house was a small craft made of *kolorite* white gold. Its shell shimmered like fine porcelain. The vessel contained no windows except for the cockpit, which included a small oval semi-dome.

The side door opened, and three armored guards stepped out and stood on the ramp with weapons drawn, ready to fire at anyone who advanced toward their Dominee. A fourth guard approached Warnom and exchanged words. He turned and walked back into the ship and emerged with the most beautiful being Li-ara had ever seen.

She was tall and thin. Huntsmen's armor covered her body, made from the same material as her ship - kolorite white gold. The clothing visible beneath the armor was also white, as was the *Pervian* cat fur that wrapped around her neck and shoulders. She walked down the ramp, her back straight, a figure of grace, beauty, and authority. Her very presence demanded respect. The Dominee spoke not a word to anyone as she approached Li-ara.

"So, you are the one who stole my best Hunter from me." Her voice was powerful yet feminine. Reaching up, she lovingly placed Li-ara's face in her white-gloved hand and turned her face right, then left. She released the female's face without comment. "We will talk. But first, I must see BiiJun."

"This way, My Lady," Li-ara said, bowing deeply. Warnom instructed her and Umae on the proper etiquette and greetings, and she hoped she was performing everything correctly. As they ventured inside, a circle of Huntsmen guards surrounded the cabin, their bodies erect with weapons drawn.

When the small group reached the bedroom, Warnom reached out his arm and stopped Umae from following. "Only BiiJun and his wife are allowed." He closed the door and stood in front of it, barring any attempt to enter.

Li-ara walked over to her unconscious husband and took his hand. "He hasn't woken since Warnom injected him with his medication two days ago."

The Dominee moved closer and pulled the covers from Hunter's side. She unwrapped his bandages and examined his wounds. "These are healing well, but slowly. We need to correct this." She resealed the bandage.

In silence, she walked around to the other side and pulled up a chair beside the Hunter. Reaching up, she removed her helmet and placed it on the floor. Li-ara stared at a youthful woman with long, wavy white hair. She remembered Hunter telling her that the Dominee was at least a hundred years old, yet before her, she saw the face of a thirty-year-old.

"BiiJun, can you wake for me?" the Dominee whispered. Hunter's body stirred. The Dominee opened a vial on her wristband and laid it alongside the Hunter's nose. A green vapor escaped and drifted up into his nasal passages. She bent forward and whispered in his ear. "I am here, BiiJun."

Hunter's eyes popped open. He stared into space, seeing nothing. He blinked several times, trying to focus on the face before him that was not Li-ara's.

"Dominee," he said, as his vision cleared.

"It is I, BiiJun."

Li-ara jumped as Hunter sprang up into a sitting position. "J'Dar. They took him." Li-ara's eyes filled with tears as she witnessed the look of desperation and fear on her husband's face. "You know what they'll do to him, Dominee. I must find him. Give me the strength to find my son before the Traders hurt him."

The Dominee pressed Hunter back down into a prone position. "You still remember the horrors of those days, don't you? No matter how many times I tried to remove them from your memory. I failed."

"Help me."

"That is why I am here." She replaced her helmet. "Li-ara, would you kindly open up the windows in this room so BiiJun can view what I brought him."

Li-ara ran around the room, joyfully opening the curtains and shutters to reveal what waited outside. Hunter stared in disbelief. "Two hundred thirty Huntsmen ships filled with almost a thousand Hunters at your disposal. Fifty ships with three hundred Huntsmen will remain here with me and protect your family until you return."

Disbelief filled Hunter's mind. Surely, he misunderstood her statement. "Why would you do this? Why would *THEY* do this?"

"Because they took your son," the Dominee said. "As you are my godson, dear to me, so is J'Dar. The Huntsmen come at my request to help you rescue him. And Umae's daughter."

"Umae's daughter?" Hunter turned to Li-ara for clarification.

"The Traders stole Willomay just hours before they took J'Dar. Umae was on his way back here for your help when he found you."

"I remember. I came out of the cave, and they shot me. Twice. Am I dead? Is this all a dream?"

"No, my son. Your wounds are serious, but you thankfully wore your breastplate. The metal stopped the shot from penetrating your heart."

"I remember. I planned to use the armor when I trained J'Dar on the technique of using his knife. Placing it inside my shirt was the easiest way to carry it." Hunter paused, a look of desperation on his face. "The knife. I lost my father's knife, Dominee. I gave it to J'Dar for his tenth birthday."

Li-ara walked over to the dresser and removed an object from Hunter's satchel. Holding something reverently in her hand, she walked back and laid a knife on her husband's abdomen.

"Kolor's knife. How?"

"I found it inside your pack," Li-ara responded.

"J'Dar had the knife with him. Somehow, he hid the knife inside my satchel when they took him. He didn't want me to lose it."

"The instinct of a true Huntsman," the Dominee said.

"Dominee, while I am thankful for the fleet and your presence, I still do not understand," Hunter said. "You never leave Kolora. The fact that I am your godson is not justification for such a grand gesture."

The Dominee smiled. "The fact that you are my godson is more than enough justification. Did you forget you called me away from Kolora once before?"

"Yes, when the *Büloot* brought me home."

"You are correct. The reason I left Kolora this time differs vastly from last time. Today, I come because you are the *Kiquan*, the bringer of truth. Thanks to you, our teachings and way of life are spreading across this galaxy. Your land is filled with strangers who willingly put aside their differences and work towards making this world a better place. Without you, there is no peace, no tomorrow for the Huntsmen or any clan. And I am here because hidden inside you is the location of where the Traders are hiding, the place J'Dar and Willomay are being held."

"Dominee, such information is not inside me. I didn't even know *Rogarian* Traders stole my son."

"They weren't *Rogarian* Traders, BiiJun. These traders are a more corrupt, more putrid form of scum called the *Bollo* Traders. You must stop them."

"How?"

"You must tell us where their stronghold is."

"I told you, I don't have any idea."

"Their hideout is the same one the *Rogarian* Traders used. It is where your *Kentite* master took you."

"He never took me there."

"He did, BiiJun. That awful place was your home for two years or longer."

"Then why can't I remember?"

"Because I made you forget," the Dominee said. "They did such horrible things to you and my Sooh Rey, unimaginable things, things no being, especially a child, should endure."

"Your Sooh Rey?" Li-ara inquired.

"Sooh Rey was my first-born son, as J'Dar is yours," The Dominee's voice broke under the emotion of reliving the memory. "Sooh Rey's agony ended the moment he died, but BiiJun's lived inside him. For weeks, he screamed in terror, afraid to let any of us near him. I did the only thing I knew to do - remove as many of his memories as possible."

"Is that why he has little recollection of his past?" Li-ara asked.

"Yes. I never intended for it to happen, but my treatments erased much of his childhood. That's why, if I restore your past, I can't seal it away again. Not this time. If I try to lock it back, you could lose everything - your memories of Li-ara, your children, your life as a Huntsman."

She paused, her voice lower now, burdened with truth.

"What I offer is not healing, it's a burden. One you'll carry for the rest of your life. But it will give us the location of the Trader's base."

She stepped back.

"Rest now, my son. Speak with Li-ara. Decide together what's right for your family. When you're ready, give me your answer."

"I don't need time, My Lady. And I have no time for rest. My son must be rescued now." His voice was low, grounded in something deeper than resolve. "The memories of my captivity have remained hidden for too long. Let them bleed. Let them scream. I'm not afraid of them anymore."

He raised his eyes, squeezing Li-ara's hand gently. "Searra told me that Li-ara's and my love was my salvation. She was right. It's the only thing that ever truly held me together. Li-ara is more than my strength. When the bear attacked me on Proxima Prime, it was her light I crawled toward as the darkness tried to pull me under. She is still my light. The reason I breathe. The reason I fight."

A silence settled, thick and unyielding.

"What you show me will be pain, yes. But pain is a shadow. As long as Li-ara stands with me, the past can't own me." He stared at the Dominee, unflinching. "I will walk through it. I will not break."

"So be it, BiiJun."

"Is Warnom here, or did I imagine him?"

"No, he is here," Li-ara said.

"I need to talk to him. You said Umae found me?"

"Yes."

"Is he still here?"

"He's with Warnom outside the door."

"I need him, too. We'll need my ship. She is one of the few flyers the Traders cannot detect. Umae must take Warnom to where she is hidden. And he needs to retrieve the rest of my armor. I can't launch a battle with only a breastplate and an arm vambrace."

"Hunter, you're still too injured to go," Li-ara said.

"I will not stay behind while others try to rescue my son. As the Dominee said, I'm the only one who knows where they are. Somewhere hidden in my memory is the station's layout, where the children will be housed, where the weapons are. But more importantly, where the secret passage inside is located."

Li-ara looked at the Dominee for help. "I am afraid he is right. Only BiiJun can get inside. I can speed up his wound recovery and bind his skin with *kolorite* binding. But, BiiJun, you must promise me you will not engage in open fighting. If you take a blow to your side, the wound will reopen, and you will die. Do you understand?"

"Yes."

Li-ara stood still for a moment, then forced herself to the door and opened it. "Warnom, Hunter asks to speak with you and Umae."

Warnom and Umae stepped into the cave, shadows swallowing them as the cool, mineral-scented air closed in. Guided by Hunter's instructions, they navigated past the jagged outcroppings until they reached the large, blue-speckled stone nestled against the wall.

Warnom knelt, pushing the rock aside. He drew a small shovel from his pack and began digging. The soft grains gave way inch by inch until something caught the light - a corner of an aged cloth.

Carefully, he brushed the sand away, revealing the edges of the bundle buried beneath. His fingers slipped under it, slow and deliberate, as if afraid to disturb what lay within. Lifting it with care, Warnom set the bundle gently on the ground. He bowed his head, voice low and steady as he murmured the sacred Huntsman greeting. He began to unfold the cloth, his

290

hands reverent, until the familiar shape of Hunter's armor emerged beneath his touch.

"As good as the day he buried it," Warnom whispered, his voice barely more than a breath as his fingers glided across the smooth metal, lingering on the etched lines of the Huntsman insignia.

Umae stood motionless beside him, his eyes wide, lips slightly parted. He had seen armor before, but nothing like this. There was a weight to it, a presence that filled the cave and wrapped itself around his chest.

"That's not just armor," Umae murmured. "It's … him."

Warnom nodded once, solemn. "It remembers. Just like we do."

He sorted through the pieces, looking for the right wristband. Once he found it, he raised it to his forehead in homage to the Huntsman whose armor it was. He removed his own armor vambrace and clamped Hunter's brace to his forearm. The clasp clicked into place with a tight hiss. For a moment, he paused, then pressed the activation node. A soft hum rose, vibrating in the stillness. The wristband came to life, crimson lights flickering across its surface like coals waking from slumber.

Warnom folded the cloth around the remaining pieces of armor once more, each movement slow and precise. When the last fold was in place, he gathered the bundle into his arms, cradling it against his chest like something fragile, sacred.

Together, the two emerged from the cave and made their way to the cliff's edge. The wind greeted them like an old ghost - cold, restless, and full of whispers. Below, the lake stretched out in shimmering silence, its surface rippling with silver light.

Beneath the gentle waves, the truth slept – hidden, deep, untouched, waiting.

"You're sure his ship is down there?" Umae questioned, looking over the side. "I see nothing but clear water."

"The lake is a crafty temptress," Warnom said, passing the bundle of armor to Umae. "She is deep and hides many secrets beneath her waves. Watch." He punched in the code Hunter gave him.

Nothing happened.

"Maybe she disintegrated," Umae said. "Or her batteries died. She's been hidden for a long time."

"No," Warnom said, his eyes locked on the still water. "Kolorian ships are built to last for centuries. She's just taking her time to wake up."

A single air bubble surfaced - small, silent, almost insignificant. It burst with a soft *plop*.

Warnom pointed toward the center of the lake. "See? She stirs."

Then, thirty seconds later, another *plop*. Then another.

Within moments, the surface fractured into chaos. Bubbles rose by the dozens, then hundreds, until the water boiled with motion. The sound was deafening, like rain falling upward, like the breath of something ancient exhaling all at once.

Warnom's jaw tightened as the churning water frothed and surged. "She remembers."

From beneath the waves, something massive reached for the sun.

"I see something!" Umae shouted, his voice nearly lost in the roar of the churning lake. He stepped forward, eyes locked on the heart of the disturbance. Through the storm of bubbles and spray, a shape began to emerge. Ghostly at first, little more than a blur beneath the writhing surface.

Then, it grew clearer.

A massive gray silhouette pushed upward, slow and relentless. What began as a smudge took on shape and purpose - smooth plating, angular ridges, faint glimmers of light along its hull. It moved like something ancient, a creature shaking off centuries of silence. The water frothed around it, hissing and boiling

"There she is," Warnom said as the spacecraft floated inches below the surface.

"I don't believe it," Umae shouted. "I can't believe she's still in one piece."

With a thunderous surge, the *Li-ara* erupted from the lake. A deep, resonant hum vibrated through the cliffside. Sheets of water streamed off her hull, cascading like silver rain as the upward thrust lifted her into the open air. Thick strands of algae clung to her like tattered robes, swaying in the air - but no snails, no barnacles adhered to her sides.

Umae stared, transfixed. As the vessel glided closer, he saw it. A narrow gap existed between the floating greenery and the ship's skin. Not a single leaf or tendril touched the metal. The vegetation hovered, suspended, repelled by an invisible barrier.

"So that's why she didn't rust. A force field protected her from the water's corrosion and destruction."

"Can't keep a ship hidden underwater for six years without a decent force field," Warnom chuckled.

The ship hovered before them, humming with restrained energy. Slowly, Warnom turned her, her engines whispering. She glided toward a wide patch of flattened meadow stretched out before the cave.

Hovering low, the *Li-ara* paused, her shadow draping over the grass like the wings of some great bird. Then, with a barely audible hum, she descended.

The landing struts settled into the soil with a soft, satisfying *thump*, compressing the grass beneath them. A gust of warm air vented from her flanks, stirring wildflowers and scattering loose petals across the clearing. The engines wound down, their last breath hissing through the tall blades.

Umae exhaled slowly. "She's beautiful."

"That she is!" Warnom pushed a combination of three buttons, turning off the force field. The water vegetation crashed on the ship. He softly grasped Umae's shoulder. "Let's pull all this green gunk off. Next stop, Hunter."

———————

"Before I can open your mind, I must seal your side wound," the Dominee said. "Have the children been taken somewhere they cannot hear their father's scream?"

"Yes. A caregiver took them to her house in the village." The thought that it was necessary to send their children far away sent shivers down Li-ara's spine.

"Normally, I would allow no one in the room to view what I am about to do, but you are his rock and strength. What you are about to witness, you must tell no one. You must never talk about it, even amongst yourselves. You must forget."

"As you wish," Li-ara said.

The Dominee removed two white ropes from her waist. "Take one," she said, handing it over. "Bind his wrists to the headboard. I'll secure his ankles at the foot. It is important that he not move. When I begin, hold on to his hands. Under no circumstances, let them go."

The Dominee leaned forward. "Hunter, you are no stranger to pain and are skilled in the Huntsmen training of ignoring it. Such training will not help you here. What I am about to do will feel like the very fires of Hell are burning through your body. Because of the extent of your injury and the necessity that you must leave within the next few hours, I cannot give you anything for pain except this *junisper* root. It will help some. Are you ready?"

"Yes," he breathed. It was barely a sound. More the whisper of a ghost than a man. Hunter opened his mouth and positioned the root between his teeth, preparing himself for what would come.

"Roll over on your side."

"Hold on to me," Li-ara said as she intertwined Hunter's fingers in hers.

"Recite with me. BiiJun, the Warrior's prayer."

The Dominee began the prayer, her voice low and solemn, each word carrying the weight of ancient power. Beside her, Hunter's lips moved in time, echoing the sacred rhythm.

As she continued to recite the chant, the Dominee uncorked a small, weathered jar, releasing a faint, acrid smell into the air. She tilted the jar over Hunter's gaping wound, and a fine, dark powder spilled out. For a fleeting moment, nothing happened.

Then, the powder stirred.

Hundreds of tiny black spiders spilled from the dust, no larger than grains of sand, emerging in a dark, glistening wave. They surged over Hunter's side, drawn to the torn flesh like predators to blood. Their legs moved in eerie unison, a nightmare given rhythm. Each shimmered like polished obsidian, glinting with unnatural light as they crawled into the wound.

Li-ara froze. She opened her mouth to scream, but terror crushed the sound. Her eyes snapped to the Dominee, pleading, searching, but the woman's expression remained calm, resolute. Unshaken.

With arms lifted and palms outstretched, the Dominee chanted a new song, low and ancient, a melody born from a time before memory. The Kolorian healing rite. The air vibrated.

The spiders stirred at her voice.

They began to grow - doubling, tripling in size until their limbs dug deep into Hunter's skin. Their fangs pierced his flesh, and they began to feed. The sound was sickening - wet, slurping, methodical. With each bite, a shimmer of green spread across his blood.

Acid.

It sizzled where it touched raw skin, smoke rising in thin, curling tendrils. The spiders spun frantically, casting silk soaked in acid into the wound. The web glistened, stretching wider, sealing the torn flesh in burning threads.

Hunter gritted his teeth, veins bulging in his neck. The *junisper* root in his mouth snapped in two with a sharp crack. He twisted on the bed, sweat pouring from him in torrents. His jaw locked in agony, every muscle in his body fighting the fire under his skin. The room filled with the stench of scorched flesh, thick, cloying, unmistakable.

"Dominee, STOP!" Li-ara cried, voice trembling, breaking. "You're killing him!"

But the Dominee gave no answer. Her voice only rose, commanding now, echoing off the walls. Her fingers carved glowing sigils in the air, drawing the pain into purpose. The spiders obeyed, weaving faster, sealing deeper, burning more.

Hunter yanked his hand free from Li-ara's grip

"Hold his hand," the Dominee called out.

Li-ara swiftly entwined her fingers around Hunter's. Hunter fought her, trying to reach the searing heat and brush it away.

Hunter convulsed. His body lifted off the bed in one final, brutal arc, and from his throat came a scream that shattered the stillness of the chamber. It was not the cry of a man. It was the roar of something being torn apart and remade in fire.

The Dominee chanted.

The spiders spun.

An intricate lattice of acid-laced silk tightened across Hunter's shredded side. The searing threads burned like fire laced with needles, each strand biting deeper as the wound disappeared beneath smoldering webbing and a frenzy of skittering obsidian bodies. They moved with merciless purpose, stitching him together as if he were nothing more than torn hide.

Hunter thrashed, his back arched off the table, but the bindings held firm.

Still, he screamed.

Again.

And again.

For five eternal minutes, his screams echoed through the chamber - raw, inhuman, tortured. They rose in waves, broke in sobs, then rose again, a sound so primal it bypassed thought and struck directly into the soul.

Each cry sliced into Li-ara, reverberating through her bones. Every instinct screamed for her to run, to cover her ears, to shut out the agonizing symphony of his suffering, to save herself from this unbearable sound.

But she didn't move.

Her hands remained clamped around his, trembling from the force of his convulsions. Her grip was iron, forged from desperation and devotion, refusing to loosen even as her arms ached. If she let go, he would be alone in the fire, and that, she knew, would break him.

Hunter screamed again, long and shuddering. Then he collapsed, breathless, his body limp beneath her grip.

The chanting ceased. A deafening silence followed, thick and oppressive, as if the room itself were holding its breath.

The Dominee stepped forward, her expression unreadable. She held a small vial filled with glowing orange liquid in her hand. In silence, she uncorked it and poured the contents over the wiggling mass of spiders.

The response was instant. The spiders' legs curled inward, their bodies shriveled, twitching violently before going still. Within seconds, the entire swarm lay lifeless, collapsed in a dark mound atop the sweat-soaked sheet.

Smoke coiled from the pile. The healing was done.

The Dominee bent down to Hunter's ear. "It is over. You did well, My Son." She straightened and turned to Li-ara. "As did you. You can let go of his hands now. But his wrists must remain tied for a bit longer."

Li-ara slowly loosened her grip, her fingers trembling as she untwined them from Hunter's hand. She stood, turned quickly, and crossed the chamber in a few swift strides. Her hands shook as she lifted the water bowl, its surface trembling with each breath she took. Grabbing a clean cloth, she returned to his side.

She washed away the sweat clinging to his skin. She brushed the cloth gently across his brow, over his cheeks, down his neck and chest, careful to avoid the glistening, acid-sealed wound.

"Are you still with me?" Li-ara whispered.

Too weak to speak, Hunter nodded, his movement slow and deliberate. His breaths came in deep pulls, the air rushing to fill lungs that had fought to keep going. A hint of color returned to his cheeks.

The Dominee scooped the dead spiders across the bed into a container. "Rest, Hunter. Remain on your side. The webbing must harden before I place the *kolorite* weaving over your skin. The weaving must enhance the seal, not adhere to it, and become a part of it. Once the webbing hardens, I will remove your restraints."

"How long?" his words wavered as if each syllable cost him more strength than he could afford to give.

"It should take about thirty *clotnocks* for the web to harden. Once the seal has formed and I have bound you, I will begin restoring your memory."

"So soon?" Li-ara shrieked. Her eyes snapped to the Dominee, pleading. "Can't he rest? Just for a few hours? Look at him. He's barely breathing."

"No," Hunter whispered. "Must … leave."

Li-ara bent down to his eye level. "Hunter, you can't. You just endured the most horrible pain I've ever witnessed. You need time to recuperate."

"No. Restore now."

"I can't restore your memory until I bind your wound with the *kolorite* weaving," The Dominee said, examining the solidity of the webbing. "In your agony of remembering, you might tear open the wound."

"Agony? How bad can the memory restoration be?" Li-ara asked, her face even paler. "How much suffering can one man endure before he breaks completely?"

The Dominee's face grew solemn, her features carefully composed into a mask of practiced calm authority. Beneath the stillness, a storm of remorse and sorrow churned.

"The intense pain BiiJun just suffered is nothing to the emotional agony he is about to experience. I need you to be very, very strong, Li-ara. Your husband is a strong Huntsman, a Bounty Hunter, afraid of no one or nothing. But when I restore his memories, he will return to that terrified and tortured boy his father brought to me. Do not think less of him, but celebrate the hero he is today. He relives his past to save his son and Umae's daughter."

"I could never think less of him," Li-ara said.

The Dominee removed from her pocket a mesh-chained cloth made of tiny rings of *kolorite* metal. The metal weaving would bind Hunter and keep his blast wound sealed. And him alive.

Warnom gritted his teeth as he eased the controls forward, lifting Hunter's ship into the air. The vessel groaned in protest, her systems sluggish from years of dormancy.

She rose, but not cleanly. The nose pitched slightly left, drifting off trajectory. Warnom corrected, but his change was too late. The ship scraped against the rocky outcrop with a metallic screech, sparks flashing in the rear view.

"Maybe I should have walked," Umae said, pulling his seat belt tighter.

"BiiJun's made too many damn modifications to this heap of junk," Warnom offered as an explanation. "Makes it hard to understand what to do."

Warnom's hands flew across the controls, trying to coax the ship into balance. The left thruster sputtered, then caught, and she began to level out. The ship bucked again, then settled into a slow, trembling hover above the ground.

"You sure you can fly this?" Umae asked.

Warnom smiled. "Hey, she hasn't flown in six years. She's got a right to complain."

The Li-ara lifted gracefully into the air, her engines humming with surprising steadiness. Warnom kept a firm but relaxed grip on the controls, guiding the ship toward her owner. She swayed gently in the wind, dipping slightly as she adjusted to full flight.

Aside from the occasional gust that nudged the ship off-center, the journey home was uneventful. The rhythmic thrum of the engines filled the cockpit. Below them, the landscape rolled past in shades of green and gold, familiar terrain welcoming them. Twice, the ship took a sudden dip, barely missing a collision with the ground. Each time, Warnom corrected her course.

"She flies better than I thought she would," Warnom murmured, half to himself.

Umae offered a quiet nod, eyes scanning the horizon. Finally, the cottage came into view.

Warnom set the Li-ara down with a *thump* and lowered the ramp. The moment the hatch hissed open, Umae bolted. His boots pounded down the ramp, the feel of solid earth beneath his feet a welcome relief after the tense flight. He didn't slow. He headed to the cottage. But as he reached the porch steps, the air split with a scream.

It was sharp, raw, and utterly inhuman, filled with such pain, such primal torment, that it stopped him cold.

"What is happening?" Umae inquired. "It sounds like someone is butchering a *glisperzen* alive."

"It's BiiJun," the Huntsman said quietly, his voice barely carrying. He sat slumped on the front porch steps, hands hanging between his knees. The screams echoing from the bedroom were too much. His legs had given out beneath the weight of it, and he hadn't bothered to stand again. His eyes remained fixed on the ground.

"What are they doing to him?" Umae asked as he ran up the steps, determined to end whatever was happening.

The guard stood blocking the Ki-wan's advancement, grabbing Umae's arm. "You may not interfere."

"The hell I can't."

"Umae, he's right," Warnom said, climbing to stand beside the Ki-Wan. "The Dominee is restoring the memories BiiJun forgot. He is reliving the horrors of his childhood. He does this with free will to save his son and your daughter. If you try to stop the proceedings, you will never lay eyes on your daughter again."

Another bone-piercing cry thundered through the air. Umae flinched, his stomach lurched. He glared at the guard. "How can you sit there and listen to those screams?"

"To do so is my duty. I am assigned to guard this door and will remain here until my commander or Dominee tells me I may leave."

The glistening of tears on the Huntsman's breastplate caught Umae's attention. Beneath his helmet, the soldier was crying as he lived Hunter's pain. Yanking his arm free, Umae covered his ears and ran from the yard.

"How long has he been like this?" Warnom sank onto the step beside the guard.

"For over an hour. His cries keep getting worse." He turned to Warnom. "Do Huntsmen survive this?"

"No one's ever gone through this before."

"BiiJun is the first?"

"And hopefully, the last." Another scream exploded into the air. "What did those heathens do to that poor boy?"

After two hours, the screams ceased. Li-ara sat on the floor, cradling her sobbing husband, her tears mixing with his. The Dominee sat in a chair, crying her own tears. Her soul ached for the pain she caused her Huntsman. She remembered the horrors of BiiJun's time with the Rogarian Traders. But her knowledge did not prepare her for the truths BiiJun remembered.

When able to control her emotions, the Dominee replaced her helmet and went to the door. "Onk, BiiJun remembered where the Trader's hideout is. Tell the fleet to prepare to launch. They leave within the hour. BiiJun will emerge momentarily to give them the coordinates."

"Might I ask where the stronghold is, My Lady?"

"They hide in the *Unis* Asteroid Cluster."

"But no one can navigate through the boulders."

"No one except the *Bollo* and BiiJun. He remembered the secret route."

"You can't possibly expect him to leave within the hour," Li-ara spat, her temper flaring. "He can't even stand."

"Li-ara," Hunter said between sobs, fighting to control his emotions. "You witnessed what they did to me. Time is not our friend. If we don't rescue J'Dar, they will do the same to him. They may have already."

"Don't say such a thing," Li-ara shrieked, covering her mouth with her hand to stifle a scream.

"Dominee, please ask Warnom to bring in my armor," Hunter said.

"In a moment." The Dominee removed another vial from her pocket containing a yellow powder. She poured it into a glass of water and swirled it, mixing the ingredients. She handed the glass to Li-ara.

"Help your husband drink this. It will help restore his strength."

While Li-ara helped Hunter drink the medicine, the Dominee opened the door. "Warnom, BiiJun is ready for his armor."

Warnom entered the bedroom and saw Hunter crumpled on the floor. He placed the wrapped bundle on the bed and reverently opened the package, putting the pieces across the bedding. When completed, he walked over to Hunter, his screams still echoing in Warnom's mind.

"Li-ara, perhaps you can help me raise BiiJun to his feet."

Li-ara clenched her fists, every fiber of her being screaming to cry out "No", begging them to leave her husband in peace. The urge surged up her throat, raw and desperate, but she swallowed it down. She stayed silent.

She knew if Hunter didn't go, their son would suffer the same unspeakable horrors her husband had just relived.

For J'Dar's sake, Hunter had no choice. And neither did she.

Li-ara took a deep breath and steadied herself. She stood, slipped her hand beneath Hunter's arm, and helped lift him to his feet. With Warnom's help, she guided him to the edge of the bed and eased him down.

The Dominee checked Hunter's side, running her fingers across the *kolorite* mesh. "Warnom, help Li-ara wrap BiiJun's side."

Warnom folded a towel in half and held it against the shimmering weave. Li-ara wrapped a length of gauze around his waist, each pass snug but gentle.

"You doing okay?" Li-ara asked.

"Doing better," Hunter whispered. "The Dominee's medicine is working."

"I need an undershirt and a long-sleeved shirt to put on him," Warnom said. "Also, a fresh pair of pants. And, if you happen to have a scarf, I'll take that as well."

Li-ara moved swiftly to the dresser. She gathered the shirts and trousers, then turned to the closet. Her eyes scanned the shadows until they landed on the scarf tucked away, forgotten yet waiting. She retrieved it and returned to Hunter's side with all three items.

Li-ara gently lifted Hunter's arms as Warnom eased the shirts and his vest over his shoulders, guiding them down carefully over the tender lines of his healing frame. The trousers followed, replacing the sweat-soaked pair clinging to his legs. Li-ara wrapped the scarf around his neck, smoothing it flat against his collarbone.

The armor came next.

In silence, Warnom connected the breastplate to the backplate, the polished metal clicking softly into place. He guided the completed piece over Hunter's head, fastening the side straps securely. Each motion was deliberate, ceremonial, more than dressing a warrior. It was restoring one.

The scapula armor followed, resting against Hunter's shoulders like a mantle of responsibility reclaimed. One by one, Warnom fitted the boots, ankle guards, shin plates, and leg armor, the pieces locking together in a rhythmic sequence.

He slipped the gloves over Hunter's hands, then carefully fastened the wrist armor in place, sealing the final piece of the second skin Hunter had once worn so effortlessly.

Standing him up, Li-ara held him as Warnom placed a padded strip across Hunter's abdomen, an added barrier for protection and balance. Over it, he secured the armor belt, tightening it with a practiced tug. Hip plates clicked into place, followed by the broad strap of a weapon harness, secured firmly across the front.

Then, the final moment.

Warnom turned, lifted the helmet, and held it out.

Not to Li-ara

Not to Hunter.

But to the Dominee.

Only she could complete the rite.

Only she could anoint the warrior reborn. She stood, still unsteady, and walked to her Huntsman.

"BiiJun, I stripped you of your Hunter's title six years ago and banned you from Kolora. Today, with this helmet, I restore to you the title of Huntsman, Hunter Extraordinaire, with full privileges." She placed the helmet over Hunter's face. Hunter struck his heart with his right hand and tried to go down on one knee.

The Dominee reached out and stopped him from bending his knee. "Not today, My Brave Huntsman. Today, I bow to you." The Dominee bent her knee slightly and bowed to her knight.

Warnom and Li-ara assisted Hunter in going to the kitchen. The room was filled with the newly arrived commanders and Umae. More Huntsmen lined the porch, gazing through the doors and windows.

Hunter struck his heart and bowed. He knew it was the only thanks his fellow Huntsmen needed. They returned the gesture.

Hunter activated the holographic projector on the table. A detailed star map appeared, focusing on the Unis Asteroid Cluster. He gestured toward a tight grouping of asteroids at the cluster's core. "Inside this cluster is their fortress. It is where they are holding my son and Umae's daughter. It is impenetrable. But a safe pathway *DOES* exist. And I know it." He enlarged the Asteroid Cluster and drew a squiggly line through the field of floating boulders. "Because of its secrecy, it contains no cannons, no radar to detect our presence."

"The corridor is narrow. Only six vessels can enter at once. Since I am unfamiliar with many of you, I will rely upon you, commanders, to choose the best pilots and aircraft. I need aviators who can fly by instinct rather than instrument, who feel the ship's pulse as if it were their own heartbeat. The flyers must be capable of executing abrupt, razor-sharp turns and exhibiting outstanding maneuverability. Only with such pilots and aircraft can we hope to traverse this treacherous pathway successfully."

He turned to Umae. "Our children will be held here, in this building." Hunter drew a basic schematic of the compound. "We will land first. Umae, Warnom, Gutz, Kled, and I will enter here, the back closest to the prisoner housing."

"Me?" Warnom asked. "I'm not a Hunter. I'm a teacher."

"Today, you are a Hunter," the Huntsman said. Warnom lowered his head, hiding his smile. "Two of the accompanying vessels will maintain their positions here and here. If reinforcements are needed, they will supply them. If we fail in our objective, it will be their mission to get the kids out."

"The other three ships will position themselves at the front of the complex. They will concentrate their fire here." Hunter switched the map again, drawing another schematic. "Their weaponry should draw most of the *Bollo* Traders away from the hostages. But only artillery fire. Save the cannons until we're out."

"Once I hear your weapons, we will slip inside and rescue the children. The moment the children are safe, all ships are to evacuate. No one is to wait for me or any other vessel. Understood?"

"Yes," came a variety of voices.

"Do not, I repeat, *DO NOT* blow up the compound. The explosion will disrupt the asteroids, and we will all die. You can bet some Traders will pursue us in their ships. Do not fire upon them. Wait until everyone is out of the corridor, then give it everything you've got."

Hunter looked at the many masks before him. "Trust in your training, trust in each other, and let's bring J'Dar and Willomay home."

A mighty cheer rose amongst the commanders. The sound spread across the lawn and down amongst the ships. As the joy dwindled, Li-ara heard, "BiiJun, BiiJun, BiiJun."

22 THE RESCUE

Hunter removed his helmet and kissed his wife goodbye. He held the kiss for a long time, taking in all the love she had for him. When he broke the kiss, he wiped the tears from her cheeks.

"I have something for you," Li-ara said. She nodded to Umae. He stepped forward, holding a wrap in his hand. Li-ara opened it and presented to her husband the knife he had given his son.

"*D'nang do Unamae.*" Hunter raised the weapon to his forehead, then placed it inside his belt. "I will plunge *D'nang* into the being who dared take our son and carve out his heart."

"Good," Li-ara said to Hunter's surprise. His screams still resonated in her mind, reminding her of what they might be doing to her son. For the first time in her life, Li-ara wanted revenge.

Reaching into her pocket, Li-ara withdrew the silver coin with Beta and Kii's etched pictures. "This brought you back to me once before." She slipped the keepsake inside his vest next to his heart. "May it bring you back to me again."

Hunter took a step to the side, standing before the Dominee. "I remember, no knee bending." He imagined she smiled beneath her helmet.

"You are correct, no knee bending. But only for now. When you return with your son, I expect a bend to the ground."

Hunter laughed. "As you wish, My Lady."

The Dominee held a hand over each of Hunter's shoulders. "BiiJun, may the spirits of our ancestors guide you and the fleet to victory. May the will of the One be done. Good Journey."

"May His will be done," Hunter said. Raising Li-ara's hand to his lips one last time, he kissed it, turned, and replaced his helmet as he ran to his awaiting ship. As he neared the ramp, he noted a deep scrape on the port side. Running his fingers along the deep grooves etched into the metal, he felt the raw edges where the hull had been torn. She was pristine when he left her on the lake floor. His jaw clenched as his voice thundered through the ship. "Warnom! Did you scratch my ship?"

Scanning the area inside for the elusive teacher, Hunter climbed the ladder and took his seat behind the wheel. He started the engines, listening to her purr.

"Let's go get our boy, Girl."

Hunter lifted his ship into the air, delighting to feel her vibrate beneath his grip once more. After removing his helmet, he turned the flyer to the side. Raising his hand to his lips, he blew Li-ara a kiss. She blew one back. Then, he and the fleet were gone.

Li-ara watched the departing ships ascend into the azure expanse, their forms growing smaller until they became mere specks against the vast sky. Beside her, the Dominee stood.

Li-ara's lips parted slightly, the one question haunting her lingering on the tip of her tongue, yet fear anchored it there. She had to know the truth and grasp any sliver of hope, but the terror of hearing an answer she couldn't bear paralyzed her.

"You are wondering if you will see him again," the Dominee said.

"Yes."

The Dominee turned and placed her hand on the fearful wife's belly. "Your daughter still awaits in the spirit world to be born. Something happened last time, and she had to return to the unborn world. She still longs for the day she will meet her father and mother."

"My unborn daughter? Oh, no, Dominee. Hunter wants no more children. He fears their loss too much. And he fears for me."

"You must change his mind, for she must be born. She is an important part of the peace that will travel across this galaxy. And the only way she can be born is if her father returns and plants his seed inside you. Yes, Dear Sweet Child, he will return."

"With my son?"

"His future I cannot see."

"Have they done things to J'Dar as they did to Hunter?"

"I do not know."

The fleet emerged from hyperspace outside the *Unis* Asteroid Cluster. The belt was packed densely with asteroids ranging from a few yards to hundreds of miles across. It was believed the field contained nothing of value. But Hunter knew the truth. At its heart lay a minor planet the *Rogarian* Traders discovered decades earlier. Scattered across the sphere were countless gems and precious metals which funded the pirates. And it was the perfect hideout with an unpredictable entrance.

The doorway changed configurations as the asteroids drifted, yet the pathway remained constant. Any vessel veering a tenth of a degree off course would be pulverized. When the Biiloot killed Hunter's master, the secret to entering their domain was lost to all outsiders except one – BiiJun. The path had remained etched into his memory, vivid and unyielding. Thanks to the Dominee, he could navigate it as though he had sailed through its treacherous field just yesterday.

"We're looking for two large cylinder asteroids," Hunter said over the radio. "One is made of carbonite and the other of green pyrite. That is the entrance. Everyone, fan out and search for these two stones."

"Looking at them now," came a voice over the radio.

Hunter drifted into position, and there it was - the entrance, a doorway into his past.

"Are you sure, BiiJun? Their orbits don't appear very stable."

"That's because their orbits aren't," Hunter said. "The asteroids are constantly moving up, down, or sideways, but the distance between two adjacent stones remains constant. Remember, you can't maneuver the field by coordinates - only by landmarks. Mimic the fighter before you. If you deviate even a *tripod*, you will be squished like a bug in your boot. Is that understood?" Confirmations sounded across the air. "Remember the landmarks. If we run into trouble, retreat and hit the asteroids with everything you have. The asteroids will destroy the planet."

"BiiJun, they will also smash your ship."

"If I'm not leading the way out, I'm already dead."

Hunter maneuvered his ship into position. The five accompanying pilots followed suit, forming a line behind Hunter's lead ship.

"To my knowledge, this is the only entry and exit point. But there may be other routes I am unaware of. Commander Hil, deploy the remainder of the fleet to encircle the asteroid field's perimeter. Should any Trader vessels attempt to escape, neutralize them."

"Will do," came the answer.

"For those of you going in, follow me." Hunter flew past the two boulders. "It gets tight in here real quick, so stay alert. Keep close together. Watch your wings."

Each ship followed in close formation, swerving around boulders, flying upside down to squeeze through a narrow spot, keeping their fighters' wings tight against the ship.

"This is insane," Warnom said as Hunter made a sharp left turn. The teacher's eyes opened wide with fear as he witnessed boulder after boulder try to smash them. "How much longer?"

"A little claustrophobic, Warnom?"

"No, a lot afraid of being squashed like a bug."

"About another five minutes, and we'll be clear. I see the glow from the compound's lights up ahead." Warnom's stomach churned as Hunter did a three-hundred-and-sixty-degree flip.

Hunter's ship slipped into an expansive void as they cleared the last asteroid. Ahead loomed the Trader's stronghold, its shadowy structures punctuated by dark windows that seemed to peer into his very soul. The cold seeped from its walls, as cruel and unforgiving as the soul who inhabited it. Hunter stared, his stomach's acid rising into his throat. He coughed and swallowed, closing his eyes, calming his insides.

"Just sneak inside, get J'Dar and Willomay, and leave," Hunter said to himself. *"And, if possible, kill the bastard who stole my son."*

"Everyone, turn off your lights," Hunter said. "Switch to stealth mode. Vignew, take your three flyers to the front."

The three ships moved past Hunter and traveled to the right. The other two remained suspended behind Hunter, like silent sentinels ready to strike if needed.

Hunter nudged his ship down, setting it silently upon the compound's platform. He pushed the ramp button and cringed as he heard the gears groan as it lowered.

"Should have remembered to oil that damn thing," Hunter mumbled.

Umae and the four Huntsmen softly walked down the ramp, weapons drawn and ready. Warnom and Umae looked past the compound walls at the floating asteroids only yards away from the structure. Each one, like the asteroids in the passageway, remained constant, neither straying closer to the structures nor drifting away, their presence a perpetual reminder of the razor-thin line between survival and obliteration. Warnom tried to swallow, but his mouth had no spit.

Hunter and his team slipped into the shadows, waiting. "Cunat and Rigel, there are more Traders inside than I estimated. I need another six Hunters down here.

As Hunter prepared to enter the compound, Vignew and the other two ships took their positions in front of the compound. They opened fire, sending a barrage of bullets into the structure, pulverizing the stone blocks, sending chunks of stone and concrete into the air. Flashes of light erupted across the metal door as bullets ricocheted off the impenetrable entrance. Within seconds, Rollo Traders emerged, firing at the fighters but inflicting minor damage.

"They're using hand weapons," one pilot said. "They're bullets can't reach us."

"Guess they're too afraid to use any kind of launcher or heavy loaders," another replied. "They're afraid to disrupt those asteroids behind us."

"Really poor military defense planning," Vignew laughed. "Heads up. They're making a run for those flyers. Don't let them lift off the ground."

"Got them." The two accompanying ships opened fire and blew up the flyers resting on the flight pad. With nowhere to hide, the Traders ran back to the compound. Vignew fired his guns. No one made it back.

The moment Hunter heard the shots, he gave the silent command to proceed. He reached out and grabbed the teacher's shoulder. "Warnom, I need you to return to the ship and keep the engine running. Make sure no one but us boards her. If we don't make it back, get out of here."

"Hunter, I can't fly your ship. I'm not a pilot. You saw what I did to your ship just flying her back to your cabin. In here, I'll crash within minutes and take everyone with me."

"With luck, Gutz or Kled will return and fly you out. But if not, have Cunat or Rigel pick you up and take you out in their craft. I believe in you, Warnom."

"Glad he does," Warnom said to himself as he ran back inside the flyer, withdrawing the ramp and closing the door.

The team ran across the platform, moving like shadows, their presence swallowed by the silence of the stronghold. The double doors loomed ahead, a barrier against the unknown. Then, the faint echo of hurried footsteps shattered the quiet. Hunter froze, raising his fist, and the team melted into the darkness. Weapons drawn, silencers clicked into place, they waited, motionless.

The doors burst open with a thunderous crash, slamming against the walls as eleven Bollo Traders stormed through, weapons ready. Silent bullets zipped through the air, striking with unerring accuracy. One by one, the guards crumpled to the floor, their lifeless bodies sprawled in unnatural stillness. The Huntsman remained motionless until the final Trader fell.

Hunter stepped forward, his boots barely audible as he crossed the bloodstained stone. His sharp gaze swept over the bodies, confirming the kills before signaling the all-clear. The team followed silently, their movements synchronized as they pushed deeper into the stronghold.

A narrow corridor stretched before them, its dim light casting long shadows on the walls. Hunter motioned to take the right-hand path. With each step, the air thickened, carrying a vile stench of sweat, blood, and urine. The acrid smell clawed at his senses, dragging him back to a past he could never forget. Nothing here had changed.

Hunter clenched his jaw as the passageway stretched ahead, familiar and haunting. He bypassed the offices lining the hall without so much as a glance. He knew they'd be empty. His focus lay at the end of the corridor, where the hall widened into a vast, open room.

As the hallway ended, BiiJun abruptly stopped. The sight before him stole his breath. His legs trembled. Four metal cells lined the far wall, each crammed with wide-eyed children, their faces pale with fear and exhaustion. Their small bodies huddled together for warmth, their bodies shaking from fear. For a moment, Hunter saw his younger self staring back at him through the bars. He blinked, and the image was gone. He wasn't inside the pen but outside, ready to rain hell on those responsible.

Hunter raised a finger to his lips, silently commanding the children to remain quiet. Their frightened nods were the only response. Hunter and Umae moved quickly, scanning the faces in desperation. Their eyes searched every corner of the cells, every terrified expression, but their son and daughter were not among them.

Hunter's fists tightened around his weapon, his knuckles white with rage. The sight of the children fueled his resolve. This was no longer a mission, it was a reckoning. Whatever it took, no matter the cost, he would end this nightmare.

"J'Dar or Willomay?" Hunter mouthed.

"J'Dar is down the next hall," an older boy whispered back. Hunter noticed the scars on his arms. A gash covered his face. "I don't know where Willomay is."

"We will get you all out, but I need you to stay here and be quiet for now. Can you do that?" The children nodded their heads.

Hunter continued, progressing silently down the hallway, checking each cage they passed for the missing children. Halfway down the hall, Hunter stopped. Up ahead, the passageway branched out in three different directions. Hanging by a heavy chain in the intersection hung a lone body. His hands and feet were bound. Blood covered his body. Hunter rushed forward as he recognized the prisoner's clothing. It was J'Dar.

"J'Dar? J'Dar, can you hear me?" Hunter asked, trying to keep his voice low while not panicking. His son was severely beaten. His nose leaned to the side, and his face was swollen, displaying various shades of black and blue. One eye was swollen and closed, and the other half-shut. Dried blood and blood clots matted his hair towards the back of his head.

"Is he alive?" Umae asked as he ran over and released the chain. The links made a loud clanking sound as it lowered, alerting two Traders. As they came forward shooting, Gutz and Kled took them out.

"Hurry, Hunter," Gutz shouted. "They know we're here."

As the still body of J'Dar descended, Hunter took him into his arms. He grabbed his knife and sliced open the ropes that bound the child's hands and feet.

"J'Dar, are you with us?" Hunter asked again.

J'Dar opened his half-closed eye in terror. Unable to determine who spoke, he shook and tried to fight. "No, don't hurt me. Don't beat me anymore."

"J'Dar, it's me, your father," Hunter said, removing his helmet. "I'm here to rescue you."

J'Dar recognized a blurred outline of his father. "Dad?" He threw his bloody arms around Hunter. "I thought you were dead."

"Where is Willomay?" Umae asked.

"Umae? I … I tried to s … s … ave her. Traders tried to rape her. I stop … stopped them. He … he killed them. Said she wa … was for some general. M … m … ust be a vir … virgin. He was grate … grateful. Beat me. No wh … wh … whip. He b … b … be … beat me over and over."

"Who took her?" Umae asked.

"Konk," J'Dar and Hunter said simultaneously.

"You know him?" Umae asked.

"He was the one who gave me my scars. He rewarded me the same way for so-called 'good' deeds. Umae, take J'Dar back to the ship."

"No, I must find Willomay," Umae said.

"I've got this. Trust me, My Friend."

"Dad, I'm coming with you," J'Dar said, trying to stand.

"Not this time, Son. You go with Umae."

A Trader came out of nowhere and grabbed Hunter around the neck. Hunter raised his gun, placed it alongside the Trader's temple, and pulled the trigger. J'Dar stared as blood splattered across his father's armor. "Kled, take Gutz and another, and take Umae and my son back to the ship. The rest of you with me."

"It will take more than the six of you to retrieve her," Kled responded. "I can get them to the ship. Take Gutz with you."

"The alarm has gone out. It will take all of you to get J'Dar and the other children to the ship. I can do what I must, but only if I know J'Dar is safe. Go before more Traders arrive."

"Hunter, I'm going with you," Umae said, grabbing Hunter's arm and stopping him from leaving. "I'll not abandon my daughter. It is my obligation to rescue her."

"Yes, it is. And the way to fulfill that obligation is to let us do our jobs as Hunters. You are an exceptional warrior, but you are out of your element here. Your presence will only slow us down and hinder our rescue. Trust me, Umae. I will rescue her. For now, I need you to rescue my son."

"And what of the bastard who took our children? I want to be the one to kill him."

"If I can, I will bring Konk to you for your pleasure. Now go. We are wasting precious time."

Umae did not want to forfeit the right to slice open the being responsible for his daughter's kidnapping. But he also understood that if he wanted his daughter back, he had to trust Hunter. The Huntsman could only work his magic if he knew J'Dar was safe. Retracing their steps, Umae and the others took J'Dar down the hall.

"Cunat, Rigel, we need more help down here. Land and send the rest of your men in." Gutz shouted into his radio, feeling no need for silence anymore. He heard firing across the link.

"We're kind of busy up here."

"I don't care how busy you are. One of you needs to land."

"On my way," Cunat said.

"Come through the double doors and take the hall to the right. You'll see several Huntsmen there with a group of kids."

"Did you say kids?"

"That's what I said. Take them to your ship. We'll rendezvous shortly with Hunter's son."

"Roger."

A bullet ricocheted off Gutz's shoulder armor. He turned and fired, killing two Traders. Kled took out a third. The sound of running boots alerted them that more were coming from different directions. Throwing J'Dar over his shoulder, Umae ran towards the cells. Kled and Gutz followed, shooting anything they encountered.

"Hurry. Help me push these beds over and against the bars," Umae shouted to the children as he laid the blind J'Dar on the floor. "We just need to hold them off for a few minutes."

The children scrambled in panic, overturning their cots and shoving them against the bars that lined the hallway. Blankets, thin mattresses, anything soft, were hastily piled behind the wooden frames in an attempt to build a barrier. Whispers turned to cries. Then, footsteps. Ten Rollo Traders stormed into view, rifles already raised. Muzzles flashed. The air exploded with the thunder of gunfire. They were shooting the children.

"No," Gutz shouted, removing the pulsating rifle from his back. He opened fire, cutting the Traders into pieces. Kled did the same. Umae hurried amongst the children, getting them to lie on the floor behind the barricade. He crawled over to one of the shot children and dragged her to cover. Blood poured from a gaping hole in her chest.

"You will be okay," Umae said, ripping off his shirt and pressing it into the wound. "We will get you medical attention, and then you will go home."

"I don't know where my home is," she replied, looking up into his face.

"Then you'll come to live with my family and me," Umae said, holding the young girl's hand. "I have three daughters, so you'll fit right in."

"Thank you." She smiled. Her eyes glazed over. Her head fell back.

With trembling hands, Umae reached up and closed her eyelids. "Sleep, my child. For you are home." Enraged at the child's needless death, Umae stood and fired, shooting into the still bodies of the dead Traders.

Gutz walked over, put his hand on Umae's weapon, and lowered the barrel. "They're dead, Umae. They can't hurt her anymore."

The sounds of weapon fire and yells echoed down the hall, followed by pulsating rifles and the sound of running feet. Prepared to fight their way out, Umae and the other saw three bleeding Traders running towards them. They were fleeing, not advancing. From the west, twenty Huntsmen emerged, firing their weapons.

"Where in the hell did you guys come from?" Kled shouted.

"One of the pilots recorded the path Hunter took. When he heard Hunter request more men, he asked for two volunteers and brought in more fighters."

"Who's crazy enough to try such a crazy stunt?"

"Some young kid barely old enough to shave named Qui. He's one hell of a pilot."

"Open these cells," Cunat ordered, breaking the lock and slamming the door open. "Take the children outside and put them on the ships. Carry the wounded and the weak. Take J'Dar to Hunter's ship." He scanned the area. "Where is Hunter?"

"He went after the leader and my daughter," Umae said, lifting the dead girl into his arms.

Cunat looked at the still body. "Umae, I think it's too late for her."

"I'll not leave her behind."

Cunat did not argue.

———————

Hunter walked down the center of the corridor, back straight, intent on only one purpose - to rescue Willomay and apprehend Konk. Alive, if possible. But one way or another, Konk would be his.

Reaching the hallway leading to Konk's luxurious suite, he paused. The door stood ajar, a silent invitation that reeked of a trap. Hunter's jaw tightened as memories of that room filled his mind, threatening to unnerve him. He took a deep breath and stepped inside. Once in, he looked around and realized what waited for him were only memories, and they couldn't hurt him anymore.

The suite was as gaudy and grotesque as he remembered, its decadence masking the filth of its purpose. To the left, a man in a crisp uniform stood near the shadows, his posture rigid. Is this the General J'Dar spoke of? Or just another scumbag hiding behind power and lies?

In front of the man, four young girls stood, their small frames trembling. Their clothes, little more than scraps, did nothing to hide their fear or their vulnerability. His stomach churned at the sight, rage bubbling beneath his cold armor. He scanned their faces, his heart pounding. They ranged in age from eight to twelve. None of them was Willomay.

"I am sure this appears worse than it is," the male explained. Fear filled his voice.

"You are right. It's worse." Without any hesitation, Hunter raised his gun and fired, hitting the male in the groin. The man crumbled to the floor, screaming in agony. Hunter walked over to the now eunuch male and rested the barrel of his gun alongside the man's temple. "Where's the other girl? The one named Willomay?"

"Konk took her to another room." Hunter pulled the trigger.

Keeping his eyes focused on the entranceways, he asked the girls, "Which way did they go?"

"That way." The oldest pointed to Hunter's right.

"You four go with these Huntsmen. They are here to rescue you. Run as fast as you can." Accompanied by two Huntsmen, the girls ran from the room and down the hallway. Hunter listened as their footsteps faded.

The last four Huntsmen guarded his back as Hunter surveyed the next room. It was empty. Stepping into the hallway, he shouted, "Konk, where are you, you bastard?" His voice reverberated off the walls. Silence. Hunter inched forward, looking inside every room with his night vision, searching for hidden dangers. The rooms were empty. Where was Konk hiding?

"Show yourself, Konk," Hunter shouted. "Or do you only fight children?"

"As I live and breathe, a real live Huntsman," Konk said as he emerged from the shadows behind Hunter. He held Willomay with his arm, a long hunting knife resting on her throat. "What do I owe this pleasure to? Here to purchase a few slaves of your own? Gets lonely on your ship at night?"

"I came for my son." Hunter nodded towards Willomay. "And that girl."

"Your son? Your son, you say?" Konk thought hard. "There are no Kolorian children here. You've made a mistake."

Hunter removed his helmet. "I don't make mistakes."

Konk gawked hard at the male before him. The male seemed familiar. "Do we know each other?"

"Let's say I'm familiar with your ways of praising those who do good deeds."

Konk's face lit up in remembrance. "You're that skinny little kid, the one the old *Kentite* master kept around. Your kid's the one hanging in the hallway. I thought he looked familiar. I told Jimsy something was familiar with those blue eyes. Sorry, if I had known, I would have returned him. After all, you were my greatest pupil." He smiled, showing a mouth of broken black teeth.

"Give me the girl."

"What's she to you?"

"A girl."

"Sorry, no can do. There's this big-time General due here tomorrow with lots of money who plans on buying her. If she's gone when he arrives, I'm afraid he'll be quite upset. And I don't want to disappoint him."

Hunter stepped closer, his gun never straying from its intended target. "I said, give me the girl."

From the blackness of the adjacent room, six Traders emerged, firing their weapons at Hunter's companions. Their bullets penetrated between the armor plates of two Huntsmen, killing them. The remaining two Huntsmen quickly eliminated the threat.

"Nice try, but not good enough," Hunter spat, his anger boiling inside. A sharp pain erupted inside his shoulder. A *Bollo* Trader emerged from behind and pushed a knife into Hunter's body between his breastplate strap and his shoulder armor. Hunter swung around and fired, hitting the attacker in the chest. His attention diverted for a moment, Konk grabbed his gun while keeping his other hand with the knife at Willomay's throat. As he prepared to fire on Hunter, another shot ran out. Konk screamed in pain, dropping the knife, his weapon hand in pieces. Willomay elbowed him in the ribs and ran the moment he eased his chokehold. Hunter spun around to find out where the second shot came from. Warnom was against the wall with a gun in hand, a trail of smoke emanating from its barrel.

Hunter's instincts ignited at the sound of rapid footsteps echoing through the corridor. In a fluid motion, he spun around, weapon raised, every muscle coiled for the anticipated attack. His mind braced for Konk's assault. But instead, emerging from the shadows, was Willomay. Hunter looked past the girl, but Konk was nowhere in sight. Umae's daughter closed the distance between them in seconds and collapsed into his arms.

"Are you okay?" Hunter asked Willomay. She nodded in affirmation. "Did you see which way Konk went?"

"No."

"Come on, Warnom, we need to get Willomay to the ship." When no response came, he turned, his eyes searching for his companion. To his astonishment, he saw the elder Huntsman sitting against the wall, his face pale and drawn.

Warnom stared at the red circle growing below his breastplate. "Guess I should have asked the Smithy to make me a longer plate." He tried to laugh but cringed in pain. "I don't think I can do as you ask, Hunter. Go, get her to safety."

"I'll not leave you behind."

"Go. I'll only slow you down."

"You will if you keep talking." Hunter hauled Warnom to his feet, slinging an arm around his waist. Another Huntsman rushed in, locking his grip on the opposite side. With the wounded warrior supported between them, the two sprinted down the corridor. Their boots pounding against the metal floor as shouts and gunfire echoed around them.

"Willomay, do you know a way out?" Hunter shouted. "We can't go back the way we came."

"Yes. There's a service door up ahead. It's not far. Down the next hallway to the left."

At the next junction, the small group veered left. Warnom's steps became increasingly sluggish, his body sagging with exhaustion. Each movement turned into a struggle, his weight nearly overwhelming his companions as they labored to support him down the dim corridor.

As they rounded a corner, the corridor exploded with the deafening crack of gunfire. Bullets whizzed past, their supersonic snaps slicing the air, while others struck the walls with sharp, echoing thuds. Sparks erupted as rounds ricocheted off their metal armor. The acrid scent of gunpowder filled their nostrils, stinging their eyes.

Hunter pulled Willomay behind the wall, shielding her body with his armor.

"Stop," Warnom said, sliding against the wall. "I can't go any farther. You have to leave me, Hunter. You said our priority was your son and the girl. Fulfill what you came to do. Allow me a warrior's death. I can stay and keep them from following you." He reached inside his ammunition belt and withdrew two blasting bombs, each the size of a quarter.

"We can make it. All of us," Hunter said.

"You know we can't. Now, go."

Hunter removed an ammunition belt and laid it beside the injured teacher. "We will sing your praises in the grand hall. Give them hell."

"Good Journey," Warnom said.

"Good Journey," Hunter repeated.

"We can reach the service door down this other hallway," Willomay shouted as she ran forward. "It's a little longer, but it gets us to the same place." The two Huntsmen ran behind her.

"It's just up ahead," Willomay shouted. "Down this hallway to a set of double green doors. That will take us outside."

As the light from outside drew closer, Hunter detected movement at the entrance. Were they cut off? Had the Traders realized their retreat? Placing the girl behind him, he prepared to fight their way out. To his relief, Cunat and ten Huntsmen ran towards them.

"Willomay, go with the Hunters. They will take you to your father," Hunter stated.

"And where are you going?" Cunat asked.

"Warnom's hurt back there. I'll not leave him to die."

"Nor will I," Cunat said. He turned to his men, signaling out three. "Take her back to the ship and prepare to leave. Tell the Commander to get the fleet out of here and prepare to destroy this place. You two with us." The five Huntsmen followed Hunter back down the hallway and through the double doors. Firing echoed through the hall.

"Appears Warnom has them pinned down," Cunat stated, thinking he underestimated the teacher.

Hunter ran. "That's not all he has for them. Warnom plans on using a blast bomb to stop them. We must hurry."

23 JUSTICE

"I understand your canines show intelligence equal to ours," the Dominee said as she followed Li-ara into the kennel.

"On some occasions, I would say they even surpassed ours," Li-ara answered.

"Is it true that after the Traders shot BiiJun, a canine pack protected him? And a female canine led BiiJun's friend to his wounded body?"

"Yes. She and her pack also protected them on their way here, diverting any predators who thought Hunter was easy prey."

"Amazing." The Dominee knelt and scooped up the fluffy brown pup, its oversized paws dangling as she raised it to her vision visor. For a long moment, she stared into its eyes. "There's wisdom here," she murmured. "And a depth of feeling far beyond her months."

The pup wagged its bushy tail and stretched forward, planting a wet lick across the Dominee's helmet. Her vision blurred with slobber.

With a soft chuckle, she set the pup gently back into the pen. "But wisdom alone won't teach discipline." Using her sleeve, she wiped the puppy drool off.

"I only began training the new pups last week."

"How long does it take to train a canine?"

"Their intelligence and character determine the length of time, but generally, we can sell the pups when they reach three or four months."

"How long for in-depth training?"

"Two years for basic training. Four to six for in-depth."

"Six years ago, I sent BiiJun to Rigel Three to purchase eight puppies from you to use in our Hunting program."

"Yes, I remember," Li-ara replied. "Your directive was how he found J'Dar and me."

"I'm sure that after seeing you, he realized you were my real purpose for sending him to Rigel Three. But I still would like a return on my investment and to incorporate the canines into our Hunter program. When might I expect my eight pups?"

"I'm, I'm sorry, My Lady," Li-ara said, her face turning a soft red. "I owe you eight pups." She looked around the kennel. "I don't have that many canines trained at the moment. I can give you two now and two within a few months. I can take four out of the litter due next week."

"And it will be two years before they are completely trained?"

"Yes. But if you do the training, I can send the remaining four in four months."

"Do you possess any black canines?"

"No, My Lady. Black canines are rare. I have only seen three: Kii, the leader of the wild canine pack, and the foundling pup Umae has."

"Is it true the black canine possesses more intelligence?"

"Yes, from what I've witnessed. Kii solved complex problems better than any of the other domesticated canines. His great-grandson sired the litter due next week. Perhaps we'll be lucky, and a black pup will emerge." Li-ara paused. Tension crept into her jaw, and the light in her eyes dimmed, replaced by something raw and wounded. Her face, once animated, now held a haunted stillness. "My Lady, why do you think those Traders did those horrible things to Hunter?"

"Who knows why beings' hearts turn black and evil?"

"Are you going to tell Hunter Sooh Rey was your son?"

The Dominee's face lost its color, drained by the weight of memory hidden deep inside her. "I did not know BiiJun told you of the other stolen Kolorian boy." The Dominee walked to the window and looked outside. "I am grateful BiiJun did not remember the truth of my son. And, no, I will not tell him what he forgot. I fear the identity of the boy who saved his life would only add to his sorrow.. Best for it to remain forgotten. The truth of who Sooh Rey was will be our secret." The Dominee turned to face Li-ara. "Since you inquire about Soo Rey, I fear you have not forgotten the horrors you heard BiiJun speak of as you promised."

"No, My Lady. I don't think I ever can."

"Then I wronged you as well. And for that, I am sorry. Perhaps you can promise me this. If you cannot forget what you witnessed, then take some pleasure in knowing his horrors are the catalyst that molded BiiJun into the Hunter he is today."

"That I can do."

———————

Warnom remained hidden around the corner, safe from the Bollo's bullets hitting the surrounding walls. He leaned around the corner and fired, taking out two Traders brave enough to advance. Ducking back behind the mortar protection, he looked at his two guns. He was running low on ammunition, even with the extra belt Hunter left him.

"I believe it's time for the big guys." Warnom lifted the blast bomb from his ammunition belt. He listened for the sound of running feet and pushed the red button. "May the spirits of my ancestors show me the way home." He closed his eyes, awaiting his death.

"Not today," Cunat shouted as he ran by, grabbing the explosive from Warnom's hand. He ran into the hall and stopped, surprised by twenty Bollo Traders almost upon him. Debating what to do, he shouted, "Good Journey. Now, get Warnom out of here."

Cunat ran forward, bullets hitting his metal armor as he charged. As the last few beeps from the explosive sounded, he screamed a cry of victory, leapt into the air, and landed on the front five Traders. The bomb exploded, killing all the Traders and Cunat.

Hunter and another Huntsman hauled Warnom upright, each gripping an arm as his legs buckled beneath him. With grim determination, they half-carried, half-dragged the wounded warrior down the corridor.

"Why did you come back? Warnom asked. "I was ready to die."

"I wasn't ready to let you go," Hunter replied.

"Why did Cunat do that? Sacrifice himself for me?"

"You, of all people, should know the answer. You were and still are our teacher," Hunter said.

"Because I was injured and unable to save myself. He saved me because he was a Huntsman. And Huntsmen protect the innocent and purge the guilty."

"It is our most sacred code of conduct. I am glad your loss of blood has not clouded your memory."

Inspired by Cunat's sacrifice, Warnom forced his body to run. He wouldn't give up today. As they rounded the next corner, the green double doors came into view.

"Doing okay, Big Guy?" Hunter asked Warnom as he stood before the doors. "Just a few more feet. There's a nice crate waiting for you to sit on inside the ship."

"For Cunat's sake, I will reach the ship."

Hunter pressed his eye to the narrow gap between the doors, switching to heat vision. The corridor beyond glowed in muted reds and blues. Clear. No heat signatures. No movement. But he didn't relax. A cold void could still mask hidden enemies. Danger didn't always announce itself. With his hand hovering near his weapon, Hunter braced himself and moved to advance.

"Our journey begins now or never," Hunter said as he ran forward once more with Warnom. The five Huntsmen ran as fast as possible toward the waiting ramp. Hunters stood outside the landed aircraft, with weapons ready, waiting to shoot any Trader dumb enough to try to stop their retreat.

Hunter raced up the ramp into his ship. Then, abruptly, he stopped and turned.

The air was unsettlingly still, as if the world itself was holding its breath. The chaos he expected, the shouting, the gunfire, the Traders rushing to intercept, never came. Instead, an eerie silence enveloped him, oppressive and unnatural. A chill crawled down his spine. Konk was near.

"Take Warnom up and find him some medical help," Hunter said. He remained motionless on the incline, panning the area.

"Show yourself," Hunter shouted. "I know you're here."

Konk stepped from the shadow. The dim light flickered across the blood-soaked rag wrapped around his mangled hand, dark crimson oozing through the fabric in slow, sickening pulses. His grin was a predator's smile, hollow and cruel, something barely human. But it was his eyes, flat and merciless, that rooted Hunter in place. They burned with a hatred so intense, so personal, it needed no words.

Notably unarmed, Konk took a step forward, his eyes locked on Hunter's, unblinking, unrelenting.

When he finally spoke, his voice was a low, razor-sharp whisper that sliced through the silence, each word dripping with the unspoken promise of imminent revenge.

"Going so soon?"

"Not until you're dead."

"As you see, I'm still alive, Huntsman."

The Huntsmen raised their weapons, preparing to fire on the Rogarian Trader.

"He's mine," Hunter yelled. "No one fires on him."

"Are you going to kill me?" Konk sneered. "The big, brave Huntsman? You're nothing but a pathetic piece of dung. A scared little boy afraid to fight me."

"I see no one worth fighting," Hunter said, his voice cold and detached. "All I see is a pathetic shell of an old man who never amounted to anything. Someone so small, so weak, that the only power you could grasp was through the suffering of children. Is that why you tortured us? Was your existence so meaningless that the only way you could feel anything was by defiling those too young to fight back? You're not a man. You're a parasite, something from the bowels of hell."

"I know who you are now, Huntsman," Konk spat. "You can't hide. I'll hunt you down and take all your family. Every night, you can watch while I ravage your wife."

Hunter took two steps closer, each stride deliberate. His body trembled with barely restrained fury. Every fiber of his being screamed for vengeance, demanding that he end this hated creature's existence with a single pull of the trigger.

"Should I tell you the sounds your son made or how much he enjoyed what I did to him?" Konk screamed, grabbing his groin. "How do you live with yourself knowing your young Huntsman friend died because of you? Or did you forget? Let me refresh your memory."

A shot rang out, shattering Konk's kneecap. Blood squirting out of the leg, the Trader screamed in agony, dropping to the ground. "Aaahhh, why did you shoot my knee?"

"Because Hunter's right," Umae said as he walked up to the Huntsman, his weapon in his hand. "You are nothing. You're not even worth a bullet to the head." Umae turned to Hunter. "Come, My Friend. Leave him here to die a dishonorable death. Hurt him by denying him what he wants - a Trader's passage to *Breehalla*."

Hunter smiled. He turned and walked up the ramp, his back to his oppressor.

"There's no place you can hide," Konk screamed. "I'll never stop hunting you."

Hunter stopped in the doorway, staring at the pathetic creature below. He reached up and pushed the button. As the door closed, the sound of the defeated Trader screaming his name was music to his ears.

Hunter walked over to his son and took him in his arms. Fearing the worst, he asked, "Did he touch you?"

"No, Dad. He only beat me."

Hunter kissed his son on the head. "Let's go home. Strap yourselves in." Turning, he climbed the ladder up to the cockpit. Two soldiers followed him.

"Hunter, you need your neck wound attended to," one said. "You're losing too much blood. And you haven't recovered from your last injury."

"Is Vignew's group back?" Hunter asked, ignoring the Huntsman.

"Yes, they arrived five minutes ago. They're waiting to follow us out." Hunter flicked switches and pushed buttons. His craft's engines roared to life as thirty Traders emerged from the buildings, firing upon the aircraft.

"You can't make those turns in the field injured, Hunter," said the young Huntsman. "Vacate your seat now, or I will forcefully remove you."

Hunter cocked his head to the side in surprise. "You think you're grown enough to take me out of this seat?"

"Yes, Sir."

"And, if you do, who will fly my ship?"

"He will," the young Huntsman said, pointing to the other Hunter. "He's the one who brought in the other fliers that saved your ass."

Hunter looked at the second Huntsman. "I have the way out all memorized up here," the Huntsman stated, tapping his finger on the side of his right temple.

"Do we have a problem with our pilot?" came Umae's voice from below. "If we sit here much longer, those Traders will shoot the hell out of this ship."

"Do we, Sir?" the second Huntsman asked.

In silence, Hunter rose from his seat. The new pilot quickly slid in, making a few adjustments to the knobs and dials. Hunter's eyebrows raised as he observed the young pilot's choices. They were excellent ones. Why hadn't he ever thought of that configuration?

Taking a seat in the back, Hunter removed his breast and backplate. The first Huntsman applied a field bandage to help with the bleeding until they exited the asteroid field.

One by one, the ships thrusted upwards and waited. The young pilot lifted the Li-ara. He revved the engines, purposely creating a powerful wind that blew across the platform, knocking the remaining Traders off their feet. When he reached the entrance, the junior pilot slowed and entered. The others followed closely behind.

"Keep close together," the new pilot said over the comm. "Nine ships making it through safely is pushing the safety barrier."

"And what happens if nine flyers are one too many?" Hunter asked.

"We all die," Qui said.

Hunter's eyes narrowed, a flicker of skepticism crossing his face. "I plan on kissing my beautiful wife again, so you'd better be right on your estimate."

Hunter soon discovered why so many became ill when traveling through the field as Qui twisted and turned through the passageway. Thrice, the food he ate yesterday did its best to resurface. Below, someone vomited. He wondered if it was Umae. Hunter closed his eyes, but the blackness only made things worse. An alarm sounded on the console.

"We're being followed," the young pilot shouted. "I count three groups of eight Traders."

"Looks like they think eight is the maximum safety number," Hunter said, looking over at the display. "Are you really an ace pilot?"

"The best there is."

"Let's hope so. How far back is the first set of Trader ships?"

"One hundred and sixteen *quips*."

"It's going to be close, but doable. Okay, this is what I need you to do. Once our flyers have passed the entrance, swing a hard right and re-enter the passageway. Fifty feet in, you'll spy a large purple-blueish boulder. I want you to blast it at mark 45.2 by 198.8 *nips* the second you spot it. Then immediately bank at a fifteen-degree angle straight up."

"Yes, Sir."

"Everyone below, strap in tight," Hunter shouted. "This is going to get dicey."

As the flyers emerged, Qui looped the Li-ara in a three-hundred-and-sixty-degree loop and zoomed back inside, almost clipping the tail of the last flyer. As they sped down the passageway, Qui watched the blips on his radar.

"They're getting pretty close, Sir," Qui said.

"Give her a little more gas," Hunter said. "Raise your speed to eighteen *glinks*."

"Do you think that's a good idea? It's kind of narrow inside here. I'm barely keeping her within parameters now."

"You said you were an ace pilot. If we don't increase our speed, we're going to run straight into the nose of that first flyer headed our way."

"Here goes." Qui pushed the throttle forward.

The Li-ara sped up.

The blips grew closer.

The parameter alarms sounded.

Hunter held his breath.

The roar of the ship's cannon fire filled the cockpit. An immense force pressed Hunter's body into the back of his seat as his vessel catapulted upwards.

The blasted boulder slammed into a neighboring asteroid, cracking it open with a sickening crunch. That rock careened into another, setting off a brutal chain reaction through the corridor. The passage collapsed in a thunderous roar, sealing the path and crushing the Traders in a violent storm of debris.

Hunter wondered if Konk was on one of the destroyed ships. He hoped not. He wanted his nemesis to meet a slow, painful death and remember it was he who denied him a warrior's death.

Qui slammed the lever forward, and the ship surged upward, punching through the jagged gap. Ten seconds later, the boulders collided behind them with a deafening crunch, sealing the passage in a brutal cascade of stone and dust. The narrow escape left no margin for error. Only the echo of what could've been their tomb.

"Contact the fleet and advise them we're clear," Hunter said. "Tell Commander Hil to open fire and blast the hell out of the asteroid field."

As Qui brought the flyer back around to join the fleet, everyone watched the destruction through the port windows. The ships opened fire, sending a barrage of cannon discharges into the field, creating a cataclysmic event. Massive explosions reverberated from inside the asteroid bed. Geysers of flames shot into space, covering the area in their red glow. Hunter watched as the station and the horrors of his past were destroyed, along with the male who perpetrated them.

"Not bad," Hunter said to the young pilot as the second Huntsman attended to his neck wound. "You really are as good as you claimed. What's your name, Huntsman?"

"Qui, Sir. That's a considerable compliment coming from you," the pilot replied. "You're a legend on Kolora."

"A legend?"

"In flight school, we all learn the BiiJun flying maneuvers."

Hunter smiled.

"Sir, it appears the knife did some damage to several muscles. You're still losing considerable blood. I need to seal it with coagulant powder and stitch it closed. But this is only a temporary measure. You must have it attended to the moment you return home." The young Huntsman paused as he held the powder over Hunter's wound. "This will hurt."

"When doesn't it?" Hunter asked, closing his eyes and preparing for more pain.

Hunter woke up several hours later.

"Do you want to take the controls, Sir?" Qui asked.

"She's all yours. Take us home."

Swinging his leg onto the ladder, he climbed down to the cargo hold. His hunch had been correct - Umae was the person who became ill during

329

the flight through the passageway. Warnom didn't appear much better. The deck was covered with vomit.

J'Dar and Willomay stood at one of the port windows looking out into space. "She's a beauty, isn't she?" Hunter asked.

"I imagined nothing as beautiful as this," J'Dar said. "No wonder you spent your life traveling through space. The sights you must have seen. I want to see them someday."

"None as magnificent as that," Hunter said, pointing towards the Huntsmen fleet.

"Where did they all come from, Dad?"

"Do you remember when one of the Traders shot me the day they took you?"

"Yes," J'Dar hauntingly said. He didn't think he would ever forget that day or the sight of his father being shot.

"His bullets didn't penetrate my heart, but they did some major damage. No matter how I tried, I was too injured to come after you. Like it or not, even Huntsmen must sometimes admit their limitations and accept help from others. The Dominee foresaw my need for help and brought part of the Kolorian fleet to rescue you."

"The Dominee? You said she never leaves Kolora."

"She doesn't." Hunter pulled both kids into his arms, kissing first J'Dar and then Willomay on the head. "She understood how much you meant to your mom and me. And she remembered another innocent boy who endured the horrors of the Traders years ago."

"That boy was you, Dad. Right? Konk gave you those marks on your back. He beat you as he beat me."

"Yes. Take off your shirt, J'Dar. I want to inspect your injuries."

"Dad," an embarrassed son shouted. "I told you I'm well."

"I must see for myself." He started to unbutton his son's shirt.

"Dad, stop. I can do it myself." His cheeks red, J'Dar removed his shirt. Hunter turned J'Dar around, his eyes scanning every inch of exposed skin. The whip marks crisscrossed his back and shoulders, a brutal map of torment. Most were shallow, angry red streaks that stung to look at, but others were deeper, raw, and seeping. Blood oozed from three of the deeper gashes, trailing down his skin in slow, red rivulets.

J'Dar's face and arms bore their own share of abuse - cuts and welts scattered amongst black, blue, and yellow patches of skin. But it was his ribs that drew Hunter's worry. Angry purple bruises with veins of black ran across both rib cages.

"Inhale deeply," Hunter instructed, placing his hand lightly on his son's ribs.

"Oh, that hurts."

"I know. Just bear with me for a moment. Inhale." Hunter concentrated on whether he felt any ribs moving out of alignment. "Any sharp pain or trouble breathing?"

"No."

"Does it feel like your ribs are moving awkwardly?"

"No."

"It appears no ribs are broken, but I'll ask one of the Hunters to bind you to be sure. A few of your slashes are infected. They'll rub antibacterial ointment on them and across your back. Two may need stitches." He examined the closed eye. "It will be a week or longer for the swelling to go down. Keep a cool compress on the eye."

"Are the stitches going to hurt?"

"Yes."

"How bad?"

"I have learned that closing wounds is usually more painful than opening them. I'll ask the attending Huntsman to give you something to bite down on. Oh, and one more especially important instruction. When we arrive home, you must wait inside the ship until I talk with your mother."

"Why?"

"Because if I don't explain to her what your injuries are, she will freak out when she sees you." J'Dar glanced at his reflection in the window. He did appear pretty bad. "And she will do more than remove your shirt. She will want to inspect every inch of your body, from head to toe. If you think I just embarrassed you, wait until she examines you before the entire fleet and everyone back home."

A horrified expression crossed the young male's face. "Dad, you won't let her do that, will you? I mean, in front of everyone?"

"No promises."

Hunter felt Willomay's arms gently surround his waist. "Thank you, Hunter, for saving me."

"I had to." Hunter smiled down at her. "Your father is like my brother, which makes you a member of my family. Besides, you may be the future mother of my grandchildren." Hunter laughed when he saw the disapproving look on his son's face.

"Great, Dad. Nothing like embarrassing me again. Besides, Umae's pretty much explained how he feels about me."

"That was before you saved his daughter. I believe his view of you may have changed. But I'd still avoid kissing her. No sense ruining your good standing with her father."

"Dad." This time, both youths blushed in embarrassment.

"Willomay, would you mind if I spoke to my son in private?" Hunter asked.

"I need to check on my Dad. All the flying upside down and weaving made him sick." As she left, Hunter softly grasped his son's arm and escorted him to a corner of the cargo hold where he could speak in private.

"J'Dar, I must ask you something, and you must tell me the truth. I want you to look me straight in the eyes when you answer. I realize this will be embarrassing, but I must know." Hunter took a deep breath, preparing to hear the answer to the question he feared the most. "Did Konk or anyone else touch your private parts or do anything to you, you know, sexually?"

"Dad!" J'Dar's face turned bright red. "I told you I was okay."

"That is not an answer. Did they violate you?"

J'Dar saw the look on his father's face and, for the first time, realized what really happened to his father. Konk not only beat him, but he, and possibly others, sexually accosted him. No wonder his father didn't talk about his scars. They were the source of unbearable horrors. J'Dar gained a new respect for his father and a deeper understanding of the Hunter.

J'Dar looked directly into his father's eyes. "No, Dad, no one sexually violated me. You came in time."

"Do you know if they violated any of the other children we rescued?"

"A couple of boys and several girls were." J'Dar reached out and wrapped his arms around his father, thinking of what would have happened if Hunter hadn't arrived in time.

Hunter hugged him tightly, not wanting ever to let him go. "As of this moment, this topic is closed to everyone except you and me. You cannot discuss these things even with your mother. However, if ever you need to talk about Konk's treatment of you or what happened to the others, I will always be here to discuss what transpired with you. Is that understood?"

"Yes."

Li-ara reminded herself to breathe as Hunter's ship landed outside the back porch. She stared at the helmeted pilot. Fear gripped her heart when she realized the pilot wasn't her husband. Why wasn't Hunter flying his ship? He never allowed anyone else to operate her. Did her greatest fear come true? Had the Dominee lied to her?

Li-ara darted across the ship's side to the ramp in preparation to run inside and discover the truth. The seconds ticked by as she waited for the door to open and the ramp to extend. The report the Dominee received stated Hunter and J'Dar were fine, but reports often omitted details, exaggerated the truth, even lied. A Huntsman grasped her arm and moved her back into the safe zone.

"You cannot enter, Li-ara. They have wounded needing attention. And the pilot has not invited you aboard. You must wait down here."

The gears groaned and turned as the ramp extended. The Huntsman maintained his grip, preventing her from moving. Li-ara tugged, trying to advance. She needed to discover what happened to Hunter and her son.

"He is well," the Dominee whispered in her ear. "You must be patient."

At the sound of the Dominee's voice, Li-ara's breath slowed, her pulse reluctantly beginning to calm. There was power in the woman's words, and it was pulling Li-ara back from the edge. She cupped her hands above her eyes, peering through the swirling shadows at the doorway. Four Huntsmen stepped into view, a stretcher gripped between them. Li-ara's eyes strained, desperate to make out the figure lying still beneath the bloodied armor. Broad shoulders. Full gear. Too short to be Hunter, too husky to be J'Dar. She exhaled hard and closed her eyes, a rush of guilt and relief slamming into her at once. It wasn't them.

Next came Umae, and Li-ara's breath caught again. His face was ashen-green, drawn tight with something deeper than exhaustion - grief. Cradled in his arms was a small, cloth-wrapped body. Willomay?

The name screamed in her mind. Li-ara's vision blurred as she strained to see. Each step Umae took felt like a lifetime. She took a step forward. The Huntsman tightened his grip. The seconds stretched unbearably long. She squinted harder. Then, a head popped out from inside the ship. Willomay.

Alive.

Peeking, cautious, unharmed.

Li-ara's knees nearly gave out. Her lungs remembered to breathe. She pressed a hand to her chest, grounding herself, the surge of relief nearly as crushing as the fear that preceded it.

Three more followed behind Umae, all bloodied. One limped, aided by another. They passed before Li-ara, standing before the Dominee, heads bowed, bending a knee, accepting her whispered blessing like a lifeline in the dark.

But Li-ara couldn't tear her eyes away from the small, lifeless form cradled in Umae's arms. If it wasn't Willomay… *then who?* The question struck like ice, lodging deep in her gut and spreading through her veins with slow, paralyzing dread.

She slowly turned and scanned the landing site. More children were emerging from the other Kolorian flyers. Some were limping, others smeared with blood, wide-eyed and silent. A few were carried, their faces gray with shock or pain. One child sobbed quietly into a Huntsman's chest. Another dragged a bloodied blanket behind her like a ghost of comfort.

Her stomach twisted. Once more, the horrors of Hunter's captivity flooded her memory. Did these children endure the same abuse he did?

She turned back sharply, locking onto the ramp of Hunter's ship. The corridor beyond loomed like a gaping maw, and still no sign of them. No Hunter. No J'Dar.

Li-ara didn't move. She stood rigid, eyes locked, muscles trembling. The world narrowed to that ramp. That doorway. That silence.

Finally, Hunter appeared at the top of the ramp. His armor was off. His shirt clung to him, streaked with blood. How much was his, how much was someone else's? His right arm rested in a makeshift sling, and there was a weariness in his posture that spoke of battles far beyond the physical.

But he was alive.

Li-ara didn't wait. She tore free from the Huntsman's grasp and sprinted up the ramp, tears spilling before her feet even moved. The breath in her lungs turned to sobs as she closed the distance.

Hunter saw her and ran, despite the pain. He caught her in his uninjured arm, pulling her against him with a desperate strength, as if afraid she'd vanish if he let go. She rose onto her toes, his lips crashing into hers - fierce, trembling, and hungry with the ache of survival.

"I can't believe I'm kissing you again," Hunter whispered, breaking their kiss, resting his forehead on hers. "I feared I would never taste your lips again."

"You're hurt," Li-ara said. "And you're bleeding. Did you re-injure your side?"

"No, the side's doing fine. The Dominee's web held. Most of this blood belongs to the Traders I slaughtered. But a little is mine. I got stabbed in the neck."

"Your neck?" Li-ara's voice rose several octaves in alarm. "Who stabbed you in the neck?"

"I'll tell you all about how and who later. First, I must talk to you about J'Dar."

"J'Dar? Where is he?" The frantic mother glanced past Hunter, but she did not see her son.

"He's fine, but I must speak to you about him."

"What aren't you telling me? What did they do to him?"

Hunter lifted her hand, closed her fingers, and kissed her fist. "We reached him in time. Nothing terrible happened to him or Willomay."

"What terrible thing DID happen?" She imagined the worst. A severed arm or foot. Crippled. Cut in half. Beheaded. A million real and unrealistic ideas popped into her head.

"He's pretty beat up. But don't worry, the injuries are superficial. He has no broken bones or muscle damage. His face took the brunt of their mistreatment. It's black and blue, and one eye is still swollen shut. I think one of your poultices will help with the swelling. They had to stitch a few whip slashes on his back."

"I want to see him," Li-ara said, pulling away from Hunter.

Hunter pulled her into a holding embrace. She struggled against his grip, determined to find her injured son. Hunter held tight despite the pain she was causing him.

"Li-ara, stop. Listen to me. You can't go running up there like a mad woman and make a fuss. You'll embarrass him in front of everyone. He's not a baby anymore, but an adolescent male."

"He's *MY* baby."

"Yes, he is. But today, before all these Huntsmen, you must show them he is a man. Let him walk down the ramp with dignity. When he comes up to you, you can hug and kiss him briefly. Understand? Briefly. And no hysterical crying. And save all the gushy mother stuff for inside the house. Promise me." Hunter waited for a response. "Li-ara, he won't come out until I tell him it's okay. Do you want him to come out or remain inside forever?"

"I want to see my son, Hunter. I want to know he's okay."

"All right." Hunter released his embrace, ready to grab her if she left his side. "Take my hand and squeeze it if you start losing control. Here he comes." Hunter raised his arm and waved, then grabbed Li-ara's hand.

J'Dar poked his head out from behind the door. Everyone cheered as he stepped on the ramp. Li-ara froze, squeezing Hunter's hand as tightly as possible. Her heart sank as she saw how badly he was beaten. His face was so discolored, so distorted from the swelling. Not only was one eye closed, but the other was barely open. Willomay guided him down the ramp, meaning he had trouble seeing.

"He's well, Li-ara. Just remain calm."

Standing beside her husband, Li-ara raised herself up and down on her tiptoes. Every nerve in her body shouted for her to bolt and run to him, but she kept her stance, squeezing Hunter's hand so hard it was cutting off his circulation. After what felt like hours instead of a minute, J'Dar stood before her.

"Mom," J'Dar said, grabbing his mother.

Li-ara hugged her son, keeping her tears at a minimum. "Welcome home, J'Dar. Your father said they beat you, but you suffered no major injuries."

"He did a job on my face. But his beatings put me in good standing with Umae, so I guess they were worth it."

Li-ara lifted her eyebrows in surprise. She turned to Hunter for an explanation. "Another story for later."

"Willomay, I am so glad you are well. Were you beaten?"

"No, Mam."

Li-ara hugged the young girl. She pulled J'Dar back into her arms, then added Hunter. The sound of giggling surrounded the four as three younglings hugged their legs.

"Daddy. J'Dar," they chirped.

Trying not to fall over, Hunter broke free and knelt, hugging and kissing each of his three youngest.

"Daddy, did you get another Ouchy?" Nataa-a asked.

"Just a little one." Out of the corner of his eye, Hunter noticed the Dominee approaching. He lifted Nataa-a into his arm while the twins clung to his legs. He bowed. "My Lady. I fear my legs cannot bend."

"Children clinging to their father's legs and preventing a proper homage is the best reason to give none. It gladdens my heart to witness you united once again with your son. You did well, BiiJun."

"It would not have been a victory without the Huntsmen and you, My Lady."

"Qui tells me we lost twelve brave Hunters, including Cunat and Kled."

"Yes."

"True Huntsmen," the Dominee reverently said. "All will be greatly missed. Their families will be proud they died in battle. Cunat's wife is pregnant with his first child. Let us hope it is a male to carry forth his father's bravery."

"I did not know he was to be a father. I will be sure to send his widow a token of my esteem and thanks for her unborn child. I will also send something to the other families as well."

"As is our custom. Qui also reported that you did not kill the one who harmed you, even when he taunted you. Why didn't you plunge your knife into his heart as you had planned?"

"Every microbe of my being screamed for me to kill Konk. Then I realized that thanks to you and your teachings, he no longer had a hold over me. I wasn't a scared little boy anymore, but a true Hunter. I saw him for the pathetic being he was and, in doing so, realized he wasn't worth the price of a bullet. Nor did he deserve an honorable death. Plus, I realized if I wanted to bring peace to this world, it needed to begin with me." The Dominee smiled, although Hunter could not observe her satisfaction beneath her helmet.

"How many children did you rescue?" Li-ara asked.

"Only forty-eight," Hunter said. "When the Traders realized they were losing their captives, they purposely shot and killed as many as they could. Of those rescued, I fear at least five will not survive."

"That's appalling. Why would they kill them?" Li-ara asked.

"To preserve their secrets," the Dominee stated. "Had BiiJun been killed instead of rescued, we would not have known the entrance to the Trader's fortress. For beings such as the Traders, they prefer to destroy what is theirs rather than allow it to fall into the hands of others."

"But children aren't property."

"To them, they are," Hunter replied.

"Is that who Umae carried down the ramp? One of the shot children?"

"Yes. She died in Umae's arms. She was so young, she didn't even know where her home was."

"What will happen to the other children?" Li-ara asked.

"My Huntsmen tend to their injuries," the Dominee answered. "We will return those who remember where they came from to their home planets. Any children who do not remember or who have no one to return to will be adopted into our clan as Huntsmen. We will love and care for them."

"Several of the villages lost children," Li-ara said. "If they wish, might they adopt some children to replace the ones they lost?"

"A wonderful idea," the Dominee replied. She turned and addressed the Huntsman beside her. "*Glindar*, instruct *Minn* to separate the children with mild injuries and no known family. We will allow the villagers to adopt them first. Any children not selected, I will take with us to Kolora for adoption."

"Thank you, My Lady," Hunter said. "The children can never replace the ones lost, but they will help ease the parents' agony."

"As it should be. I take my leave. Take care of your family, BiiJun. Warnom will remain behind until he heals. I am also leaving twenty-four Hunters and their ships to help protect your family and patrol your land while you recuperate. I do this so you will take the time needed to recover. I leave another three Huntsmen for Li-ara to train on the breeding and training of wild canines." She turned to Li-ara. "I expect to receive the first two canines in three months, the next two in thirty-eight weeks, and the remaining four canines at the end of two years."

"As we agreed, My Lady."

"She's taking canines back to Kolora?" Hunter asked.

"A story for later," Li-ara said.

"While I enjoyed my time here and seeing my Hunter once more, do not give me a reason to leave Kolora again, BiiJun."

"I will try, My Lady."

She placed her hand on Hunter's cheek. "No mother could be prouder of a son."

"Thank you, Dominee."

"Take your leave."

She extended her hand to Hunter. After setting Nataa-a on the ground, he grasped the Dominee's hand, raised it to his forehead, then lowered it to his lips and kissed it. "Good Journey."

"Good Life." The Dominee slightly bowed her head and turned to leave.

"Tell my parents I send my love," Hunter blurted out as the Dominee withdrew.

She turned. "As you know, such emotions are not our custom, BiiJun."

"No, Dominee, but perhaps they should be."

"Perhaps."

"Might I inquire how they are doing?"

"You are a Hunter of many surprises today. It is the parent's job to worry about the child, not the child's to worry about the parent."

"Again, Dominee, maybe it should be."

Hunter sensed that hidden behind her helmet was a guise of approval. "Like all ex-Hunters, your father is grouchy and longs for the days of battle. Time is not always a happy present to our Huntsmen."

"And my mother?"

"She was stricken with *Trigillian* Fever three years ago. Her health has continued to decline since then."

"How many breaths remain for her?"

"I expect she will not live another three *daedoos*. That is the reason your father did not come to help save his grandson. He does not leave your mother's side but waits for both their deaths."

"He's always loved her dearly."

"Yes, he has. I will inform each of your accomplishments and deeds. And how proud I am of their son."

"Thank you, My Lady."

The Dominee paused at the base of the ramp, casting one final glance over her shoulder. Then she turned and strode aboard her ship, her guards following behind her, the hatch sealing shut with a metallic hiss. Engines rumbled to life, their thunder rolling across the field. One by one, the sleek warships lifted off, their underbellies glowing with fire. As the Dominee's vessel soared skyward, the fleet followed in perfect formation, rising like a storm into the darkening sky, until only contrails and trembling earth remained.

"Hunter, if your mom's that sick, perhaps you should take a trip back to Kolora and visit them. Sounds like she doesn't have long."

"The Dominee said she has less than three *dedoos* left. She will pass on to the next life before the Dominee returns home."

"Since you have no siblings, maybe you should bring your father back here to live with us," Li-ara said.

"He will die the next day."

Li-ara grabbed Hunter's injured arm. "What do you mean he'll die?"

"When a Huntsman finds their true mate in this life, they cannot and will not live a life without that mate. The Huntsman, be it either male or female, will seek the *Cattamalla*. We seek an enemy or a wild animal that cannot be defeated. Armed only with a knife and with no armor to protect us, the two will fight until the Huntsman dies. Reunited, the soulmates will journey together into the afterlife."

Li-ara's expression changed as the meaning of his words carved themselves into her heart. Fear surged in her chest like a rising tide, swallowing everything else. Her eyes, stormy and glassy, locked on his.

Hunter quickly looked away. "This has been the Huntsmen tradition for thousands of years."

"Do you plan on killing yourself if I die first?"

"It is the Huntsmen's tradition," was all he said. Dragging his twin sons still clinging to his legs, he walked as fast as possible into the house.

24 THE SLAP

Umae and Willomay stepped into the kitchen, now functioning as a makeshift medical unit, and froze. The air inside was thick and volatile, like the moment just before lightning strikes.

No one spoke.

No one *dared* to.

Hunter sat at the table, shirt peeled down to his waist, blood crusted along the side of his neck. He didn't move. Didn't blink. Just stared ahead, his jaw clenched, the line of his mouth as flat and unforgiving as iron. His brow was drawn so tightly it carved shadows into his face. He looked like a man holding back a scream. Or worse.

Li-ara stood beside him, tending the wound with careful, practiced movements. But there was no softness in her touch. Only precision. Her face was taut, lips pressed into a thin, bloodless line, and her eyes, those storm-dark eyes, never once lifted.

She cleaned the gash as if it offended her. Her hand trembled only once. Barely. But Umae saw it.

He didn't say a word. Neither did Willomay.

This wasn't a room for words.

Umae had no idea what had happened. He leaned toward one of the Huntsmen. "A little tense in here. What happened?"

"They're fighting," he whispered.

"Fighting? They should be in the bedroom enjoying each other's company, celebrating he's still alive. What are they fighting about?"

"The *Cattamalla.*"

"What's that?"

"A Huntsman's ritual of death."

"Who's dying?"

"No one, yet."

"Then why are they arguing?"

"Tell you later," the Huntsman replied as he noticed Hunter direct an angry stare at him.

"Umae, have you decided when you are leaving?" Hunter asked, his voice loud and strained.

"Actually." Umae cleared his throat, a small, habitual sound meant to ease the tension in his chest. But in the stillness, it rang out like gravel scraping over stone. Sharp. Dry. Embarrassingly loud.

No one looked up.

No one moved, except for the few attending to the injured.

Umae shifted his weight, wishing he could step back out the door and erase the moment completely.

"I was coming to tell you that Willomay and I are leaving within the hour. It's a lengthy journey home, and my wife will be waiting for me."

"It's comforting to know someone will receive a warm welcome."

"Perhaps Umae's wife welcomes him warmly because he doesn't cling to stupid ideas," Li-ara said, her voice clipped as she poured disinfectant over Hunter's cut.

Hunter flinched, just barely, but the tension in his jaw snapped tighter. His shoulders stiffened. A muscle jumped in his cheek. His eyes narrowed, brows knitting into a darker scowl as the sting bit deep.

"I don't think that's true. She tells me all the time how dumb my ideas are," Umae quickly stated, laughing nervously. Neither Hunter nor Li-ara laughed.

"Umae, instead of making the trip by land, tell Qui I said he is to take my ship and fly you and your steeds home. There should be enough room in the cargo hold for everyone. You can be home within four hours."

"Are you sure?"

"He's a talented pilot. I trust him. And one of us should have a decent welcoming and a night in a warm bed."

Li-ara slammed the bloodied cloth she held down onto the table. The impact echoed across the room, sharp and final. "Gee, I'll finish doctoring J'Dar's eye. You can clean out Hunter's wound." She took several side steps, turned her back to Hunter, and put a poultice on her son's face.

Believing his presence was complicating the current situation, Umae took his leave, hugging Li-ara. Her stance was rigid, and her muscles firm.

"Hunter, I can never repay you for what you did for my family. If ever you need anything, I will be there for you." He bowed his head.

Hunter bowed back. "Good Journey. Until our paths cross again."

The door whispered shut behind Umae, and the silence that followed was deeper than before. Thicker, heavier, as if the air itself had stopped moving.

The sounds that did remain - the soft clink of metal, the quiet drag of fabric, the distant hum of equipment - felt strangely intrusive, like they didn't belong. Each movement was cautious, mechanical, as though the wrong gesture might set off something volatile.

The tension hadn't left with Umae. It had grown.

Finally, at his threshold, Hunter stood. "Enough. Li-ara, outside now. These beings cannot treat J'Dar, Warnom, and the other injured with our bickering disrupting the entire place."

Li-ara walked to the door, saying not a word, her footsteps pounding across the floor like hammer blows, each one echoing through the house like a warning. Hunter followed a beat behind her, his jaw locked, his expression thunderous.

In the kitchen, the others tried to focus on their work - bandaging wounds, tending to the injured. But the effort was futile. Voices rose from outside, sharp, cutting, unmistakably heated.

Then came the shouting.

J'Dar turned his head slightly toward the sound, wincing not from pain, but from disbelief. Through the window, he saw them. His mother stood toe-to-toe with Hunter, her finger jabbing wildly in the air, inches from his chest. Her body trembled, not from fear, but fury. Hunter stood rigid, a wall of silence in the face of her fire. He didn't interrupt. Didn't shout back.

J'Dar blinked slowly. After everything that had happened over the past three weeks, he wondered how either could act in such a manner.

345

After nearly ten minutes of sharp words and raised voices, Li-ara spun on her heels and stormed back into the house. She crossed the kitchen like a force of nature, fury radiating off her in waves, then disappeared into her room and slammed the door with such force the walls shuddered.

Hunter followed close behind. He heard the lock click.

He tried the handle. Locked.

Then again.

Still locked.

He stood there, hand on the knob, jaw clenched, as if trying to decide whether to knock or punch through the door.

"Li-ara, I'm not done talking to you. Open this door."

No response.

"Open it, or I'll break it down."

Still no response.

He hit the door with his uninjured fist, cracking the wood.

"Damn your temper. Maybe you would be happier if the knife had entered my heart instead of my neck. Then you wouldn't have to worry about the *Cattamalla*."

The lock clicked, and the door swung open with a forceful bang, the sound reverberating through the room like a gunshot. Hunter turned toward it, but the moment his eyes met Li-ara's face, his heart sank. Her expression was a storm of betrayal and fury, her trembling lips unable to contain the rage that radiated from her.

She stepped forward, her movements sharp and deliberate, her arm already rising. Before Hunter could utter a word, her palm connected with his cheek in a crack that seemed to echo louder than the door's impact. The slap wasn't just a strike; it was a statement, a line drawn in the sand.

"Don't you ever say that to me again," she hissed, her voice low but laced with venom. The room, which had been buzzing with hushed murmurs, froze. Gasps of alarm and dismay punctuated the tension, but they were fleeting, swallowed almost instantly by a suffocating silence. All eyes darted between the two, waiting, watching.

Hunter's hand snapped out and seized her arm.

Hard.

Not in anger. In control.

His grip locked around her like iron, immovable. Li-ara froze, her breath catching, eyes wide. The sudden contact jolted through her like a current, but it was the look in his eyes that stopped her heart cold. They weren't just angry. They were lethal.

Piercing, unblinking, and merciless. His gaze cut straight through her, tearing past every defense, every illusion of safety she thought she still had. It was like staring into the heart of a storm that no longer knew how to pull back.

In that paralyzing silence, she understood. Truly understood what he was capable of. Who the Hunter was beneath the armor of love and memory.

And it terrified her.

He said nothing. Not one word. And that silence was the loudest thing she had ever heard.

Thirty long seconds passed, his eyes never leaving hers, before he released her. Just let go.

No apology.

No explanation.

Hunter turned and walked away, the door creaking open and shutting behind him with a finality that made her flinch.

She stood frozen in the silence he left behind, her arm still tingling where he'd held her. Then, her body jolted into motion. She stumbled back into the bedroom, slammed the door, and twisted the lock hard.

"Did Hunter return?" Li-ara asked Warnom as she exited the bedroom. "He never got his wound attended to." Her eyes were puffy and red. Even though she had tried to wash them off, tears still stained her cheeks.

"He returned about a half-hour ago," Warnom replied. "I believe he's sitting on the north porch talking to J'Dar."

"Probably trying to explain his crazy wife." Li-ara gave a slight giggle. "J'Dar never witnessed such an outburst before."

"It was one for the books, but mild when compared to the fights Huntsmen couples have. I have known mates to lose a hand or foot in such quarrels. Sometimes someone actually died."

"For real?" She couldn't grasp if Warnom was teasing or telling the truth.

"We Huntsmen are a passionate race. We do nothing small, including fighting amongst ourselves. Which, if you think of it, is bizarre. If you killed your mate in anger, you would then kill yourself the next day in *Cattamalla* because your mate is dead."

"I wish I had never heard that word."

"Li-ara, the *Cattamalla* is not an everyday occurrence on Kolora," Warnom explained. "It rarely happens, probably because few Hunters live to old age. Most die before the age of thirty. And for those few who beat the odds, finding one's soul mate is near impossible."

"Do you think Hunter would?" She could not look at Warnom's face.

"Do I think you're BiiJun's soulmate? Yes. That is undeniable. Could he live without you? No. The moment you die, he ceases to be. You are his life, his reason to exist. Would he take part in the *Cattamalla*? I hope so."

Li-ara stared at the injured Huntsman. "Why would you say such a thing?"

"Because the Hunter I know could never survive your loss. If you died tomorrow, I have no doubt BiiJun would stay behind long enough to raise his children. He loves them nearly as much as he loves you, and he would never abandon them to a life without either parent. But the man we know? He would vanish. What remained would be a shadow. A shell. A being moving through the motions of life with no light behind his eyes."

"I will not wish that fate upon someone as extraordinary as him. He deserves more than survival. He deserves an ending worthy of the love he gave in life. A warrior's death, and to walk eternity beside the only soul he ever gave his heart to."

"You make this ritual sound like a gift."

"It is for the one in pain. Li-ara, I am the last one to tell you what needs to be done. Talk to him. Explain to him your concerns, why you fear the *Cattamalla*."

"I do fear it."

"He knows that. Plus, that fact is clearly written on your face for all to see, especially in your eyes. Remember, this ritual has been ingrained in his soul since he was a small boy. Because you do not agree with it, you cannot expect him to abandon his beliefs. It would be like asking your canines not to howl at the full moon or for a razorback not to snort. A fish cannot live in a field of grass. It is not in their nature. It is not in ours to live without our mate. But BiiJun will do whatever he can to ensure you remain happy."

Li-ara sank into the chair beside Warnom's bed. "I slapped him, Warnom. In front of everyone. You should have seen the look in his eyes."

"I didn't need to. I felt it. Do you not think he feels bad for the horrible thing he said? You reacted with equal emotion. He already forgave you, as you have forgiven him. It will be a past event once your lips meet. He is in pain, Li-ara. Go to him."

She smiled at the Huntsman. "How did you ever get so wise, Warnom?"

"I'm a teacher. I have listened to the woes and regrets of Hunters for over seventy years. The story is always the same - a regret of lost love or the absence of one. Hunter is one of the few who achieved a more fulfilling life than killing for a living. Go. He awaits your forgiveness."

Li-ara exited the house and walked around to the north porch. She beheld Hunter sitting on the walkway, his legs dangling over the edge. He was speaking with J'Dar, possibly about their quarrel. Taking a deep breath, she approached them.

"Hunter, I . . ."

Hunter reached out, took her hand, and pulled her to his body. Laying his head on her abdomen, he encircled her waist with his arm. "I don't want to fight anymore," he whispered. "I will honor your request."

Li-ara wrapped her arms around her husband's head, holding him lovingly against her. "No, Hunter, I was wrong to ask it of you." She dropped to her knees, raising his head to look into his face. "And I was wrong to strike you. I am so sorry. I had no right. Can you forgive me?"

"You warned me of your temper."

"That is no excuse."

"Nor was what I said."

"It is forgotten."

"Might take a few days to forget that slap," he said, rubbing his cheek with a mock wince. "You hit hard. It still stings." Hunter laughed, and Li-ara's smile, hesitant at first, bloomed. That was all the invitation he needed. He leaned in, kissed her gently, and pulled her into his arms.

CRACK!

The deafening report of a weapon shattered the air like a lightning strike. Li-ara's scream followed an instant later - raw, high-pitched, and filled with terror. The sound ripped through the air.

Li-ara slipped from Hunter's arms, collapsing like a puppet with its strings cut. She hit the ground hard. At first, Hunter didn't understand. Then, he saw the color. Her khaki pants were no longer brown. They were soaked in red.

Blood.

His instinct overriding shock, Hunter lunged, grabbing J'Dar and yanking him off the porch, shielding him with his own body as they dropped beside her.

"Stay down!"

Hunter remained in front of Li-ara and J'Dar, his arms spread, body tense.

Another shot rang out.

The blast slammed into the ground inches from his chest, sending dirt and splinters flying into his face.

He scanned the trees, eyes sharp, adrenaline surging. Where were the Huntsmen? They should've been here. Protecting them. Covering them. But he had no answers. Only shouting. Chaos.

Another shot screamed past, slamming into the earth beside him. This time closer.

Movement caught his eye. A flash of reflection. The attacker broke cover. Armored. Helmeted. A Huntsman? Impossible.

The traitor charged forward, blaster raised, shots exploding in rapid succession, chewing up the earth closer and closer to Hunter's chest. He gritted his teeth, refusing to move. If he shifted even slightly, Li-ara or J'Dar could die.

A blast tore through his lower leg. He didn't cry out. Didn't flinch. Just locked his jaw and held the line.

More movement to the west. Two more attackers sprinted from the trees, weapons raised, charging hard. Without a gun to defend them, Hunter estimated they only had seconds to live. The only thing he had to protect them was him.

From behind the shed, two shadows exploded into motion. Blurs - fast, low, lethal. Then, clarity as the black she-canine and her companion launched through the air like living weapons. They hit the armored attacker with bone-crushing force, knocking him off his feet in a tangle of limbs and snarls. The blaster flew from his hand.

Snarls filled the air, guttural and wild. The assailant's scream ripped out, high-pitched, and panicked, only to be drowned beneath the canines' furious growls. Their teeth tore through the weak points in his armor, ripping into flesh and cloth - arms, hands, legs, abdomen. Blood sprayed across the dirt as the attacker withered beneath them, powerless.

Figures emerged from the side of the house. The Huntsmen had arrived. They surged forward in formation, blasters raised, forming a protective circle around Hunter, Li-ara, and J'Dar. The sharp staccato of gunfire cracked through the air as they dropped the two remaining assassins mid-charge. Their bodies hit the ground.

Then, the guns turned toward the canines.

"No!" Hunter shouted, his voice like thunder. "Do not harm the canines! Protect them!"

The order landed with the weight of command, halting the Huntsmen's movement mid-step. Their fingers twitched near their triggers, eyes wide with confusion and fear. The canines were still tearing into the fallen assassin, blood splashing across their muzzles. But the Huntsmen obeyed. Because Hunter had spoken.

The canines froze. Both lifted their heads, blood dripping from their jaws. Without a sound, the black she-canine turned. Her companion followed. As quickly as they had arrived, they vanished into the trees.

The Huntsmen didn't move. Couldn't. They stood there, stunned and silent, watching the place where the beasts had vanished as if unsure whether they'd just been saved or warned.

"Li-ara, how badly hurt are you?" Hunter shouted, rising to his knees.

"He shot me in the leg. Was J'Dar injured?"

"I'm fine," J'Dar said. "Just shook up. Who was that?"

"I do not know. But I'm about to find out. Huntsmen, take my wife and son into the house. Get them medical attention."

"Hunter, you need attention yourself," a Huntsman said. "You're bleeding." Hunter didn't answer. Didn't slow. The words behind him scattered like dust, meaningless, weightless.

His focus was absolute.

"Where are you going?" Li-ara yelled, although she knew the answer. Someone had attacked Hunter's family on his home ground. The Huntsman in him would do whatever was necessary to find out why and who ordered it.

"To get some answers."

Hunter moved with the kind of purpose that couldn't be reasoned with, driven not by thought but by fire. Every step pulled him closer to the one person who held the truth, who had the answers he *had* to know. It wasn't a want. It was a hunger, a compulsion burning through his veins.

Nothing else existed. Only the answer. And the one person who dared to hold it.

"Stand him up."

Two Huntsmen seized the stranger by the arms and hauled him to his feet, boots dragging through the dirt. Hunter stepped forward, eyes blazing. Without hesitation, he grabbed the helmet and ripped it off with a violent twist. Beneath the helmet was no assassin. No rogue Huntsman. It was a Rollo Trader. Sweat-streaked, bloodied, defiant, but unmistakably one of the nomadic merchants.

"I thought we killed all of you."

The male spat in Hunter's face. "I'm not saying anything, you piece of *contonk*."

"Where is the Hunter you stole this armor from?" Hunter asked, his eyes glaring with hate as he wiped away the spittle. The assassin stared into Hunter's eyes. "Do any of you recognize this armor?"

"I believe it belongs to a recruit," the Huntsman on the right said. "I recognize the dent in the helmet. Rigger bent it when he and the recruit disagreed."

"Rigger the Terrible?" Hunter asked. "That guy's still around? He was a mountain when I trained."

"Still is. I don't remember the kid's name. Skinny cadet, red curly hair."

"I know the one. Gets sick from space traveling," the other Huntsman added.

"Yes."

"Who's his commander?" Hunter asked.

"General Ranford. But his immediate commander is Hellsworth."

"You," Hunter said, pointing to another Huntsman. "Find Commander Hellsworth and ask him to conduct a headcount. Tell him one, perhaps more, Huntsmen are slain. The attackers may have stolen their armor and are now disguised as Huntsmen. Then, radio Commander

Hightower at the fleet and advise him of what has happened. Tell him there's another base and I will be obtaining its location shortly."

Hunter turned his attention back to the bleeding assassin. "You killed a good Huntsman. We are no strangers to death and accept the loss of a warrior. But my wife and son are innocents. For attacking them, you will pay. I will make sure your suffering is short if you tell me what I want to know. I will give you one chance. Answer my questions, or I will extract the truth from you. And believe me when I say the pain I will inflict upon you will show you my rage."

The assailant sneered at Hunter. "Do your worst."

"Stretch him between those trees," Hunter ordered, nodding towards two nearby maples. Three Huntsmen dragged the kicking Trader to the trees. They tied each outstretched arm to a different tree trunk. Tying a separate rope to each ankle, they pulled the male's legs apart and secured the line to the same trees as his arms. The ropes taut, the assassin could not move. He was ready for Hunter.

While the Huntsmen prepared the Trader, Hunter built a small fire. Borrowing several of the Huntsmen's knives, he placed them in the flames.

"Strip off his clothes."

The first knife flared red in the fire's glow, the metal pulsing with heat like a living ember. Hunter reached in without hesitation, gripping the hilt with steady hands. The heat radiated up his arm, but he didn't flinch.

Turning, he moved toward the wounded male, his eyes scanning the torn flesh, the mangled tissue, searching for the worst of it. He found it near the ribs, raw and ragged.

"The canines did a fine job tearing you apart," Hunter said, his voice low. "But I need you alive long enough to bleed me the answers I want." He lifted the glowing blade, white-hot and wicked, and pressed it to a deep laceration across the man's rib cage.

Sssshhhhhh.

The skin hissed. Tissue bubbled. The scent of seared flesh filled the air, thick and metallic. Hunter's nostrils flared, and a slow, cruel smile curled across his face. The assassin flinched violently, but made no sound.

Hunter's eyes narrowed. "You hold your tongue well," he murmured. "But you won't hold it forever."

353

He shifted the blade to another wound, this one raw and deeper. He pressed again. The metal bit into the flesh with a sharp sizzle, smoke curling into the air.

Still, no screams.

Hunter extended his hand. "Another blade."

A Huntsman stepped forward without hesitation, placing a freshly heated blade into his palm. Hunter barely paused as he walked around the restrained male, his gaze locked on a new target.

"Let's see if your silence holds when it's your throat under the fire."

He pressed the blade against the side of the man's neck.

The Trader screamed. Sharp. Guttural. Primal.

Hunter didn't blink. His face was carved from stone, but his eyes … his eyes burned. With fury. With focus. With unrelenting purpose.

He worked methodically, sealing one wound after another, each blade discarded and replaced as the metal cooled. The screams came faster now, louder, rawer, until they echoed through the wind like the howls of a dying animal.

The Trader thrashed against the restraints, but it was hopeless. Hunter kept going. This wasn't cruelty for cruelty's sake. This was controlled. Calculated. And he would burn his way to the truth if that's what it took.

"Where is the young Huntsman you stole this armor from?" Hunter asked again. The Trader's eyes glared with hate. Hunter reached down and withdrew his hunting knife from his boot. "It appears pain will not entice you to tell me what I need to know. Perhaps another form of motivation will." Hunter reached down and grabbed the male's testicles. Dragging his knife across them, he made a small incision. "You know you will die for attacking my family. But I will allow you to choose if you die as a male or a castrated it. I will only ask one more time, and then I will slice your sacks off. If you continue not to answer, I will slice off your penis as well. Where is the Huntsman?"

The Trader's eyes squeezed shut, as if shutting out the sight of Hunter's steely gaze could lessen the weight of his words. A shiver ran down his spine, a primal reaction to the unmistakable menace in the man's tone. The threat was not a bluff. He could feel the sincerity of it in every syllable, and it chilled him to his core.

"He's in the ravine behind the woodhouse," the Trader blurted, his voice trembling. He prayed the answer would be enough to spare him the unthinkable.

Hunter nodded to a Huntsman who took off running towards the location. "Is there only one, or did you kill others?"

"I only killed the one," the Trader replied. "I don't know if the others killed more or not."

"How many of you are there?"

"Four, counting me."

"Where is your outpost?"

"I don't have one."

"Don't lie to me," Hunter screamed, releasing the male's private parts. "No Traders survived our destruction of your headquarters. Therefore, you hailed from another location. Where is it?"

"I can't tell you that. Go ahead. Cut them off. I'm dead either way."

Hunter raised his knife. Fresh crimson blood glistened from its blade. The prisoner tried to swallow, but there was no saliva in his mouth.

"No. You answered my questions. I will not send you to that next place as half a man. But I still need answers." Hunter cut a one-inch square into the Trader's left breast with the tip of his knife, then peeled the skin back. A blood-curdling scream escaped the prisoner's mouth. Fresh blood ran down the male's chest and dripped onto the ground. Hunter held out his hand for another scalding blade. As he pressed the red-hot steel into the fresh opening, the blood splattered and sizzled. The pungent odor of burning flesh refilled the air.

The Trader's eyes rolled back in his head as he neared unconsciousness. Hunter slapped him across the face, bringing him back to awareness. "Why did you attack my family? Where is your hideout? I will cut pieces of you off all night if I need to. TELL ME."

"Hunter, there." One Huntsman motioned his head to the south. Three Huntsmen were dragging another Trader towards them, the last member of the assault team.

Hunter glared at the attacker before him. "You're in luck. Another comes to take your place." Grasping the hunting knife, he plunged it into the assailant's chest, twisting the blade and severing his heart. The last thing the dying Trader saw was his heart beating in Hunter's hand. "No being threatens my family in my home." He turned to the closest Huntsman.

"Dispose of him and the other two. I don't want my family to see any evidence of this. And keep the other one alive. I want to talk to him after I attend to my family."

Hunter hobbled as fast as possible towards the house, Qui and three other Hunters beside him. Halfway there, he stopped and surveyed the surrounding area. As far as he could see, there were tents, huts, and hundreds of people moving around.

"I can't defend my family with all these people. Any enemy can be hiding amongst them, waiting for their chance to strike, kill my children and wife. I want everyone cleared out by tomorrow."

"Are you abandoning the training school?" Qui asked.

"No, only moving it. There is a suitable field located ten miles to the east. There's a river nearby and plenty of room for both the training grounds and living areas."

"I'll tell our men to get on it right away."

"No. I want the Huntsmen to patrol the grounds, protect my family. Go to the tents with the blue stars. Ask for Conari. He is a *Delamite*. Tell him my wishes to move the inhabitants to the new location."

"Yes, Sir."

"I also need a five-member guard to go to Searra's hut in the village. My three youngest are with her. Tell her what has happened and ask her to keep them a little longer. I don't want them returning home and hearing their mother while they attend to her wound. The guards are to remain with the children until I send for them."

Hunter entered the kitchen. Once again, it was a makeshift medical unit, except this time it was Li-ara lying on the table. As he entered, she screamed as the attending Huntsman poured disinfectant over her wound.

"You okay?" Hunter asked his son.

"Yeah, Dad. Not a scratch." J'Dar peered over at his mother. "Mom wasn't so lucky. Why did they shoot her? She's never hurt anyone."

"I don't have an answer, Son. Possibly to hurt me by harming her and you. If you're sure you're okay, I have an assignment for you. I want you to go with the Huntsmen to the village. Stay with your siblings. Can you do that?"

"Yes. My vision is getting better." Hunter gave his son an encouraging smile.

Li-ara lay on her belly while a Huntsman medic examined the blast to her leg. A sizable pool of blood was visible beneath her thigh. It followed a depression in the table and dripped onto the floor. Hunter watched each drip splash into the growing puddle, cursing himself for getting surprised.

"How bad is it?" Hunter asked as he stepped over the growing red pool beside the table.

"She was lucky. The shot hit the outside of her leg, so there should be no mobility damage. But she's bleeding badly. I need to cauterize the wound. And we used most of the painkillers on you, J'Dar, and Warnom yesterday. I have little to give her. She will feel it." He noted the expression on Hunter's face. "Before you ask, there isn't time to find more painkillers. I need to seal the veins now."

"She's luckier than you realize. The assassin meant to hit her heart. Had she not stood when she did, she'd be dead now." Hunter walked to the head of the table, pulling up a chair. He sat down and smiled at his wife. "How are you doing?"

"It hurts."

Hunter forced himself to smile. "Yeah, I've had the experience a few times. But I'm afraid it will hurt worse in a moment. They can't stop the bleeding, so the wound must be cauterized. Remember what you're always telling me?"

"This will hurt?"

"Afraid so." He leaned down and kissed her. "Someone bring me two pillows." One of the attending villagers hurried into the bedroom and retrieved two cushions. "Rise on your elbows," he instructed Li-ara. When she did, he placed a pillow below her breast and one above. "Lie on these. I want you to hold my hands." The medic was ready. "You will feel some pressure on your leg and foot. It's imperative you don't move, so two Huntsmen will hold your leg down with their hands." Several men stepped forward. After removing their gloves, they firmly wrapped their fingers around her leg.

The medic unscrewed the lid from the vial. He meticulously poured the coagulant powder into the wound. The top of the opening burned. Then, heat radiated down into the wound. Li-ara grimaced, biting her lip. and squeezing her eyes tightly shut against the pain.

"Li-ara, open your eyes. Look into mine. Don't break our connection. Just focus on the blue inside them. It will be over in a flash." Without breaking his stare, Hunter nodded to the medic.

A flash of light ignited, followed by the smell of burning flesh. Li-ara threw her head back, her eyes wide in terror. A scream of excruciating pain escaped her throat, ripping Hunter's soul apart. She frantically yanked at her hands, trying to pull them away from Hunter, but he clenched them tightly. She tried to move her body to make the pain stop, fighting against those holding her down. Unable to bear the pain any longer, Li-ara collapsed, her head falling on the pillow.

Hunter rested his forehead on the top of her head, tears flowing down his face. "I'm sorry," he whispered. "I'm so sorry, Li-ara."

"Hunter, we're ready when you are," came Qui's voice in Hunter's ear. Hunter straightened up. He watched the medic's fingers spread a healing ointment over Li-ara's wound.

"The bleeding's stopped," the medic said, noting Hunter observing him. "If no infection sets in, she should make a complete recovery."

"How bad will the leg be scarred?"

"Over time, it will lessen, but she'll have a considerable mark." The medic glanced down at Hunter's bleeding leg. "You need attention, as well. And, if memory serves me correctly, your neck wound has not been attended to."

"It can wait."

"Only if you want them to get infected," Warnom shouted from his bed. "You're no use to them dead. It will take five minutes for your injuries to be cleaned and bandaged. He can live for another five minutes."

Qui softly placed his hand on Hunter's shoulder. "We have time."

"They don't." Hunter kissed his unconscious wife. "Bind the leg. The neck can wait."

25 SHADOW AND SUEMAY

"Send a runner up to the house and grab me a clean change of clothing," Hunter ordered as he pealed the blood-soaked clothing from his body. "Burn these. No scrubbing will wash the blood out of them."

Hunter knelt at the stream's edge and plunged his hands into the current. The cold bit at his skin. He dragged his palms across his forearms, smearing off the blood in thick, rust-colored streaks. It clung like oil, stubborn and slick.

The stream clouded instantly. Pink, then red, then the deep, murky shade of a slaughterhouse floor. Blood matted his hair, drying in stiff clumps. He dunked his head beneath the surface, held it there, then came up with a sharp breath and pushed the wet strands back from his face. More blood loosened, slithering down his neck, curling into the water like dye.

Hunter splashed his face. Rivulets of red ran down his neck, dripping from his chin. He scooped up handfuls and poured them over his shoulders, over his chest, over the dried patches that had already begun to crack. Red dripped from his elbows, his fingertips, disappearing into the current without a trace. Hunter scrubbed the remnants of that truth from his body but not his mind. Inside him, the stain remained.

Tonight, he was not simply a Huntsman. He was a Hunter. Trained. Unforgiving. Necessary. There was no room in him for peace. No space left for mercy. Li-ara's screams echoed in his soul, haunting and raw, replaying each time his blade had opened a new wound in the assassin's flesh.

And he had not flinched.

He told himself it had been the prisoner's choice. That he'd given him the chance to speak freely. To confess. To offer up the truth. But the man had stayed silent. So Hunter made him bleed the truth instead.

Steam curled faintly from his skin in the cool evening air. A slow exhale fogged in front of him, long and steady. His eyes swept the trees. Once. Twice. Then stilled.

Behind him, the stream kept flowing.

Ahead, the world waited.

He rolled his shoulders, bones cracking faintly beneath the weight of effort. A thin line of blood trickled down from his temple, missed by the water, and curled along his jaw like a reminder.

Still, he didn't speak.

No words. No thoughts spoken aloud. But the surrounding silence tightened, as if something unseen was holding its breath.

Watching.

Waiting.

Deciding.

Qui stepped beside him, breath hard, chest rising and falling beneath a shirt soaked in blood. It stuck to his body like a second skin, stretched tight over muscle. His face was spattered, his eyes sharp and unreadable.

Without a word, he grabbed the hem and peeled the shirt over his head. It resisted, dried blood binding it to skin, before coming free with a sound that was part rip, part grunt. He dropped it beside the stream and knelt.

The stream, already tinged crimson, welcomed more.

Qui dipped his arms in, flexing his fingers underwater. Red drifted from his skin in loose, cloudy ribbons. He scrubbed at his palms, between each finger, over the knuckles where blood had crusted like armor. Some of it came off. Most didn't.

A long breath left him, sharp, controlled.

Beside him, Hunter remained a solid presence, silent.

When Qui finally looked over, the corner of his mouth twitched - not quite a smile, not quite anything. *"Cavingau,* I never knew a *kapoo* Trader had so much blood. I didn't think he'd ever stop bleeding."

"When my children return from the village, have them pick out two older pups from the kennel," Hunter continued, not commenting on Qui's statement. "I want them brought up to the house, and their training to start. This attack would never have happened if Kii were still alive. He would have warned us."

"Should I burn the body like the others?"

"Burn the body, but not the severed head. I want it mounted on a pole and set at the entrance of the airfield. Gather the skulls of those already burned and place them on each side."

"The ancient practice of *Kii Rii Lee.* Show your enemies what will become of them before they attack."

"I want every assassin, assailant, and bearer of ill will to understand any hostile action against my family will end in an unspeakable death. My wife will never again scream in pain as she did today."

"Yes, Sir."

"And Qui, contact Commander Hightower and give him the coordinates of the compound where these assailants hailed from, along with the other two outposts' locations. Send a special dispatch to the Dominee and tell her I humbly ask that all three be obliterated. This system will be safe under *my* watch. Traders will never steal another child."

"Gladly, Sir."

"Feeling better?" Hunter asked his wife as she opened her eyes. "How's the pain?"

"Have you been sitting in that chair all night again?" Li-ara asked. He hadn't, but she'd never know. She rolled over, grimacing. "The pain's still bad."

"You know I can't sleep without you in my arms." He gave her a loving smile. "And I feared lying beside you with your leg wound." Hunter leaned in and kissed her. *"Tuwaan* is trying to locate some more pain medication for you. Cook is brewing up *cackleberry* leaves to help for now."

"Are the kids okay?"

"See for yourself." Hunter nodded, and a caregiver ushered the children in, along with a three-month-old canine pup.

"Look what Daddy gave us," one twin shouted. "Can he sleep in my bed?"

"No, not in your bedroom," Li-ara said.

Nataa-a came running in with a second pup. "Are you okay, Mommy?"

"Two canines, Hunter? I hope they're from the potty-trained group."

"We both know yesterday would never have happened if Kii were still alive. He would have sniffed those guys out the moment they arrived. And had they been able to hide their presence, he would have stopped them before they got close to the house. We need their protection."

"I agree. The pups can stay in the house. But not in the bedrooms."

"Hooray!" the three little ones shouted, their voices bursting with delight as they spun in circles, laughter ringing through the air.

J'Dar stood a few steps back, hands folded behind his back, a faint smile tugging at the corner of his mouth. The excitement was there, but he held it still.

Since the Traders, everything was different. He wasn't a child anymore. Not after what he'd survived. So, he watched in silence, taking delight in his siblings' happiness. His gaze was steady with eyes that had seen too much, too soon. They were older now, wiser. The innocence he once carried was gone, stripped away by fear, by captivity, by truths no child his age should know.

"Kiss your Mom, then off you go. Remember, you must stay inside for the next couple of days. *Patma* will remain with you to make sure you do as told."

Kolo followed behind the new Huntswoman. "Are you going to shoot us with your weapon if we don't listen?"

"Not today." Kolo's eyes opened wide. He turned and looked at his father, an expression of worry in his eyes. Hunter turned his face trying to hide his smile. Maybe a little fear would keep the twins in line.

"Can I hold your weapon?" Huns inquired.

"That's a definite no," she replied.

"Two canines AND a female Huntsman? Isn't that a little overkill, Hunter?"

Hunter's face muscles tensed, his temple vein throbbed. "The assailants almost killed you yesterday. I will never allow another attack again."

"You can't stop everyone. You always told me the Hunter is also the hunted."

"Not this time. Maybe I can't stop assailants, but the canines can. I told you about the wild she canine and her companion stopping the shooter. They tore him apart, yet she purposely didn't kill him."

"What do you mean?"

"She allowed him to live. It was like she knew I needed to talk to him, find out information on who ordered the attack, and why."

"I assume he is dead now." Hunter did not answer. Li-ara did not pursue the subject. "This is the third time she has saved you. And the fact that she purposely did not kill the assailant is almost incomprehensible. Do you really think she understood you needed to interrogate him?"

"I have no doubt. What does Umae say about his black canine?" Hunter asked.

"He is extremely intelligent, shows exceptional abilities in protecting, and can problem-solve as Kii did. Umae reports his canine occasionally anticipates what he needs and reacts accordingly."

Hunter kissed her. "Topics for us to discuss later. I'll tell Cook you're awake and ready for your tea." He stepped away, then stopped. "Before you ask, and we have another fight, had you died yesterday, I would not have abandoned our children. I would have stayed until they were old enough to care for themselves."

"Thank you," she said softly. "I never truly doubted you'd stay for the children. But hearing you say it eases something in me I didn't realize I was still holding on to. And just so you know, I would've waited for you at the gates of *Breehalla* no matter how long it took."

"Pups are all loaded," the Huntsman stated. "The next stop is Kolora. The Dominee is eager to receive her next shipment of canines."

"This makes four," Li-ara said. "Please remind her it will be another eighteen *quin* until I train the last four and am ready for delivery."

"I shall. You ready, Warnom?"

"Time for my departure," Warnom said, a tone of sorrow in his voice. "Thank you for allowing me to recuperate in such a beautiful place. I will miss it. And the children."

"So, you won't miss Li-ara and me?" Hunter teased. "I mean, we're the ones who fed and kept you."

"Of course, I will miss you," Warnom stammered. "That goes without saying. Had it not been for you, Hunter, my atoms would be floating in the Outer Rim along with all those Traders. And Li-ara, without your sweet accommodations, I would have slept with a bunch of snoring Huntsmen." Warnom sighed as he took a long glance across the property.

"Warnom, you don't have to go. If you wish, you are welcome to stay. The training center enjoyed your teachings on the Huntsmen's ways. And a few village females were asking about you."

"Really? About me? What did you tell them?" A quirky smile spread across his face. "No, I couldn't. The Dominee is expecting me. I am Kolora's teacher."

"The Dominee sent word giving her permission for you to stay," Hunter stated, enjoying the surprised expression on his friend's face. "Her decree is your reward for helping me save J'Dar."

"She said that?"

"You doubt my word? I have never lied to you, Warnom. I received a communique earlier this morning stating such. I can show you, if you like."

Warnom shook his head. "That's not necessary."

"She also said any Huntsman who wishes to remain here on Orallia may do so with her blessing. And, if they choose, may remove their armor."

"Our armor? In public? No, I couldn't. Could I? Not that I doubt you, but are you sure she said that?"

Hunter chuckled. He handed Warnom a folded sheet of paper. "Here, read it yourself since my word does not seem to be sufficient."

Warnom's shoulders straightened, but his eyes glistened with something between disbelief and quiet gratitude. He didn't speak right away. He just stared at the paper as if absorbing the weight of the words.

"I didn't help rescue J'Dar for any reward."

Hunter's smile deepened. "I know. That's why you deserve it. Plus, your Huntsmen's teachings here on Oralia have helped bring peace to this section of space. It would spread faster if you continued to teach at the school."

"If I stay, could I have a place of my own? Sharing a room with J'Dar for the past weeks was a bit cramped."

Hunter and Li-ara laughed. "I'm sure we can find something."

Two years had passed since the attack, but the memory of it remained etched into every choice Hunter made. He took extreme precautions to ensure Li-ara never set foot near the airfield again. Hunter's grisly warning of five severed heads now stood at nineteen, each one mounted high along the perimeter of the airfield, blackened by sun and time. A brutal message to anyone foolish enough to come close.

None had.

With the unwavering discipline of the Huntsmen and the fierce loyalty of the now fully grown canine pups, no threat got within miles of Hunter's family.

Hunter adapted fully to the Huntsmen's way of life. The structure. The training. The code. He thrived in it. Though the wound in his neck, left untreated for too long, cost him partial mobility in his right arm, he considered it a fair trade. A scar earned. A price paid.

Li-ara, too, had healed, physically and otherwise. Her leg bore a three-inch scar, angry and pink, but no deeper damage remained. Still, the sight of it never failed to bring a chill down Hunter's spine. A reminder. A warning. *Beneath every bush waited an attacker.*

So, he remained vigilant. Always watching. Always ready.

The children had blossomed in the peace that followed. Strong, curious, full of life. The quiet years had brought a rhythm to their lives, one Hunter had never dared to hope for. And for Li-ara, that hope took shape as something more.

One quiet evening, wrapped in Hunter's arms as they lay in bed, she tilted her head against his chest and whispered the unthinkable.

"I've been thinking about something. And hear me out before you say no."

Hunter waited.

"In a few months, J'Dar will attend the Learning Center on Kolora with Warnom for a year. When he returns, chances are he will continue his

365

education at the Training Center. Natta-a attends school in the village, and the twins will join her in a few months."

"All true."

"I thought maybe, just maybe, ah, if you wanted to. . ."

"Woman, what do you want to ask me?"

"Maybe it's time we have another child."

Hunter stiffened, his breathing halted. The subject had been forbidden, unspoken since her miscarriage. But now, it hung between them, delicate and full of dangerous hope.

"No." The word burst from Hunter's lips as he threw back the covers and shot to his feet, his voice sharp, final. He began to pace, dragging a hand through his hair, the tension rolling off him in waves. His breath came hard and uneven.

"You know how I feel about another child," he said, stopping mid-step, staring down at his open palm, frozen. "But every time I close my eyes, I still see her. Meg. Her body, so small, so still, lying in my hands like a broken bird. I couldn't save her. I . . ." His throat closed around the words.

He looked at Li-ara, eyes burning.

"And you. That night. I almost lost you. I watched the light leave your eyes. Your blood was everywhere." His voice dropped to a whisper, full of pain. "I won't go through that again. I can't."

He turned away. "No. No more babies. No more chances."

Li-ara rose from the bed, silent for a moment, then crossed the room slowly, her expression not angry, not wounded, but filled with something deeper. She stopped in front of him, placing her hand gently on his chest, feeling the storm in his heartbeat.

And then, softly, she spoke. "Hunter, we didn't lose our daughter."

"What are you talking about? Have you seen her playing outside? Have you heard her laughter? No, because she never got to live. I won't witness the death of another son or daughter, Li-ara. Please, don't ask me to father another child."

Li-ara took his hand and led him to the bed. "Sit. I want to tell you something."

"You can't change my mind."

"Just listen. It's all I ask." Hunter sat on the edge, prepared to jump up and object if she pursued the present subject. "Do you trust the Dominee?"

"That's a silly question. You know I do."

"And you agree she possesses ways of knowing things we do not."

"Yes. What does the Dominee have to do with another child?"

"When you went to rescue J'Dar, I asked the Dominee if she foresaw you returning to me. She said you would because our daughter was still waiting to be born. You needed to plant your seed in me."

"Be born? She *was* born, Li-ara. She was born too early, and she died."

"Her body died, Hunter. Not her soul. The Dominee said she waits in the spirit world for me to become pregnant so she can come and meet her PaPa. She also said our daughter would be an important part of understanding the wild canines and using them to bring peace to this quadrant."

"The Dominee said that?"

"Yes, Hunter. She said she needed to come into the land of the living."

"But what if something goes wrong?" Hunter asked, his voice barely above a whisper. "What if one, or both of you, die?"

"We won't."

"How do you know that?"

"Because the Dominee told me. You never questioned her before. Why are you now? Believe in what she told me." Her words struck deeper than he expected. Not because they were forceful, but because they were true.

Hunter looked at her, truly looked into the eyes of the woman who had stood beside him through war, through pain, through near death. The woman who now stood asking him not to be strong but to have faith. He swallowed hard, torn between memory and possibility. His mind screamed caution, but his heart, damn it, his heart was leaning toward hope.

He exhaled slowly, his fear slipping from his shoulders. "And when would you like me to plant this seed?"

"I think tonight would be a perfect time." Li-ara's eyes twinkled as she leaned forward and passionately kissed her husband, to which he equally responded.

Eight months later, under a full moon with the wild canines howling, Suemay entered the world of the living: seven pounds, six ounces with black curls and her father's blue eyes.

Hunter claimed that, besides Nataa-a, she was the most beautiful baby girl to be born. He held her close, heart thundering with a joy so profound it bordered on ache.

Tears slipped silently down his cheeks. He closed his eyes and offered a silent prayer to the Dominee, gratitude swelling in his chest. "Thank you for healing what I thought could never be whole again."

———————

In all, thirty-two Huntsmen chose to remain with Hunter and the family. Each removed their armor and now lived near the house, either sleeping in tents or in their flyers. Some taught their tactical form of defense at the school, while others joined the patrol to protect the grounds surrounding Hunter's family.

The School of Huntsmen Teachings evolved beyond its humble beginnings, blossoming into a renowned center of learning and discipline. What once served a handful of people became a beacon for many, drawing beings from across the galaxy, each seeking the wisdom, strength, and honor the Huntsmen lived by.

Some stayed only long enough to learn. Others remained for years, rising through the ranks until they themselves were named teachers. These guardians of knowledge returned to their homeworlds, carrying the sacred lessons with them like torches into the dark.

And with each torch lit, the light spread.

The age of peace, once fragile and fleeting, was growing, rippling from one world to the next. A quiet revolution built not on power but on purpose. The Huntsmen had become more than warriors. They were the foundation of peace and understanding.

Hunter continued his morning ritual of Gaball, his children often taking part. When not hunting or patrolling with the Huntsmen, he spent time with his family or helping Li-ara. When in the kennel, Baby Suemay accompanied him. She seemed more at peace with the canines than with people.

"I received word from the Dominee today stating the new canines are working out well," Li-ara said as she placed Suemay in her crib.

"Did she order more?" Hunter asked.

"Yes, another twelve. She said they are working fantastically with the Hunters. Their bounties have tripled."

"Perhaps I should go back into the bounty hunting business," Hunter laughed. "Nah, I'd miss you too much." He went to kiss her, but she stopped him. A puzzled look crossed his face.

"At the door," Li-ara mouthed.

Hunter turned slowly. There, standing in the doorway, was the black female canine, her massive form framed in shadow. Clutched gently in her jaws was a small black pup, no more than four weeks old.

She didn't growl. Didn't move. She just stared.

Hunter's heartbeat quickened as he instinctively tightened his hold around Li-ara, shielding her within his arms. Without a word, he bowed his head. Not in submission, but in respect.

The canine blinked once, then lowered her head in return. She stepped forward. One deliberate paw. Then another. The sound of her claws clicking on the cement echoed throughout the room.

Li-ara tensed in Hunter's embrace, breath shallow, eyes locked on the approaching beast. Her gaze flicked to the crib. To Suemay. Her maternal instinct screamed to move and grab the child. But Hunter's arm pulled tighter.

"Don't move," he whispered, barely audible.

With a subtle motion, he slid his hand down, fingers brushing the grip of his sidearm, ready to draw. If she lunged, he'd fire.

The canine walked with eerie calm across the room, her eyes never leaving Hunter's. At the edge of the crib, she reared onto her hind legs, resting her front paws gently on the railing. With the care of a mother, she lowered the pup into the crib beside the human baby.

Suemay stirred, opened her eyes, and reached up. Her tiny fingers brushed the canine's muzzle. The mother canine licked the child's face once, soft, slow, as if marking her with something more than scent. Then she turned and padded swiftly through the doorway.

Hunter released Li-ara and rushed to the door. He watched the canine disappear into the underbrush. Her body halfway through, she stopped and looked back once, lifting her head to the sky. A long, haunting note echoed through the trees like a farewell or perhaps a promise. And then she was gone.

"I don't believe it," Li-ara said, looking into the crib. Her daughter was asleep, the small pup curled up alongside. "She purposely brought the pup to Suemay. I've never known of a mother to give up her pup willingly."

Hunter glanced down at the small ball of fur. "And not an ordinary pup. A rare black one." He tasseled his daughter's black curls. "I think the Dominee was right. Our daughter has a special connection with the canines."

That evening, after finally settling Nataa-a and the rambunctious twins into bed, Hunter and Li-ara collapsed into their own, limbs tangled, breaths heavy, exhausted. Sleep claimed them almost instantly. But it lasted less than ten minutes. A sharp cry pierced the silence, raw and relentless.

Suemay.

Li-ara groaned softly and rolled out of bed, her body aching as she crossed the room and lifted their daughter into her arms. "Shh, shh," she murmured, rocking gently, her voice strained with fatigue. But the crying didn't stop. For over thirty minutes, Li-ara paced the floor, whispering, bouncing, and humming every lullaby she knew. Nothing worked.

"Why won't she stop crying?" she asked, glancing at Hunter with tired, pleading eyes.

"You're sure she's not sick?"

"She has no symptoms. She's not running a fever. It doesn't appear she has a bellyache or headache. I don't understand why she's behaving like this."

A knock sounded at the door. "Now, what?" Hunter stumbled to the bedroom door.

"Sorry to disturb you, but Anxel reports he has a problem out in the kennel."

"Did he say what kind of problem?" Hunter asked.

"Only that you or Ms. Li-ara needs to come right away."

"You go," Li-ara said.

Before he even reached the kennels, Hunter heard it - sharp barks, restless whines, the scrape of claws on metal. The canines were on edge.

"What's wrong?" Hunter shouted, trying to talk above the noise.

"She is." Anxel pointed to Suemay's new pup. "She hasn't stopped whining since you went up to the house."

"That was three hours ago."

"I know. She has the whole place upset. Can you please take her someplace else?"

The black pup was pacing in its enclosure, its tiny frame tense, tail curled low, emitting tiny, high-pitched howls.

Hunter approached slowly, crouching by the gate.

The pup's eyes locked on him. She turned toward the far wall, whining again. Hunter followed her gaze. She was looking toward the house. Toward *Suemay*.

He exhaled quietly, understanding settling in his chest. "You don't want out, you want her." Hunter reached for the latch. "Let's get you where you belong."

Li-ara looked up as Hunter stepped into the kitchen. She never stopped pacing, yet Suemay continued to cry. "What was it?" she asked, her voice laced with exhaustion. "What upset them?"

"This little lady." Hunter held up the happy pup.

"No, Hunter. Not another canine inside."

"The pup wouldn't stop whining. She had the entire kennel in an uproar. What else could I do? I think she wants Suemay. It's just for the one night."

"I'm too tired to debate that. There's a box in the pantry. You can use it for a bed." Suemay struggled to get down, nearly falling out of Li-ara's arms. "What is wrong with you tonight? I almost dropped you. Here, sit on the floor. Hunter, I have an old blanket in the cupboard. I'll grab it, and you can toss it in the box."

Hunter stopped. "Listen."

Li-ara froze. "It's quiet. She stopped crying."

The two tip-toed to where Suemay was. She was already asleep on the floor, the pup curled up beside her.

"I'll carry Suemay to bed," Li-ara whispered. "You put the pup in her box."

"Shouldn't we take the pup with us?"

"Definitely not. No canines in the bedroom until they're housebroken."

Hunter placed the sleeping puppy inside the box. Slinking back into the bedroom, he checked on the sleeping Suemay as he passed her cradle. Pulling his wife into his arms, he settled down for a night's sleep.

"Not again," Hunter said, waking to Suemay's cries. "We haven't been asleep for five minutes." The pup howled, followed by the house dogs barking and the children yelling.

"Please don't tell me the rest of the kids are awake," Li-ara said, stumbling out of bed.

"Dad, make Suemay stop crying," a groggy J'Dar complained. "I have a test tomorrow and need my sleep."

Next, Huns and Kolo appeared in the doorway.

"What are you two doing up?" Li-ara asked as she bounced Suemay up and down in her arms.

"The dogs woke us," Huns replied. "Make them stop."

"Where's your sister?" Hunter asked.

Huns shrugged his shoulders. "Probably still asleep."

"At least someone is," Li-ara stated.

"No, I'm not." A sleepy Nataa-a appeared in the doorway. "Can I go out to the ship and sleep?"

"No." Hunter and Li-ara said at the same time.

"Why is Suemay crying so much?" J'Dar asked.

"We don't know," Hunter sighed.

"I do." Nataa-a yawned.

"You know why she's crying?" Hunter asked.

"Yes. The puppy and Suemay want to sleep together. You can't separate them."

"Who told you that?" Li-ara asked.

"She did."

"Nataa-a, Suemay can't speak yet."

"Not Suemay. The puppy."

"The puppy told you she wanted to sleep with Suemay?" Hunter asked.

"No, she said Suemay wanted to sleep with her. You can't separate them."

Hunter gave Li-ara a bewildered look. "It's worth a try."

Hunter bent down and scooped the howling pup into his arms. The small body squirmed for a moment, then stilled as he cradled it against his chest.

"Give me Suemay," he said quietly.

Li-ara placed her daughter in the crook of Hunter's free arm. The change was instant. Suemay wrapped her tiny arms around the pup, resting her head on its soft fur. With a soft yawn, she closed her eyes and drifted into sleep.

The puppy lifted its head just enough to nestle against Suemay's cheek and followed her into slumber.

Hunter lifted his eyebrows, staring at Li-ara. "I don't believe it. It worked," Hunter whispered.

Keeping the child and canine together, Hunter laid them in the cradle. He stepped back, pulling Li-ara into his arms. "Finally, quiet. You go back to sleep. I'll tuck the kids in."

Li-ara didn't say a word. She shuffled across the floor and collapsed onto the bed, barely bothering to pull up the covers before sleep took her.

"Okay, everyone, back to bed." With a sweeping motion of his arms, Hunter herded them down the hallway. Feet shuffled. Nataa-a rubbed her eyes. Kolor bumped into a wall.

"Will you read us a story?" Huns asked.

"No, it's bedtime."

"But I'm not tired. Can we stay up and play?" Kolo inquired.

"Well, I *AM* tired. To bed. And I don't want to hear one peep out of you."

"Peep." Kolo giggled and ran to his room, hopping in bed. Hunter tucked them and Nataa-a in, kissing them good night for the second time. He returned to his room, grateful for the sleeping child and pup.

Hoping to stay in bed for over five minutes, he brought Li-ara into his arms. "Should we be worried about what Nataa-a said about hearing the canine dog?"

"Too tired," Li-ara yawned. "We'll worry tomorrow."

The little black pup was never more than a step behind Suemay, trailing her like a fuzzy shadow with paws. It was a wonder the girl didn't tumble over her five times a day. And even more of a wonder that the pup didn't seem to care. So, Hunter gave her the only name that made sense - Shadow. Suemay's personal, four-legged attachment.

Suemay and Shadow were a matched set. Separate them for even a second, and the wailing could wake the dead. Bath time? A joint operation. If one went in, so did the other. More than once, Hunter found himself drying off both a squealing child and a soggy pup, wondering who'd made the bigger mess.

"Li-ara, Suemay won't eat her lunch again," Hunter shouted from the kitchen. "What did you say to do?"

"Give Shadow some food, then put Suemay's plate on the floor near Shadow's bowl," Li-ara shouted back. She was bathing the twins. "But watch Suemay. If you don't, she'll eat Shadow's food, and Shadow will consume her food."

After a few minutes, Li-ara appeared with the twins. They ran to their waiting lunch on the table. Li-ara chuckled, seeing Hunter standing between Suemay and Shadow, trying to ensure they didn't swap plates.

"I'm not sure this is a good idea," Hunter said. "Our daughter's not a canine. She needs to eat at the table like the rest of the family."

"You are more than welcome to try to persuade her. I've tried everything I can think of. So have the two caregivers. She only eats with Shadow."

"No, that's not yours." Hunter picked up his daughter as she crawled over to Shadow's dish. "You do not eat canine food. You are a Huntsman and eat Huntsman food." Suemay gave him a disapproving look. "Don't give me your mother's pouty face. It won't work, Little Girl." He turned to his wife. "Have you been teaching her your tricks?"

"I don't have the foggiest idea what you are talking about," Li-ara replied, raising her eyebrows, tilting her head to the side, and smiling.

"I said no," Hunter repeated as he caught Suemay dashing for the canine food again. He picked her up and gave her a slight swat on the behind. Shadow pounced and sank her baby canine teeth into Hunter's pant leg. "Hey, she bit me."

"Well, you spanked her protectee." Li-ara laughed.

"This is getting serious, Li-ara," Hunter said. He placed Suemay in her chair, dragging along the puppy who refused to let go of his pants. "We need to break this habit now. If not, we won't be able to discipline her at all once the pup's grown. She'll tear us apart." Suemay gurgled some words, and Shadow released her hold.

"Did you see that?" Li-ara asked. She lifted the young pup. Shadow licked Li-ara's face. "It's like they can communicate. I've seen the two do this interaction before. I didn't imagine it, did I?"

"Who knows? Remember what Nataa-a told us the night we brought Shadow in, that she spoke to her?"

"It was a dream."

"Are you positive? You, of all people, understand how smart they are. And you've always said that black canines possess more intelligence. Those two Huntsmen who stopped by the other day said they are astounded by what their canines are capable of. One said the legends of old were right - Huntsmen and canines not only work together but talk to each other. Actually, talk to each other."

Li-ara looked into Shadow's eyes. "Can you understand Suemay? Can you understand me? Is that why you are so extraordinary?" Shadow barked in response.

"Only time will tell," Hunter said.

And in time, it became undeniable. As Shadow and Suemay grew, so did the bond between them. Deep, strange, and unlike anything anyone had witnessed before. There was no longer any doubt: they were communicating.

Sometimes it came in bursts of playful barking, other times in quiet, watchful listening, as if Shadow understood Suemay's words down to the intent beneath them. But on rare, almost sacred occasions, it went beyond that, glances exchanged in stillness, a tilt of the head, a pause before acting. As if they spoke telepathically.

One day while hunting just short of the tree line, Hunter caught a slight glimpse of movement between two trees. He raised his head and filled his lungs with the crisp morning air. There was no smell of urine, fermented vegetation, or rotten meat. It wasn't a bear or wild boar. It was at times like this that he wished he had brought his helmet so he could scan the area with his heat vision. But today, good old-fashioned eyesight would have to do.

His hand resting on the hilt of his weapon, he scanned the area three times before spotting her. The black she-canine stood between two trees, silent, unmoving, nearly invisible. She was watching him.

Hunter raised his hand over his heart and bowed his head. He concentrated on sending her a silent message to raise her right paw, but if she received his request, she gave no indication.

"You're being ridiculous," Hunter told himself. "She can't hear your thoughts. You're letting everyone's crazy ideas warp your thinking."

Then, she moved. It was subtle, a deliberate gesture that made the hairs on the back of his neck rise. A shift in her posture. The slightest raise of her right paw. In the next second, she was gone.

"Wait, don't go," Hunter shouted, rushing forward. Did he imagine it? Had she heard him? He stood there, waiting for a return that did not come, replaying her movement in his mind. Was there a bond between him and the black canine like the one Suemay shared with Shadow?

Hunter never spoke of what happened. Not to Li-ara. Not even to himself aloud. But sometimes, late at night, he'd lie in bed reliving the incident in his mind, wondering.

––––––––––––

Hunter stepped into the house and held out an envelope. "The Dominee sent you a communique," he said. "I imagine it's about what the Kolorian library has on *Gloxdirian* canines, specifically their history working alongside the Huntsmen."

Li-ara read the communique, her eyes narrowing. "That's odd."

"What did she say? Didn't she send you the requested information?"

"No. She said she could find no recordings of that period or the fact that Huntsmen used canines."

"That doesn't make sense." Hunter took the paper and read it himself. "We all know the legend of the great partnership between Hunter and canine. That relationship is the reason Kolorian Huntsmen attained such high status in the galaxy. It shaped our history and existence. Why are there no records of it?"

"Do you know why they stopped using canines?"

"No. As far as I know, one day, they just stopped. I never heard a reason why."

"Do you think Warnom might know?"

"I doubt it. If he knew, he would have taught us. But you can ask him."

"Do you think someone took the texts or moved them?"

"No," Hunter said. "All of our history is housed in the Great Library inside the Dominee's palace. Although the general population has access to the information there, security is tight. No one would be able to sneak information out."

"I guess this means I'll just have to keep studying them myself, then.

Li-ara documented everything, meticulously recording the canines' behaviors, gathering data from owners across regions, and constantly refining her research. Page by page, observation by observation, her knowledge deepened.

As her work expanded, so did her reputation. Word of her dedication and insight spread far beyond her homeworld, reaching across the quadrant. Among scholars, Huntsmen, and trainers alike, her name became synonymous with understanding the ancient bond between human and beast.

"Hunter," Qui called as he approached. "TiDo reports a mother *tumack* emerged from her winter den with three new cubs. I thought the children would like to see them."

"Can we go, Dad?" Kolo shouted. "PLEASE."

"I've never seen newborn cubs. We have to go," Nataa-a added.

"One of you go into the house and ask J'Dar if he wants to go too," Hunter said. All four children ran inside after their older brother.

A tug on his pants compelled Hunter to glance down. He noted a small canine pup trying to climb up his leg. "Where did you come from?" He searched the area and observed Li-ara running towards him.

"I'm sorry. He somehow got out of his pen when I wasn't looking." She picked up the pup and carried him back, placing him inside his enclosure.

"J'Dar said he has too much studying to go," Huns shouted first as the children returned. "Warnom is giving him an important test tomorrow."

"Okay, let's go. And remember, we must remain quiet. We don't want the mother *tumack* to see us, or she might charge."

"We'll be quiet," they all shouted.

Hunter took a step forward and tripped. A soft yelp followed. The pup had returned and was sitting unnoticed at the Huntsman's feet. "You guys go with Qui to the ship. I'll be right behind you." He carried the lost pup back to his pen. "Li-ara, you lost something. I tripped over him."

"How did he escape again?"

Hunter kissed her on the cheek. "Qui and I are taking the youngest four to watch a mother t*umack* and her newborns. J'Dar's in the house studying."

"Tell me if you spot any canines."

The children and three canines ran up the sidewalk to tell their mother all about the cubs.

"Did you see any canines?" Li-ara asked.

"I didn't witness her, but the black leader was somewhere close."

"Why do you say that?" Hunter removed from his pocket the coin of Kii and Beta he now wore on a chain around his neck. "You lost the coin last month when you went hunting with several Huntsmen. I thought you said you hunted near Tannis Port?"

"We did."

"Did you find it on your ship?"

"We went by steed, remember? The coin was resting on a rock fifteen feet from where Qui sat the ship down. The ground contained canine prints."

"You think the she canine found it and knew you'd be in the meadow today?"

"Yes."

"Hunter, that's too far-fetched, even for me. It's way beyond anything a canine is capable of."

"What if it's true, Li-ara? What if she can foresee the future?" Both heard a soft bark. Standing beside Hunter was the small canine.

"No, Hunter. We have three canines in the house already. There isn't room for a fourth."

Hunter stood in the kitchen with the canine pup in his arms. "Li-ara, he finds me two to three times a day. You can't figure out how he's escaping from the kennel. He finds a way out even when the kennel door is closed and locked. He's broken the screen on the kitchen door three times now. One of these times, I will seriously hurt him when he trips me, or he will kill me. I don't know why, but he wants to be near me."

"Or do you want to be near him?" Li-ara teased.

"No. Maybe. All right, yes. I feel a connection like I did with Kii." He held up the pup and allowed him to lick Li-ara's face as an enticement. She loved puppy kisses. "Besides, he's not black. He's golden brown. He will give you more data on non-black canines and help determine if they can communicate, too."

"But four? In the house?" Hunter gave her his best begging smile. She laughed. "Okay, but not in the bedroom. No canines in our bedroom. Agreed?" Hunter nodded. "Have you named him? A proper name would be better than the name 'Little *Kaapoo*' I call him now."

Hunter laughed. He did like the name "Little *Kaapoo*", but he didn't want to encourage the kids to swear. Especially the twins. "Brox. It means escape artist."

Li-ara ruffled the pup's fur. "Welcome to the family, Brox."

III

The moment you die, he ceases to be. You are his life, his reason to exist. Would he participate in the Cattamalla? I hope so.

Warnom

26 A PARTING

Li-ara immersed herself in the study of the canines, both domesticated and wild. She hunted answers in every howl and glint of eye, peeling back the layers of legend and myth to uncover startling realities. Some did speak. Many solved puzzles. All bore an intelligence far beyond their two-legged keepers. And a rare few - like Kii, the fierce guardian, and Shadow, the silent sentinel - saw slivers of the future.

She filled journal after journal with her observations. Every new discovery left her breathless, each insight another crack in everything she'd once believed. The canines weren't just smart. They were *aware*.

But aside from Hunter, no one else knew. She kept the majority of her findings close, hidden away from the world. She knew people wouldn't understand. Admitting the canines were more than animals, that they could think, reason, maybe even *feel*, would shatter too many comfortable lies.

With her through the years was Hunter - silent, watchful, unwavering. He never strayed far from her side, his existence reshaped by a single vow: she would never feel pain again. Where threats arose, he erased them with brutal precision. If her joy faltered, he restored it by any means necessary. Every few years, another head was added at the airfield, grim testimony to his dedication. By the end, forty-six grim trophies stared blindly at the sky.

But time has no master. Even the fiercest devotion can't hold back the slow, inevitable drift. It came quietly. Without warning. Not from an enemy Hunter could tear apart or a threat he could see coming. Death had not challenged him. It had simply stepped around him.

Li-ara's eyelids fluttered open, the room still wrapped in the hush of early morning. Her gaze shifted, and there he was. Hunter sat slumped in the chair beside her bed, his hand wrapped around hers like it was the only thing anchoring him to the world. His head tilted slightly, lips parted in sleep, a shadow of weariness etched across his features.

She squeezed his hand gently. "Hunter?"

His eyes blinked open, hazy at first, then sharpening with relief and something deeper, something tender. A slow, boyish smile spread across his face, warm and immense, like sunlight breaking through clouds.

"Have you been sleeping there all night again?" she asked, her voice a breath above a whisper, already knowing the answer.

He gave a soft shrug, brushing the hair from her forehead with the backs of his fingers.

"Where else would I be? You know I can't sleep in the bed without you. How are you feeling? Should I have Cook make you some breakfast?"

"About the same as yesterday. I'm not hungry."

"Maybe later." He leaned over and kissed her lovingly yet carefully.

"Did Suemay get that shipment ready?"

"I don't want you worrying about the canines. Suemay can run the business. She has for the past five years."

"Has it been that long?" Li-ara asked. "It seems like only yesterday she came into our lives."

"That it does. J'Dar and his family arrived last night after you fell asleep."

"You should have woken me."

"You needed your rest."

"Hunter, we both know rest will not make me better. Not this time."

"Don't say that," he whispered, the words strained, barely holding back the weight behind them. He diverted his eyes to the floor, as if meeting hers would make it real.

Li-ara reached out and touched his face. "Look at me, Hunter." He didn't. "Hunter, please." Hunter slowly raised his eyes. "For almost fifty years, you have given me the best life any being could want. Not one day passed that I did not feel loved tremendously. You've given me five beautiful children. There is not one moment I would change." Li-ara paused. "Except one."

"The day we fought, and you slapped me," Hunter sorrowfully stated. "It still haunts me, too." He kissed her hand. "It was not your fault, Li-ara. You reacted to the horrible thing I said."

"I've never forgotten that look in your eyes, Hunter. No matter how we fought, I never felt your hate, but I caused you to hate me that day."

"Not you. Never you. I hated myself."

"Only because I asked for something you could not give me. And, for you, death was better than disappointing me. You loved me, and still do, that much. Just as I love you. But now, it is time for me to go ahead without you and prepare for our next life together."

Every word Li-ara spoke rang with truth, and Hunter hated it. Hated how powerless he was to stop the clock from running out. She was slipping away from him, and there wasn't a single battle he could fight to save her.

His lips parted, but no sound came. The weight in his chest was too heavy for words. He just shook his head, slow and desperate.

"You know I'm right."

"Can't go on without you," came an almost silent whisper.

"Our children are grown now, living good lives because of you, because of the peace you brought to the quadrant. And they've given us five beautiful grandchildren. They'll need their PaPa to guide them, to pass down the way of the Huntsmen, so they too can become something extraordinary. I know what the *Cattamalla* means to you. And I will not ask you to refrain from partaking in the tradition. But, is there any way you could give them a few more years? A little more time before you join me?"

"No," came a haunting whisper.

"I thought that was too much to ask. How about a few months?"

Hunter shook his head negatively.

Li-ara smiled. "How about until J'Dar returns home? He will take your leaving the hardest. Can you promise me a few days?"

Hunter looked into the face of his only love. "I will try."

"That's all I will ask of you. And one more favor, Hunter. Can you please take those heads down? The ones you staked on posts at the airfield."

"You know about them?"

"I've known about them since the day you stuck that first Bollo Trader's head on a post. The one who shot me."

"Why didn't you ever say anything?"

"Because after that horrible fight we had over the *Cattamalla*, I vowed never to attempt to amend your beliefs again." Her cheeks reddened a little. "Plus, I was glad you did it. Every time you added another head, I was glad because I knew they would never hurt you, me, or our family. My only regret was that I wasn't there to see the life drain from their eyes. But I don't want the kids or grandkids to see them. So please take them down."

Hunter smiled, a low snicker escaping his throat. "I hate to tell you, Li-ara, but the kids have known about the heads for decades. Even some of our older grandkids have seen them. No one ever talks about it because we didn't want you to know."

"As it should be, My Most Beautiful Bounty Hunter."

Four days later, in the soft hush of twilight, Li-ara lay cradled in Hunter's arms, weightless, as if already halfway between this world and the next. Her skin was cool beneath his touch, her breath shallow and fading. The family knelt in silence. The grandchildren held back tears they didn't yet understand. The older ones frozen in the helplessness of watching their mother slip away.

Hunter stroked her hair, his lips brushing her forehead as if he could anchor her to this life with tenderness alone.

Li-ara opened her eyes, just barely, and found his. Even now, there was love there. Fierce. Endless.

Then, with trembling lips, she gave him one last kiss. It was soft, fragile. But it held everything: their history, their battles, their laughter, their children, and all the words she no longer had the strength to say.

It was goodbye.

And then, Li-ara exhaled. A breath so faint, he almost didn't hear it. But Hunter *felt* it, like something sacred leaving him.

Her body went still in his arms. Hunter froze. His heart seemed to stop with hers.

Then, the silence shattered.

His scream -raw, guttural - tore through the air like a wounded animal, echoing throughout the house and across the yard. It wasn't just pain. It was annihilation. It was a soul breaking open. A love ripped from his grasp.

Hunter buried his face in her neck, sobbing against skin that had already begun to cool, his tears soaking her gown. His arms clung to her, holding her tight against his chest.

"Please," he whispered, again and again, voice cracked and broken. "Please, come back … just one more breath …"

But there was no reply. Only the sound of his own grief and the weight of a world without her.

For three long hours, Hunter clung to her, whispering desperate pleas, willing her to open her eyes, to breathe again, to stay with him. The world beyond his pain ceased to exist. There was only her and the unbearable reality that she was gone.

It wasn't until a mournful howl echoed through the night, a sound so haunting it pierced his shattered heart, that Hunter stirred. The black female canine stood on an adjacent hill, her head raised to the sky, a sentinel of grief honoring the loss. The sound broke something inside him, yet it also gave him the strength to loosen his hold.

"I'll see you in our next life together," Hunter softly whispered, kissing Li-ara's forehead.

And then he let go.

A Huntsman walked over and stood before Hunter. With quiet reverence, the man lifted her gently, cradling her like the sacred thing she was, and carried her through the doorway into the kitchen. Three village women waited in silence to wash her, dress her, prepare her for the rites reserved for a beloved Huntsman.

Hunter remained where he was, watching the Huntsman leave the room. Wrapping his fingers around the chair's arms, he stood. But his knees buckled, and he hit the floor with a thud. No words escaped his mouth. No cries emanated from his throat. He sat there in silence, a shadow wrapped in grief.

J'Dar and Kolor rushed forward, lifting their father back into the chair. Nataa-a scurried to the kitchen and retrieved a glass of water, a mild sedative hidden inside.

"Come on, Dad," J'Dar said. "Let's get you cleaned up."

Three days later, as the sun climbed high and cast its golden light over the gathering, Hunter stepped through the crowd with Li-ara cradled in his arms. The mourners parted in silence, heads bowed, hearts heavy.

To honor the love of his life, he wore his full Huntsman armor. Polished, ceremonial, and gleaming in the light. Each piece was a testament to duty, to tradition. And to her.

Umae and Qui walked beside him, ready to give support if needed. J'Dar, Willomay, and their three kids followed with Brox. Nataa-a, her girls, and Kolor and Hans followed. Then Suemay and Shadow. A Huntsmen Honor Guard of eight came last.

The procession moved in solemn silence toward a hill at the southern edge of the yard. Hunter had chosen the location because it was there, beneath the open sky, that he and Li-ara had spent countless days over the past decade. Talking. Laughing. Simply being.

At its summit, Hunter saw the funeral pyre, crafted with care by the Huntsmen. They constructed it from golden Orallian aspen, its grain glowing softly in the light. A crown of Orallian white daisies, Li-ara's favorite, encircled the top, their petals trembling in the breeze like whispered farewells. Wildflowers of every hue spilled down the sides, vibrant against the solemn backdrop.

At the center, a layer of *Tillosian* silk stretched smooth and pristine, pure white, like snow untouched. It waited to receive her, as if the fabric itself understood the honor. Around the base, kindling and autumn leaves were carefully arranged, a quiet promise of flame and release.

Warnom waited at the base of the hill. His hand rested on a floating stretcher, its gentle humming interrupting the stillness in the air. The climb would be too steep, too cruel, for Hunter to carry Li-ara, so the stretcher would carry her the remainder of her journey.

Hunter laid her still body on the stretcher, his hands trembling as he placed her inside. His hands lingered, unwilling to let go. Hidden beneath his helmet, a single tear slipped down his cheek. Qui stepped forward and gently took his elbow. Hunter released his hold and stepped back.

Warnom guided the stretcher upward. Hunter walked beside it, his hand resting along the edge to keep from collapsing. Step by step, Hunter climbed. Brox walked alongside him.

Halfway up the hill, his legs faltered. He dropped to one knee, the crushing weight pressing on his chest too much to withstand. His breath faltered. His vision blurred. For a moment, time seemed to pause.

No one spoke. No one moved. They simply waited, giving Hunter the silence to grieve without judgment, honoring him as a Huntsman with too much sorrow.

A long, shuddering breath sounded from beneath his helmet. Hunter pressed his fingers into the edge of the stretcher, and pushed himself upright, not out of strength but sheer willpower.

He continued toward the place he *never* wanted to go.

Warnom guided the stretcher to its side of the pyre and stopped. Hunter stepped forward, slow and unsteady, each footfall dragging through the dirt like it was fighting him. He gathered Li-ara into his arms, clutching her to his chest, his arms tightening.

He stood there, frozen, holding her with both strength and desperation. The silk-lined pyre waited for her, but he didn't move. His fingers curled into the fabric of her clothing, jaw trembling. Tears ran unchecked down his face.

She was gone. But he couldn't let her go, lay her inside. It would make her leaving real. And he wasn't ready for that.

J'Dar, silent and pale, stepped forward. He approached his father with quiet steps, tears flowing from his own eyes. Wordlessly, he placed both hands on Hunter's arm.

Hunter looked down at his son. Their eyes met, and in that gaze shared between a grieving father and a heartbroken child, something shifted.

"Dad, can I help place Mom inside?"

With a trembling breath, Hunter nodded. Slowly, painfully, with J'Dar's help, he laid the woman he loved more than life itself onto the pyre.

His hands lingered. He reached up and removed his helmet, allowing it to drop to the ground beside him. Taking her hand in his, he brought it to his lips and kissed her for the last time. Then, he stepped back.

Warnom walked in silence, placing a lit torch in each hand of those gathered around Li-ara. One by one, the children stepped forward. Then Umae, Qui, Warnom. Friends, villagers, and the Huntsmen followed. Each lowered their torch to the base of the pyre.

The flame flickered violently in the wind, dancing at the edge of Hunter's vision, a cruel and vivid reminder of the final rite he was expected to complete. He remained stationary, his torch clenched tightly in his shaking hands. His jaw locked. His feet rooted. But his body screamed to run.

He couldn't do it. He *couldn't* set fire to the woman who had once breathed life back into his broken body, who had brought laughter into his quiet moments, who had battled beside him, wept with him, and loved him without hesitation or condition.

Nataa-a stepped forward. Her eyes were red and swollen, but her hands were steady as she reached for his. She placed her palm over his fingers, small yet stronger than the grief weighing him down.

"It's okay, Dad. You don't have to."

Then, gently, reverently, she took the torch from his hands and lowered it to the grass, extinguishing the flame without ceremony, without shame. The decision was made. His fire would not be part of her passing.

The flames rose higher, consuming the pyre in crackling waves, casting flickering shadows across the faces of the mourners. Sparks floated into the twilight like tiny stars into the sky. Fragments of Li-ara drifted upward - embers, ash, bits of fabric curling like petals in the wind. They rose slowly, weightless, carried by the fire's breath.

Hunter didn't move.

He didn't speak.

He didn't blink.

He just watched. Watched as the last visible pieces of her slipped beyond his reach, one glowing flicker at a time.

Nataa-a slipped her hand into his, grounding him to what remained. Unable to withstand any more grief, the tears came. Not silent, but sudden, violent, unstoppable. They tore from his heart, searing hot, falling fast, born from the weight of everything left unsaid, every heartbeat he thought he'd have with her, every second that slipped through his fingers like ash. They came from the deepest part of him, where love had taken root. And now, where grief had hollowed it out.

J'Dar, Suemay, and the twins rushed forward, wrapping their arms around their father and Nataa-a. Together, they cried, allowing Hunter to release his grief.

Qui stepped forward and read the Huntsman's Farewell, a prayer for the fallen, an honor reserved only for the bravest of souls. His voice was steady, solemn. It cracked only once - when he spoke her name.

The Huntsmen bowed their head, many wiping away their own tears. In unison, they sang the *Glory Song*, a haunting melody sung through the ages for fallen Hunters. It rose softly, swelling with reverence, then falling into silence again like a breath held too long. The final note faded as the first howl broke from the trees - long, low, and full of mourning.

From the forest, from the hills, from the shadows, wild canines lifted their heads to the stars and cried out as if the Earth itself was grieving. Brox raised his head and added his voice. A tiny smile crossed Hunter's lips. Li-ara would be pleased.

The flames diminished. The mourners turned and began the descent down the hill. No one approached Hunter. They knew they had no words to ease his sorrow. Many embraced the children, offering soft condolences, saying to advise them if there was anything they could do for the family.

Hunter remained with Nataa-a, Qui, and Umae nearby, ready to catch him if he went down. But Hunter didn't falter.

J'Dar returned and stood on the other side of his father, his hand finding Hunter's and holding on as tightly as he could. There, the three stood, Nataa-a, J'Dar, and Hunter, watching the last of the flames dwindle and die.

"Dad, it's time to go back down," J'Dar finally whispered

Hunter said not a word. He only stared at the place the pyre had stood, where his Li-ara had rested.

"He won't leave until he collects her ashes and takes them to where he will release them," Qui said. "You and your family should go back to the house. Warnom, Umae, and I will stay with him."

"Shouldn't we stay and go with him?" J'Dar asked. "Or at least me, as the first born?"

"This is something your father needs to do alone," Qui replied. "He has shared her departure with you five, your children, and the rest of the world. Now, he must say his final goodbye alone. Can you understand that?"

"Sort of. What about Brox? Should I take him back to the house?"

"No. He will not leave your father's side. He will go with us when it is time."

J'Dar explained to his siblings the need to return to the house and why. None questioned him.

When they reached the house, J'Dar and Suemay sat on the porch. There they waited, keeping vigil over the man they loved.

Once the embers cooled enough to handle, Warnom gathered Li-ara's ashes and placed them in the holy chest. To aid Hunter in the rest of his journey, Qui brought the airship around. The box of Li-ara's ashes held tightly in his hands, Warnom and Umae guided him onto the ship.

Qui flew to the mountains and gently set the ship down on the landing above the deep, still lake, the same hidden place where the Li-ara had once remained concealed beneath the waves. It was where Hunter had first met the black canine. But more importantly, it was where he had stood at a crossroads, torn between running from his responsibilities or stepping fully into the life he'd built with Li-ara. Thankfully, he had chosen her.

Hunter could think of no place more fitting for her to rest. It was surrounded by quiet, watched over by the wild, and rested in the place where love had once overcome fear. It was where she would wait for him.

His legs shaking, Hunter turned to his friends. "Qui, I fear I am not strong enough to carry Li-ara's ashes. Would you carry them for me?"

"I would be proud to."

"Umae, I fear I have stood too long. Would you and Warnom help me down the ramp?"

"First, you couldn't pee while riding your steed, now you can't walk down the ramp. You are getting old, my friend," Umae said.

"That I am," Hunter chuckled.

Warnom and Umae slipped their arms around his waist, steadying him. They felt the frailty in him, a dangerous, brittle weakness that hadn't been there before. Holding him tighter, they guided him carefully down the ramp and onto the bluff. Every step was a battle, and though Hunter said nothing, his body betrayed him, sagging heavier with each stride. Somehow, by sheer will, he reached the edge of the cliff.

Afraid his strength would give out, they never let go.

Qui stepped forward, wordless, and placed the chest into Hunter's hands. Hunter gripped it tightly, anchoring himself to it, to her. When he gave a faint nod, Qui opened the lid.

Inside, a soft layer of ash and soot lay undisturbed, delicate as moon dust. It was all that remained of the woman who had once filled his life with stubborn laughter, fierce devotion, and a love that had made him believe in something beyond survival.

How could he let her go?

But if her soul was to fly to *Brehalla*, he had to release her.

Closing his eyes, Hunter whispered an ancient Kolorian prayer under his breath. Then, with a breath of his own, he tipped the chest.

The ashes poured into the wind like a silver mist, swirling and dancing as the cliff's breeze carried them outward. The light caught them, spinning them into the air, and for a moment, the mist took shape.

Li-ara.

She appeared to him, young and vibrant, just as she had been when he first laid eyes on her, fierce, beautiful, alive. His heart broke all over again.

"Thank you for loving me," Hunter whispered. Li-ara blew him a kiss. Hunter's hand lifted slightly to reach for her, but the vision thinned, stretching into the sky, becoming one with the endless blue.

From the forest, the black canine howled.

"Dad, Willomay, and I can stay for another week or two," J'Dar said as he closed his suitcase. "It's no problem."

"There is no reason," Hunter replied as he played with his grandson and the new pup he was taking home. "My strength is returning. Suemay and Huns are here, and it's almost impossible to get Qui, Warnom, or Umae to leave my side. I don't need any more people making sure I eat and rest. I'm likely to die just because there are so many people around me, and I tripped over one of them. Besides, you're the governor of the eight planets now. You have lots of work waiting back at the capital. Don't you have a treaty to arrange with the *Hiique*?"

"When they learned of Mom's death, they backed off and gave us as much time as needed," J'Dar replied. "So, I really can stay."

"A bit of advice, J'Dar. Never believe what the *Hiique* tell you. They always lie."

Qui poked his head in the door. "Ship's ready to take off when you are."

Hunter escorted his family out to the waiting ship on the lawn. Everyone kissed and hugged each other. Hunter watched as Willomay and the kids walked up the ramp.

"You're sure you will be okay, Dad?" J'Dar asked, not wanting to leave.

"I will be fine," Hunter replied, forcing a smile onto his face.

"I'll finish the Hiique treaty and return within the month. Promise me you'll be here in a month." Hunter smiled. "Dad, I'm not leaving unless you promise me you'll still be alive in a month. No *Cattamalla*. Do you understand?"

"J'Dar, in over forty years, your mother never got me to promise such a thing. Why do you believe I will make such a promise now?"

"That's because she never asked you anything after that fight. Promise me. Or I'm not leaving, the treaty will not be signed, and the galaxy will go to war. It will all be your fault."

"You should know guilt trips don't work on me," Hunter laughed. "I will be here when you return." Under his breath, he added, "If I can."

"Promise."

"I promise. Good Journey."

J'Dar took his father into his arms. "I love you, Dad, so much. Thank you for everything you did."

"As is a father's duty," Hunter replied, hugging his son back. Hunter waited for his son to let go, but J'Dar held the embrace. "You're going to miss your flight."

The son forced his arms to release the person he loved the most. "See you in one month."

"Yes. Now go."

Slowly, J'Dar climbed the ramp and sank into his seat near the window. As the ship rose, he kept his gaze fixed on the retreating cabin, on his father's face. A heaviness settled in his chest, the quiet, unshakable fear that he had just spoken with him for the last time.

The hum of the engines filled the silence between his thoughts. During the entire flight to the city, J'Dar wrestled with the urge to cancel his trip home. He couldn't shake the unease gnawing at him, even though Hunter had promised, sworn, he'd still be there in a month.

J'Dar didn't doubt his father's love. Not for a second. Hunter had always been there for him, for all of them. But now, with Li-ara gone, the fire in his father's eyes had dimmed.

He dug through his memories, desperate to find a single time when his father had broken a promise. Nothing. Not once. And so, he clung to that. He forced himself to concentrate on his own obligation - a treaty with the Hiique that, if ignored, could spiral into war. He couldn't let fear dictate his choices.

The moment they reached the hotel in the capital, J'Dar called Suemay.

"Is he alright?" he asked immediately.

"He's quiet," Suemay said. "But he's alright. Really. Umae left this morning, but Qui and Warnom are still with him. We never leave him alone."

J'Dar closed his eyes, letting out a breath. "I know he hates that. Dad's never been one to enjoy the presence of others hovering around him, except Mom."

"Don't worry, J'Dar. He'll be here when you return. He gave you his word. And you know our father. He doesn't break it."

The next morning, J'Dar and his family rose before dawn and made their way to the city's bustling airport, bracing for the long journey ahead to Quazar Three. As final boarding was announced and the family gathered their things, J'Dar's youngest approached quietly and held out a small bag.

"Here, Daddy."

"What's this?" J'Dar asked.

"PaPa wanted me to give it to you when we got home, but I'm afraid I might lose it. Is it okay if I give it to you now?"

"Sure," J'Dar said with a distracted smile, opening the bag and gently pouring its contents into his palm.

The smile vanished.

Resting in his hand was a silver disk strung on a chain, worn, familiar, etched with the faces of Beta and Kii. His father's coin. The one Hunter never took off.

J'Dar's fingers curled around the metal as if he could will it not to mean what he knew it did.

"No…" he whispered.

Willomay stepped closer, her expression shifting from concern to alarm. "J'Dar?"

"Take the kids home. I have to go back," J'Dar shouted, running across the platform and out into the terminal.

"Why?"

"He's going to engage in the *Cattamalla.*"

"But he promised he wouldn't," Willomay shouted.

"He lied," came the answer echoing through the station.

It took J'Dar hours to secure a transport, each passing minute feeding the storm inside him. He called again and again. No answer. No response.

By the time he reached the house, dusk was bleeding into the horizon. He barely let the flyer land before running down the ramp. His boots pounded against the earth as he sprinted toward the door, throwing it open with a crash.

"Dad!" he shouted, his voice already breaking. "Dad!"

He tore through the house, shouting louder with each room he cleared. "*Dad!*"

He reached the bedroom. Laid out on the bed with meticulous care were Hunter's armor, his long rifle, and the hunting knife he never traveled without. Resting at the head of the bed, positioned precisely on the pillow, was his helmet.

Facing backward.

Refusing to believe what the helmet meant, what it *had* to mean, J'Dar tore across the grounds toward the kennel. He burst through the entrance, the dimming light casting long shadows across the space. Shapes moved. Canines yipped. But he saw none of it.

His eyes swept the room like a storm, searching, hoping, begging, until he found Suemay. He sprinted toward her, shoving past a handler. Reaching her, J'Dar seized his baby sister by the shoulders and spun her around.

"Have you seen Dad?!" he asked, his voice wild with panic.

"Aren't you supposed to be on a flight home?"

"Have you seen him?"

Suemay saw the panic in his eyes, felt it wrap around her chest like a closing fist. "Not since dinner last night. *Illiu* went into labor last night, and I spent the evening out here. She just gave birth to six pups an hour ago. Is something wrong?"

J'Dar held out his hand and showed Suemay their father's necklace. "Dad lied to us."

"No, he wouldn't do that. He's probably off somewhere with either Warnom or Qui. I'll look for Warnom. You go find Qui."

It took J'Dar fifteen minutes to locate Qui. "Have you seen my Dad?"

"What are you doing back here?"

"Have you seen my Dad?" J'Dar shouted, his voice wild and desperate.

"Not today. We're supposed to get together for evening meal."

"When was the last time you were with him?"

"Warnom and I stayed up with him last night until he fell asleep in his chair. Warnom said he'd stay with him through the night and today, so I came back to the ship for some sleep. Did you ask Warnom where he is?"

"Suemay went to find Warnom."

"Your dad's probably sleeping in."

"He's not. I was just at the house. There's nobody inside."

"I'm sure there's nothing to worry about. He and Warnom probably went down to the stream for a bath. You know how your father likes bathing in the stream this time of year."

"No, Qui, you don't understand. Dad's armor was laid out on his bed, along with his long rifle and his knife."

The blood drained from Qui's face. "What about his helmet? Was his helmet there?"

"Yes."

"Which way was the helmet facing?"

"I don't remember."

"Think."

"I think it was backward. Yes, it was facing backward."

"Show me." The two ran up to the house and into the bedroom. When Qui saw the armor, he crumbled into the nearby chair. Tears filled his eyes.

"I'm sorry, J'Dar. We're too late. When a Hunter is ready to die, he lays down his armor with reverence. Every piece is placed with purpose. The backward helmet … it means he's finished his journey. He has no further use for the suit."

Qui looked J'Dar squarely in the eyes, not hiding the pain in his own.

"It's his final message asking for his armor to be returned to Kolora. There, the Metalist will melt it down and forge it into new armor for another Hunter." A shadow crossed Qui's face as he added. "He asks this so that no Hunter ever walks alone."

"Maybe there's still time. We have to find him."

"Wait. Where's Brox? Maybe they went somewhere together."

"I haven't seen him either." J'Dar whistled. "Brox? Here, Boy." Barking sounded down the hallway. Following the sound, they discovered Hunter's dog tied to the bed in the twin's room. It was evident the canine was waking from an induced sleep.

"Why would he drug and tie Brox up?"

"Because he didn't want Brox to follow him and get hurt," Qui said. "But let's not jump to conclusions until we see what Suemay found out."

"Why did he lie?" J'Dar asked. "Dad's never lied to me before."

"We don't know yet that he lied. And if he did, it was because your father said the words you wanted to hear, just like he did with Warnom and me. I am surprised he waited this long to join your mother. He is as one with no heart, no soul, a ghost of flesh and blood."

"But he promised!"

"He promised because he loved you and your siblings. If it's any consolation, I think he tried to stay. But he couldn't bear another day without her."

Suemay came running into the house. "Warnom hasn't seen Dad either. He said Dad told him Qui was staying with him until tonight's meal, and Warnom should take the opportunity to get some rest."

"Stop. Don't let Brox out," J'Dar shouted. But the warning came too late. Brox made a mad dash out the door, down the steps, and ran towards the mountains. The wild pack sounded in the distance as the three ran out onto the porch to catch the canine.

"That's the black leader's pack," Suemay said. "I recognize their howl. They're howling the canine death song."

"We'll take the ship. We can follow Brox from above." The three ran towards the airfield. Qui shouted into his radio, "*Tytoo*, get the Li-ara started and ready to lift off. I'll be there in fifteen minutes."

Once everyone was onboard and strapped in, Qui lifted the Li-ara off the ground. He veered toward the direction Brox had gone.

"I see Brox," Suemay shouted. "He's at your two o'clock position just past that large *kicklegum* tree." Qui turned the ship farther to the east and saw the canine running at a full lope.

"Where's he going?" J'Dar asked.

"He's headed to the huckleberry fields," Qui said. "It's where the *tumacks* gather this time of year."

"*Tumacks?*" A cold shiver ran down J'Dar's spine. "Dad plans on fighting a *tumack?*"

"I fear so."

"How much further?" Suemay asked.

"Right past that grove of trees ahead. The ground flattens out some and is covered with various berry bushes. There's a small clearing where I think I can sit down."

Up ahead, a flock of birds circled.

"Are those buzzards?" J'Dar asked.

"Crows, I think," Qui replied. "But still not a good sign. I believe they're circling something dead."

Qui slowed the aircraft, guiding it gently over the treetops as the canopy parted beneath them. His hands trembled on the controls, and a sob caught in his throat when the scene below came into view. Tears welled in his eyes as he bowed his head in reverence.

There, beneath the cloudless sun, lay Hunter. Lifeless. His body sprawled in a warrior's rest, and the black female canine lay across his chest, her muzzle buried against him in eternal loyalty. Around them, her pack stood guard in a solemn circle, silent and unmoving, like sentinels carved from grief.

Beyond them lay the great *tumack*, the beast Hunter had faced in his final trial, the *Cattamalla*. Its massive body sprawled in death, a testament to the price Hunter had paid for honor and peace.

Above, a storm of black wings circled - crows waiting to descend, drawn to the scent of blood and silence. Others perched in the branches, heads cocked, patient and still, ready to claim what remained of the battlefield.

Qui closed his eyes momentarily, letting the grief wash over him. He silently recited the Huntsmen's prayer.

"No," J'Dar screamed, slamming his hand against the metal wall and pressing his face against the window. "Get us down, Qui."

Suemay placed her hand on her brother's shoulder. "We're too late. He's gone, J'Dar."

Qui sat the ship down close to the bodies. J'Dar waited impatiently at the door, ready to run out. But the door did not open. J'Dar reached up to press the release button, but Qui stopped him.

"The wild female canine lies on your father's chest," Qui said. "I can't tell if she is alive or not. Plus, there are at least twenty wild canines waiting. I don't know what they're doing. But I do know this: If you go running out there, they will perceive you as a threat and attack. It appears the *tumack* did a lot of damage to your father. His blood covers the ground. With the strong wind today, every predator and scavenger for fifty miles will smell it and come. We must proceed carefully."

"What do you expect us to do?" J'Dar yelled. "Stay on the ship? Shoot the canines? What?"

"I expect you to act like the Huntsman you are. Do what your father would expect you to do. Observe and assess the situation, then act." Qui turned to Suemay. "You are the canine expert. What do you suggest, Suemay?"

Suemay looked out the window at the ring of wild canines. "I don't know what they're up to. I've never seen canines act like this. It's like they're protecting Dad." She thought for a moment. "Open the door and extend the ramp. Shadow can speak with them and determine whether it's safe for us to step outside. She can tell them we are here to take his body, not harm it."

Qui nodded and opened the door. As the ramp lowered, the three witnessed a gory, bloody scene. Fur, feathers, and body parts of scavengers littered the ground. The earth was a deep crimson stained by the blood of the dead. Birds and small mammals scurried amongst the dead, tearing pieces of flesh from the scattered bones.

"What happened here?" J'Dar asked, his stomach churning.

His eyes wide, Qui studied the scene. "I think the canines killed anything that tried to reach their leader and your father."

"They protected them," Suemay said. "That's what the circle is for – to keep the bodies safe."

The moment the wild canines spotted the three figures standing atop the ramp, their reaction was instant. They dropped low, hackles raised, lips curling back to reveal sharp, gleaming teeth. Growls rumbled, primal and threatening.

Shadow stepped forward, descending the ramp until she was halfway down. She paused, lifted her head high, and howled.

From the treeline came the answer. Brox emerged, his tawny coat streaked with dirt, eyes locked on Shadow with unwavering focus. He bolted up the ramp, his paws pounding the metal like drumbeats of war.

He stopped beside Shadow, raised his head, and howled. Their voices twined together, deep and high, sorrowful and strong. The wild canines joined in, a chorus of sorrow floating across the wind.

Then, silence.

Complete.

Absolute.

Shadow turned and looked at Suemay. "She says it's okay to go to Dad, J'Dar," Suemay said. "But keep your steps slow and calm. Brox will accompany you. Qui, Shadow will escort us."

"What about the leader?" Qui asked. "Is she dead?"

"Yes, but I don't know how."

Fighting every instinct he had to run, J'Dar forced his legs to slowly walk down the ramp. Brox stayed beside him. Suemay and Shadow followed. Qui brought up the rear, pushing a hovering stretcher forward.

As they approached the clearing, all eyes flicked briefly to the massive, fallen form of the tumack. The beast was a mountain of blood and muscle, its thick fur matted with fresh gore. Blood still oozed from a dozen savage wounds, deep, deliberate slashes carved by Hunter's hand in the final, brutal fight. His warrior's knife remained buried to the hilt in the creature's chest, a final signature of defiance and victory.

Crows swarmed the carcass in a black frenzy. They squawked and hissed as the party passed, angry at being interrupted mid-feast.

As they drew near to Hunter's body, the pack shifted. Their circle split just wide enough to allow the two-legged beings and their domesticated companions to pass. Once they were inside, the canines closed ranks behind them like a living wall.

J'Dar stepped forward slowly, his eyes locked on his father. His hands trembled as he reached for the black female, hoping to lift her gently from Hunter's chest.

The moment his fingers brushed her fur, the pack erupted like a storm. The canines surged to their feet, teeth bared, snapping jaws just inches from his hands.

"Wait, J'Dar," Suemay said, placing her hand on her brother's arm. "They think you're going to hurt her. Shadow, tell them we must move her to retrieve Dad's body." In silence, Shadow conveyed the message. "Qui, she says they will permit *you* to move her, not J'Dar. Gently place her alongside Dad." With the canines' eyes watching him, Qui reverently lifted the female canine and placed her to the side.

With the black canine no longer shielding him, Hunter's injuries were laid bare beneath the fading light. His chest had been torn open by the tumack's claws, a deep, ragged gash exposing bone beneath shredded muscle. His left arm was mangled beyond recognition, the wrist twisted, fingers obliterated into a ruin of flesh and bone. From his right leg jutted a splintered bone, white and sharp, piercing through blood-soaked skin. A pool of dark crimson blood had gathered beneath him, still glistening, as if refusing to dry, refusing to accept the finality of his death.

There was no question. Though he had chosen death, Hunter had not fallen quietly. He had fought like the Huntsman he was - fiercely, fearlessly.

He had earned a warrior's end.

J'Dar dropped to his knees with a choked cry, his breath coming in gulps as he gathered his father into his arms. The weight of Hunter's body slumped heavily against him, lifeless, still warm, but gone.

"You promised," J'Dar whispered, his voice cracking. "You promised you'd stay."

His sobs tore from his throat in broken gasps as he rocked back and forth, clutching Hunter. "Why did you go? Why did you leave us?"

Beside him, Suemay knelt in silence, her voice lost to sorrow too deep for words. She leaned into her brother, resting her head on his trembling shoulder, her hand closing around her father's fingers. Fingers that would never move again.

Brox padded forward slowly, ears flattened, eyes dull. He laid his head gently on Hunter's leg and let out a soft, keening whimper, low and mournful, a sound soaked in despair.

Shadow sat beside her fallen mother, her golden eyes wide and unblinking, her body perfectly still. Only her slow, deep breaths betrayed her pain.

Qui stood nearby, his face stoic, but his eyes shimmered. And then, the tears came. He didn't hide them. Didn't brush them away. They spilled down his cheeks openly, silently. Tears not of weakness, but of respect, of heartbreak, of love. A rare thing for a Huntsman to display.

For a moment, no one moved.

The forest stood still. The canines stood watch. And grief, thick and all-consuming, wrapped around them all like a storm cloud unwilling to break.

"We need to go," Qui said sharply, his voice low but commanding, eyes narrowing on the pack.

The wild canines had gone still, their ears pricked, bodies rigid, hackles rising in unison as they turned toward the trees. A deep, unsettled growl rippled through the circle, low and instinctive. Something was out there.

From the dense forest came the sound of rustling. Slow at first, then heavier. Branches snapped under the weight of something large. The wind carried the coppery tang of blood, and the predators it lured.

"*Tumacks*," Qui muttered, scanning the treeline. "Or worse. A wild cat, maybe. Drawn by the scent of death."

He turned to the children, his expression tightening. "We need to leave. *Now*. It's not safe here anymore."

Suemay stared up at him, frozen, clutching her father's hand.

"Suemay," Qui said, softer this time, kneeling to meet her eyes. "I need you to ask Shadow to explain. We're going to lift Hunter's body onto the stretcher and take him home. Please. Now."

Another branch snapped, closer this time.

Suemay turned to Shadow. "She said the wild canines request that we take their dead leader with Dad. They don't want her body eaten by those approaching."

The three lifted Hunter's broken body. They folded his arms gently across his chest, the posture of a warrior at rest. Qui laid the black canine beside Hunter, positioning her head across his arms as if she had simply fallen asleep in the place she belonged.

The pack parted, forming a path to the ramp. Qui nodded and pushed the stretcher forward. Just before he reached the top, Brox turned and trotted down the ramp. He climbed onto the *tumack's* bloodied chest and pulled Hunter's warrior knife free from its heart, the blade slick with blood.

Shadow waited halfway up the ramp. She barked once, sharp, purposeful.

"What is it, girl?" Suemay asked.

The canine stepped forward, pressing her head gently into Suemay's chest. After a lingering moment, Shadow pulled away. and trotted down the ramp, stopping at the bottom. She looked back, her eyes meeting Suemay's. Then she ran to the waiting pack. The wild canines surrounded her, their bodies moving as one. Together, they vanished into the forest.

"Where's she going?" J'Dar asked.

"To take the place of her mother," Suemay said. "She is now their leader."

"But she's your canine."

"They need her more than I do."

Within seconds of the Li-ara lifting off, two massive *tumacks* crashed through the bushes. They sniffed the blood-soaked ground where Hunter had lain. Roaring in frustration, they sauntered to the fallen bear, sinking their teeth into the waiting flesh.

"Do you think she died defending Dad?" J'Dar asked as he held his father's right hand against his heart.

"I didn't see any wounds on her," Suemay said, running her hand through her father's hair, absentmindedly picking out leaves and twigs. "Nor is there any blood. Somehow, I think she was connected to Dad. And when he died, so did she. It was like they were two halves of the same spirit, neither able to live without the other."

"Like him and Mom."

"Yes. That's why the female canine lived so long. She must be at least … what? Sixty years old. No canine lives that long?"

J'Dar looked over at Brox. "Then why didn't Brox pass?"

"He was Dad's canine, his companion. They weren't connected on a spiritual level like the black canine."

As the sun set the next day, Hunter's body was consumed by the purification flames beneath the stars. Cradled against his chest, her head resting over his heart, lay the black she-canine.

There was no fancy pyre, no great gathering, no sea of mourners as there had been for Li-ara. This farewell was quiet. Private. Sacred. Only those closest to him stood witness - his five children, Nataa-a's daughters, Warnom, Umae, Qui, and the Huntsmen. A small circle of souls bound together by love, loss, and the weight of a goodbye too great for words.

One by one, those gathered stepped forward. Each shared a story - some with laughter, others through tears. Tales of battles fought, lessons learned, lives saved. Many spoke of Hunter's discipline, his loyalty, his quiet strength.

Umae recounted the day he first saw Hunter tame a wild beast with nothing but patience and steel in his gaze.

Warnom shared the memory of the day Hunter saved his life, dragging him across the Trader's compound, a bullet in his gut.

Qui, voice hoarse, spoke only one sentence: "He never asked to lead, but he never once let us walk alone."

When the final words were spoken, J'Dar took his place before the pyre. The fire had died down, the flames replaced by glowing embers and the fine ash that would soon carry his father to the stars. He stood there, just as Hunter had done for Li-ara, motionless, reverent, guarding the remains of the one he loved most.

From the trees, a shape emerged. Shadow. She approached the pyre, her eyes reflecting the glowing embers, and bowed her head low - once. Then, she turned and slipped into the blackness of the forest, the rest of her pack vanishing behind her like mist.

The next morning, Qui flew J'Dar, Warnom, and Umae to the cliffs above the lake, where Hunter had previously scattered Li-ara's ashes.

No words were spoken as the three stepped from the ship. J'Dar's boots crunched softly over stone as he approached the edge. The last time he had stood here, the Traders had stolen his childhood, his father thought dead, his world thrown into chaos. Now, he returned not as a boy but as a son carrying his father home.

He stepped to the edge, his hands holding the box solemnly. Umae and Qui flanked him, heads bowed, offering presence but not intrusion. J'Dar looked out across the lake.

"Are you okay with dumping his ashes?" Qui asked. "Umae or I can scatter them if you wish."

"No, I am the oldest," J'Dar said. "Sending his soul to *Breehalla* is my responsibility."

"That it is, Young Huntsman," Qui complemented, clasping his hand on the oldest son's shoulders. "You bring your father great honor."

"Qui, I am almost fifty," J'Dar said. "And, with my father's death, I am now head of the family. Don't you think it's time to drop the word 'young' from my nomenclature?"

"Now that J'Dar senior is gone, perhaps," Qui teased. "But you must remember this. Huntsmen have an average lifespan of two hundred years. Your father was only middle-aged when he died. You must live another fifty, sixty years before attaining an age not considered a youth."

"I'm always going to be a youngling," J'Dar sighed. J'Dar lifted the lid of the golden box and peered inside. It did not seem feasible that the larger-than-life male he loved was contained in such a tiny box.

"May you and Mother begin your life anew in *Breehalla*," J'Dar whispered. He turned the small box over, and Hunter's ashes slipped free, tumbling into the air. At that moment, a soft breeze stirred off the lake, lifting not only Hunter's ashes but some of Li-ara's as well. The two streams twisted together, dancing in the sunlight, weaving into the faint silhouette of two figures reaching for one another.

J'Dar stood motionless as he watched the delicate image form, his father and mother, their faces alight with joy. Hunter leaned forward and kissed Li-ara, her arms folding around him. She had been waiting for him, as she had promised. Together, they turned toward him, smiles bright and full of peace, and blew him a final kiss. Then, hand in hand, they drifted higher into the endless sky, until the wind carried them out of sight.

A profound stillness settled over J'Dar. Though his heart ached with the weight of goodbye, he finally understood. His father wasn't lost anymore. He was reunited with his Li-ara. He was home.

27 HUNTSMAN ARMOR

Qui flew the five children to Kolora to personally return their father's Bounty Hunter's armor.

"This is a rare honor being given to you," Qui said as they walked towards the Dominee. "And for an off-worlder to enter the armor furnace is unfathomable."

"But Dad was an off-worlder," Nataa-a stated.

"That is not entirely correct," Qui said. "He was from *Ribos,* our sister planet. Anyone born on *Ribos* is a citizen of Kolora. We are one nation that lives on two planets. Now, remember what I told you and mind your manners."

The children halted at the foot of the steps leading to the Dominee's throne, their heads bowed in respect. Only Qui moved forward. He ascended the steps with measured grace, dropping to one knee before her. With solemn reverence, he took her hand in both of his, pressing it first to his forehead and then to his lips. Rising to his feet, he stood motionless, his gaze steady, waiting for the Dominee to speak.

"You bring visitors for us today, Qui?"

"Yes, My Lady. I bring before you the five children of Huntsman BiiJun D'Kolor. They respectfully bring their father's Huntsman armor back to Kolora to join with the *kolorite* of those long gone."

"Come forward," the Dominee said as she stood.

As the oldest, J'Dar went first, climbing the stairs and stopping four steps from the Dominee. J'Dar bent his knee, saying not a word. She looked exactly like he remembered her - a suit of white-gold armor accented with a wrap of pure white fur embracing her neck and shoulders. But, today, she did not hide her face beneath the white-gold helmet.

J'Dar's eyes grew wider as he viewed the beautiful leader. Her face contained the most delicate facial features complemented by the bluest of blue eyes, like his father's. Waves of silken white curls rested against her shoulders, light and airy. She appeared in her mid-thirties, yet J'Dar knew she was over a hundred years old.

"Welcome, young J'Dar," the Dominee greeted, nodding. She held out her hand.

J'Dar advanced. He took the Dominee's hand in his, raised it to his forehead, and then to his lips as Qui had instructed him to do. He hid his smile, remembering seeing his father do the same the day Hunter returned from rescuing his son.

"It is with much sorrow that I welcome you and your father's armor to Kolora."

"Thank you, My Lady. My siblings and I are honored and humbled to enter Kolora to return his *kolorite* armor. We are thankful it will protect other Huntsmen on their dangerous journeys. With your permission, I would like to introduce you to BiiJun's children." The Dominee nodded.

One by one, J'Dar introduced his siblings. Each announced the item of armor they brought along with a brief tale about how their father used the covering. When completed, they stepped to the side and waited.

"BiiJun was a renowned Huntsman. We will celebrate his life in our songs and legends. His armor will combine with the coverings of those before him and continue in the shielding of new Huntsmen. May his time in this world never be forgotten."

When the Dominee took a step forward, Qui intervened. "My Lady, before we continue to the furnace, young J'Dar has something he would like to give you." Qui beckoned the young Huntsman.

J'Dar walked back to the Dominee. "I didn't know if this is appropriate, My Lady, for I found nothing in the Huntsmen's teachings. Warnom said, although not a normal part of Huntsmen tradition, he thought you would appreciate this." He reached into his pocket and removed a small golden box. He held the gift out for the Dominee. "Since my father loved Kolora so much, I thought part of him should remain here.

I brought some of his ashes, hoping you would return him to his beloved planet."

Tears filling her eyes, the Dominee reached out and took the small box. In silence, she lifted the lid and observed a fine layer of Hunter's ashes. After reclosing the lid, she slipped the precious gift into her pocket.

Taking Qui's arm, the Dominee walked down the steps, her legs unsteady as she fought to compose herself. She embraced the young J'Dar, something she never did. Qui recalled only one other being the Dominee hugged years earlier, and that was BiiJun D'Kolor.

"Thank you," she whispered. "His return home means much to me."

The streets of Kolora were lined with people. Huntsmen in full ceremonial dress stood shoulder to shoulder, their armor gleaming in the midday light, polished to perfection. Old warriors stood with clenched jaws, tears in their eyes. Children, too young to understand, waved boughs of Kolorian beakwood palm. Civilians, nobles, and soldiers alike lowered their heads, some falling to one knee as the procession passed.

There were no cheers, no drums. Only silence. The people of Kolora had not come to watch. They had come to *grieve*.

In the carriage, the children rode through the sea of bodies, their hearts overwhelmed. They had always known their father was respected, but here, on Kolora, they understood the depth of it. BiiJun had not only belonged to them. He had belonged to everyone.

As they entered the last part of their journey, they beheld the street embellished with hundreds of skulls on top of stakes.

"For eons, Huntsmen have displayed their slain enemy along the Road of Victory," Qui said. "To do so takes power away from the enemy and gives it to the clan."

"Now we know where Dad got his idea from," Suemay whispered to J'Dar.

The carriages rolled to a halt before two towering golden doors, their surfaces etched with intricate designs that caught the light and shimmered like living fire.

Following the Dominee's lead, they stepped inside into a vast, cathedral-like chamber rimmed with soaring stained-glass windows that bathed the stone floor in rivers of shifting color. At the heart of the room stood an enormous golden cauldron, suspended on six ornate legs. Beneath it, pillars of blue flame roared upward, their heat rippling the air as they hungrily licked at the cauldron's underside.

Behind the cauldron, two metal workers stood like sentinels, each clad in a thick leather apron and heavy gloves. Their faces were hidden behind helmets crafted from rare red *kolorite*, giving them a fierce, almost otherworldly appearance in the dance of flame and light.

"Today, we return a Huntsman's armor back to the *kolorite* of the ancients," the Dominee said. "We are sad that one we loved we will see no more, yet we rejoice in the knowledge he is with his beloved Li-ara, and together they live in *Breehalla.*" She signaled to Qui.

Qui led Suemay to the tray holding Hunter's armor. Using a pair of thick tongs, she picked up one of his shoulder shields and carried the armor over to the caldron. She lowered the shield into the melted *kolorite*, hearing the faint sound of melting metal.

"I return you to the metal from which you were forged." Tears streamed down her face. "Goodbye, Daddy. I love you so much. I wish we had spent more time together. Thank you for not forgetting me and for giving me a second chance to enter this world. I promise I will not squander the life you and Mother gave me." She turned and carried the metal tongs to Huns.

One by one, the remaining children brought their piece of armor to the furnace and lowered it into the liquid, each saying the appropriate statement, followed by their thoughts.

Only one child remained - J'Dar.

His hands and legs trembling, J'Dar grasped his father's helmet in the tongs. As he turned, the Dominee placed her hand on his arm. "Tradition dictates that the oldest places the Hunter's helmet in the furnace. However, I wish for you to select a different piece. I have something another purpose for BiiJun's helmet." Without question, J'Dar picked a thigh shield and carried the piece to the furnace.

"I return you to the metal from which you were forged." The sound of metal melting hissed again. "Dad, I was so angry at you when you left us, when you left me. I studied the Huntsmen's teachings most of my life, but I didn't understand why you chose death over us. The day I took your ashes to the cliff, and they mingled with Mom's, I saw how happy you both were. And I understood; I understood the Huntsmen; I understood their creed; I understood why you could not live without her. She was the half of you that held your joy, your life, your very existence. You two were one and the same being. Willomay and I will never achieve such a love, but I will try. Thank you, Dad, for everything. For saving me from the Rollo Traders, for acknowledging me when you learned I was your son, for teaching me the ways of a Hunter. I love you, Dad. I miss you terribly, but you will always be in my heart and at my side. Until we meet again, Good Journey."

J'Dar stepped back, wiping tears from his eyes. With the acceptance of his father's decision, the heartache of Hunter's death disappeared, like his ashes in the wind. When he directed his eyes up, J'Dar saw everyone crying, even the Dominee.

"You do your father proud, young Huntsman," the Dominee said. She handed J'Dar Hunter's helmet. "Return this to Orallia and place it in the university BiiJun's training began. Thanks to your father, our creed is taught across this star system and spreading across the universe, bringing peace to the downtrodden, forgotten, and oppressed. He eliminated the threat of child slavery. He established the *Kun D'Kolor,* an elite fleet of Huntsmen who patrol this system, ensuring peace remains. I want all to know and remember the name of BiiJun D'Kolor, of J'Dar Jen, a child of Tallus, Ribos, and Kolora, the son of Kolor and Meg, a Hunter who defeated the odds and found happiness in the arms of a woman. Never must his name be forgotten."

Upon his return to Orallia, J'Dar commissioned a glass case to be built to hold his father's helmet. He displayed the helmet in the entranceway leading to the classrooms his father inspired. Below the case, he nailed a plaque inscribed with his parents' names and a brief description of their love and accomplishments.

In the years that followed, a statue of BiiJun and Li-ara was erected in the hallway to honor the Dominee's request that the great Huntsman's deeds never be forgotten. To honor Li-ara's accomplishments, a bronze statue of Kii was erected beside them. Thus, the legacy of Bii-Jun D'Kolor, the woman he loved, and the existence of the wild canines continued for future generations.

The Dominee wandered through her garden, the soft fragrance of blooming flowers trailing in her wake. She made her way to the golden pool, its surface glimmering in the afternoon light, and lowered herself onto the stone bench, the same bench where she and BiiJun had once sat together so often. She closed her eyes, remembering how she had reached gently into his mind, easing away the lingering terrors of his captivity. Memories stirred of countless hours spent cradling him against her, his small body trembling with fear, yet finding solace in the steady beat of her heart and the unbreakable shelter of her love.

Those hours had etched an unspoken bond between them, one born not only of blood, but of something deeper

Removing J'Dar's gift from her pocket, she unclasped the lock and peered inside at BiiJun's precious ashes. A warm breeze blew through her hair, carrying with it the sound of his laughter. She lifted her eyes and witnessed a young BiiJun running through the fields of flowers chasing butterflies, the tortures of his slavery at last forgotten. His image neared, and her body longed to feel his embrace once more. But she could not satisfy such a longing, for her BiiJun was but a memory. He existed as one with his beloved in the other world. No one would ever hurt him again.

She stood and turned the box over, allowing its contents to spill out onto the breeze. As his ashes spread across the garden, she gave thanks for the boy she loved as her own.

Please leave an honest review on Amazon. It helps me write better when I understand what you liked and didn't like.

Coming Summer, 2025 The Bounty Hunter II: Canine Conspiracy

**The deadliest betrayal doesn't always come with a weapon.
Sometimes, it comes on four legs.**

Suemay never saw it coming. One moment, her trusted canine companion was at her side. The next, its teeth were sinking into her flesh. Bleeding, stunned, and betrayed, she tries to make sense of the attack—but the terror doesn't end there. Across the galaxy, whispers grow louder. Canines are turning. Violence is spreading. Fear is rising.

Desperate for answers, Suemay and her siblings unravel a forgotten chapter of Huntsmen history—a dark secret buried so deep that those who knew it chose silence over survival. The truth is more terrifying than anything they imagined: the bond between canine and Huntsman was never broken by choice. It was severed for a reason.

Now, with old allies becoming threats and an ancient conspiracy closing in, Suemay must confront the horrifying question: **What do you do when your greatest protectors become your greatest danger?**

Bounty Hunter II: Canine Conspiracy is a pulse-pounding tale of betrayal, survival, and the terrifying cost of trusting the wrong instincts.

ABOUT THE AUTHOR

P.R. Garcia grew up in rural Michigan and is the youngest of three. She became a lover of Science Fiction at an early age when her parents took her to the movies. She was hooked the moment she heard Patricia Neal tell the robot, Gort, in The Day the Earth Stood Still, "Klaatu barada nikto." Inspired by what was possible, she and her dog spent many days in the fields behind her home, fighting aliens and investigating unfamiliar planets. During the late 1960s, while in high school, the series *Star Trek* hit television, boosting her fascination with what might be out there. Her friends still comment on her refusal to attend the Friday night high school football games. Instead, she stayed home and watched that week's episode.

She became an award-winning basket weaver in her thirties and continued in this craft for three decades. After retiring from her thirty-year job, she moved to San Diego, California. She volunteered for five years as a guide on Whale-Watching Boats, teaching people from around the world about gray whales and other Pacific Ocean aquatic life.

At sixty-two, Ms. Garcia began to write her Europa Saga, a tantalizing, ten-part sci-fi series of intrigue, suspense, and mystery. Her saga is a fresh retelling of the story of Atlantis and its inhabitants. The books span six thousand years and three generations. Her story launched her into the world of a best-selling author.

Global warming, deforestation, pollution of our air and water, species loss, and the devastation of Earth itself are all subjects dear to Ms. Garcia's heart. She has incorporated those themes into her later books, including books seven through nine of the Europa Saga and *Extinction 2038*. In 2021, she published the first novel in the Guardians of Earth series, followed with *Guardians of Earth II* the same year, *and Guardians of Earth III* in 2024. She is currently working on a sequel to *The Bounty Hunter*. It should be available in Summer, 2025.

In 2024, Ms. Garcia turned her love of fairies and her belief in Healing crystals into a stone guide for beginners and experts entitled "*The Magical Fairy Guide to Healing Crystals*.".

The majority of the above books are available for free on Kindle Unlimited.

In addition to novels, Ms. Garcia also writes children's books. *A Cat for William* is based on an authentic story about how a stray cat helps a man cope with a disabling disease. *The Christmas Crayons* is based on a true story about a homeless, neglected girl who finds happiness in a box of crayons on Christmas Day. She has also started a series about Granny Ducks.

In addition to writing, Ms. Garcia designs adult coloring books. All are available on Amazon under the author name of Pamela Garcia, or you can find them on her website: http://www.prgarcia1.com.

In 2024, Ms. Garcia added her fairy designs to Redbubble and Zazzle for sale at the following stores:

www.redbubble.com/people/Labadie2024

www.zazzle.com/store/whisperingwillows

THE EUROPA SAGA

She was never meant to be human

When Europa wakes, her world is already gone. Her mother assassinated. Her life, a carefully woven lie. And now, she's the next target.

The Europa Saga is a bold reimagining of the myth of Atlantis, told through the eyes of a twenty-year-old woman whose entire existence was never meant to be what she believed. Spanning four generations and two thousand years, this sweeping saga reveals the hidden truth: Europa's parents are not human at all, but the exiled rulers of an aquatic alien race from Jupiter's ice moon, Europa.

Driven from their dying homeworld by civil war, the Atlanteans fled to Earth and built a secret city beneath the Pacific Ocean. But time and betrayal have nearly wiped them out. No Atlantean child has survived beyond the age of five in over two millennia. Their last hope: a child born human to survive the enemy's curse.

Now, with her mother dead and her enemies closing in, Europa must uncover the true history of her people, claim the throne she never asked for, and transform herself into what she was destined to become, an Atlantean.

But to save them, she must sacrifice the one thing she has left: her humanity. And if she fails, Atlantis will fall forever.

For more information, go to .www.prgarcia1.com or the Europa Saga website, www.europasaga.com

MORE STORIES BY P. R. GARCIA

Extinction 2038: When Antarctica's ice finally yields to global warming, a discovery thought to be the greatest scientific breakthrough of the century turns into humanity's deadliest nightmare.

Beneath the melting glaciers, a perfectly preserved dinosaur corpse emerges carrying inside it the original, prehistoric strain of Ebola. Within hours, the virus claims its first victim. Within days, it spirals into a global extinction event.

As the death toll explodes, civilization collapses. The Internet dies. Electricity vanishes. Fuel and food become relics of a lost world.

Now, the few survivors must fight not just the deadly plague, but the brutal lawlessness rising from the ashes of a shattered society.

The clock is ticking. Humanity's final chapter has begun.

Guardians of Earth: An unstoppable alien force is racing toward Earth, determined to strip the planet of her water, minerals - and life itself. One guardian, sworn to protect Earth, stands in their way. But he can't do it alone. He needs help from an Earthling he has never met — a woman who holds the key to humanity's survival.

Her name is Sarina Spalling. And she thinks she's just launching a science fiction novel.

Sarina's new book about alien guardians defending Earth from annihilation is a work of pure imagination. Or so she believes. Until the impossible starts to bleed into reality.

A secret government agency, exposed in the pages of her novel, abducts her, accusing her of espionage. Her husband is implicated. Her life, as she knows it, collapses overnight.

Held against her will, Sarina is desperate to prove her innocence until a message from the Moon reaches the facility. She is ordered to call her childhood home, a house demolished years ago.

When the line connects, her dead mother answers.

With everything she believed shattered, Sarina is thrust into a hidden war for Earth's survival, where fiction is fact, guardians are real, and her destiny is greater, and more dangerous, than she ever imagined.

Guardians of New Earth II: **The Watcher** Six months from New Earth, humanity's future shatters when a catastrophic breach cripples the great space station ferrying Earth's last survivors. Systems fail. Tensions ignite. Survival hangs by a thread.

When Head Commander Glogg is gravely injured, reluctant but battle-tested Renn Spalling is thrust into command, and into a nightmare he never saw coming. The breach wasn't an accident. It was sabotage.

What begins as a desperate repair mission spirals into a deadly hunt through a maze of lies, conspiracies, and secrets buried deep within the station's android core. Enemies walk among them, hidden, calculating, and deadly, even as the station's very structure buckles around them.

Now Renn must uncover the traitors, protect the last living cargo of Earth's animals, and save the station before it collapses into the void. But survival demands sacrifices Renn may not be willing to make sacrifices that could cost him everything.

In *Guardians of Earth II*, alliances will fracture, loyalties will be tested, and the fate of humanity's last hope will rest on the shoulders of one man, a man who never asked to be a hero.

Guardians of New Earth III: **The Emissary:** For the first time in thirty-eight years, Earth has sent a desperate signal to the Interstellar Space Coalition. Captain Tim Spalling, grandson of the legendary Renn Spalling, is ordered to lead the mission to find out why.

It's a journey he never wanted. A burden he fears he can't bear.

Haunted by the shadow of his family's legacy, Tim arrives to find Earth worse than he ever imagined. The northern hemisphere is a wasteland of ash. Of eight billion souls, only two hundred thousand cling to life in the radiation-choked south.

Every decision he makes could save them or doom them all.

Now stranded on a dying planet, Tim faces an impossible task: stop the radiation that's killing the survivors and his own advanced android team. But something far darker lurks in the ruin, a hidden alien threat watching, waiting to strike.

As the pressure mounts, Tim's growing bond with an Earth woman threatens to blur the lines between duty and desire, clouding his judgment when he can least afford it.

With time running out and betrayal closing in, Tim must confront the question that will define his legacy. How far will he go to save a dying world?

Please leave an honest review on Amazon.

Amazon Author's page:

https://www.amazon.com/stores/Pamela-Garcia/author/B00GH4F8TG

Li-ara finds a dying stranger

Bear Attack on Orallia

Should he stay, or should he go?

Heartache

Li-ara's home on Orallia

The Bounty Hunter